THE DRAGON OF DREAD DEEP

Some of the greatest heroes
were once the villain.

C.D. MCKENNA

The Dragon of Dread Deep

A Vorelian Saga Novel

Cover Design by Cherie Foxley

Map Illustrations by Eve's Worldbuilding

Editing by Busy Quill Press and The Missing Ink

Cassian and San'yila Illustration by Dalisacg

Interior Design and Formatting by Bryan Kamtsios and C.D. McKenna

No water is as restless as an untamed soul.

Eiyrǎl
Sorréle
Ashen Sea
Volkori Island
The Shade
Merrél Sea
City of Liral
Warión Sea
N
Greve's Point
The Gulf of Beritisian
Diyrǎ
Hil Islands
Creitón
Grave of Seas
Venkar City
The Vore World

Ereitón
Greve's Point
Hil Islands
Delion's Port
Barnäl's Port
Tyrik Village
Rvby Village
Warón Sea
Delion
Saveen's Port
Barnäl
Saveen
Venkar City
Crescent Lake
N
Pynsole Mountains
Vor'Gal

Contents

PART 1

"Destiny doesn't wait for the restless.
She takes what's hers."
~ The Vorelian Scrolls

The Queens' Bidders

Pirates were thieves. They stole gems, precious goods, food, but most of all . . . they stole freedom. Cassian learned that in his ten summers out at sea, sailing the vast waters and bartering for rope and gems. The people of the Vore World liked to believe that being a pirate meant being poor, but it was quite the opposite. Some of the grandest ships to set sail were pirate-owned. These were the fiercest men and women the world bred. Rulers paid high coin for men like him to do their dirty work.

Cassian tied the knot, slapped the wood railing for good luck, and leaned over to get a better look at the ship they were chasing. *Torment* was faster—one of the fastest—and their target didn't stand a chance—lowlife pirates who skipped out on paying their fees to the Red Queens. Every pirate served the Queens. The White Horns, Cassian's clan, were one of the Queens' Bidders, a fleet of ships that did anything the Queens ordered, enforcing rules and stomping out traitors. Cassian's clan and a few others, like the Su'rüles, were given lists of ships that refused to acknowledge the Queens' reign, like now.

Pirates had a hierarchy. Just because they didn't live on land didn't mean they didn't have laws, structure, and an order for how things were run. Pirates weren't brutes thrashing in these waters. They lived and breathed the sea, and when someone disrespected the way of the pirate, they were punished accordingly.

The Red Queens owned the sea. Had done so for centuries. With the highest number of ships across the world, they were everywhere. And with that kind of reach, they declared the seas as theirs, creating the laws that now dictated every pirate's action . . . a way of life that hadn't been challenged in centuries.

With rising tensions between the members of Red Queens, *Torment* worked overtime to keep the peace. Talks of a prophecy uprooted the decades of strong rule the Queens once held. Brewing wars and stories of strange events spilled from the tongues of many who came from the north; Energy Harvesters, people who could summon energy to do their bidding, called on souls in forbidden rituals, nightmarish plagues, and reports of resurrection added to already fragile partnerships. Some even spoke of great beasts crawling out from the depths of the ground to reclaim the land they once called theirs.

"Gainin' on them!" Glass yelled from the crow's nest. Below, waves broke as the ship slammed into them, wind in their favor, and the groan from the hull Cassian heard told him they were picking up speed. The sails strained, hungry, shoving *Torment* ahead. The fabric was new, replaced the last time they docked, about sixteen days ago. A fresh polish on the wood protected it against harsh conditions as well. Three masts, cannons—front and side-facing—and spacious decks to store, transport, and hold prisoners. This ship had been Cassian's home for a decade.

Life hadn't always been the endless waters. He was the son of criminals. A mother and father who worked the underground market, constantly on the run. Every kingdom wanted their heads. He knew that now. Back then, though, he was only worried about getting a meal and their love, which he got neither. When he was ten, he was traded as payment for passage, abandoned at Junok's Port, screaming as dirty men kept him still with iron grips. He kicked, slashed, and punched, but he was too small to make an impact. His parents left without ever looking back.

He worked his way up the ranks, earning the respect of some of the most seasoned sailors through the summers. Though not all. Some thought his blood was dirty; pirate slang for a man who didn't have the right to the sea. Much like the royalty that ruled kingdoms, pirates operated the same way. One was born into the world. Outsiders were hardly welcomed, even as orphaned children.

A burly man with a penchant for throwing crewmembers overboard, Captain Ricard gave him a chance. Missing three fingers and proudly carrying a silver beard that hung down his chest, he'd practically raised Cassian. The crew had a part, too. Cassian was loading cannons by the time he was eleven and ransacked a destroyed ship at twelve. By fourteen, he killed his first man. As the blade sank into flesh and muscle, he didn't squirm or gag; rather, he was elated. The men who raised him encouraged the twist of the sword, to never hesitate in the face of the enemy. Control came to those who took. Life at sea wasn't meant for the weak.

Cassian grabbed a bundle of rope just as four other men did the same. Calloused hands worked fast, looping some around the railing and knotting it so it stayed in place. They would board the ship with the remaining ropes, and the crew needed to ensure the knot didn't slip. Scum's knot is what pirates called it. A knot meant to never loosen.

One loop. Another. Cassian yanked as hard as he could to keep it in place, then checked the sword and dagger strapped to his hip. Satisfied, he hopped onto the railing, grabbing onto the shroud to keep steady. Having done this a hundred times, he didn't flinch even as the slick wood made his boots slide. The rest of the crew followed.

Now, they waited.

The ship swayed, striking a larger wave. Water splashed up along the side, coating wood and men. Sarok slipped to his right, catching himself with the shroud. He nodded at Cassian. Anyone unwise to stand on the railing without holding onto something was better off at the bottom of the sea.

They were nearly upon the ship. Shouts started aboard *Torment*. Beneath, in the gun deck, cannons were loaded and prepped, slotted through the designated openings. More men stood behind, ready to dock the ship once Cassian and the others made the leap.

Their target, a ship poorly named *Blue Bells*, had blue ribbons tied along the railings. A pitiful attempt to stand out, perhaps. Cassian had seen a lot of unique ships, but this one was the worst. Cracked wood, frayed sails, and sun-bleached rope that probably would snap at the slightest inconvenience. A disgrace. A two-mast ship such as this one would last proper pirates a lifetime.

At the sight of *Torment*, a few of the *Blue Bells'* crew jumped overboard. Cowards. They'd get swept into the current, left to die, and be eaten by the beasts below. Others grabbed rusted blades with untrained hands and gathered in a tight circle on the main deck. This would be easy. They weren't defending themselves from the *Torment* crew boarding. No sign of cannons either.

Cassian held his breath. Closer. Two heartbeats passed. Closer. One heartbeat.

Torment collided with the target, and he launched off the railing, using the momentum in his favor. He loosened the rope, giving it length as he crossed the short distance and landed with a heavy thump and a huff. *Blue Bells* was smaller, which made his landing easier. Men followed, and they quickly tied ropes to the railing, securing their ships together. *Torment* rammed the ship again, causing Cassian to stumble as he finished the scum's knot and unsheathed his sword. The helpless crew, dressed in rags and covered in grime, finally reacted, coming to life in a futile attempt to defend themselves.

Behind, the rest of *Torment's* men boarded, surrounding the crew, blades drawn.

Splintered wood groaned underneath Cassian's weight. Wide-eyed youngsters gawked, hardly a day old on the sea. Wes shoved a *Blue Bells* seaman toward the center of the main deck—the one manning the wheel—and took his place.

"W—who are you?" a woman asked, standing on the outskirts of the cornered *Blue Bells'* crew. Her voice shook and her hands trembled. These pirates had never fought a single day in their lives.

"Consider us collectors," Captain Ricard announced, coming up from Cassian's left. He unraveled a scroll, sealed with the Queens' symbol of a skull wearing a crown, and stopped before the small crew. "Quite the chase, hm?" Sarcasm dripped from his sneering lips with that question.

Anyone who wished to call these waters home had to place their loyalty in the Queens. Fees were paid every few moons. Ranks were earned through countless seasons of service. The White Horns earned their high title through centuries of hard work and dedication to the Queens, even declaring their faith in the Red Goddess to earn respect. Not that they practiced religion—prayer didn't belong at sea, though some still tried before the waves took them under. Better to be serving the ruthless savages who worshipped the Red Goddess than running from them. That was how Cassian thought.

The Red Goddess, the deity that the Queens worshipped, was a woman who once roamed the world, able to take and give life with a single kiss. Though paintings portrayed her as lovely and delicate, she became one of the most feared deities in the history of faith. She would walk into a village and kill everyone as retribution for a petitioner being spited by a lover. Or she would grant a mother a healthy child. To the Queens, she embodied the viciousness needed to end wars, but the gentle nature of new beginnings. The unforgivable winds of a maelstrom, but the warm touch of the sun at dawn.

"Spare the lads, yeah?" Greg joked, black hair braided down his back. "Probably scared out of their wits." To make his point, he lunged, and the imprisoned crew jumped back. Laughs filled the deck. "Say, what if we toss them into a black spot? The Queens made those, you know. Keep bilge-sweatin' barnacles like yourselves from ruining these waters."

"Easy now, mate," Captain said, raising an eyebrow. "I might just toss you in with them for fun." At that, he cracked a wild grin and flashed a gold tooth. "Let's get to it, shall we?" He tapped the parchment. "You lot been runnin' from the Queens for about a moon now. Avoiding the fee and deliberately setting fire to an innocent crew's ship to divert attention. Who's the captain?"

Nobody replied. The wind shifted. A storm was coming from the east, from the Grave of Seas. Cassian felt the humid air settle onto his clothes with a foreboding warning. Anything from the Grave was bound to be nasty. They'd need to wrap this up soon if they intended to find an island to hunker behind before the wind got too bad.

Captain took a step forward, the scroll unmoving. "Are you all deaf? Who's Captain?"

A few glanced at one another, but no one spoke.

Cassian scoffed, eager to get this over with.

"All right." Captain motioned at Arian, a man with little to say but a lot to offer. Orders weren't verbally given—didn't need to be—when Arian wrapped his hands around the head of the woman who first spoke and twisted hard. She raised her hands in protest, but it was too late. Her neck snapped, the crew gasped, and Arian tossed her body to the side. Cassian said a silent farewell to the dead woman, as he knew many others did, too. Failure to wish the dead luck could result in a vengeful haunting, and nobody wanted that.

"Are you all done being swabs?" Captain rolled the scroll up and handed it to Glass, who tucked it into his back pocket. "Let's try that again. Who's Captain?"

This time, several shipmates pointed at a young woman in the front. Dark hair braided with rogue strands and freckles, she looked like she belonged in a shop sewing dresses and not out at sea. Hands weren't scarred, skin wasn't red from the sun, and garments weren't tattered and torn from overuse. A sea infant, an apprentice who barely had her head on straight and couldn't possibly tie a scum's knot to save her life. That's who he made her out to be: a woman who disowned her family name and fled to the sea, hoping to find freedom. The only problem was that these waters had already devoured her whole. Just like the rest of them.

"Come on, now." Ricard motioned for her to step forward like he was trying to earn the trust of a frightened child. "Little thing, aren't ya? Been to sea for a whole day?"

"A moon," she mumbled.

"Well, keep your head up when you speak. You're Captain. Act like it."

She did as she was told. "A moon," she repeated, stronger. Her tongue didn't carry the same heavy accent that most pirates had. Her words were sharper, clearer, while pirates, especially the older ones, often rolled their words like they were slurping soup.

Captain nodded. "More like it." He took in the poor conditions of the ship with a quick sweep of his head. "Seen better. You buy this one?"

He was dragging this out, playing with his prey before sinking his teeth in. Cassian grew antsy. Ricard liked to put on a show when he was feeling abnormally cruel.

"Stole it," the woman replied. The chipped sword in her hand didn't waver. She was growing bolder. "Don't have the coin to buy."

"Hm." He wagged his finger, flashing chunky silver rings. "And that's why you won't pay your fee?" The question hung in the air, and after several moments, she finally nodded meekly, averting her gaze. "Shame. Just not lookin' good for you, is it?"

"We're working on it," she said. Too fast. Too abrupt.

"Don't look like it." Captain jerked his chin. Cassian and his men stepped forward, squeezing the crew against the railing. "The Red Queens don't take kindly to disrespect. The seas aren't a place for runaways." Even in the insult, Ricard spoke gently, feigning compassion.

Her head swiveled, reality setting in. This was a losing battle. Cassian's mouth watered. He loved the taste of fear. Sweat made the hilt slip in his hand, and he switched arms. He was one of the few who could comfortably fight with both hands.

Captain motioned again. Another step forward.

"Wait," she blurted. Her crew squeezed in, no longer brave enough to hold their own. Weapons quivered or dropped completely with bitter clangs against the wood, and a few even got on their knees, mumbling about forgiveness and the Gods. Cassian's lips curled up, annoyed. The only Gods they needed to worry about were the ones that lived beneath the waves.

"We were working on it," she insisted, voice high-pitched and frazzled. Her sword wobbled as the ship tipped and her body staggered too close to the railing. Cassian watched with revulsion. This woman didn't and wouldn't ever earn her sea legs. "We had a plan. We're on the way—"

"You're wasting my time," Captain said. He was growing irritated, evidenced by the bulging vein in his neck. The veil hiding the cruel monster underneath finally slipped.

She pointed to the horizon with a trembling hand. "Greve's Point. A man. We're on our way to meet a man who promises a large payout. If we can get to him and fulfill his request, we can pay the fee."

The White Horns exchanged curious looks. This was news. "What was it that he wanted you to do?" Captain asked.

In a meek whisper, she answered, "Steal a dragon egg."

Cassian laughed, angry enough to stab her. Absurd. "You're lying," he spat. Relics were one thing, dragon eggs were preposterous. Pirates bought and sold unique items all the time, especially him. *Torment* had earned a violent reputation, but the crew was also known for its exceptional work with the underground market. Talisman, amulets, people, relics—nothing was off-limits if the price was right. They'd traded a woman to a rich Lord, only to take the family heirloom after following the man back to his ostentatious home. The buyer paid a hefty fee for the mirror, which was said to show the loved ones of the user. They went back for the woman, sneaking her out as promised before dawn crested the horizon. She got a cut of the payout—Captain's orders.

Their latest expedition was big. If they found the Crown of Gods, they would sell it to a man in the Nighthunter Federation, the small city north of here. He'd been odd, a bit reserved, and spoke of the relic like a former lover—sweet, bitter, but yearning for her. Called it Rül'Cril, the proper name for the relic. Questions and information were exchanged, a fee was paid upfront, and Captain Ricard agreed to the work. The payout would be more than they could ever imagine—six times over what Cassian had ever made. Each. Each shipmate would see that. He was eager to return to their original goal, not hunt down pathetic excuses for pirates for the Queens.

"I'm not." The woman stepped forward, and Cassian raised his sword in warning. "We were docked when Igor"—she shoved her thumb in the direction of a scraggly-looking man who couldn't lift a sword—"overheard something about a king searching for a crew brave enough to do his bidding. He'd pay a large payout if the crew succeeded in retrieving the dragon egg. We asked around a bit more and learned he would be at Greve's Point three days from now."

Captain grinned, planting his hands on his hips. Behind, *Torment* swayed and knocked into *Blue Bells* again. The deck and masts shook. "And you think you swabs can do that?"

She shrugged. "We were going to try."

"And how do you know this dragon egg is real?" The dreaded question. The one on everyone's mind. A Dragon Rider hadn't been alive in nearly eight centuries. All anyone could talk about when they docked at these cities was the black-scaled dragon that was seen leaving the city of Geral several seasons ago. Recently, people spoke of the white dragon, spotted in the country of Diyră. Wild talk is what Cassian called it. People growing desperate under the growing political tensions between countries.

Dead queens, murders-for-hire, and new rulers always got the land-walkers, what pirates called 'citizens' who lived ashore, chatting like fearful baby birds left alone too long in a nest. Crewmen would talk crazy, too, when the storm got bad enough. Talk about the Life Eaters that spun the waters and made the sea impossible to sail, how the Gods had made these beasts to target those who questioned their authority. It wasn't the first time a Dragon Rider story circled, and it wouldn't be the last.

"We don't," she said, shoulders slumping. "But can you blame us for trying?"

"Yes," Cassian mumbled. Captain shot him a glare. He was overstepping. If he didn't watch his tongue now, he'd earn a black eye or be gutting fish for two days.

"You mentioned a king," Captain said. "Do you know who?"

He swallowed his agitation. He knew that tone—Ricard was interested. Double the payout if this egg was real. Cassian didn't have the title to speak against the captain's wants. If they were already heading to Greve's Point for information on Rül'Cril, then they would try to learn more about this egg, too.

She shook her head. The fight in her was dying. Maybe she realized just how ridiculous this all sounded. "Only that he would be wearing a gold ring with a red jewel," she told Captain. "As far as I know, he's only there one night. I don't know anything else."

The groaning wood from the rocking ships filled the silence. The horizon darkened, and the wind intensified. Greve's Point was a two-day sail from here on good waters. If they managed to hunker down behind an island and wait the storm out, they'd lose time. Cassian didn't care about the egg. It was likely a façade to get the attention of desperate impostors like *Blue Bells*, who thought they'd earn their right as pirates. Buyers always did that. Talked up the prize to get a pirate's attention.

Pirates didn't care about landwalker laws or royal titles. If coin was involved and it increased status, they did it. The more a crew succeeded, the higher their cost was for working with those on land. Being a pirate was a business. One at which *Torment* was exceptional.

Captain turned without warning and walked back to their ship, footsteps final. "The fee must always be paid."

That was their cue. The one Cassian had been waiting for. He and the others moved swiftly, polished in the art of execution by surprise. Latching onto the woman who called herself a captain, Cassian pinned her instantly. He couldn't hesitate or show her mercy, not now. She struggled as the others shouted, fumbling with their weapons. They never had a chance. Cassian dragged the blade across the woman's throat, fingers digging into her jaw while he kept her pressed against him to restrain her. Blood broke free, pouring down her clothes and staining the poorly-kept wood. She spasmed, reaching for the wound, and he pulled her to the railing. She didn't even put up a fight.

"They say that the Tsu'ran take souls like yourself and put them to work for eternity. If you're lucky, you'll be turned into one of their own," Cassian told her. Best to warn her of what was to come. He'd spent many summers learning all that he could about the merciless Tsu'ran. If he could have given her a chance to run, he would have simply because he recognized the look of terror in her eye—the very same he'd had the day he was abandoned—but not with the captain watching. Any show of kindness would earn him a place right next to her at the bottom of the sea.

Color drained from her, her movements became more sluggish, and when she opened her mouth to speak, the muscles in her neck reacted, but nothing came out. "May you find peace among the dead," he whispered into her ear. At that, he shoved her overboard and watched her strike the water headfirst.

Out here, where the sea was Judgment and the winds were Destiny, he believed in the Tsu'ran. Any pirate foolish enough not to should be killed on the spot. The Tsu-ran were shape-shifters and protectors of the Grave. They took on the form one most desired and hunted for restless souls. In their most natural form, they were anything but beautiful or alluring. Tentacles, orb-like eyes, and massive. A madman wouldn't strike a deal with one.

The rest of the *Blue Bells'* crew was taken care of, tossed overboard like their captain. Cassian gave the orders, directing them to loot and pull all resources. Men got to work, quickly finding that *Blue Bells* had hardly anything worth value. Food was scarce, and water was plentiful. One starved goat with its ribs showing was near death. A few spare boots, flint, and rope were found below where the cannons were stored. The few chickens were taken. A pile of discarded items was placed on the main deck. Once that was done, the *Torment* crew piled back onto their ship, and Captain Ricard gave the order.

"Burn her."

Cassian and a few others passed a lantern around, dousing sticks and rags in fire. One by one, they threw the burning item aboard *Blue Bells* as several crewmembers pulled the ropes back. Captain turned the wheel, giving them space as the ship lit up. Shrouds and sails caught the flames as the pile burned higher. The victorious crew watched, as was customary. A ship shouldn't ever burn, but an abandoned one shouldn't ever be left to wander the sea. Souls could find their way aboard and never leave. Pirates who died honorably needed safe passage to the Afterlife, a paradise into which all souls in the living realm passed. An abandoned ship would grant them no such right.

The sea was no place for the restless.

Rough Waters

Rains drenched the main deck. Winds tore at the sails so harshly that the men loosened the ties and lowered them. A storm like this would rip those in two and leave their ship stranded unless they paddled their way to the nearest dock, which was countless leagues from here. Pulling out the long paddles was never a good sign. It either meant the ship was destroyed or a lot of men were dead. Otherwise, best to keep the paddles where they belonged—tied securely to the walls of the gun deck. Easy to pull cannons back and stuff paddles through the same windows they shot out of when needed. Cassian hadn't ever run into that problem yet.

He took a sip of water from the canteen. Stale and lukewarm. Old. Nobody ever talked about how nasty water could get once it sat aboard for a moon under the grueling sun. Moisture turned the canteens into stewing pots of mold, and if they weren't cleaned out regularly, the crew got sick. Most skins used for canteens were burned and sanitized with fire and liquor, but those out at sea were hardly ever made properly. Call it pride, but the pirates on these waters had a different way of making things.

Belts were created with braided leather taken from raids. Shirts, boots, and pants were stolen from the disrespected dead—they didn't need clothes where they were going—and weapons were sharpened against their opponents' swords. Few had whetstones. The Queens did. They had everything a pirate could ever need and more.

He leaned his head back. Coffee sat in the galley, ground and ready. A good drink to curl the toes and knock the life right back into any man or woman on sea. A staple to cure any hangover or to cleanse the tongue from the stale taste of nothingness after a long stretch of not talking. Coffee was harvested from only one place in the world: along Hyle's Lake in the northern country of Eiyrăl, where the climate was just right for optimal growth. Prices were high to get hands on ground coffee, but pirates never recoiled at the cost.

Once this storm passed, they'd set off for Greve's Point to find the king with the gold ring. Captain Ricard tore Cassian a new one when they left *Blue Bells* behind for overstepping, disrespecting the captain in front of the crew. Nothing much ever needed to be said, but those few words could gouge a hole the size of a city in a man's pride. Cassian's tongue still tasted the sour interaction. Speak out of turn again and Captain would have to make a public example out of him, make sure the crew understood who was in charge.

This was the second time in a full moon that Cassian overstepped his boundaries; five times if he counted the season. One of the rules on this ship was not to question or speak over the captain, and he'd done both. Respecting authority because of titles troubled him. Not because he didn't like Ricard, but because he was crawling out of his skin to do more than just tie ropes off and obey an order. He wanted—no, *needed*—more than that. He deserved to be the captain, to be the one everyone respected. But power like that didn't come by accident. It was earned.

So, off to Greve's Point for the mad king. Rül'Cril was still a priority, but nobody denied the underlying buzz in the air with this new prospect. This could change *Torment's* entire reputation—pirates wouldn't dare call Cassian dirty-blooded anymore. A dragon egg could start and end wars, more than some relic from a dead king. Greve's Point was home to the pirates, a place where beggars became kings, royalty were thieves, and the only law was none. Not even the Seven Sea Laws held a place on the large island. A Queen was just another pirate, a king a nobody. The perfect place to disappear if one was ever hunted.

Coin was on Cassian's mind constantly. Ricard told him they'd have more than they could ever need in four lifetimes if they succeeded in obtaining the relic and agreed to the king's heist for the dragon egg. He couldn't deny the allure with that . . . if the egg was real. Ships cost money, a lot of it. A simple fix could put a normal family in debt for the rest of their life. If a mast broke, they'd be docked at port spending more coin than a tradesman working with a king. Labor costs. That's what they all said. Labor costs more than any jewel.

The crew's quarters were cramped, mostly full of resources that a pirate could need, like extra clothing and belts. One could never be too prepared at sea. Having additional resources was essential if they were stuck for a long while. Hammocks were tied on either side, waterskins hung from hooks above, and the galley was just ten paces away, up a narrow set of stairs. A nice ship for long stretches of travel. Landwalkers always thought pirates were scum. Cassian couldn't stand the landwalkers. Ignorant scoundrels who didn't ask the right questions and always said the wrong thing.

He kicked the scratched chest in front of him. Off-duty until sunrise. Generally, Cassian tried to only work nights, but with a sick seaman and the storm, Captain adjusted the nightly duties, which forced schedules to shift. During the day when the sun was hot, he could lay his head down without worry. At night, he never quite rested as well.

Out at sea, when black tendrils wrapped over the sun and dragged it below the horizon, the voices started. They lived in the floors, the water, and the walls. Everywhere. The dead came out at night, seeking refuge from the madness of their eternal suffering. Loud splashing sometimes caught the attention of the crew, followed by shouts. Drowning victim. A spirit reliving their final moments. Shipwrecks were usually near—close enough to catch the attention of the crew in fear of a collision—and the captain often barked orders to change direction.

The restless dead not yet claimed by the Tsu'ran were best avoided. If the voices grew too inviting, anyone could be dragged into the prison these souls were chained to. When Cassian was on-duty, he could keep his thoughts busy, but in the crew's quarters, where the silence was more damning than the howl of a cannon, he was left listening. At night, when he slept, he was plagued by terrorizing dreams; dreams where he was locked in a box at the bottom of the sea, trapped, and others where he was running.

To keep himself busy, he carved a piece of wood with the short utility knife he carried. The blade needed sharpening, but it still did the job. Slow and careful, he dug wood away, creating a small pile of shavings beside him. Whenever extra wood was around, he took pieces and carved things; whales, boats, daggers, figurines. The crew thought he was talented; some even went as far as to request a couple of pieces several summers ago, but Cassian didn't think there was anything special about his work. All he did was dedicate a little bit of time. Dedication could get a man anything, good or bad.

When they docked, he usually gave his creations away, not finding the need to hold onto them. Children loved them, but he often found single women or unloved wives appreciated them most. After a few times, he found he enjoyed the process of gifting. It gave him fulfillment to do good when his days were often filled with ending lives and obeying orders he didn't like. Some might call it purpose, but that was a word he still wasn't sure he quite understood at the age of twenty.

Boots echoed and the floor groaned. The lantern in front of him flickered as the ship swayed again, waves lapping against the shore they'd anchored themselves close to. Most of the winds pummeled the other end of the island. Thunder cracked, though much less than earlier. The rains likely wouldn't let up until dawn.

Glass appeared, soaked. Scraggly hair stuck across his face, no shirt, and holding a piece of dried fish. Fresh fish was plentiful, but the crunchy dried skin and seasoning could appease any pirate on a hot, sweltering day, or warm their bellies after sailing in cold winds. It was a pirate's favorite meal. Glass was covered in tattoos—depictions of ships, swords, and symbols special to him. Wherever skin was, ink followed. Hardly a day over thirty, and the man carried himself like a curmudgeon of fifty. Rings decorated his hands, and he had earrings of gold and silver. Strangers wouldn't approach him, and if Cassian didn't know better, he'd avoid him too. But this was Glass. The kind of man who'd take a sword to the heart for him.

"Thought you'd be down here," Glass said and settled in next to him. The necklace he always wore shimmered. The skull with crossbones was as iconic as having coffee aboard for those days when the liquor took a bit too much life out of a pirate's step. There wasn't a day that Cassian hadn't seen that necklace. "Captain relieved me. Storm's dying down out there. Not as nasty as we thought it'd be." He reeked of ale.

Cassian nodded, returning to his carving. "Think we'll pull the anchor sooner?"

"Nah." Glass bit into the fish. "Don't want to foul the anchor. Best to see the sun before we move out. You know how it is," he said through a mouthful. "Want some?"

Storms like this were unpredictable. Act too fast, and they could be another lost story, killed because the storm kicked back up once they moved. Or it could be what they hoped—quiet. Cassian shimmied the edge of the blade into a crevice and pushed gently, not wanting to crack the wood.

"No."

Glass took another bite. "Your loss. It's better than whatever Wes bought last time."

Cassian raised his brow in acknowledgment. "How are Elliot's studies coming along?" he asked. As the youngest, Elliot was taken under the wing of the crew to be taught everything he needed to know, including reading.

The pirate snorted, amused. "He's clever. Come a long way. I think he's done after this season. Knows everything he needs to be successful." Glass shook his head. "Wild. I taught him to read, you know. Practically taught that kid everything he knows."

Cassian waved his knife in warning. "Don't take all the credit. I did, too." Long nights of swordsmanship training and talks filled his head. Sometimes, he felt like the older brother; other times, like the swabber who got lucky. Instead of washing the decks, he was teaching the son of Traz everything he knew. Traz was Captain's second-in-command. If the lad wanted his son aboard the same ship he worked, then Cassian wasn't paid enough to argue. The only thing he cared about was Elliot not getting killed under his watch by slipping off the shrouds or pissing off the wrong pirate.

"Whatcha carving this time?" Glass asked.

"A dragon," Cassian answered. He hesitated as the chunk of wood fell away. "Does it look like one?"

"How am I supposed to know? Ain't ever seen one. Not unless you count the Life Eaters. You know what the stories say about those." Glass mumbled his forgiveness to the sea and finished off the last of the fish, then motioned with his dirty fingers to the piece. Many thought Life Eaters were once dragons who fell in love with the water, but when they tried to leave, the sea wouldn't let them go. "Those are wings, right?"

Cassian nodded. "Yes, and this will be the head, and here's the tail." He pointed with the knife to the spots, hoping they were accurate.

After the run-in earlier with *Blue Bells*, he couldn't shake the woman's words or his captain's wild glimmer of glee. A dragon egg. They'd burrowed into the darkest places of his mind and settled in for the long stay, far more than any relic ever would. Coin could get him almost whatever he wanted, but a dragon egg would give him the respect he deserved.

On *Torment*, men had learned to stop asking questions, accepting what was, but out there, where the Queens ruled, he still got told he was dirty because he wasn't born on a ship. The dragon egg would give him the chance to fulfill his purpose of wanting his own ship, crew—a new life where he was in control of his own destiny.

"Looks good to me." Glass leaned back, pushing his legs out. His left boot was torn along the top; aged leather that was well past its prime. "Hear anything tonight?"

He meant the dead. "No. Not yet," Cassian replied.

"Hm." Glass looked around at their small crew's room. "Quieter than usual lately, don't you think?"

He wasn't asking questions about Cassian's disobedience with the captain, which was a relief. Ricard didn't necessarily make it a secret when he requested to speak to anyone. Captain loved to make a scene. More often than not, men waited to pry and humiliate any poor soul pulled into the captain's cabin, jeering and cackling their added insults. Thankfully, none of that had happened tonight.

Cassian cleared his throat. "Isn't that a good thing?" he asked.

"The dead only get louder when they're not being heard," Glass said. "Now they're quieter than they've been for a decade. Ain't normal." He shuddered and kissed the palm of his hand, paying his respects. Customary habits for the more traditional pirates.

Cassian's knife hovered over another section, not quite committed. "Well?" he pressed. "What are you trying to say?"

"Sometimes I forget you weren't born in these waters," Glass mumbled, shaking his head. "You best watch your tongue. Don't be asking absurd questions like that off this boat. You might just piss off the wrong man." He sighed. "I should have gotten more fish."

The dragon carving still needed a lot of work. He hoped to do detailed scales along the body and dig out little horns, but his creativity waned the more Glass spoke. The crew didn't understand the motivation behind creating. Once it was gone, it wasn't coming back. Stubborn, he continued, wanting to at least get the wings better displayed before he stopped for the night. Each motion felt like he was digging through mud. Not even the knife worked right, and frustration flared.

"Doesn't that wing look a bit smaller than the other?" Glass asked, leaning too close.

"Details," he snapped. "I'm trying to get the wings to look similar." The response was harsh, even for him, and he dipped his head. "Are you going to tell me more about whatever this is about the dead?"

"Oh, you want to know?"

The tip of the knife burrowed into the base of the wing. "You brought it up. Finish the story."

"It ain't just a story, depending on who you ask," Glass replied, annoyed. "The children are taught about the dead. The young ones are too curious for their own good sometimes. Go exploring while men are working and sleeping, following the voices, and next thing you know, kid's gone. Victim to the dead." He scoffed. "Watched a girl get dragged right over the railing when she took the dead's hand when I was only six. Hand reached up and wrapped grimy fingers around her little wrist. She had no idea what she was doing. Never got a chance to find out either. It's real. All of it."

The creativity was gone completely. All his attention was on Glass. Everyone knew of the dead and the superstitions around them, but he'd never known Glass witnessed a real taking. Witnessing that left a mark—black and cold—on the soul. Some thought the dead could sniff that out and came looking when their time was up. Others went as far as to throw those who witnessed a taking overboard to please the dead.

"The dead grow louder when they're not being heard," Glass repeated, softer. "When they grow quieter, it means someone's listening. Old legends talk about a collector. Someone who ends the suffering and brings the souls where they need to be. A peacemaker that establishes balance between the dead and living." He studied his fingernails.

Cassian waved his knife. "And you think this is happening?"

"Strange timing, don't you think? The dead grow quiet, and now there's talk of a dragon egg?"

The question sat between them, stifling. Strange was an understatement. Put it that way and Cassian couldn't help but wonder if none of it was a coincidence. The carving was still in his hand, waiting, but he made no motions to try anymore. "You think it's real?" Cassian's question came out hardly audible.

Glass nudged his shoulder. "You saw the look in that woman's eyes, didn't you?"

He nodded. Afraid. Desperate. Raw.

"She wasn't lying. You know that. We all do."

That didn't settle anything. "Has Captain mentioned what he plans to do if we get a dragon egg?" Cassian whispered. The question tasted sour. His intentions weren't honest, but at sea, nobody had honest intentions. "How can anyone be certain of this? There's not been mention of dragons in centuries, save for the wild rumors. We all know those are made up. Landwalkers are always telling crazy stories."

"Take it back to the buyer and get a big payout," Glass said and shrugged. "What else are we doing with a dragon egg? Maybe it's fake. Maybe it's just got coin inside it or some special necklace. I don't know, and at the end of the day, I won't ever know. You ever see a dragon egg?"

Cassian shook his head, deflated.

"Nobody has," Glass told him. "Would we even know if it was real or not if we picked it up?"

"Probably not," Cassian muttered. "Could be a rock carved to look like one."

"And if it was real, we're carrying around a dead dragon. Morbid."

Glass made sense. No way a dragon could live for centuries in an egg. Some said dragons could survive that long; something about the energy they were made of helped preserve them, but that defied logic. If it was real, it would be hardly anything more than just a shelf piece. Still, Cassian could leverage it.

"This talk of the Queens and their prophecy." Glass's voice was soft. "It feels different."

Cassian wasn't sober enough for this conversation, and he cursed himself for not grabbing anything to drink prior to camping out in this cramped room. Change made anyone nervous, but any sort of shift in the power dynamics of the rulers of the sea kept him up at night. If anything changed, it would disrupt the entire flow of how these waters were run.

Glass didn't wait for a reply. "They speak of war like they've waited for this day for centuries. Makes me wonder if these black spots are intentional, some sort of sign of the end of times. The Queens are hungry for more than just the sea—"

"The extremists," Cassian corrected. The crew believed the Queens opened gateways to the Soul Realm, the home of the dead, as part of some bargain for power. Black spots. They swallowed ships whole. Cassian didn't know what he believed. "Zinfel doesn't want to take the land. Pirates belong at sea." Zinfel and her current family had ruled the Queens for three decades now—peaceful, but with a strong hand on control and authority.

Glass scoffed. "For how long?"

Cassian squinted, confused. "For what? For all this to wash over? Give it a season."

"No," Glass shot back, shaking his head. "How long until pirates want to claim the land as their own?"

"That's an outrageous statement." Cassian's response came out hot, angry. "We wouldn't be pirates if we took land. We'd be commoners, Lords, kings—you get the idea. Landwalkers."

"They say the Red Goddess will return." Glass was quieter than usual, like he'd seen a ghost and was afraid it might hear him speak. "That the King of Monsters will court her. That to ensure she is reborn into the flesh of you and I, the Queens must fulfill their oath in ensuring the world knows her name."

It was true. The power struggle occurring between members of the Queens was founded on a warring belief in what their future held. Some wanted to keep the peace, believing the Red Goddess didn't seek to be reborn. Others felt differently. With the world changing, many Queens were certain this was the start of the prophecy. War amongst the landwalkers, strange plagues wiping out thousands, unpredictable weather patterns, and quakes were a few signs the Queens believed were markers for the start of the end. Cassian didn't like what was happening either, but he didn't think it was because of a prophecy, so he chose his next words carefully.

"Don't you wonder if some of this is bolstered by those who wish to do the world harm?"

The pirate smiled, so faint and weak that it troubled Cassian to see. "You speak just like them," Glass mumbled. "Desperate to bury your head in the sand and ignore all the signs around you. Every now and then, I am reminded of just how different you are from those who were born on the sea."

The insult stung. He bit his lip, trying to refrain from saying anything that would be rude. Glass never meant it to be unkind. He was one of the only ones who could speak freely to Cassian about his upbringing on land. Still, he'd worked hard to bury the troubled childhood and embrace this life he'd been given.

All Cassian wanted was to be accepted by these men and women who called the waters home. The harder he tried, the more he was shoved back. No matter what he did, he would always be the dirty-blooded pirate who craved the acceptance of those who wished to make an example out of him. It was cruel how life sometimes turned out.

Glass shifted. The space was confining, making him too close. "What would you do if you got a dragon egg?"

Cassian raised an eyebrow.

"If the crew didn't exist," Glass clarified. "If only you found it. What would you do? I like to think I'd sell it, but I don't know. Would be interesting to keep around, too."

Cassian stuffed the knife back into a short sheath on his belt. "Sell it and get myself a ship. Be captain." The answer felt right. He'd wanted his own ship for several summers now. Working as a deckhand was old. He was restless, ready for more, and the idea of serving Captain Ricard for another decade made his skin crawl. He needed out.

"You never doubt yourself, do you?" Glass asked. His eyes twinkled, amused.

The question was odd. Cassian wasn't sure how to answer that. "What do you mean?"

"Ever since we brought you aboard, you have always spoken with such certainty," Glass observed. "Didn't matter if you were wrong, either. Never seen a boy take a life so fast when you were told it was how things were done, how we survived. And here you are, as certain as ever. Some men would pay anything to be that way."

Being unforgiving and quick was all Cassian knew. He'd spent his first ten summers running. Hesitation got criminals killed. His parents taught him that. If he learned anything, it was that nobody questioned him when he spoke with confidence. In the silence, that's when he let his guard slip.

"I'm getting more fish and taking a piss." Glass stood and stretched. "Want some?"

"Piss or fish?" Cassian cracked a wicked smile. "Just don't go overboard," he said. "That would be a humiliating way to die, yeah?" The beakhead—the worst-smelling spot on any ship, and sometimes endearingly nicknamed the Dead's Rot because of the aroma—was where men and women went to relieve themselves, just below the bowsprit. Rains from storms like tonight cleaned the area up, washing away sometimes countless days of rancid piss and shit that could make the toughest man heave if the waves didn't do their job. And when the drunks used the head to retch? Cassian wanted to gag just thinking about it. Captain had a private spot for himself, like most captains did. Occasionally, Cassian snuck to the back of the ship to use it when hot days turned the head into a rotten feast for the nostrils and forced tears to the eyes.

"Suit yourself," Glass replied and left the room, shutting the narrow door on the way out. The ship tilted from the fighting waves, and he realized he'd not heard thunder in a while. Maybe the rains had let up by now. Based on the lantern's flame, the night was still young. He'd filled it with oil just before sitting down.

The dragon statue stared at him, expectant. He grimaced. Still so much to be done, and he worried he wouldn't make it look good. The body was still chunky, the wings disproportionate, and the tail only noted by the small line he'd carved into the lower base of the body, wrapping around. When he was done, he'd dip it in oil, give it a nice, finished shine and set it out to dry. Someone would appreciate it. It wouldn't be done by the time they reached Greve's Point, but perhaps by the next time they docked.

He sat there, glad for the silence. Glass was right. The dead were quiet. Too quiet. His eyelids drooped, his head bowed, and he succumbed to slumber.

Wretched Queens

The gun deck was where most of the heavy artillery was stored. Below the main deck, cannons lined each wall, ready to be used at any time. In front, placed on either side of the bow, were two more cannons. They could be useful in a chase that wasn't going well. Hardly used, though.

Cassian checked the cannonballs, cleaned the cannons, and surveyed the ropes keeping the weapons in place. Last thing they needed was to have one of the ropes snap during a storm and send that weight rolling around. It would upset the ship's balance, damage other cannons, and potentially kill someone. Maintenance like this happened regularly, sometimes three times a moon, depending on *Torment's* activity. After the storm last night, it was good practice to inspect the artillery. Captain always asked Cassian to do it because he was the best.

He switched a few ropes out, taking the old ones and bundling them in a chest of extras—used primarily for binding prisoners or dragging cargo that didn't weigh as much. Then he cleaned the chamber of every cannon. Grime packed up over time, and that could impact speed and precision.

Chains hung along the back, useful in destroying enemy masts. Last summer, they were only used once when a fleeing ship refused to abide by their requests, firing cannons back. *Fearless* was the ship's name. Cassian still remembered. The crew fought with everything they had. Respectable but senseless.

The White Horns weren't always the Queens' Bidders. Centuries ago, before the Queens expanded their reign and took over the seas, they were the most feared pirates of the world. They raided villages, slaughtered anyone who stood in their way, and practiced traditions that were unique to the tribes of Assane. Some of the older generations that still sailed upheld those, but many, like *Torment*, were captained by a newer generation of White Horns, one bred by the Queens.

A handful of summers ago, a weathered crewman joined the ranks for a short time. An older White Horn named Lacky, who found their ship after losing his from an attack by a Life Eater, a creature that lived in the darkest corners of the sea. Uncommon, but it did happen. Lacky brought tradition with him, lighting sage on full moons and carrying bones strapped to his belt to ward off any unsettled spirits. When he worked the nights, he hummed a song that had been passed down for generations, promising that it soothed the restless and kept the malicious dead from getting too close, causing bad luck. He spoke of the Gods as if they walked among them all, even going so far as to test each crewmember, believing any one of them might be a deity. Captain Ricard wasn't fond of that part. Threatened the codger for it. Didn't stop Lacky, though. He just got better at hiding his actions.

Too much pride in the older generation kept anyone from killing him—one of the few times everyone agreed on something. At the next stop at Greve's Point, they dropped Lacky off and told him to find a new ship.

A distant horn sounded. Cassian tensed, hand halfway down the cannon's barrel chamber. The Queens' call. Odd. The crew and he had just seen the Red Queens a few days ago to give report. The usual. How many ships were avoiding the fee, any new crews setting sail, possible strife between clans, and so on. The Queens ordered *Torment* to prioritize *Blue Bells* on the list they were handed. Cassian hadn't seen that list, but expected at least three more ships they'd need to hunt down before the next moon. Fee runners, what they called those like *Blue Bells* who had neglected to pay tribute, were increasing lately. A result of the brewing political war on land, Cassian supposed.

Pulling his arm out, skin blackened, he tossed the dirty rag over his shoulder and crossed the room to the ladder. Climbing, he saw the main deck already busy with preparations. Greeting the Queens always meant a clean deck. The horn blew again, closer. The iconic Red Queen flag soared against the blue sky—a skull wearing a crown against a red background—glaringly proud. Rulers of the sea. Cassian was lying if he said he didn't envy their power and influence. Even their ships were grand.

The dark wood of the Queens' ship was polished and finished with a glaze that reflected thousands of red specks. Three masts with red sails. Black rope because they could afford to buy the customization. The bow was carved to look like a woman reaching outward, a crown in her hands. Breasts and body were in full detail, hair taken by the unseen wind. The railing depicted small waves. Along the front, written in crimson, was *Goddess*. She had earned a reputation as a ship that hadn't ever lost a battle. The Queens spared no expense in displaying their wealth with how well-loved their ships were. If the White Horns were ruthless kings, the Queens were opulent Gods.

"Line up, men!" Captain Ricard descended from the upper deck. Coops full of chickens and ducks lined the railing, having been placed there to minimize the stench in *Torment's* hold while the weather held. Air was charged, which meant another storm could smother them today, and they didn't want to keep the livestock exposed to thrashing waves and high winds, so they would be moved below later.

Livestock were essential. They kept the ship fed and offered a continuous supply of resources—leather, eggs, meat, and bones for cleaning and decorative purposes. Any ship that failed to care for their livestock might as well be at the bottom of the sea. It was bad luck to kill any animal without reason and a blessing.

Goddess pulled herself flush with *Torment.* The Queens' crew tossed ropes to the White Horn vessel. Cassian grabbed one, securely tying it off. When that was complete, the Red Queens dropped a gangway between the gap in the railings left for such occasions—or for recovering sailors if they accidentally fell overboard. Occasionally, it happened.

Next to *Goddess, Torment* looked cheap. It was one of the nicest White Horn ships at sea, but nothing compared to the magnificence of a Red Queen ship. All these summers later, Cassian still couldn't shake the awe that bubbled up from the pit of his stomach. The Queens' crew was no less a grand exception, garnished in gold and silver along their hands, ears, hair, and wherever they could fit it. They had enough gold and power to rival any landwalker kingdom in the Vore World.

Ringlets decorated the right arms of the more respected crew, displaying their authority, while the captain wore a crown necklace and possessed a tattoo along his neck in Old Tongue. A lost language that once ruled the sea. Few could speak it, save for some of the oldest Queens, who worked tirelessly to pass the language on. Some of the most ancient Vorelian scrolls were written in Old Tongue. Cassian couldn't read it. All he knew was that the black sigil tattooed into the neck of the captain meant the sun queen, inspired by an old Goddess who once was believed to have control over light. From her, the Red Queens were born.

Captain Ricard stood front and center, hands on his hip, as the Queens' captain crossed with several high-ranking shipmates. Ebony skin shimmered with a fine layer of sweat, and his amber gaze swept the crew, settling on Cassian. Chills raced over Cassian, raising gooseflesh on his arms. He'd not met this man before, and he didn't want to. Something about the way he carried himself made Cassian want to crawl into the bottom of this ship.

The Queens' captain stopped in front of Ricard. "Greetings." The other Red Queens stationed themselves strategically close to Ricard. If Cassian didn't know better, he would say his captain was cornered—an injured bird in a den of starved beasts.

"Greetings, Captain E'ghan." Captain dipped his head, submitting to their title. "What's the inspiration for today's visit? I was just talking with Zinfel three days ago. We've already acquired the debt of *Blue Bells*. Just last night."

E'ghan grunted. "Zinfel's dead."

Cassian laid a hand on the railing, steadying himself. The crew turned to statues, and Ricard's complexion dropped a shade. Political anarchy never occurred with the Red Queens. Their traditions kept the peace and pride of their long-standing culture. Women born from the six families of the inner circle were voted in. If only one woman was the choice, then she was placed as leader in a unanimous vote. They called her Viv'an, which meant daughter of the Red Goddess, and they revered her. The Queens believed that the six families were hand-picked by their deity, but only women were to rule, certain their blood ran with the soul of the Red Goddess. She lived through Viv'an, and to honor that meant to uphold their faith. The highest priority. Anyone who threatened that was considered a traitor and executed.

To kill Zinfel wasn't just a politically-charged devastation; it was an outright declaration of challenging their faith in the Red Goddess. Centuries of practice stomped on in a single cruel act for control.

"I just spoke to her—" Ricard stopped, looking down. Cassian hadn't ever seen him so flustered. "What happened?"

"Zinfel's hand was passive," E'ghan said. "Too many issues now. Fee runners are too high, traitors getting away. The damage is worldwide. We needed to reclaim control."

Everything went deafeningly quiet. Even the lapping waves against the ships sounded leagues beyond Cassian's ears. Not a single pirate moved. Zinfel deposed. This would change everything.

"The new ruler is of the Serulic family," the Red Queen captain continued, head held high. "Kinson. You will meet her when you present your next report. I recommend trimming up the beard. She prefers well-dressed captains."

Ricard, for once, had nothing to say. He only nodded.

E'ghan gestured at Ricard. "Where are you heading?"

Cassian bit his tongue. Captain had no reason to lie. A successful heist like this would increase the Queens' status. They'd get a cut of the payout. A win for everyone.

"Heading for Hil Islands. We have reason to believe the next fee runner is hiding out there." The lie was told so smoothly that Cassian momentarily believed him, forgetting about Greve's Point and their goals. He wanted to slap his captain and ask for an explanation for all of it. He'd sworn he knew Ricard better than most—the captain practically raised him. Now, though, as he stood there, he felt out of control. Captain knew things that the rest of the crew didn't, and Cassian wanted to know why he felt the need to lie. Pride? Fear?

"Hm." Captain E'ghan surveyed the main deck, slowing as he beheld the captain's cabin, and curled his upper lip in disgust, as if the ship repulsed him. An insult—Cassian ground his teeth in response. *Torment* was one of the nicest ships the White Horns had. It didn't have the outrageous paint job or trimmings like a Red Queen ship, but it didn't need to. The Red Queen crew kept their hands on their hips, awaiting orders. The ink that decorated their skin displayed their loyalty to their clan. The Red Queens loved tattoos, far more than any other pirate clan. To them, it wasn't just ink; it was cultural pride.

"I've got another job for you and your men," E'ghan added quietly.

"But the list—" Ricard started to say.

"Will be dealt with in due time," E'ghan interjected. "You are far more valuable than hunting low-life pirates. Under orders of Kinson, you are now tasked to hunt and dispose of Zinfel's family, the Dirnals. At present, the ships we know belong to them are *Lover*, *Crown Taker*, and *Hunter*. The quicker you complete your task, the better. We have reason to believe they've fled and will abandon their ships once they find reason to."

Captain Ricard stood there, pale and sweaty. The collar of his tunic and underarms were damp. Cassian felt the same. Hunting for those they once reported to was risky. These weren't poorly-run ships or unskilled crews. These were Red Queens—or had been. Taking out three ships with full crews was impossible, even for *Torment*. Cassian's stomach twisted as frigid dread blossomed. They weren't supposed to live through this.

"Uh . . ." Ricard scratched his chin, laughing nervously. "Can I ask what this is about?"

Captain E'ghan smiled, revealing silver teeth that were branded with tiny skulls that caught the sun. "Do you really want to know?"

Ricard cleared his throat. "Well, yeah. White Horns don't normally dabble in political disagreements between the Red Queen families."

"Of course." E'ghan moved his fingers. The gesture was so subtle that, if not for his angle, Cassian would never have seen it. A high-ranked Red Queen stepped forward, decorated in more jewels than Cassian owned, and drove a short blade right through Ricard's back. The tip of the sword came out the other side, glistening red, before the pirate twisted and yanked the blade free with a blood-curdling *squelch*. Ricard stood there, staring at the blood spreading across his tunic. The *Torment* crew startled, taking a step back, but no one reached for their blade. Cassian sank further into the railing.

"It's fitting you would say that." E'ghan raised his chin, lip curling in disgust. "Your work with Zinfel is no secret. Not anymore."

The wind stilled. No one dared move. The horrifying nightmare unraveling before Cassian strangled the little bit of courage right out of him. The life he'd known was falling apart before his eyes. The captain he'd worked with for many summers stood there, stoic despite the blood that poured from the wound through his chest. Even in the face of Death, Ricard didn't flinch.

"When Zinfel lay dying in her own bath, it was your name she spoke," E'ghan hissed. "Why?"

Ricard sputtered, blood dribbling down his chin. No response came. In one final act of defiance, he collapsed without answering. Dead.

"Tre'lang ungahr," E'ghan whispered. *Destiny loved the sea.* The bold statement hung over everyone, hushing the winds. Anyone who denied Destiny what she wanted had no right to call the sea their home. A Red Queen's farewell.

A long silence followed, once brewing with frustration, now bubbling over with a despair so thick that the winds died against the sails. The Red Queen leader's chest rose and fell several times as he inspected the dead captain, nudging him with his polished boot. "Questions are not welcomed," E'ghan finally said, turning away from the scene. "It's time we establish boundaries. If I or Kinson ask you to do something, you do it without question. Am I understood?"

The *Torment* crew didn't speak, paralyzed. In response, the Red Queens who stood at the ready dropped a hand to the blade strapped to their hip. A silent warning.

"Am I understood?" Captain E'ghan yelled. Cassian flinched, nodding instinctively. *Like a coward*, he thought. He felt like he was eight again, being pummeled by his father for failing to steal as much jewelry as he was supposed to. The sudden memory made the ship feel too small and like Cassian might suffocate on the air he breathed. Instinctively, he squashed that memory, infuriated that E'ghan could make him feel that way. He'd kill the Red Queen captain just for that. The rest of the *Torment* crew followed, nodding in understanding.

"Good," E'ghan said, twisting one of his rings around his finger. "Now, you are in a bit of a predicament, aren't you? No captain, which means you need to vote one in. That takes time you don't have, causes problems about who thinks they're worthy. A mess. So I'll make the decision for you." E'ghan scanned the crowd with maddening slowness. No questions were asked and nobody dared move. If he cared about skills, he didn't make it obvious.

That ugly appraisal passed over everyone, while blood continued to soak into the floorboards from Ricard's heart. That would stain. The main deck's floor was more porous, a result of the constant sun exposure. Cassian gritted his teeth. That wouldn't be good for morale. A bloody mark where the Queens had murdered their captain would do nothing but cause more friction that they didn't need. It would serve as a constant reminder that they were on borrowed time, waiting to be slaughtered like cattle.

Ricard was a good man—had been. Tough to please, but clever and strong. The only captain Cassian had ever served. That was true for many of *Torment's* crew. He kept his ship orderly, an impossible feat for most, and that kept men aboard. The shock left them numb, unwilling to accept what was obvious. This wasn't *Torment* without Ricard.

"How about you?" E'ghan suggested.

Cassian blinked. The Red Queen was in front of him. "Me?"

"Is there anyone else?"

Cassian's mouth was so dry that he couldn't find the spit to speak, when he did, the reply came out in a jumbled mess. "I don't, um, think—"

"I don't care. I picked. And if you're successful, we might just spare your life. Try anything foolish, and I'll string you and your crew up for the birds," E'ghan warned. "You don't want us thinking you're in support of Zinfel, do you?" The Red Queen captain squeezed Cassian's shoulder in what should have been a friendly exchange, but it felt like a final threat. "You're Captain. The next time I see you, act like it. Kinson will expect as much, too. Questions?"

It was a trick. Cassian knew better. Ricard had questions, and it got him killed. The Queen was testing him. He tried to swallow but couldn't. "No." As his first word as captain, that was pitiful.

"Someone has ears. Good." E'ghan turned around and motioned back to *Goddess*. "You know your orders. Follow, and there won't be any problems. Refuse, and you'll know why the Serulic family took control. Best you avoid that. Long live the Red Goddess." E'ghan crossed the gangway without looking back. The other Queens followed, pulling the board once they were across.

Several men stepped forward, then hesitated, looking to Cassian. The ropes. Cassian yanked one loose and the others did the same, tossing them back to the Queens. As *Goddess* steered away, Cassian still couldn't move. His legs felt like iron, and he couldn't get a full breath of air. This couldn't be happening. He wanted—dreamed—of being captain, but not like this. The Queens sacrificed him to the crew. They'd eat him alive. Nobody took kindly to breaking one of the Sea Laws. Voting a captain in gave everyone a say. Kept the peace. He'd have to sleep with his sword in hand. Some were bound to want his head, no matter what'd just happened.

Slowly, Cassian lifted his eyes. Men crowded around Ricard. Some knelt, placing hands on him to say their appreciation. All Ricard's belongings would remain on him. To ensure his spirit crossed into the Afterlife without being tethered to the sea, his body would be burned on the nearest island. Until then, his body would be wrapped and kept in the crew's quarters.

A few glanced over their shoulders at Cassian. Arian was amongst them. Unhinged lunatic. Out of everyone aboard, Cassian feared Arian the most. Arian would slit his throat right here if the spirit moved him. Nausea stormed Cassian's insides, turning his limbs cold and his skin clammy. He didn't know what to do.

Glass approached, cautious, like he wasn't sure he was committed to the idea of talking to Cassian. He didn't blame the old salt. The true colors of the crew came out when a captain was announced. The tattoo-covered pirate stopped before him.

"You want a word?" Glass asked quietly.

Cassian scoffed. "And get stabbed?" The ship swayed as fiercely as the contents in his stomach did. He gripped the railing tight, trying to tame his nausea.

Glass raised his brow. "Most will understand. Nobody wants to cross the Red Queens."

"They killed him," Cassian said, frantic and low. He didn't want the others to hear how much of a coward he was. "They had no reason to." He tossed his arms up. "I'm not a captain. I can't be."

"You have to be," Glass insisted, irritated. "They'll expect it."

Did Glass doubt Cassian's abilities? Not that he blamed Glass—Cassian doubted himself, too. What he wanted to know was why he'd been chosen instead of someone far more capable and experienced. The Red Queens never made a poor decision. They were already anticipating something out of Cassian. Perhaps failure. Perhaps loyalty. He didn't know.

"What you want to tell me is that you all will be spared after they drive a blade through my heart." He crossed his arms. "I can't."

"Afraid to die?"

"I'm not afraid of the Queens. I'm afraid of the men on this ship." Cassian saw Arian mumble something to Wes. "I can't take this title in good heart. It breaks one of the Sea Laws. Let's vote someone in. Have them be captain, and when we see the Queens again, I'll act the part. At least let me do that."

"And risk the whole crew getting slaughtered?" Glass motioned behind him. "If we play your game, everyone is at risk of being killed. If we listen to the Queens, then it's only you."

Cassian leaned over the railing, submitting to his stomach's cries. Salty vomit coated his tongue and lips, tasting of fish and old ale. He retched a few more times, painting the side of *Torment* until nothing more came. He dry-heaved, cold under the sun's heat, and slowly stood. Wiping his lips, he blinked tears away and met Glass's gaze once more.

"When we get Captain moved, we'll get your tattoo done. Choose which hand you want." Glass patted his shoulder and then walked away. If he was worried that Cassian would damn them all, he didn't let it show. In fact, Glass acted like they were chatting about supper, and it only made the storm of nerves worse.

The crew didn't wait for him. They were already dragging the body off the main deck. Cassian tried to regain his composure, but was unable to.

The blood stain from where Ricard had been killed glared at him, hideous in its garish color. No amount of salt water would strip that, not unless they replaced the floorboards, and that wouldn't happen anytime soon.

He leaned over the railing again and retched.

Salt and Sea

Captain Ricard's body was propped in the seat where Cassian had sat the night before. His private space for wood carving was now taken up by the dead. He'd avoided that area for the rest of the day, not wanting to see Ricard in such a vulnerable state, worried that he might run into the captain's ghost. Keeping the ship moving was easy. Men got to work, finding their places in the crow's nest and main deck, overseeing the surrounding areas and watching for shallow reefs, and manning the wheel.

Grounding the ship was the last thing anyone needed. They were heading for the outskirts of the Hil Islands, where they'd put Ricard's body to rest once and for all. No ceremony accompanied the fire. Pirates weren't poetic and didn't spend time making speeches. Everyone said their peace before they moved his body. Following the right steps would spare his soul from eternal imprisonment.

Cassian sat in the captain's cabin, arm stretched out on the table, feeling like an interloper. Cabinets that he'd yet to explore were latched closed to keep them from flying open when the waves got too wild. Drawers, too. The bare table where he sat now was nailed into the floor. The cot was nailed down, too. Ricard had slept here almost every night, and now Cassian was expected to do the same.

They'd not cleaned anything out. Everything could be used by the next captain—clothes, leather, quills, parchment, maps, all of it. Things that Cassian was supposed to know how to do, like writing letters to other captains and guiding the crew, were supposed to be taught by a mentor. He had no idea what he was doing. Days ago, he'd been so certain that becoming captain would be the answer to all his problems. But now, with all that handed to him in such a brutal manner, he realized he didn't know anything about being a captain. He didn't ask the right questions when Ricard was alive or pay enough attention to the details that made a ship run as smoothly as *Torment* had. He was completely unprepared.

He hissed. The small needle burrowed into his knuckle with a sharp sting.

"Sorry," Elliot said. The son of Traz had the steadiest hand aboard and was tasked to do everyone's tattoos. Only fitting he'd do the captain's mark, too. A silhouette of a rose on his right hand, stem and all. Crest of the White Horns. A rose was chosen as the crest because, as the story goes, the first White Horn was gifted a rose from the woman he loved in her dying breaths. With that rose, he sailed across the Vore World, seeking retribution for her death. Nobody would ever question him when he showed up and displayed this. He was Captain of *Torment*.

Elliot worked meticulously, dipping the needle in a bottle of black ink he kept in one hand and driving the tip into Cassian's skin with the other hand. It was a slow process, but the young man was fast because experience made him so. At only sixteen, Elliot was already decorated with a few tattoos on his arms. It was common practice that every pirate earned their first tattoo on the top of their left foot. Good luck. Not getting it was as bad as asking a Tsu'ran to marry—poor and reckless.

Elliot had earned his at thirteen. Cassian got his—a small anchor—when he was ten, but it was severely faded now. Liquor for sterilizing the needle was now in Cassian's left hand. Seaman's Water . . . what the pirates called the bitter and flavorless liquor with one job: to get a man drunk. He'd drunk half the bottle already, hoping to suffocate the nerves. It was working.

"So, uh—" Elliot poked his skin again. "Busy day, yeah?"

Cassian stared out the window. Water rippled where the ship passed. Captain's cabin was at the back of the ship, far from the crew's quarters. It felt strange to stare at where they'd been and not at where they were heading. He wasn't sure he would get used to that.

"Yeah." Cassian took another drink.

"Save some for afterward. Gotta cleanse your hand once I'm done." Silence passed before Elliot added softly, "Captain."

The word made him cringe. "Don't call me that."

Elliot's needle hesitated over his skin. "You're Captain now, right?"

"By force," he clarified. He hadn't earned the title, which had been what he wanted. Earning it would have given him respect, not a target on his back.

"Orders are orders," Elliot replied, poking his skin. "Orders keep the peace. If the Queens call you Captain, then that's what you are to me."

Spineless. Cassian nearly smashed the bottle into the young man's head for saying such a thing. "Orders aren't just orders," he hissed. "If I ordered you to jump ship without any island nearby, would you do it?"

Elliot subtly shook his head.

"Then don't say something so ignorant again. Orders aren't just orders; they impact our lives. We had peace before the Queens showed up. Now I can't walk the decks without checking over my shoulder."

The needle bit his knuckle again, and he took another drink. The liquor was helping immensely. Elliot worked quietly for a moment, starting his second trip around the tattoo.

Finally, Elliot asked, "Are we going to do what they want?"

Cassian raised his brow. "Hunt the Dirnal ships?"

Elliot nodded, grabbing more ink.

He'd not given it too much thought yet. The frenzy of the day still clung to him, making his thoughts mushy and unreliable. But now that he was forced to face what the Queens said, he dreaded it. "It's a suicide mission."

"You think?"

"I know," Cassian replied, stern. "These are the Queens we're talking about hunting. More specifically, one of the inner families. They didn't get that title for no reason. They are some of the toughest fighters out there. We'd never make it. Our crew is half that of a normal Queen's ship."

"Then why ask us to go after them?"

"To get rid of us," Cassian snapped. "Aren't you listening?" Elliot's dark eyes flashed up to his, halting his progress. "Ricard was the target. He was dead before they even boarded the ship. But we're his crew—were his crew." The correction tasted sour. "To Kinson, we're a liability. No certainty about what we know without torturing all of us, and that takes time that the Queens crew didn't have. We owe it to ourselves to find a way out of this."

Elliot resumed his work. "You think this could be a test?"

"Perhaps." Cassian took another drink. The bottle was getting low, which meant he would have to slow down so that Elliot could use the rest when he was done with the needles. "A way to see where our loyalties lie." The dishonesty about the situation with the Red Queens didn't sit well with him. "But I think they want to get rid of us this way. A final cruel joke to make us scramble to try and stay alive. We'll never make it out alive against three fully-crewed ships like the Dirnals have."

Silence passed between them. Cassian didn't have to clarify or go into detail, and based on the young pirate's lack of reply, he knew Cassian was right. This wasn't a test. It was a death sentence.

"So"—Elliot poked again—"what are we going to do?"

His skin was starting to go thankfully numb from the incessant prodding. If they refused the Queens, they were as good as dead, but they were dead anyway if they obeyed. Cassian studied the dingy liquor bottle, too cloudy to see inside. "We go to Greve's Point."

"What?"

The decision came instantly. Had to, now that he had a crew to lead—not that he was certain it would work. In all the emotions that stormed his senses, the only thing he could cling to was the next step. If he spent too long focusing on what his life was turning into—a shitshow with a clear end at the mercy of a blade—anxiety rippled through him like a fast-moving parasite. He took all that fear and the memory and stuffed it in a chest deep within himself, where no one, not even himself, dared venture.

Down there, he stored chests full of memories he'd not thought of in many summers—including memories of the day his parents sold him. Certain moments in time created chasms in the soul so wide that no amount of healing would ever fix them. Time didn't heal those wounds, only made the grief more manageable.

Information on the Crown of Gods and the mad king were supposed to be at Greve's Point. They were a little over a day's trip from the island still, if the winds were in their favor. Plenty of time to get there by tomorrow night if they sailed soon after Ricard's funeral. Cassian knew there was little guarantee they would find the information they needed for the relic. Nothing that old and unique was ever easy to acquire. But they would perhaps find someone who knew someone, who also knew someone who knew something about the relic or where it could be. That's how this trade worked—know the right people, and anything was possible.

That left him with the obvious: the king. The dragon egg. The little itch in the back of his mind returned, gnawing at his composure. A dragon egg would change everything. He had his doubts that it was real, and if it was, the dragon inside was most likely dead, but that didn't staunch the growing excitement about laying his hands on one. The king was tangible, an easy target to find. He might not be thrilled at the idea of putting his trust in a dead woman's claims for coin, but it was all he had. The other option was obeying the Red Queens and getting him and the crew killed. Finding the king could give him and the rest of the *Torment* crew a second chance. They could start a new life, get new identities, even a new ship. The possibilities were endless.

"Captain didn't tell the Queens about Greve's Point for a reason. Whatever his work was with Zinfel was big enough to get the Queens' attention. If he didn't speak of our intentions, then that's because he knew something we don't about what's going on. So I think it's best if we keep on track and follow our original goals. Keep an ear out for the relic, but find the king—if he's even there. If not, then we can work on maybe breaking the crew up and abandoning the ship."

The needle went too deep, striking muscle that was still very much responsive. Cassian jerked his hand. Elliot apologized profusely. "I'm sorry. I didn't mean to. I just—you want to abandon *Torment*?"

"It may be the only choice we have," Cassian replied. Couldn't this kid see the double-edged sword they were faced with? Abandoning a ship was about as bad as spitting on the respected dead. Bad luck. An abandoned ship like *Blue Bells* should be destroyed to help the dead move on. A ship like *Torment*, where the crew still lived and served, was bad luck. "Stay, we're killed. Flee, we're killed. If we can find other crews looking for extra shipmates, we can find safety."

"All due respect, Captain, but for most of us, this is the only ship and crew we've ever had." Elliot started his third round on the rose. "And if you're thinking about leaving, why am I doing this?"

Because he wanted to leverage the tattoo. With any king or captain, he could display this and make up a lie. Nobody checked stories out at sea. He'd be able to earn himself a crew and ship and take off, find a new identity. The Keeper of Ships on Greve's Point documented all active captains. Eventually, if he lived long enough, he would seek out the Keeper of Ships and state his name with several shipmates who could vouch for his title. Failure to report within three moons of becoming captain would earn Cassian a hefty fee or execution, depending on the severity of the crime. With that documentation, he could go anywhere. But he wanted to give the Keeper of Ships a different name and ship, so that the Red Queens couldn't track him.

"In case things go wrong," he said, the words hollow on his tongue. "Queens wanted a captain, right? I'm your guy." The lie came easy. Cassian had no intention of being sacrificed to the brutal Queens.

Elliot worked quietly for a little while longer, letting the answer fester between them. Cassian didn't feel bad lying, but he didn't feel good about abandoning the men. Most of them had raised him. They were strong, loyal men who worked because they loved it and had the sea in their blood. And he was willing to toss them aside . . . for what? A chance to find a new beginning? He'd built up this dream of manning his own ship and crew. Now given that, he didn't think he wanted it anymore. Earning the title of captain like this was bad luck. Nothing was honorable about how Ricard died or how Cassian became captain. If he and the crew weren't careful, *Torment* would end up at the bottom of the sea.

"We'll find the king," Cassian whispered, more to himself. "When we do, we can focus on getting that egg and getting a payout. If we do that, we can get a new ship and keep the crew together. Change our names, so the Queens don't think twice. Spread rumors about finding *Torment's* wreckage. They'll blame the Serulics, and we can go on chasing low-life pirates like we were."

It wasn't the strongest idea, but it was all Cassian had. He knew the Red Queens would doubt the rumors—they were too clever—but all Cassian needed was for the savage pirates to hesitate long enough to give him and the crew a running chance to get to the other side of the world. Ashen Sea was far north, had fewer pirates, and was avoided because the colder waters made fishing harder. A perfect destination to disappear and figure out the next steps. Cassian couldn't hide forever, but he could disappear long enough to start a new life. Maybe on land, away from the Red Queens' reach. He didn't want it to come to that—he loved the sea—but he didn't want to die either.

"I hope," Elliot replied. "Because I don't think your other plan will work."

Cassian needed more Seaman's Water. "Why not?"

"This crew doesn't want to see this ship abandoned. You know that." Elliot surveyed his work, twisting Cassian's hand around like it didn't belong to a body. "You won't find a more loyal crew than this, Captain."

He almost told the kid to stop calling him that, but stopped himself. "How can you be so sure? A Sea Law was broken. Half of these men probably want me dead just for that." Voting a captain in was one of the seven laws. He wasn't starting this new title with honor, only trepidation.

Elliot touched up a few more spots. "Because we'd be more afraid of the bad luck that might follow us if we split up and scuttled the ship."

He knew the superstitions. Still, he hoped the men would be more desperate to get out from underneath the Queens' critical gaze than worry about taboos. For his sake, he'd hoped it would be that. Cassian wasn't opposed to keeping the crew together, but they needed to work together and get the egg. The only thing keeping Cassian from running off with the egg was that if the men all agreed to accept him as captain, he had a crew. A new ship was all that was left. Already, he envisioned it named *Wrath*. This could work.

"Then we sell the ship to another crew," Cassian said. Elliot leaned back and motioned for the bottle. He handed it over reluctantly. "It isn't our hands destroying it, right?" A little loophole, and based on how Elliot looked at him, he knew the kid believed it.

"Well, when you put it that way." Elliot soaked his hand with the liquor. Skin stung, and Cassian wanted to pull away, but knew this was the most important step. He'd be as good as dead if he lost a hand from an infection.

A knock interrupted them. "Come in."

Glass stuck his head in. "Captain." That moniker didn't sound right coming from him. "We're approaching land. It's time."

The burning. Time to bid farewell to Captain Ricard and send him off to the Afterlife. Beg whatever sea spirits might govern here that his soul didn't get dragged down into the depths of these waters and be forced to serve the Tsu'ran.

"All right," Cassian said and looked at Elliot, who gave him a thumbs up. He stood. "Let's get this over with."

White sand crunched as he shifted his weight. Captain's body was laid out, hands over his chest, with his belongings placed respectfully around him. Discolored patches from where the blood had settled decorated the back of Ricard's head, neck, and parts of his arms that were visible. The crew was careful with how they moved him. Poor handling of a respected pirate could mean bad luck or a vengeful spirit. The sun baked the back of Cassian's neck. His hand burned, red and angry, where the needles had pierced him. The captain's mark gleamed, proud. The crew beheld him with a single nod, acknowledging the meaning. Nobody tried to slit his throat yet, which he thought was a win, but he was still wary.

Ahead, tropical trees clustered. The island was small—they could sail around thrice in a day—but he couldn't see the other side with the tall trees and jagged peaks. Birds of different colors chirped, bewildered by the men's arrival. *Torment* was anchored just beyond the drop-off, where the depths of the sea were deep enough to hold the ship. They'd taken small rowboats to shore with Cassian, insistent that he give the final blessing, even if that was just to say goodbye or light the fire. He'd argued, wishing not to attend the ceremony. It felt wrong, and he knew by the brooding glances of Arian and Wes that they were waiting for an opportunity to corner him.

Just yesterday, they'd taken *Blue Bells* and learned of a possible dragon egg. Now, they were saying farewell to Ricard and trying to outsmart the Queens. No blessing worthy after the last day came to mind. Cassian fumbled for words, struggling to form a sentence that was both sympathetic and influential. He drew a blank. Finally, he turned and looked at the crew encircling him.

"We shouldn't be here," Cassian said. "None of this should be happening." He knelt and took the flint and a chunk of steel from his pouch. The wood and grass they'd piled under Ricard's body would take to the flames fast. He struck steel against flint several times before a spark jumped. He did it again, making another. Smoke rose, and he blew on it, giving the ember life. Satisfied, he stepped back and stuffed the items back into his pouch as the fire quickly spread.

Elliot's words echoed in his head. Men were superstitious, but resentment was an ugly beast. He knew some of these men were unhappy about the circumstances, and he needed to say his peace. "You don't have to respect me like we respected Captain." Cassian made sure to find Arian and Wes as he spoke, hoping to connect with them. "But I ask that you respect *Torment* and what Captain made of her and this crew. Queens will be on our tail, but I don't care. We're heading to Greve's Point, and we're going to find that king. If he's there, we might just have a chance at starting fresh. If you want to go your own way once we dock, then do it. I won't stop you. I want men aboard who want to be here, regardless of the Seven Sea Laws and tradition."

Flames cracked, engulfing Ricard's body with ferocious delight. If Cassian believed in the Gods of the Vore World, he'd have said a prayer, but his faith belonged to the sea and what lived within, so he pleaded that the Tsu'ran let Captain's soul pass.

Nobody moved. Cassian wanted to return to *Torment* and be off. No point in standing there and watching Captain's body burn. Men gaped, and he wondered if they expected something more. He'd said his peace, and he didn't care who left. Those who didn't find him fit to be captain would go on their way, which meant he could hopefully sleep at night without the worries. It was the best compromise he could make.

"Dirty," Arian commented, spitting on the ground close to Cassian's boots. A blatant insult. Cassian tensed. He'd known this was coming.

"Damned Captain's soul with your dirty hands and unclean ways." Flames snapped, gaining height to match the growing hostility.

"We've got no choice," Elliot defended Cassian before anyone else could speak up. He shrank, wheezing, when Cassian elbowed him in the ribs to make a clear warning. Elliot would get himself killed faster than a newborn turtle crawling across the sand while a hundred birds circled above. Come to think of it, Elliot *was* a baby turtle—ignorant and gullible.

Arian poked Cassian in the chest with a bony finger and spat, "Captain kept you around because he was too soft with orphans." Several nodded vigorously, as if they'd waited for those words to finally be said, including Wes. "We ain't as kind as Captain."

Cassian knew that was coming, but his heartbeat still thundered. "I'm not asking you to like me. I'm asking that we just get to Greve's Point without killing each other."

Wes scoffed. The man was missing a front tooth—knocked out by a fight he got into many summers ago. "Ship's cursed already. What more could go wrong?"

"Don't speak like that," Traz snapped. The big man belonged on a battlefield. The rooms aboard *Torment* could hardly fit him. "Dead are listening. We don't need them down our backs because you can't keep your mouth shut."

"Listen," Glass started, baring his hands to the crew. Always the peacemaker. "Nobody here's happy, but we have to work with what we've got. That's our ship out there, waiting for us. If you don't like her anymore, then get out of her way when we get to Greve's Point. But if you like the ship, then stick around. A captain's a captain. Every ship needs one, but nobody can sail without a crew."

"He'll sail us right into the Grave," Arian declared, face red with fury, gesturing wildly at Cassian. "Why'd the Queens pick you, anyway?"

Cassian opened his mouth, but Elliot spoke first. "Queens' orders."

That kind of talk would get the kid killed. Cassian almost backhanded the boy for speaking out of place again—a loose tongue like that would get him strung up faster than any bounty or angry drunk—but he never got the chance.

Arian yanked free a short dagger with a jagged edge from his belt. Everyone stepped back. Cassian's fingers instantly wrapped around the hilt of his old sword. Adrenaline surged through him, and his boots slipped on the sand like it was made of ice.

"I want a fight," Arian hissed, spit flying from his cracked lips. "Let's settle this properly."

The second Sea Law. Cassian instantly felt cold. He hated Arian, and he knew the pirate was as wild and unpredictable as the waters they sailed. Arian would cut Cassian's tongue out and fry it up. Wear his fingers as a necklace and skin him alive. A fight with him would be suicide, like wrangling a Life Eater with no hands. But Cassian had been dreaming of this day for many seasons. He hated Arian just as much as fire loathed water. A fight with Arian would prove to everyone that he wasn't to be doubted.

"You're upset—" Glass pleaded.

"Watch your tongue," Cassian snapped. He unsheathed his weapon, the glimmer of metal a bold challenge in the silence that followed. He wouldn't be bullied by Arian, and if this was what it took to prove his worth, then so be it. "You want a proper one?" Rage from the last day boiled over, making him shake. "Terms?"

Arian spat on the ground and smashed his boot into the sand as if he was trying to uncover a secret beneath. "To the death. If I win, I'm Captain."

Flames cracked. The acrid odor of burning flesh filled the space between them, stomach-churning. Behind, the towering trees with leaves wider than any man shook as several dozen birds took to the sky. Some wings were vivid blue, while others had massive beaks that curved downward, perfect for plucking meat right off the bone. "And if I win, I let the birds have their way with your body. Savvy?" Cassian suggested. A disgrace. Crewmembers mumbled, upset. Arian would spend the rest of his life stuck with the restless dead if he lost. Letting birds have their way would damn his soul. The pleasure of that thought gave Cassian all the courage he needed to follow through with this.

Arian lunged, dagger aimed low for Cassian's stomach. Cassian stepped out of the way, swinging his sword at the pirate's arm. Too slow. Arian tossed his dagger into the other hand and jabbed him in the side. The cut was shallow, but surprising. In the same breath, Arian's fist connected with his ribs with enough force to rip the air right out. Cassian wheezed and ducked to avoid another oncoming punch and kicked out. His boot smashed into Arian's knee, bending it sideways. The pirate stumbled and cursed. Before Arian could act, Cassian dragged his sword across the man's leg, shredding fabric and skin. Arian drove his dagger down, narrowly missing Cassian's shoulder as he rolled out of the way.

Heat licked Cassian's skin with blinding intensity. Flames crackled, delighted for another feast. Cassian stared at the charred leather of Ricard's boots. With one hand, he dug his fingers into the sand beneath the flames and threw it at Arian, sword gripped in the other, ready. Nobody declared the rules of the fight.

Arian screamed—the kind of scream that made the heart skip a beat and the victorious salivate. Cassian stood in time to see the pirate swipe at his face, where the flames had licked. Blisters had already sprouted, and Arian's left eye was crimson and glassy. The others didn't move. According to the second Sea Law, no one was to intervene in a fight. Not until the terms were met.

Cassian drove his blade forward before the pirate could react. Metal sank into flesh and muscle just underneath the heart. Arian froze, staring at the weapon, and then at the captain he'd disrespected. Enraged, Cassian stepped forward, forcing the blade deeper with a sickening *crunch* as a rib cracked. He twisted, feeling muscle and tendon give. Arian's body spasmed. He dropped his dagger.

"May your eternity of suffering begin," Cassian whispered. With that, he pulled free the blade, and the pirate collapsed. Cassian wiped his bloodied blade across Arian's shirt before sheathing it. His hands trembled with the shock of it all, but he balled his fists up in hopes that nobody would see. To the left, Ricard still burned. Arian wouldn't join him. Ever.

The others awaited Cassian's statement as the victor. He stood there, staring at the fire. He'd expected more. Perhaps a better fight after so long of worrying about the dreaded confrontation, but instead, it had ended just as fast as it started. Cassian had practiced more than anyone on this ship on how to swing a sword, and he'd known that it would one day come into use against someone as vile as Arian. What Cassian hadn't anticipated was how easy it would be to defeat Arian. He'd dreamed for many moons of the two of them fighting, always imagining how it could go. A slight misstep, a slip of the hand—all the possibilities that could end badly for Cassian. Instead, the fight had gone as smoothly as it could have under the circumstances.

Cassian sucked in air, still fueled with untempered rage . . . rage for Arian that he'd kept buried. He swallowed the sensation. Now was not the time. He needed to keep his emotions under control. The other part of him wanted to add to the body count, kill anyone who might ever challenge him, or consider calling him a *dirty-blooded pirate* like Arian had. He was tired of being treated like he couldn't hold his own.

"If anyone wants to hold a vote, then let's do it here and now." Cassian planted his hands on his hips. He already had the captain's mark on his hand, but he couldn't stand the way his promotion had unfolded. If there was a problem, it needed to be resolved now. "Who wants to do this the old-fashioned way?"

Wes and two others raised their hand instantly, but nobody else. Looks were exchanged. Cassian knew why. Glass was right. Queens needed a captain—a victim if things went wrong—and nobody wanted to take that place, save for the imbeciles too worried about his dirty blood.

"Majority wins. No vote," Cassian observed. His voice didn't shake. He couldn't tell if he was relieved or terrified. What he did know was that he needed a drink and to get as far from this island as possible. "Let's get on with it. Ship's ready, and we have a heist to plan. If you're parting at Greve's Point, pack your things and say your goodbyes. We've got a day and a half left. If you think you want to challenge me, I'll make sure you join Arian."

The crew gawked like it was the first time they'd ever seen him. Their eyes were wide, and their heads held high as if they didn't want to cast doubt on Cassian's new title. The behavior bolstered Cassian's newfound confidence. Killing Arian was the best thing to happen today. The victory reaffirmed the Red Queens' decision to make him the captain. Nobody on *Torment* would challenge him again. Maybe he could make this new title work, after all.

Men shuffled, some muttering farewells to Ricard's half-destroyed body. Arian's remained untouched. Nobody was absurd enough to deny the terms—his soul was damned. The birds circling above cried out, perhaps sensing the impending feast. Cassian stayed behind, falling into step behind Glass and Traz, who hardly looked his way. What lay ahead kept his mind preoccupied. The dragon egg gave him purpose. Find that, and he could get out from under the Queens and start a new life. Fail to do that, and he might as well lie down and burn to death with Ricard.

The Hollow Market

Greve's Point. Home to the pirates. Where criminals came to be traded or sold off, and where pirates came to do business. During the Hil War, it was decided that Greve's Point would be dedicated to the pirates. A place to kick their feet up and relax without interrupting normal business in the cities. Landwalkers believed pirates were uncivilized. But they'd never spent a day in the life of a pirate, so they had no idea what the everyday life looked like—the pride in culture, the love for the sea, the way of life they'd known for centuries.

The dock was massive, stretching a league to accommodate the massive number of ships that came and went. If the dock was full, ships were anchored beyond the drop-off and paddled in with rowboats. That didn't happen often, save for the festivals and meetings that required most, if not all, captains to be present. Such summonings were reserved for times of major changes and threats. Cassian hadn't ever seen anything like that, but he'd heard of it from others. The dock was almost full when they tossed ropes to those awaiting their arrival. As *Torment* was securely put into place, Cassian turned to the crew now in his charge, not that he was sure he knew what that meant yet.

Wes was packed and ready to go, lost without his merciless partner, Arian. He'd not spoken since they returned from the island several days ago, and whenever he looked at Cassian, he scowled. It wasn't uncommon for pirates to fight for the captain's title, but how it had all happened—the arrival of the Queens and the murder of Ricard—caused enough tension to raise the dead from their graves. Cassian hoped that with those who didn't want to be here leaving, the somberness that drenched *Torment* would also be gone. A few others were unfortunately packed too—stragglers who popped onto different ships to help where needed, so they wouldn't be missed much, but they were hard workers and would need to be replaced. Nobody ever took the time to learn their names. Just called them *the crew*. Relief was an understatement. Getting the unwanted and the dissidents off the ship would put Cassian's mind at ease, but he was surprised to see Traz and Elliot packed too.

Cassian opened his mouth to say something, then thought better of it. Not here. Not in front of the others. "If you're leaving, I don't want to see you again. If you're staying, then we'll meet back here at sunrise. If you find the king with the gold ring, find me. If you hear anything about the Crown of Gods, find me. Keep your wits about you and don't sell your soul to one of the undead. I'll hop the pubs to see what I can learn."

Instantly, the men broke and started their way down the gangway. Some would find new work, like Wes and the few stragglers. The rest would seek a good time and return at dawn to set sail with Cassian. Traz and Elliot remained behind, making up the rear. When they got close, he stopped them before they could disembark with the rest.

"What's this about? I thought you supported me." Cassian choked on the words. Desperate. That's how he sounded.

Traz looked down at his son, Elliot, who refused to say anything. "I do. And if it was just me, I'd stay, but I got my boy to worry about. If something happens to you, he's going to go the rest of his life being known to have served . . ." Traz trailed off.

"Dirty blood," Cassian finished. He didn't need more. Traz wanted his son to serve a captain who was highly respected, not a sacrifice to the Red Queens if this all went south. "I understand."

The crew was loyal to Traz, and he'd earned it. By the sea, Traz had been here for nearly thirteen summers; came aboard when his son was only three. Without Traz's influence, Cassian feared there'd be problems aboard *Torment*, but he wouldn't want them to stay if they wanted to go. "Find a good ship and let the sea have her way," Cassian whispered. He squeezed Elliot's shoulder, who still didn't meet his gaze, and nodded at Traz. This hurt. "I'll see you out there."

"Aye," Traz replied. A smile crept across the man's lips, but it was somber. Taking his son, Traz departed. The fading echo of their boots against wood deafened the sound of the shouts that came from below.

Cassian stood there for a bit, not wanting to intercept Traz and Elliot when he departed the ship. He looked at the masts, shrouds, entrance to the captain's cabin, and hatch to the decks below. *Torment* was his, at least for a short while. This was every pirate's dream. Yet, now standing there without the scrutinizing gaze of the crew, he felt like a fraud. Alone on this ship, he was left with only his torturous thoughts of doubt and uncertainty.

The tattoo on his hand was still red and sore, but the swelling had become manageable. They'd need more Seaman's Water before setting off again. He'd used that several times for sanitizing and drinking. Most of the crew drank. Having liquor and ale on board was just as important as water and food. Kept the nerves at bay when storms got bad, or the stress low when one's life was in the hands of a dirty-blood captain. Cassian scoffed. He needed off this ship.

On the ground, men and women worked to check ships, receive payment, and answer questions. Just like any port, Greve's Point had a fee each ship must pay. Kept cheap criminals at bay and the unwelcome from getting too close. The Dock Keeper, a plump woman with red hair and bright blue eyes, approached wearing a man's tunic and pants, wood groaning from her assertive steps. She managed all the goings on with ships, who came and went, and took payment to dock for any ship staying more than half a day.

"Men comin' off said this was yours? You're Captain, yes?" The Dock Keeper motioned at his hand to indicate the captain's mark—the rose tattoo.

"Aye," Cassian replied. The Dock Keeper pulled back a few pieces of parchment on her board. "*Torment* hasn't been here in a while, has she?" She squinted. "Captain Ricard? I don't think that's you, is it?"

Cassian shook his head. "Lost his life." He hoped she didn't ask questions. Lying came easily to him, but he was in no mood to come up with some wild tale about bad weather and poor luck.

"Hm." The woman pulled a short bottle from one of the four pouches on her hip. Opening it with one hand, she pressed her finger over the top and turned it over. Then she took her ink-covered finger and pressed it next to Ricard's scribbled name on the parchment. "Did you see a Rü'shane carry his soul?"

A raven. Old Tongue for 'God's soul.' Carriers of the souls unwilling to pass into the Afterlife. Pirates kept a lookout for ravens when a high-ranked shipmate passed, hopeful that if they saw one, they'd earn clarification that their soul wasn't bound to the bottom of the sea. The dead out at sea rarely ever found rest in the Afterlife. But if pirates could know that the well-respected found peace as a Rü'shane, then that was better than being chained for an eternity to a Tsu'ran.

"Still looking," Cassian managed to say. "Storms were bad. You know how it is."

"Hm." The Dock Keeper seemed disinterested as she cleaned the ink from her finger with a rag she plucked from her belt. The woman had just about anything one could need strapped to her hips. "And your name?"

"Cassian."

"Captain Cassian. Your last?"

He pinched his lips together. "Blackwater." The name orphaned pirates were given, or men like him who were sold to the sea. He hated it.

The woman didn't make any fuss about it. "I'll get the records updated."

"And you're new," Cassian replied, changing the subject. "Where's Lyra?"

The short woman shook her head and plucked a quill from a bottle of ink that was clutched in her other hand. The entire scene was precarious. There had to be a better way to do that. Maybe there was, and she just wasn't interested. She kept everything still by pressing the board against her bosom. "Lyra's not working this side today. Helpin' Jack with boarding. You got me."

"And you are?" Cassian wanted to be pleasant. Last thing he wanted was a check next to his name that he knew some captains got. The check meant to avoid business if possible and charge more.

"You're a new captain, aren't you?" She raised her brow. The Dock Keeper appeared bored. "Questions like that don't happen with the experienced ones. You can call me Rasel. I'm Lyra's niece. That'll be ten Krye."

Niece. He didn't see it. Actually, it was impossible. Lyra had dark olive skin and long dark hair. He'd met her as one of the crew—always here when they docked to check them in. Rasel had porcelain skin with eyes that didn't quite match, and a round nose. A long distant cousin, perhaps. One from the other side of the world, but surely not close.

"Yes." He dug into his leather pouch tied to his belt and plucked out ten tarnished silver coins. A few had dried blood, one was so worn that it almost looked fake, and another was stamped over with a crown—Queen currency. They preferred to mark their coins. He handed them to her and unbelievably, she tilted forward to reveal her chest.

"Plop 'em right in there. Got a little basket tucked between." Cassian did as he was told, hearing them strike metal. Couldn't knock her. It was a clever way to store the coin when her hands were full. "You're all set. Ah, one more thing. How long can we expect you to stay?"

Cassian took another look at *Torment*. The sooner they could get out of there, the better. "Hopefully tomorrow morning. Just passin' by, but I'll be sure to send one of the boys down if things change." He tapped her arm and stepped aside. "Good evening, Rasel."

"Good evenin', Captain," she called back. Humming to herself, she went on her way, greeting another on the dock.

All around, people fretted over ropes, talked about their ships and their trades, and laughed. Nowhere else in the Vore World could so many pirates gather without it causing a stir. He nodded at a group of Su'rüles, iconically dressed in white leather bracers. One man bore the sun silhouette tattoo on his hand . . . the Su'rüles' captain. Queens' Bidders. The White Horns and the Su'rüles were the toughest clans at sea, serving the Queens however they were needed. Both understood their position, so respect was given, no matter the circumstances. He and the captain made eye contact, silently acknowledging each other's position. Nothing was said—didn't need to be.

The Su'rüles loved the color white; all their ships were the same color. They spent more coin keeping the image than anyone else he knew, but it worked. As iconic as the red sails of the Queens were, the Su'rüles were identifiable a league out. Along the bow of every ship, a sun was painted under the name. God's sun. That's what their name translated to. Hardly friendly, but they'd earned their place underneath the Queens centuries ago when their crews went on a bloody massacre to enact vengeance for the death of one of their ow n.

The White Horns, on the other hand, weren't known for painted ships or leather. Not even for having the finest weapons. They were simply known as the Assassins of the Sea and Courters of the Grave, a place in the sea that no ship ever came back from. Landwalkers hired the White Horns when blood needed to be spilled. On land, the people had their own killers—Nighthunters—assassins who worked for anyone if the price was right. At sea, the White Horns were just that. And when an assassination was too dirty for a Nighthunter, they were summoned.

The port was huge. Pirates too old for the sea or no longer able to work the deck set up shop and managed taverns, provisions markets, or ship repair establishments. Families that lived at Greve's Port—often those of pirates who sailed and returned—also had their own stands. Lovers waiting for their partners to return roamed the dock, checking out the ships and asking questions. Kids born at sea ran past, yelling slurs and bartering for jewels and weapons. Smells of fried fish, baked goods, and strong ale wafted through, accompanied by the putrid odor of unwashed bodies who'd forgotten baths were possible. Nothing quite came close to the glory of a hot bath on land. Cassian couldn't wait to have a proper one, and he hoped the other men took advantage of the opportunity. Once they set sail, it was the cool salt water that would be washing them.

"One to keep the dead at peace," a woman called, holding a bundle of silver beads with a small sun pendant. Hyle's Beads. The God of Courage. Cassian slowed, curious. She saw and stepped forward, raising the beads. "Protection."

He pushed her hand down. "Why do you bring that religion here?"

Drügalism was the polytheistic faith of the landwalkers. Others, like Zimbórism and the occasional misfit cult, made their rounds, but were far less popular—even forbidden in some places. Cults made their rounds every few decades, hardly ever coming to sea. Last one Cassian heard about was some manic-fueled group who gouged their own eyes out in the name of divine intuition. Very few pirates believed the Gods protected them. The last he knew, four Gods were still widely worshipped: Eazon, the God of Luck; Greve, the God of Strength; Helyna, the Goddess of Love, and Hyle. Another God existed, Sekar, but many refused to acknowledge him, simply referring to him as the Dark Lord who resided in the northern mountains of Sorréle.

Dreamer's Faith was the only religion that worshipped Sekar. The City of Liral was one of few places to publicize their commitment to the Dark Lord, citing visions from Sekar himself had granted them the ability to prosper. As far as Cassian heard, the faith's practices were extreme and often involved blood. Some didn't believe the Gods were in control, settling on placing their faith in the energies—magic, as many bards told it. Blind Man's Faith, what the pirates called the spiritualists, hadn't been seen on the sea in decades.

Hyle, though, was a different story. Once every few moons, a new preacher showed up at Greve's Point, speaking of the God of Courage until they were killed or kicked off the island. This woman was another missionary, trying to stuff her beliefs down the throats of anyone who listened. Pirates didn't tolerate landwalker religions.

She tightened her grip on the beads, jutting her chin. "Times are changing. Can't you feel it?"

He tilted his head. "No." Best not tell her about the dead. She might start to think it was the end times.

"Whispers from the east tell of an illness seeping through these lands and waters," she continued, fast and frantic, like she would lose the opportunity to share. "Mad Man's Sickness. It's back."

Cassian tensed. Mad Man's Sickness hadn't been spoken of in decades. Landwalkers called it something else—they always had a different name for things—and it was known for black blisters and hallucinations. Skin died, peeling away at the fingers first, and men and women went insane, speaking of unseen things. If they weren't killed before their eyesight went, they grew violent.

"How do you know?" Cassian asked.

"Men from the north returned, said they heard of it in Geral, that desert city. Didn't quite believe it, but then a few of their own came down with it." She forced the beads into his hands. "I fear no creature of the deep can protect us this time. Only the Gods can stop this."

Cassian didn't want the worship piece. "And you think the Gods will protect us? The same ones that have never set sail or felt the wind in their hair up in a crow's nest?" Cassian didn't know much about the deities, but he knew enough to understand that most believed Gods were once people like them, chosen when their soul was supposed to pass into the Afterlife. He'd never heard of or seen a God who was a pirate, which forced into question just how accurate the landwalkers' religion was. Or any religion, for that matter.

"We've upset them somehow," she mumbled. "It's our fault, and now we will pay." A fat tear rolled down her cheek. Passersby glanced but didn't slow. "We need their forgiveness."

Cassian scoffed, no longer amused. "The Gods don't care for us. Never have." He pointed to a frail old man crouched next to a barrel, missing an arm and foot and holding a cup for coin. "You think that's compassion? That man once sailed, maybe was a pirate, and had the respect of countless souls. And because he crossed the wrong man, he's here, begging. You tell me why the Gods are so desperate to curse us but not compassionate enough to aid the helpless."

She opened her mouth and closed it, stunned. Tears stopped, the beads hung from her hand between them.

"The only place we should put our faith in is the sea. Out there, there are no favorites. Judgment is based on a man's honor, not which celestial being he believes in." Beneath those waters, creatures that could bring cities to their knees lurked, made men savages, and turned the day into night. Nothing was more terrifying than that. No God would ever save them from such a dreadful fate if that was their future. Pirates didn't pray, they paid their respects to the beasts in the waters, hoping to keep the peace. For centuries, that's how it'd been done.

He pushed past her, glad to be rid of the woman. She would get eaten alive by others if she kept up that preaching. Cassian was nice, relatively speaking. The others wouldn't be. If the beads weren't ripped out of her hands and tossed into the waves before the end of the night, she was lucky.

Greve's Point was a collection of the most extreme people. Outcasts who didn't fit in anywhere else called this place home. Criminals on the run, traitors, murderers, the eclectic, and of course, pirates. Cassian enjoyed his time there, but he was always glad to get back on the ship. Too many people meant too many problems. He needed to find the king with the gold ring.

The deeper Cassian got into Greve's Point, the wilder the people became. Night was upon the small city, and many pirates were several drinks in and enjoying the steady ground beneath their feet. He passed Glass, who had women on either side as he placed bets with another pirate. He looked to be wagering a basic game of Survivor over some dice. Highest rolls five times out of seven won. Most wagered coin and swords. Occasionally, the boldest would bet a scar. The winner could slice skin clean open wherever they wanted on the loser's body. A scar for life. A mark. Cassian had one on his stomach from losing such a game five summers ago.

He stopped at a stand selling fried bread. It had been a long while since he'd had something like that, so he passed several coins over and raised a finger. One. Dan, stout and always dressed in the same red tunic, nodded and grabbed one from his pile of pastries. The mute was a staple on this island. He'd lost his tongue decades ago when he'd been tortured and refused to give up information about the underground markets and alliances with Nighthunters.

Dan came back a hero after escaping. Rowed halfway here before a ship spotted him and heard his tale, which they'd learned after Dan managed to draw his story. He couldn't write, so he'd conveyed everything through sloppy illustrations. Now, he served fried bread, sometimes soup, and anyone could always count that he would be right here, nestled between Shade's Pub and the herb healer's shop. The shop was run by a woman with midnight black hair and too many stories to share. The city called her Raven.

Dan passed the bread over and dropped the coins in his pouch. He smiled, revealing several missing teeth. Wide jaw, pudgy cheeks. This man ate well, tongue or not. His blue eyes asked a hundred questions.

"Been a while, hasn't it?" Cassian asked before taking a bite of the flaky bread. Dan nodded. "Not sure you heard yet. Queens dethroned the Dirnal family. Had a run in with them personally, and they killed Captain Ricard." Dan's jaw went slack. "I know. Crazy, right? I've got half a mind to think they're going to start a war." The man across from him shook his head.

"You don't think?" Cassian said and took another bite. "People are talking about the politics getting tense with the landwalkers. Makes me think we're on the verge of something big." Dan raised his hand, then wagged his finger. Cassian squinted, determining what he was trying to say.

"You think they're somehow involved with the landwalkers?"

Dan nodded.

"Outrageous." He snorted through a mouthful. "What could the Queens get by siding with the landwalkers?"

Dan shrugged.

He shook his head. "You really think it's possible, though?"

The man hummed, the only noise he could make that didn't sound like a dying animal. It was closer to a squeak than a hum, but Cassian liked to give the man some dignity. He wasn't sure how to process the idea. Pirates and landwalkers worked together, sure, but usually on smaller scales. The Red Queens would have no reason to want land or tie themselves down with a king or queen.

Patting the rough wood, Cassian said, "I best be off. Thanks again, Dan."

The man waved farewell, grinning wide. Cassian turned and bit into the bread, and was halfway done with it when Raven stepped in front of him. The woman was dressed in a purple skirt with beads dangling from her hips and a skimpy top that revealed far more than necessary. Her sharp jawline could cut glass.

"You're the one they speak about," she stated quickly, reaching for his hand. Cassian pulled it away. Too many people were trying to touch him tonight, and it was starting to piss him off.

"Good to see you too, Raven. Taking too many hallucinogens again. A day or two off the leaves won't hurt."

"You know I don't do that stuff," the woman snapped. "Keeps me from speaking with the other side."

Cassian knew the dead existed, but he didn't like Raven's job. Soul Speaker. Someone who communicated with the souls still bound to this world, land and sea. Most of the world thought people like her were taboo—that the dead and living shouldn't mingle like she was capable of doing. Raven arrived a few seasons ago from a ship leaving the Nighthunter Federation. Nobody knew her story or why she came here and hadn't left, and nobody asked. At Greve's Point, everyone's story was their own.

"That's great," he replied, unconvinced. He swore Raven was on something. If not leaves, then maybe one of the hallucination powders pirates snorted. Every time he asked, she denied it, but he didn't believe her.

"Have you received the tattoo?" Blood left Cassian's face at her question. "The captain's mark?"

The bread in his hand wavered. From behind her, the door to Shade's Pub opened, and a red-cloaked man stepped in, flashing a gold ring that had to cost more than a village. The gesture was flashy, intentional—he was a man with no concern for being robbed. The kind of man who would want a dragon egg. The pub was named after The Shade, which sat along the stomach of Volkeri Island. Where no ship ever entered and came out again. His first stop on Greve's Point. His next stop would be the sister establishment next to Shade's Pub, where grimy men like him could bathe and get new clothes.

"I have to go," Cassian said and tried to step around the Soul Speaker, but Raven grabbed his hand, knocking the rest of the bread to the ground. Shame. It was delicious.

"The dead are speaking of you," she whispered harshly. Twisting his hand, she revealed the rose tattoo. "I can't understand everything, but they warn me that you need to be careful. You can't pledge yourself."

He frowned. "Who in the dead sea's name would I pledge myself to?" Pledging loyalty or service to someone was landwalker talk. A king would seek a pledge from a city or person, but pirates didn't work the same way. Pirates worked for a fee, under the Sea Laws, not seeking kings and queens to pledge their services to. What the Soul Speaker suggested was an insult. Pirates didn't operate like that.

Raven let go. A feline ran up, snatching the rest of the bread between its teeth and leaving. He watched it go. The longer he stayed on this island, the more went wrong. Maybe he should have stayed on *Torment*.

"They don't tell me that." She shook her head. "I keep seeing your face in my dreams. I couldn't rest until I told you." Raven wrapped her arms around herself, deflated, shoulders slumping, and walked off.

Cassian gaped, bewildered. The Soul Speaker stepped into her place, shutting the door behind her. Shaken, he patted his pockets to make sure she hadn't been part of a scheme to steal from him. Everything was there, coin and all, and he wiped the sticky residue of the bread on his pants, his appetite gone. He respected the dead, but that's where they needed to stay—dead. Glass's words brushed over his mind with a frigid tendril. Someone was listening. That's why the dead were quieter than usual. With Raven's strange behavior, he felt dirty, unwanted—and like he was being watched.

It had to be a coincidence. That's all. Cassian shook his hands and spit, hoping to rid himself of whatever clung to him that was causing all these problems. Nothing was going right. Hadn't since they'd taken *Blue Bells*. Once he got the payout for the heist, he could resolve his problems. Get a new ship, new name, new start.

Shade's Pub awaited him, promising him a drink. He needed it. A big one.

Captain of the Kings

The lighting was poor, hence the name of the pub. Shadows danced across the walls, moving sporadically with the people sitting around round tables, tucked away in the corners, or intermingling. Maids dressed in corsets and plain dresses carried mugs of ale, stacked three high, dropping them off at the tables as they went. Behind the bar, Ekil poured. He came from a generation of people who served Greve's Point and its pirates but hadn't ever set foot on a ship. A few families were like that, happy to serve and stay where they were. Everyone knew Ekil and his daughter, Sasha. She would take over the pub soon enough.

Music played at the front—a group of men toying with instruments that weren't quite in tune. They sang sea shanties, cracked jokes with the patrons, and drank. Ekil kept their drinks full and in return, the musicians kept playing. On the other side, men tossed daggers into the wall, chatting amongst themselves and placing bets. Lodging rooms weren't available for most of the patrons—Ekil said they got too rowdy—but he reserved a few for the regulars or peacekeepers. Cassian was still trying to get on that list.

The pub was crowded, stuffed so full that nobody could move without brushing against someone else. Pirates didn't have personal space. Cassian peered over bodies, trying to find the man he'd seen. The ring was large enough to catch his eye, but that didn't mean anything. Anyone could have a gold ring, but he hoped this was the man *Blue Bells* was after. He didn't get a good look at his face, just that he wore a dark red cloak too thick for the night's warmth. Enough to catch the attention of anyone who knew what they were looking for.

Legs, arms, shoulders—Cassian felt it all rub up against him as he scanned the tight room. Ale-sodden breath caressed his cheek as a woman leaned in and tried to get his attention, but he shoved her off. Manners didn't exist in this world. All that mattered was who could get what they wanted and when. The woman moved on, not disappointed, quickly catching the attention of a burly man covered in enough hair to look like a beast who'd crawled out of the Soul Realm.

Cassian was surprised that he didn't see any of the crew here. Shade's Pub was popular for most, and he'd prepared himself to see a few here, even Wes. Perhaps they got turned off by how packed it was and moved to another pub. Cassian didn't mind.

He blinked. There he was, the man in the red cloak. No, it couldn't be. The ease of this search made him second-guess every decision—nothing ever came easy. A price always came with it. Cassian squinted. There he was . . . nestled at a table for two behind the musicians, sipping from a frothy mug. His hand was proudly splayed on the table, and on one finger, the gold ring. That wasn't by accident. The man—king—was making himself known to the right person. Cassian stepped forward, then stopped. He needed a drink. Both for his nerves and to play the part.

At the bar counter, Ekil threw a towel over his shoulder. "Cassian! Been a while since I've seen you. How are you?"

Cassian tucked his hand underneath the counter, not wanting to talk about his new ink. "Good. Normal stuff. Things look like they're holding up well here." He raised his voice to be heard over the madness and music.

Ekil grinned. The small mustache over his top lip reacted to the movement, stretching wide. The bartender was the only man Cassian had ever seen who took as much care of his mustache, even curling the corners, as he did with the drinks he poured. "Been better than well. This is every night! What can I get you?"

Cassian motioned at the guy next to him. "Whatever he's drinking."

"You got it." Ekil grabbed a mug from underneath and went over to a barrel stacked on top of another. A tap was inserted at the bottom, and the bartender opened the mouth, filling the mug. As he did, Cassian checked to make sure the king hadn't moved. He hadn't, but a lady was talking to him: one of the maids hoping to make a little extra coin by selling herself. She laid a hand on his, and he didn't pull away. Maybe he had the wrong man.

"Here you are." Ekil dropped the mug down in front of him. Froth spilled over the edges, drenching the wood.

"What's the cost today?" Cassian reached for his pouch.

"None." Cassian started to protest, but Ekil waved him off. "It's nice to see a familiar face. Enjoy. Next one, though, you got to pay." At that, he winked and walked away.

That was a good sign. Meant he was closer to getting on that list—the one where the select few got free drinks and special perks. Cassian picked up his mug and headed straight for the king. Getting to him was a mix of pushing and squeezing. A few patrons bumped into him, splashing more ale over the rim and onto his hand and pants. It wouldn't be a pirate pub without that. He didn't know how landwalkers behaved in pubs, but he believed they'd likely be appalled. On land, pirates acted like animals. Cassian once heard the phrase: *Keep 'em at sea to keep 'em civilized.* The more he saw of Greve's Point, the more he agreed.

His heart picked up pace as he closed in on his target. If this wasn't the right man, he didn't know what he'd do. Admittedly, everything about his future was piled atop someone he'd never met and wasn't even sure was real. The reality of that made him falter in his step.

But it was too late. The man, sensing him somehow, turned in his direction. Eyes darker than midnight met Cassian's. Stubble covered the lower half of the stranger's face, and he was wider than Cassian originally thought. He looked like he belonged on the field, swinging a sword twice his size and covered in blood, not with a crown and sitting on a throne. Instead of any of that, he was sat here in a dingy pub in the hometown of pirates.

All at once, the man's demeanor shifted. He said something to the maid, who lingered too long before the king waved her off. She left, lips pinched in a thin line, and eyed Cassian as she passed. Nothing kind came from that look—she knew he was to blame for her dismissal. The maid would have to find a new patron to sell herself to.

Cassian stood frozen. He was a fool. He shouldn't have done this, put all his faith in a delirious idea that would likely get him killed. It was this or the Queens' blade across his throat, though. He tried to remind himself that this was the better alternative, that if he could make it through this alive, he could start over. But now, standing there, he realized this could be a massive mistake.

Mingling with landwalkers was dangerous for the inexperienced. Cassian had watched the crew of *Torment* do the same, and it was always risky. Captain Ricard knew what to do, how to speak, what was acceptable, because he'd done it for decades. Cassian had been captain for less than a day and had already lost part of his crew.

The man raised his mug, flashing the ring intentionally. He was telling Cassian to sit if he was here for business. That brought the newly-branded captain to life, forcing his legs forward. He sank into the chair across from the man in the red cloak. Instantly, Cassian stopped noticing all the commotion.

"Unwise decision to do your business here," Cassian said. "More men die in these walls than out at sea." Pirates knew better than to conduct any sort of formal discussions in this pub. He'd anticipated to find the king with the gold ring in a quieter place, maybe an inn with a couple of patrons neck deep in their drink, not in the liveliest place on the island.

The king eyed him up and down like he was surveying an animal to buy. "I was expecting someone a little more . . . *seasoned*," he replied, taking a long drink and ignoring the comment. He was wide-shouldered and had a rich olive skin color that promised centuries of ancestors in Creitón.

Cassian wanted to stab him for the insult. Just because he was young didn't make him incapable. Youth was relative to pirates. At twenty, Cassian was more experienced than any soldier who served the cities on land. "Am I wasting your time?" he asked.

"Only if you aren't interested," the king remarked.

Cassian took a drink. The ale was smooth and was far too sweet for his liking. His hand didn't shake like he thought it would, but the nerves were eating him alive. "I'm interested." Even his voice sounded as bold as he wanted it to.

The king narrowed his gaze and asked, "You a captain?"

Cassian laid his tattooed hand out between them. Redness still clung to the areas around his knuckles, but the man wouldn't know how fresh the tattoo was. Landwalkers hardly understood the difference between a seasoned captain and a new one. All they cared about was getting the job done.

It worked. The king nodded. "All right. Younger than I would have imagined, but I don't know your politics out there. I trust you have a reliable crew?"

"Best there is on the water." Confidence soaked that statement. Cassian wanted more information. Anyone could say they were a king. Landwalkers liked to think pirates were low-life maggot-infested swabs who didn't know how politics were run on land. They were wrong. Pirates kept strong tabs on all politics because it helped them decide who to work for, why, and at what price. "You're king of what? The pub?" Harsh, but Cassian knew the king was feeling him out as well. They didn't know each other. As a pirate, he needed to take control of this situation. Make sure the king knew who was in charge.

The corner of the man's lips twitched upward, obviously amused. "King Jair of Saveen, Captain."

Saveen? He wasn't drunk enough for this. He knew he was going to meet a king, but this was real. He couldn't deny this anymore. He'd found the king with the gold ring, was sitting in a pub with him, and now it was time to get to the point. The Saveen family was known to be particularly violent when they didn't get their way. Whipped their own family members to prove a point, too. Last Cassian heard, Jair executed his brother just to ensure his own son, Dameon, would have the crown.

Jair didn't dare dress as a king, not here. It worked—nobody recognized him. Plenty of pirates displayed their priceless jewelry or carried themselves like they ruled the world. But nobody had a ring like that—bulky, prominent, with gold vines that latched onto the large red stone to hold it in place. Engravings decorated the band, but the writing was too small to be read.

Cassian had never liked small-talk—couldn't stand it. If something needed to be said or dealt with, then he wouldn't waste time chatting about the weather. "What are you paying?" he asked.

King Jair raised an eyebrow. "I thought that information was passed on?" Now the king sounded unimpressed. Bored even.

Cassian cleared his throat, swallowing the wave of panic. "Messages travel differently out there. I want to confirm what I heard."

"Ah." King Jair drummed his fingers, flashing the gold ring. "I'm willing to pay anywhere between twenty and thirty thousand Krye. Depends on the swiftness of the job. You ever stolen a dragon egg before, Captain?"

Cassian choked. He'd never seen that much coin in his life. Another drink to wash the shock down. This was it. If he and Jair could come to an agreement, he would steal a dragon egg and get out from underneath the Red Queens' thumb. "Is it real?"

"What?"

Cassian leaned forward, making sure he sounded as unconvinced as he felt. "The dragon egg. Have you seen one?"

The king leaned forward and lowered his voice. "I'll do one better. I've seen a dragon egg, held one in my hands. I know it's real."

Information like this would change the world. Nobody would lie about this. Not unless they wanted a reaction, but this wasn't that. The king offered more coin than Cassian could ever spend in his lifetime. Rül'Cril, the relic they were hired to hunt, felt ridiculous now—a pathetic prize that would never mean as much as this.

Already, Cassian was halfway through his drink. He needed to slow down or he'd be buzzed before a deal was made, but this was all too much. "So you had an egg, but now you need another?" Cassian asked. He hoped he sounded as steady as he was trying to act. Inside, he reeled. Every childhood story of great dragons rushed him. Everyone grew up hearing about the Dragon Riders who once soared the skies. He'd outgrown the tales in his later summers, finding them too fantastical and wild. Now he wondered if the rumor of the Dragon Riders returning was true. If so, the entire world would change. Kings and queens would no longer be the most powerful individuals—Dragon Riders would. Politics would shift too. Kingdoms would fight tooth and nail for a place in the new era of Dragon Riders. Where would that leave pirates like him?

The king spread his hands, chuckling. "Consider it a complication of the trade." His lips quirked up, but it was shallow, thin, and strained. Like it took everything in him to use those muscles. A story hid behind that expression, dark and cruel. Cassian didn't want to know anymore.

"So you need another one," Cassian finished. It wasn't a question. King Jair nodded. "Tell me what you know, and I'll tell you if it's possible."

"If it wasn't possible, I wouldn't be doing this again," the king said.

Cassian motioned for him to continue. This man was married to arrogance. Coin bought him everything he needed.

"There's a ship that sails between Eiyrăl and Creitón. They call it *Dread Deep*. It always has contraband onboard. The crew works directly with the city of Kalic. My best guess is that Kalic and Barnăl are in discussions, maybe someone else. Whatever the case, *Dread Deep* had a dragon egg on board seven moons ago. They were traveling with it, and I had a few men intercept, pretending to be part of the crew. They took the egg before the ship docked and fled. Showed up at my door. I'm hoping to do that again."

Cassian crossed his arms. "Where are the men you hired?"

"Dead."

Cassian held his tongue. He wanted to hear what else the king had. Dead wasn't shocking. Men died at sea all the time.

"So, why do you need another dragon egg?" Cassian pressed. "One isn't enough?"

The king's gaze darkened. A storm brewed behind those eyes, one that Cassian never wanted to experience. He shifted in his seat, tempted to reach for the sword strapped on his hip.

"I lost it," the king answered. "I need another egg."

Cassian didn't press further. He was curious, yes, but he didn't like the way the king spoke—this was personal.

"Anyway," Jair sighed. "I need a group of men who I can trust to get aboard, get the egg, and get back to me. If you can do it in less than ten days, I'll pay thirty. If not, twenty."

"In a rush?" Cassian asked, keeping his voice steady. The longer he remained quiet, the more the king talked.

"If *Dread Deep* docks, you're screwed. I've got word that they swap cargo into different shipment boxes for precisely this reason. Just in case anyone onboard is thinking of taking something and running."

A ship brimming with potential. Cassian could get more than just the thirty thousand Krye. "Do you know what else they carry?" he asked.

The king shrugged. "How am I supposed to know? Bet you it's big stuff if they've got an egg aboard."

"Or mundane material to throw off the scent," Cassian countered. "Let's get straight to the point. What I care about is whether or not this is successful and my men and I get paid. How can I trust your word? What's to say you won't get this egg"—real or not—"and slit our throats? Keep your coin?"

King Jair wrapped both hands around the drink, nodding as a maid passed by. When she was gone, he narrowed his gaze. "What would I gain by slitting your throats?"

"Keeping things quiet," Cassian answered. "We might talk to the wrong people. You're royalty. That could start a war."

The king chuckled, shallow and lifeless. "And what would you gain for that?"

Cassian leaned back. "More coin."

"Ah." The king laughed. "I see now." He took a drink, downing the rest of the ale. When he set the mug down, he said, "Payment for the egg. Payment for the secret."

Cassian nodded.

"45,000 Krye. Will that suffice?" the king asked.

The muscles in Cassian's shoulders were so tense that they hurt, and when he went to take another drink, he found only a little bit left at the bottom. This king was handing over coin without thought. It made him wonder how much the first crew got paid, but he knew he shouldn't push his luck. This was more than he could ever need. It would cover the crew, get a new ship, and still set them up for a comfortable life. Then again, Jair might be telling him what he wanted to hear. There was no reason the king needed to be loyal to Cassian; he only wanted the egg. But Cassian wasn't interested in loyalty. Pirates worked in risky business, and he was willing to take the chance for a large payday.

Cassian held out his hand. "You've got a deal."

King Jair stood, taking his hand with an iron grip. In one swift motion, he yanked him forward. Cassian caught himself on the wall. Nobody around them noticed or cared enough to watch.

"I know you're young. I know that tattoo is fresh. I know you're desperate for something—it's written all over your face." The king spoke in a whisper as cold as Death. "I also know you're not who I was supposed to meet, but between you and me, I don't care as long as I get what I want. Let me make this clear: if you fail to get me this egg, I will triple that coin and put a bounty on your head all over the world. No place will be safe, not even the Grave. Do I make myself clear?"

Cassian had misread this man so severely that he no longer wanted a part of this deal. Landwalkers didn't speak like that—they called it the Grave of Seas, not the Grave. They didn't pay attention to healing tattoos or have enough knowledge to tell a new captain versus an experienced one. The king had played him, lured him in, and now had him by the throat. Jair had experience on the sea, knew pirate politics—he wasn't just some proud, greedy landwalker. Cassian couldn't back out, because he was certain the king would kill him just for that. And he needed to get out from underneath the Queens. No matter where he looked, he was pinned. One day into being captain, and he was going to get himself and his crew killed.

"You have my word." The answer came out far less brave than Cassian wished. The king grinned, mad with a disturbing glee that made Cassian want to bury his head under the table.

"There's one last thing. *Dread Deep* cuts through the Grave." The ale in Cassian's stomach soured, making him nauseous. No crew was ever mad enough to do such a thing. King Jair didn't flinch, but the wild gleam in his eye betrayed that he knew exactly how crazy the plan sounded. "When you dock at Saveen, ask for Edward. He will know what to do from there." The king separated and grabbed his empty mug. "Safe travels at sea, Captain. I'll see you soon."

Seeker of Death

The sea was no place for the restless. Cassian repeated that to himself as he wandered the streets. The moment King Jair left, Cassian bought himself a hot bath and new clothes at the sister pub and shop next door. Nothing could keep him in that pub any longer. It reeked of a terrible decision that made Cassian sick to his stomach. He'd signed his life away to a mad king with a sick sense of humor. If he told the crew the threat, they'd run. If he lied, he was burdened with the weight of their promise. The heist could get them killed if things went wrong. If the crew o f *Dread Deep* didn't slit their throats, the Grave would swallow them whole.

Stories passed on from each pirate to another spoke of the dead, how they could sniff out the difference between a weak man and a confident one. The sea was no place for the restless. That mantra was forged under the belief that if a man wandered too far from who he was, the dead would take his soul—take it and eat the life away, leaving nothing but a brittle skeleton. Restlessness got a man killed. Cassian squirmed in his own skin, feeling more like a dirty-blooded pirate and enraged imposter. This blood of his men would be on his hands if this heist wasn't successful.

He bounced his fists off the stone walls he passed, trying to compose himself. If any of his crew saw him like this, they'd spend the coming days knocking on wood, asking the dead to leave them alone, and leaving coins in odd places. Bad luck to bring this kind of anxiety aboard. The dead were probably following him already, waiting for him to stumble, so they could steal his soul and leave him for dead.

Another turn, another dingy side street. Shadows leeched off the stone. Light failed to reach most of the corners. Unconscious drunks used their arms and pieces of wood as pillows. He was careful not to step on any of them. He'd slept in these alleys before. Sometimes it was the quietest place in the city. Others, the only place he could get for free.

He'd run from the Queens' duties, desperate for a taste of something more. He'd abandoned his responsibilities as a pirate and captain, agreed to a wild plan that could kill him and all his men for a sliver of a chance at freedom. *His* men. Already, he thought like a captain, but he was so far from fulfilling that title that it made his chest hurt just thinking about it.

He wasn't a captain. Captains led the most legendary expeditions, were idolized, and earned loyalty and trust. Cassian could claim none of those. He was a fraud, a thief, and a pirate by mercy, not anything more. Some might even say that if he was killed, he earned it—being a dirty-blooded pirate. Cassian wanted to believe that maybe his fate wasn't so bleak, that someday he'd become the most respected pirate ever to sail, but he didn't believe in destiny. Never had, never would. Bad luck and terrible timing defined each mistake made. Every decision was his own—up until the point the Queens boarded *Torment* and stole his freedom.

Agitated didn't come close to describing how he felt. This was his life, nobody else's, but now, he was at the mercy of a political war that could change the seas forever.

"You going to stand there or sit down?"

Cassian looked to his left. A hooded man sat with his back to stone, sipping on a drink. The wooden cup was large—could hold three drinks in one—and was orange under the low light. The man wore gloves, his face hidden. He didn't even look up when he spoke.

"I was just passing through," Cassian replied.

"Sit down."

Cassian swallowed. A sensation he wasn't entirely familiar with soaked into his bones and made his heart flutter. Hesitation. He didn't want to, but he also wasn't sure walking away was a smart decision either. His back turned to this man could earn him a death sentence. A chill raced over him. Something about this man unsettled him. Like fifty pairs of eyes were on him at once. Cassian took a quick glance around. Only a few passed out drunks lay in the narrow street. He needed to keep going, find a place to rest his head, and sleep off the nerves. But what he wanted to do was sit down and listen to whatever this man had to say.

"Well?"

Cassian sighed. Curiosity and uncertainty won. He sat beside the stranger, giving himself enough space that if he had to bolt, he could. Sigils on the cloak caught his attention, silvery under the lantern's gaze. The fabric was tightly threaded, expensive. Cassian tried to get a good look at the man's face, but he couldn't. The hood was large, engulfing his features and leaving nothing but shadows. The only thing he was certain of was that the man had five fingers on each gloved hand.

"Good choice," the man said.

The warmth of the day still clung to the stone wall he leaned against, heat seeping through fabric and skin. It felt nice, like a hug—something he'd not had in a decade or more. "You don't strike me as the drunk type," Cassian said. No point in dragging this out.

"Good observation." The man didn't offer more.

"Did you know I would be here?" Cassian lowered his hand to the hilt of his sword. "Are you a Queen or working for them?" Wouldn't surprise him if the Red Queens hired trackers to keep tabs on their targets.

"That's unnecessary," the man replied, inclining his head toward Cassian's grip on the blade. His accent didn't belong to these waters, but one could never be too sure. Queens were everywhere. They intermingled with landwalkers all the time to gain information, even going so far as to join the councils of distant kings and queens. "If I wanted you dead, I could have done it a number of times already."

That didn't make Cassian feel any more at ease, but he drew his hand away from the weapon. "Where are you from? I don't recognize your accent."

"Not from anywhere you've been," the man answered quietly. "How much do you know about the Death Seekers?"

"What?" Cassian didn't expect that. He'd been ready to talk threats and politics, not about the Guardians of Death. So little was known about them. Few met one and lived to talk about it. Like most people, he'd never seen one. Didn't care to either. They were bad omens, bringers of death, and harbingers of destruction. Wherever a Death Seeker went—what most called them—terrible things followed.

"Well?" the man pressed.

Cassian suddenly felt he was eight summers old again, scrambling to say anything to appease the fury of his father before he was beaten black and blue. "I, um—well, they live between realms, yeah? Guide souls to the Afterlife?"

"That's the best you got?" He sounded disappointed.

Cassian bared his hands and asked, "What am I supposed to know? What they eat for supper?" A drunk five paces down rolled over into the middle of the street, snoring.

The man scoffed. "Centuries ago, Guardians were praised and celebrated. Now they can't make an appearance in most cities without being feared and ostracized. Cruel, don't you think? To be the protector of realms and treated like scum?"

"Yeah." Cassian drew his knees up, uncomfortable. Goosebumps ran up his arms in warning. He didn't like this conversation, but he didn't want to be rude and walk away. Half of him believed that if he tried, this man would pull a dagger from somewhere within his cloak and slice his throat clean open, so Cassian stayed put. Now that he thought of it, the hooded man hadn't touched the drink in his hand.

"Ve'hem," the man quietly said. "The burdened one."

Cassian nodded, still not sure what to say. He'd heard that term before in the sea shanties sang on *Torment*. Glass told him the expression was reserved for the greatest heroes of all time. Maybe he was sitting next to a madman who just liked to hear himself talk. He watched the drunk in the middle of the street cough, lean over, and retch. The pungent stench of regurgitated ale wafted over, an aroma with which Cassian was all too familiar. The man next to him shook his head. It seemed he was disappointed by everything. The drunk slumped back down with a grunt.

"The energies are changing," the man continued. "The winds no longer seek the refuge of the mountains. Shadows chase the sun, rather than fearing her. But most of all, the dead no longer wish to remain dead." Cassian's chest rose and fell, his nerves jangling inside him like loose coin. "Have you felt the change in the water?"

Cassian blinked. "If you mean the bad blood between the Queens, then y—"

"No, fool," the man snapped. "The waters themselves. Have you felt the changes?"

"Uh, no." Cassian shifted his arm closer to his sword again. Maybe he'd have to kill him to get out of here. "If the wind is in our favor and the fish are plenty, we don't worry. Those are the signs of life we look for. You're not a pirate, are you?"

"You don't need to be a pirate to know how damned the seas are." Now, the man sounded agitated, like Cassian had said something insulting. "Spend enough time listening, and you become the most clever person in the room. If you spend too much time talking, you become the fool who loses a tongue."

The warning sat between them, ugly and bold. A warning for what, though? Pirates talked, maybe too much sometimes, but the only reason Cassian spoke now was because he felt forced into this conversation. He didn't like where this was going, and he didn't need to stay any longer to listen to the insults or insanity. "I think we're done." He made to rise, but an iron grip shoved him down. Cassian's head met the wall so hard that a welt would show. "By the dead's hand, what the—" he gasped.

"Don't call upon the dead unless you're willing to hear what they have to say," the man remarked. He shoved the drink in Cassian's hands. "Drink. And let me tell you about the world."

The ale was dark. Spices wafted up to meet Cassian's nose, enticing. This didn't smell like anything he'd had on Greve's Point. "I don't need to know about the world. I know everything I need to know to survive."

"Do you?"

The stranger's tone made Cassian hesitate. He hated the feeling of *doubt*. The weakness, the vulnerability. Cassian was a White Horn, not some commoner begging for scraps. "I know enough."

"Do you know about energy?"

This man was pissing him off. "I'm not a Harvester. I don't spend my time worrying about things I can't use."

"Manipulate," the man corrected, his voice stern. "To accurately use energy, you manipulate it."

"Magic, energy, witches—why does it matter?" Cassian asked. The strength to get up and leave waned. He studied the liquid, entranced by the glittering lights suspended within. They moved, blinked in and out of existence, and calmed his racing thoughts. His breaths came slower, steadier, and the knot in his shoulders eased. This ale, the aroma—it wasn't normal. Something was happening.

"A new era is upon us. What you've experienced at sea is only a sliver of what is happening to the world. The rumors you hear—most are true. And most will continue to get worse until something is done. You may find yourself in situations that you can't predict. Perhaps you may find yourself with an impossible decision. Are you following?"

Cassian nodded, unable to look away. The lights in the ale moved when the man spoke, responding to his voice. His mind felt leagues from his grasp. He felt drunk, but not the dastardly type where he slurred or stumbled. Rather, like he could sit on the shore for the rest of the night and watch the waves lap lazily against the sand, dragging pebbles back and spitting them back out without ever having to speak.

"Remember what I tell you. It may just save your life one day," the man said.

Again, Cassian nodded.

"Light Energy is all around us. When you drink, hunt, fish, or pluck berries from a tree, you participate in establishing balance in this realm. Light Energy creates everything. The very essence of who you are—your lifeforce, your soul—is forged from that. The God's Realm, what you call *living*, is home to extraordinary things because Light Energy was given a chance to expand, evolve, and create in such ways that no other realm has seen. You know why?"

Cassian shook his head. He didn't know much of anything about energy, or what many called magic.

"It isn't pure. Light Energy is tampered with, unclean. It absorbs and bleeds, just like you or me. That makes it malleable and easy to manipulate. Harvesters call upon this when needed. But Dark Energy? You shouldn't touch it. Nobody ever should. It is volatile and intelligent. Don't let that intelligence fool you—pure energy like that will devour you. The dead are bound to it, chained for an eternity. Dark Energy seeks a host, much like a parasite burrows into your flesh when you have a gaping wound."

Cassian swallowed, finding his mouth dry. He found blinking exhausting. He didn't know why this man spoke to him about all this, and he didn't care. He was desperate to take a drink, but he couldn't find the ability to break the hold the lights and what they promised had on him.

"You are bound to the voices now." The man's voice was distant. "That mug contains just the smallest amount of Dark Energy. Water is a pure element that Dark Energy calls home. If you were not touched with the ability to harvest, you would not sense what you do now. So, I ask again, have you felt the changes in the sea?"

At first, Cassian couldn't figure out how to work his tongue. It smashed into the roof of his mouth, mushy, and with a mind of its own. He wrangled it under his control, which took everything he had. When he finally spoke, his words came out slow. "Black spots in the sea."

"Tell me more."

The answer was pulled right out of Cassian, like he wasn't in control of his own body. "Captain thinks they're the Queens' work, that it's a part of their war, but Glass talks about the dead. Says the dead were shouting for someone to listen. But he thinks someone's listening now."

"And you? What would you say?"

The lights glowed brighter, inviting him in. He wanted to dive right into the murky ale and drown. He wanted to give everything he had to hear the voices clearly. They weren't loud enough, but they didn't have to be. He knew by the sound of their song that *they* wanted *him* just as much. He lowered his head, trying to get a better look. Lights flickered faster, thrilled by his acknowledgment. He tried to tell them he could hear them, but nothing came out. His mouth wouldn't move, his tongue gone rogue. The lower he dipped his head, the heavier it got. Thoughts slowed, his eyelids drooped—

Cassian jolted awake. He blinked and looked around. The street was still dark, the lanterns flicked lazily, unperturbed. The drunks passed out against the wall didn't move, snoring. Nobody lay in the middle of the street anymore.

He shifted. Muscles in his neck strained and protested, locked from sleeping with his head stuffed against a barrel. A mug was clutched tightly to his chest, glowing orange under the low light. Cassian held it up, recalling the strange, cloaked man. He scanned the alley but didn't see him. Was that all a dream? Couldn't be. Cassian rubbed the tender spot on the back of his head from when the man shoved his head into the stone.

"That was mine," a woman croaked from behind. He turned around to see her dressed in a tight red corset that shoved her breasts to her chin, blond hair framing a round face. Her hand reached for him.

"This?" he asked, raising the mug.

She nodded, glassy-eyed.

"Sorry." He handed it back to her. She tucked the mug under her dress, between her legs. He watched, dazed. How had he gotten ahold of her belongings? He felt like he was losing his mind.

"I ain't doing business now, if that's what you're wondering," she remarked harshly. "I'm off for the rest of the night."

Cassian shook his head. "No, no." He rubbed his face, trying to gain his composure. He was in no mood for a woman. What he wanted was answers. "Was there a man here? Dressed in a black cloak?"

She scoffed. "Do I look like the street's keeper? How should I know?"

Point made. He didn't want to pick a fight with her either. Cassian forced himself to his feet. "Thanks." Not that he meant it. He just wanted to leave. He didn't know if this was all a dream or not, and right now, he was afraid to ask.

His mind was cloudy, hard to reach, and his body—stiff and sore—moved like he'd been trampled by a galloping horse. Based on the stars, though, he couldn't have been asleep that long. Maybe the Shade's Pub was brewing stronger stuff than he realized. Or maybe he'd really talked to someone and they'd drugged him. That wasn't the finest thought. He was growing weak, if so. Cassian was better than that.

He checked his belongings. Everything was there. So no thief. Just someone with a sick sense of humor. Or a dream. He wanted to wish it was a dream because admitting that it wasn't meant he'd been tricked.

No, he realized, it *was* real. The blossoming bruise on the back of his head proved it. It was so real that he could still see the lights and hear the voices.

He wasn't drunk. A single drink didn't put him over, no matter how strong. Someone had sought him out. Spoken to him like they knew his life better than he. That chilled him to the bone. He looked up and down the street, hoping to catch a sight of whoever it was, but he knew better. The man was long gone, and if he was smart, he'd already be on the other side of Greve's Point, well beyond Cassian's reach and pleas to know what'd happened.

Cassian rolled his shoulders and straightened his clothes and belt. He needed to take a walk and clear his head before dawn. Come the morning, they were setting sail for the Grave.

Sailing the Unknown

Sunrise came too fast. Cassian spent most of the night walking the streets of Greve's Point, listening to the laughter, fights, and occasional begging. Sleep evaded him, and he refused to revisit the street he'd awoken in. If he saw that man again, he realized that he didn't have the courage to lay a hand on him—a harsh reality to swallow. Cassian was bold, reckless, and spared no mercy, but put him in a room with whoever that stranger was, and he wanted to crawl out of his skin and hide.

Their conversation floated around in his head, restless and wild. He was eager to return to the Vore waters he called home, but he was shamefully dreading it after what the man said. Black spots *were* the Queens' doing. Ships were disappearing—a perfect opportunity for the Queens to strengthen their hold on the sea by wiping out enemy vessels. It had to be. He didn't want to convince himself otherwise. If he spent too long thinking about how he really felt about the sea, he was worried about what he might find. That he was tired of the same-old, same-old. That he craved something beyond *Torment*.

He returned to the man he'd seen missing an arm and foot and plopped a few coins into his can just before dawn, wishing him well. He'd learned that the man had been, indeed, a captain many summers ago and had fallen victim to a bad deal. Men turned on him, threw him overboard, and he was attacked by one of the beasts that lived beneath—a lunga, a nasty creature with rows of razor teeth that could detect fear a league out. The lunga got distracted by another creature, whereupon a fight broke out, allowing the man to escape with his life.

Cassian left the man where he was, and strolled along the coastline, listening to the waves. The stars reflected off the surface of the water. Land was good from time to time. He knew that. Resources were bought, allies were made, and it was pleasant to have a hot bath. New clothes were always needed when they docked. The new tunic and pants were nearly identical to what he already wore, but the fabric had been old and frayed. He bought more oil for the *Torment's* lanterns, as well as plenty of Seaman's Water. Then he found some leather pieces that could be cut for strapping, so he got those too.

Rope was always a necessity, so he got more than he knew they needed. Food, water—no need for extra boots when they had scavenged extra pairs from *Blue Bells*—and a few more cannonballs. Shop owners promised everything would be delivered at sunrise. The good thing about Greve's Point was that most shops stayed open all night. Most pirates preferred it that way.

Now, Cassian watched workers from each shop carry aboard the material and supplies he'd ordered. Always be prepared. Captain Ricard reiterated that relentlessly. While the crew went out and got drunk, slept around, and enjoyed themselves, it was the captain's duty to ensure the ship was well-provisioned. He liked the role. When he had been here before, he was with the crew. But times had changed.

"Where do you want the leather?" a young boy asked. Probably the son of the owner, sporting the same freckles and red hair.

"Plop them down in the crew's quarters."

"Coffee in the galley?"

Cassian frowned. "Where else would it go?" The boy didn't reply.

King Jair sat in the back of Cassian's head with the same persistence as a fly on dung. He checked over his shoulder more times than he could count, certain the burly man would be standing there, watching. Their encounter bugged him. He walked right in and made a deal with a mad king. Cassian knew he was missing something, had to be, but what? Was Jair telling him everything? The more he racked his head over it, the more frustrated he became. Maybe he was overthinking, too caught up in the politics of land-walkers. All Cassian needed to worry about was keeping the crew alive and finding the dragon egg.

Then there was the matter of telling the crew. How much Cassian should share remained in question. If he told them the king knew they weren't the crew he'd been expecting, a good number of the men would get suspicious. Start asking questions he didn't know the answer to. If he told them they were setting sail for the egg and were promised more Krye than they knew what to do with, however, the men would support it. If he told them he spoke to a stranger who foretold terrible things ahead and that he woke up confused in the street, they'd call him a drunk. Not sharing was the right answer for that one.

He was a cornered rabbit, waiting for the fangs of the serpent to burrow into his neck and unleash an incurable amount of venom. Sailing for the Grave was the only option. He'd tell the men their plans once they were out at sea, and also see if anyone had heard information on Rül'Cril. He needed to focus his attention solely on the heist. Retrieving the dragon egg, no matter how treacherous, was the only chance of freedom for all of them. Get that back to King Jair, and he'd be a free man with more Krye than he ever needed. The only thing they needed to do was outrun the Queens at their own hunt. Do that, and he might just live to see the next season.

A hand clamped his shoulder, startling him. "Men are nearly done loading everythin' up. You need anything else before we head out?"

Darryl had been on Greve's Point since Cassian was a child. The leather master always liked to lend a hand when he wasn't busy skinning and prepping pieces for armor or weapons. He was a gangly man with a scraggly beard and short gray hair. Cassian didn't think he'd ever had a family or lover. Rather, Darryl fell in love with his job.

"This should do," Cassian replied. "I appreciate your help. Always do."

"I'm sorry about Ricard." Darryl shook his hand. "Good man."

How much Darryl knew, Cassian wasn't certain, and he wasn't going to ask—word traveled fast when drinks started flowing. What was done was done. "Yeah, he was," Cassian said.

Voices came from behind. The crew. Cassian nodded at them, watching Glass stumble into another seaman before righting himself. Jules had a swollen eye, Ryl's left arm was bandaged with blood stains, but overall, the crew looked in fairly good shape. Hungover, but that was expected. Nobody was dead, so it was a good night. He only hoped someone learned something about the relic. Though based on their looks, he'd guess not. Not entirely reliable, but they were there, and that's all that mattered.

Darryl offered his hand to Cassian, who took it with a firm grip. "Let the sea be with you, Captain. We'll see you and your men soon."

"Aye." Cassian still wasn't used to that. Wasn't sure he'd ever be.

The crew made their way aboard, hardly passing acknowledgments to Cassian or the others. They knocked on the railing as they ascended onto the ship. Keep the dead at bay, sail away. A phrase Cassian repeated religiously to himself. He followed the men. Knocking helped alert the dead that the living returned, reclaiming their place aboard the ship. The lapping waves against the dock were peaceful this morning. Sun was clear, sky was crisp, and the wind was in their favor. It would be a good sail.

Wood groaned in welcome as Cassian settled on the main deck. Already, the crew was at work, prepping sails, tying things down, and securing ropes. They knew without asking that new material awaited them. Everything the ship could need sat nestled below, ready when needed. Liquor, more livestock, leather, oil, cured meats, water, ropes, clothes, and whatever else was needed—the shopping list varied with each visit to port. This time,

Cassian ordered more straw and feed for the livestock as well as whetstones for sharpening weapons. Nobody told him they were practically out of either until he did a scan through the ship's belongings before they docked at Greve's Point. The crew trusted that things got done while they played, and Cassian wouldn't let them down. He walked up the steps to the wheel. Glass was already there, line in hand, holding *Torment* in place. Those on the dock pulled free the tie-downs and gangway.

"You ready?" Glass asked.

Cassian nodded curtly. He took hold of the wheel, the wood coarse and familiar in his calloused hand. The ship didn't fight the leisurely pull from the dock. Crew pushed them out to sea with paddles. A few crews on ships nearby howled their farewell to *Torment*. Men aboard howled back, but Cassian didn't join. He was too caught up in the heavy reality settling in. No turning back. The Queens would come for them eventually, and he hoped to be beyond their reach by then. New ship, new man. His new motto. The political disaster unfolding in the Queens' ranks was uncommon, and he intended to get as far from it as possible.

Cassian gripped another spoke, feeling the tug of the ship as wind persuaded her to sail to port. He kept the wheel steady. The wind's demands strengthened as they left the safety of the island's cover. Muscles tensed, his grip tightened, and his hair and clothes ruffled. The thick fragrance of salt filled his nostrils—incredible. No aroma came close to the sea's. The vast horizon was theirs. The waves breaking against the ship was a song that no musician could replicate, and the color of the water was unmatched by any artist. He smiled. This life was all he knew.

"Captain!"

He turned in time to see Jules dragging Elliot up the steps. The kid kept his head low, steps intentionally heavy, and when he was before the wheel, he shrugged off Jules's grip. Cassian ran his fingers through his hair, unsure if he was seeing it all correctly.

"Where's your father?" Cassian demanded.

Elliot stuffed his hands into his pockets and mumbled, "At Greve's Point."

Alarmed, Cassian narrowed his gaze, gouging a hole right through the boy's skull. "You snuck on?"

"Found him behind some barrels down in the gun deck," Jules answered. "Brought him to you immediately, Captain."

"Have you lost your mind?" Cassian yelled. Anger crawled up the back of his throat, burning a path to his tongue. He smacked Elliot on the side of the head like an older brother would his younger sibling. "Do you think your father wants this?" Elliot didn't answer. Agitation flared, ugly enough to make Cassian's lip curl in disgust. "Traz wants to raise you, give you a chance, and you're here, disregarding everything he's said, so that you could what? Prove him wrong? What's this about?"

Some of the crew on the main deck stopped to watch the encounter. One glare from Cassian forced them right back to work. If they listened now, they didn't act like it.

Elliot didn't reply. *Pathetic.* His father raised him better than that.

Cassian motioned at Jules. "Get a rowboat ready. Take him back—"

"No," Elliot interrupted, desperate. That single word held countless emotions—yearning, frustration, sorrow. The boy tossed his hands up, grabbing at the air. "I'm not going."

Cassian scoffed. "And you think you're making that decision?" The audacity.

The boy—for that's what he was, even if he was sixteen—laced his fingers together. "I don't want to go back," he insisted with enough defiance to challenge the Gods. Each word was a declaration to prove his worth. A final call to be heard.

Cassian steered the wheel away from port. The ship responded with a groan. The glimmer in Elliot's eyes instantly faded, the fight gone, like a fire that choked on its last flame before going out. This wasn't a boy acting in rebellion to prove some childish point. He was running. Cassian knew the feeling all too well—he could see it in the tension Elliot held in his shoulders.

He motioned to Jules to give them space. The crewman obeyed, stepping over to the stairs but not descending in case he was needed again.

"What is it?" Cassian pressed.

Elliot sighed. "Father wants to take me to the Queens, give me a solid reputation by providing me work on one of their ships. Told me it's the best way to make sure I don't end up in some dungeon somewhere."

"Admirable," Cassian replied. Didn't matter if a Queen killed Captain Ricard, they were the rulers of the sea. If anyone could wiggle their way into earning the respect of the Queens, whether by payment or through service, it was a safe choice. "Your father wants the best for you. He has connections to make sure the Queens treat you as one of their own, give you a life that you'll never get with me. Men and women would kill you to take your place, so why are you here?"

He shrugged, kicking his dirty boot out. The leather was cracked along the top. Old and eaten away by salt. "I don't want to be a Queen. I want to be a White Horn."

Cassian checked to ensure they were sailing in the right direction. With his back turned toward the open water—the promise of a future—he didn't want to steer the ship into a rock or a shallow reef. It gave him a chance to collect himself. He wasn't fit to give advice or sympathy. The day his parents sold him, he lost that part of him. Pirates didn't sit around and have heart-to-heart chats. No time for that. Anyone who shed a tear earned themselves a reputation for being unreliable and weak. Cassian couldn't recall the last time he cried or begged.

"Why?" Cassian asked, dropping the agitation. Regardless of how he felt, he wanted the boy to be happy and fulfilled with whatever decision he made.

Elliot didn't reply right away. "I love this life. I like the people I talk to, the places we sail. I don't need all the gold and jewels."

"But you can get the life, the people, and places as a Queen. Probably more," Cassian said.

"But I won't have earned it."

The answer hung between them, fat and stifling. Cassian knew what he meant. Anyone who wasn't a Queen would. If his father knew the right Queen, Elliot would be brought in and given the new title without trying. That went against everything pirates fought for. Out at sea, only a few were given *the life* on a platter. Safety, security, lots of coin, and everything one could ever need. Landwalkers called it royalty. Out here, it was the Queens.

Cassian finally faced Elliot. Jules watched intently, ready to follow through on loading the boy on a boat and rowing him back. He shook his head. It wouldn't be necessary. He wasn't Elliot's father. He respected Traz, but he wasn't going to force Elliot into a life he'd resent. He liked the boy, sometimes felt a brotherly bond with so few summers apart. At twenty, so much separated them in how they'd each been raised, but he felt a kinship with Elliot regardless. Quietly, Jules descended the steps to return to work. The creak of wood caught the boy's attention, and he turned to see the crewman leaving. His mouth fell open, and he looked back to Cassian.

"Am I staying?" he asked.

Cassian raised a hand, halting the excitement. "I have a few questions first."

"Okay." Elliot sounded like he might scream.

"Your father—"

"I left a note. Said I was coming back to you," Elliot interjected.

Cassian reeled. "Wonderful." Now Traz would hate him. He needed another target on his back like he needed another problem. "Does anyone else know?"

"No."

"And you're accepting that if you sail with me, there's a good chance we're going to find trouble? The Queens are watching us. We might be at the bottom of the Grave by the next full moon."

Elliot nodded. For sixteen, he was incredibly decisive. "I'd rather be at the bottom of the sea than a part of something I never wanted."

Cassian smiled, albeit weakly. He liked Elliot. A lot. The boy was strong and would be a captain one day. Hard to find someone at sea with such clear loyalties and morals. He didn't want Elliot to wind up dead if this mad campaign went wrong. Cassian liked the kid, and while he'd been upset to see Traz and Elliot depart, he'd been relieved to know Elliot wouldn't be dragged into his problems. With Elliot aboard, Cassian felt a deep sense of obligation to return the boy to his father safely. Life at sea wasn't that easy, though. Cassian didn't know what the future held or if they would all make it back alive. He hoped they would.

"The rules are the same as they were with Captain Ricard. No fights, everyone gets an equal share of food and water, especially the liquor. Night crew is responsible for cleaning the galley, day crew manages livestock, and seniority grants first rest on shift changes. But"—Cassian raised his finger for emphasis—"Ricard didn't want back-talk or to be questioned. I'm quite all right with either, so long as you don't make a fool of yourself. Savvy?"

"Aye."

Cassian wasn't even sure if he comprehended everything in his excited daze, but he figured the boy was smart enough to figure it all out. "All right. Then get to work."

Elliot rolled on the bottom of his feet, a grin stretching as wide as the Merrèl Sea across his face. "Thank you, Captain."

Cassian shook his head. "Too much. Go on."

Elliot ran down the steps, taking two at a time. He crossed the main deck and saw Glass. A quick glance exchange between Glass and Cassian confirmed the boy was staying. Glass motioned to Elliot to go below deck, and the two disappeared through the hatch. Jules showed back up, scratching his stubble.

"You let him stay."

"I'm not his father. He's sixteen." That was practically a man by Vorelian standards, even if Cassian called him a boy.

Jules cleared his throat. "So what's the plan? Find the egg?"

He was glad for the subject change. "Yes. *Dread Deep* is the ship we're looking for. They take a long route on the outskirts of the Grave to help minimize unwanted run-ins. We've got some days before we're there, so keep the men busy, pass the word on, and if there are questions, come to me. I want you and Glass rotating—you'll be my eyes. So figure out who wants nights and days. Sound good?"

"Aye."

"Good. Get on with it."

Drunken Dragons

At dusk, men switched shifts. Glass took on the night watch, which Cassian was pleased about. He was good man with a big heart, despite how harsh the sea was, and an even better conversationalist. Glass was the closest thing to a friend Cassian had. When the sun dipped her head for the long night, the dead came out. Better to spend that time in good company, working, than alone or with piss-poor people. The crew wasn't bad, but many were dull.

The crew took the plans well—they were thrilled, actually. They didn't know the details, didn't need to know. Cassian would bear that weight. He needed the men to work the ship. If he decided now was the time for integrity, then he would be better off slitting his own throat and tossing himself overboard. The less the men knew, the better. They knew they sailed toward the Grave, understood the risks of that alone, but he reiterated the 45,000 Krye that would be split if they succeeded. Coin talked louder than anything else, including superstitions.

When Cassian asked about whether anyone had heard anything about the relic, he was frustrated to learn that no one took initiative. The long few days and Ricard's death unraveled them. The moment they found themselves in a pub, they drank and abandoned all promises. The only reason he knew half the story was because Elliot had accompanied them for some of the night while Traz said his piece and shared a few drinks. Cassian hid his agitation. Find the dragon egg, then seek Rül'Cril. A payout between those two would make them the richest pirates in the world. More than that, he'd never have to worry about anything again. He could buy privacy, peace, and still have enough Krye to last him four lifetimes.

Cassian took a drink of Seaman's Water and meandered over the documents in front of him. He'd napped for the afternoon, preferring to stay up and keep his mind busy during the night. The half-carved dragon statue was stuffed away in a drawer in the captain's cabin behind him. He'd return to it when he could. Until then, it was a dud with disproportionate wings. Not much else was in this room because he didn't own much else, save for his newly inherited items from Ricard still stowed in the captain's cabin. This room and Ricard's belongings were the most he'd ever owned, and he didn't know what to do with them.

Ricard left behind a sheaf of documents. Peace treaties for different cities, letters intercepted that were outdated and should be burned, and a bundle of journal entries. He separated the old letters and rolled them up, tying them off with twine. Cassian wasn't versed in the politics of pirates as well as a captain should be—it would come with time—so he would hold onto those until he better understood them. The treaties were copies. Documentation to present to soldiers or rulers to prove they were allowed to dock. Junok's Port was strict. Cassian knew from experience. Documentation was required to be presented in order to dock and not be killed or arrested. Pirates weren't welcomed but legally, they could dock because of the long-standing peace treaty.

The lantern to his left flickered. The oil had just been filled before he walked in here. Fighting distraction, he returned to the parchment: thick, coarse, and cracked along the edges. These were left out too long. The salt in the air ate anything and everything. Ships were re-oiled constantly, wood well-cared-for to ensure vessels were as sturdy as they could be, and ropes replaced frequently. Between sun and salt, nothing lasted forever. Cassian's skin looked like he was thirty, not twenty. In the next decade, he'd look twice the age he was. Probably be dead too. Pirates never lived as long as landwalkers. Life at sea didn't provide that kind of luxury.

He took another drink. He was halfway through the bottle already. His head buzzed, but his thoughts were still sharp—the kind of clarity that only comes between tipsy and drunk. He usually carved when he felt this way. Instead, he was staring at sloppy handwriting.

Ricard kept extensive notes. Things about the men, locations they sailed to, islands, thoughts, all of it. Cassian knew captains often wrote their experiences as part of a legacy process. A way to ensure that if anything happened to the current captain, the next would know the history. A generational process for each captain to pass on knowledge. He skimmed through a few pieces on islands and wind. The handwriting shifted, and the parchment was yellowed and cracked. Likely the captain before Ricard. Whoever that was. The crew didn't ask those kinds of questions. Ricard was captain for nearly fifteen summers, which was anomaly in pirate time. That predated the men who now served *Torment*.

He stopped when he saw *Dreams* scribbled along the top of one. Another gulp of the fiery burn, and he settled in to read what Ricard had written.

I had the same dream again. Walking along a forest path—why are there always trees?—with fog and darkness. I knew I wasn't alone, so I walked faster. Faster until I broke into a run because I was being chased. They were coming for me. The faster I ran, the closer they got. I knew because I feel their cold breath on the back of my neck. I always trip. Same branch, same time. And when I do, I scramble backward until I see them. Monstrous creatures with wide mouths and black eyes. They want to eat me, but they're always stopped by the same whistle.

Just like before, he shows up. Clad in black and grinning like a madman. He tells me it's my time and offers me his hand. I take it, glad to not be alone. And just like that, I wake. That's the fifth dream I've had of the man, and I can't ever remember his face afterward. Just the smile and warmth. A premonition, perhaps? My father used to tell me the dead sought you out before you were taken. I never believed it.

It ended with a half-written word. Ricard was interrupted, probably by one of the crewmen. No date. Cassian checked through the pile, finding a few more scribbled reflections of the same dream, all in various stages of disturbance and detail. He found his mouth dry, so he took another drink but hardly tasted it. The strange man he'd spoken to entered his mind. The memory brought with it the unsettling reality of going into the unknown. The entry he read now was not from the man he thought he knew.

I can't get his voice out of my head—

He's talking to me during the day now. The man. The one I call a ghost. Telling me things. Warning me that my end is coming. I dare to wonder if I have Mad Man's Sickness, but I don't have any black blotches or symptoms. It feels like while I'm writing this, he's standing over my shoulder—

Some space, followed by a smear of red. Cassian rubbed his thumb over it, curious. The blotch looked like dried blood. The entry continued beneath it. Cassian hunched over the parchment, muscles locked.

I could tell the man from my dreams was disappointed by Cassian's arrival. This man . . . he wants me to finish getting my thoughts down. He's like an itch I can't get rid of. When the boy left, he told me I needed to give him more freedom, that I was hindering his growth. Not sure what he meant by that. The next time I see my ghost friend, I'll ask. He's not here now. I think I'll have another bottle and see if I can see him again. Every time I dream, it's the same dream. The dead, the forest, him. He's waiting for me. But I don't know why.

Cassian stared at his own name for too long. He tried to recall any time that he'd entered the captain's cabin and interrupted Ricard, but there were too many to count. The crew was always going in and out of the captain's cabin—Ricard encouraged it. Cassian eyed the parchment, hoping to place an age on these entries. It felt imperative now to know when Ricard wrote this. Was it a decade ago? If so, were there more entries that had his name scribbled? Cassian didn't understand what any of this meant, or who Ricard was writing about. His stomach twisted, violent like the sea in a storm, and he pursed his lips. It felt like the whole world was watching him.

That was it. Cassian thumbed through the others, but the rest of the entries seemed ordinary commentary on the ship's daily routine and function. He reread the mysterious entry, wondering why Ricard kept this here. It was personal, unnecessary for the captain's legacy. He'd never got a chance to get rid of these before he was killed. It was possible he left it intentionally, too. No one ever knows when they're going to die. Cassian could die tonight and never finish his dragon carving.

That thought sobered him. He could be sitting here reading about dusty old thoughts or carving his dragon. He didn't know when he'd have that time again. The parchment pile glared at him, unhappy about his sudden shift in desire. Maybe he'd take a stroll below decks, see who was up or needed anything. Keep himself busy—

The lantern lights flickered again. Cassian tensed. Not just one lantern, but all three of them. That couldn't be a coincidence. Malevolent sea spirits tormented the living by stealing the light, hiding food, and shredding ropes. Their only goal was to make a pirate's life a living nightmare. He reached for the dagger in his boot, unclipping the clasp to the short sheath tightened around his calf. The flame in the lantern closest to him wavered from an unseen wind. Then it went out.

"No." He lunged for the lantern, knocking over the bottle in the process. Liquor drowned the parchment, but he hardly minded. His hands scrambled over the metal, and he lurched out of his chair to get to the lantern behind. In the dark, the demented sea spirits could make a man go mad. "No, no, no." His heart raced, adrenaline surged through him in a fiery blast that could melt iron, and he latched onto the other still-burning lantern with too much force, nearly knocking it over. Scrambling, he opened the small glass door. A candle stood to his right, unlit, and he grabbed it and stuck it into the lantern.

The flame took to the wick, and he quickly transferred the light to the dead lantern's wick. Hands shook—shamefully so—and he inhaled sharply when the flame came to life. The bruising force of his heartbeat would make his ribs tender for the next century.

Cassian grew up on stories about the dark—the warnings. At sea, sometimes the dead tried to wiggle themselves into the souls of the living by frightening them. In these tales, the dead would extinguish the light, only to sneak up on the living and grab their souls when they were preoccupied.

He set the candle aside, eyeing the small flickering flame. He should have been satisfied with the lantern relit, but he couldn't bring himself to extinguish the candle yet. Candles were reserved for when the crew ran out of oil for the lanterns and needed light. The lantern in his hands grew warmer. Cassian watched it. As he did, he realized he was acting like a fool. Lanterns went out all the time. Flames were temperamental, reacting to the slight sway of the ship or a bad wick. It'd been a while since their lanterns were replaced. Maybe it was time for that.

Rubbing his face, he cursed to himself. He wasn't ever so jumpy. What was wrong with him? Ricard's notes were odd, but so what? Men at sea were all susceptible to the occasional madness that these waters brought. People said things they didn't mean, heard whispers in the wind, and saw apparitions of long-dead ships following them. The dead were real, but only as real as the living made them. He gathered himself. King Jair, the Queens, the strange man, Ricard—they were all getting to him. Maybe a walk would do him some good.

Cassian turned and shoved himself back into the counter, lantern still in hand. A man sat at the table, dressed in black, only five paces away. He looked ready to walk the halls of a palace, not hoist sails and tie ropes at sea. He had dark eyes bold enough to resurrect the dead and hair as black as midnight on a moonless night. His olive skin did not have the same weathered look that Cassian's did. He looked ready to court Death.

The spilled liquor didn't seem to bother the man, or if it did, he made no mention of it. He reached over and picked up the bottle, shook it and chuckled before righting it. The sound stripped the heat right out of the cabin.

"You'll need more," the man said. His voice was cool, devoid of the sea accent so many pirates had.

Cassian's tongue failed him. He'd heard stories of the dead showing themselves, but he'd not prepared himself.

"You've found his dreams," the man continued and reached forward and peeled away one of the pieces of parchment from the wet pile. "Mm, what remains of it, anyway." He dropped it and leaned back, paralyzing Cassian in his spot with that terrible gaze. "I've seen your dreams, *Captain*." The last word was drawn out in mockery, sending a chill down his spine. "You're always chasing. Desperate for what? Tell me what it is."

The grasp on the lantern numbed his fingers. He couldn't move, no matter how hard he tried. "I don't talk to the dead."

The man laughed, a cold sound. "Who said I'm dead?"

Cassian didn't know if he believed him, but he didn't dare ask. "Why do you care?" His voice shook with the terror of a small boy. Faced with the unknown, now he was a coward.

"My duties are to Destiny," the man replied. He swept his arm around the room. "Well beyond your small world. I am here for you, so why don't you give me a little bit of your time, and then I'll be gone."

Cassian nodded, too nervous to ask why or who he was. "What do you want to know?"

"I just asked," the man replied, calm.

He did. Cassian knew that. He just wasn't thinking straight. The sooner he got out of this nightmare, the better. Maybe something had been slipped into his drink. Men were known to do that—add hallucinogens to bottles as sort of a sick joke. That's what this was. It had to be.

"I'm just trying to stay alive," Cassian whispered. He set the lantern down. No need to hold onto it like a pacifier. He didn't want to make more of a fool of himself. After his run-in with the cloaked stranger in the alley, he felt like his nerves were already frayed. "Your title and who you know are all that keep you alive out here. Don't you know that?"

The man ignored the question. "Then why do you fear your men will betray you?"

"Because sometimes you meet someone with more power who promises something bigger and better," Cassian replied. He was unsure if this was a hallucination or if he was talking to a ghost. Either way, he was losing his mind.

The man leaned forward, laying his arms on the liquor that stretched across the table and parchment, and lacing his fingers. "So why the terrible dreams?"

Cassian choked on the air he tried to breathe. "Excuse me?" He was too close to this man. The small captain's cabin lacked enough air for both of them. He felt like he was suffocating.

"You dream of being chased. You're always running. Sometimes you're stuck in a dark room and can't get out. Others, you're locked in a box at the bottom of the sea, pounding the door to get out before you run out of air." The man raised a finger and tilted his head. "But between those terrible dreams, you envision a quiet home, stability, and peace. A little home on the coast. Charming."

Nobody was supposed to know that. Cassian didn't talk about it, didn't even think about them. Refused to. Dreams were just tricks played by the dead who wiggled their way into one's mind when they slept. Done to mess with their confidence and certainty.

"Destiny doesn't take kindly to those who run," the man said. "She's waiting for you."

That sounded final. "Is that why you're here? You represent some inner turmoil I have?"

"Is that what you think I am?" the man asked. "An illusion?"

"You have to be, right?" Cassian squeaked out.

The light went out. All the flames extinguished, submerging the room into darkness. Cassian swung around, bewildered, and grabbed the nearest lantern. Impossible. He needed the light. He needed—

A blade kissed the back of his neck, frigid. He threw his elbow up to deflect the weapon, but he was too slow. The man forced him around and wrapped his fingers around Cassian's throat, squeezing and stilling him instantly. Breaths came out in a wheeze, and when he tried to bash the man's skull, the man blocked the assault with the flat of his blade, then tilted his head.

"Your time is up, Captain. It's time to answer to Destiny."

Cassian shot upright, gasping and grabbing at his throat. He clawed at the unseen hand, but he was alone in his cabin. He slowed his pulse, chest heaving. The bottle of Seaman's Water stood beside him, half full, and the pile of parchment was untouched, save for the saliva that pooled at the corner of the one he'd been reading. He pushed it aside and wiped his face. A splitting headache met him, harsh and unforgiving. The kind that made blinking hurt.

A dream. Nothing more. Built from what he'd read. He refused to see it any other way. Cassian straightened the parchment, done. Between this and the encounter at Greve's Point, he wondered if he was going crazy. Maybe he'd end up just like Ricard, scribbling madly about wild dreams and unseen terrors. He wouldn't be reading anything else tonight. In fact, he would have that walk now. Hopefully, it would clear his thoughts and force the shakes out of his limbs.

He stood, feeling the sway of the ship underneath him. Familiar, welcoming. Cassian went to the drawers, unclasped the lock of the one he wanted, and dug in for the carving. Dragon in hand, he unsheathed his utility knife. This would keep his thoughts steady, balance him, and keep him busy. Cassian carved so often that he could do it while he walked. Dangerous with the swell of waves, but he'd gotten quite skilled with working with the blade.

At least the bigger spots. Once he got to the mouth, scales, and face, he'd want to sit with calm waters. Make sure he got the details right. His heart still raced—pathetically so—and he checked his hand, stretching it out before him.

It trembled. Slight, but that wasn't all. Along his tattoo, where the rose crested his knuckles, he saw discoloration where that same hand slammed into the flat of the blade in the dream. By the grace of the sea, he needed to get out of this cabin.

His boots echoed across the main deck, toward the hatch. He wanted to see what the men were doing, have some company. This night was warmer than last. A fog moved in, trapping the heat and leaving a sheen of water on everything. The ship moved more slowly in these conditions, because of the dangers of running aground in low visibility. Likely not, given they were out in the middle of the sea, but one could never be too certain. Lanterns hung all around, casting a warm light in the fog that lay across the deck.

He plucked wood away with his utility knife, leaving bits in his path. A few steps from the hatch, he heard commotion to his right. "Glass?" Cassian kept the knife raised, halfway between continuing with the carving and defending himself. The dream clung to him, and he expected to see the ghostly man, whoever he was, waiting for him. The fog was too thick to see more than a few steps in front of him. One step. Stop. Another step.

"Captain?"

Cassian jumped, swallowing a yelp. Glass squinted at him, rope swung over his shoulder, and an orange terone in the other hand, half-eaten. "What are you doing?" Glass asked.

"Couldn't sleep," Cassian lied. The skull pendant around the man's neck glared at him, as if it knew the truth. "Wanted to see if you needed anything."

Glass motioned at him with the fruit. "Help with that?" He stopped and shook his head. "Sorry. You're the captain now. Shouldn't talk to you like that."

"No, no." Cassian lowered the blade. "I need that. I don't want to be the uptight asshole no one can talk to. Keep being my friend, Glass. You're all I've got."

The inked-up man scoffed. "Not sure that's a compliment."

"I like to say so." Cassian gestured at their surroundings. "This fog got us dead in the water?" Spend long enough at sea and one didn't need eyes or ears to know when the ship moved. He'd felt it just before he'd fallen asleep. The ship's movement seeped into the very essence of who he was. A change of direction could wake him up out of slumber.

"Pretty much," Glass replied. "We're moving, just slow. Can't do much when you can't see. Mist moved in a bit ago. Got a few of us manning the main deck, but most are below. Not much to do until things clear up."

"Yeah, yeah." The faster they got to the Grave, the sooner they could intercept *Dread Deep*. "You don't think we'll lose too much time on this, do you?"

"Hard to say." Glass shrugged. "If it clears out by morning and we get a good headwind, we'll make up time. If a storm blows in—well, you know how it goes." He took a bite of his fruit. Juices ran down his chin and dropped to the wood below.

"I know." Cassian nodded. "Just don't want to lose our chance. This is all we've got."

"You think we're the only ones?"

Glass's question caught him off guard. "What do you mean?"

"The only ones who know," Glass clarified. "How do you know more fools weren't hired and we aren't sailing into a blood bath?" He finished off the rest of the terone and tossed the core into the water.

Cassian returned to the wood carving, glad to keep his hands busy while his thoughts scrambled. "I don't know. We could be one of six crews. Or it could just be us. But I'd like to think King Jair is keeping this private. It would cause more problems than anyone needed if he had multiple crews going after this egg."

Glass shook his head. "No. I mean others knowing and hiring."

The tip of the blade plucked out a spot beneath the dragon's chest. "I can't make any promises, Glass. I don't know what we're sailing into." It wasn't the answer either wanted to hear, but it was the truth.

"Hm." Glass crossed his arms. "Well, I should go make sure Elliot isn't hanging off the edge of the bow, taking the hand of the dead."

He walked, but didn't make it far before Cassian stopped him. "Hold on." Glass raised his brow. Cassian weighed asking the question, but couldn't help it. "Have you ever had strange dreams?"

Glass frowned. "I don't understand."

"I found Ricard's entries. I was looking at them, and he talked about these vivid dreams. He had the same one over and over. Even mentioned Mad Man's Sickness." No point in talking about his own.

They stood there, cocooned by the silence of the fog. It felt like they were the only two on the entire ship. They'd never see anyone approach until it was too late. Glass considered his response. Whether to tell him he was crazy or that he was onto something. There wasn't anyone else on this ship Cassian could bring this up to.

Glass lowered his voice and asked, "What kind of dream?"

Cassian shrugged. "He talked about the dead and a man—"

Glass crossed his chest and spit. "A man?" Now he sounded unsettled.

"Yeah."

"Best to stay away from those dreams," Glass said. "Sounds like Captain was marked by the Dark Lord himself. Get a drink or two in his hand and he always talked about odd things. Thought blood could cleanse hands and visions came in the form of dreams."

Cassian's knees were weak. "Why didn't I know about this?"

"None of the usual crew did. Ask Jules, though. He could vouch. We worked closest with Ricard. Found him on several occasions drunk and mumbling on about a forest path—"

"He says that in his dream entries," Cassian interrupted.

Glass shook his head and pointed at him. "Burn those. They shouldn't be on this ship. Bad luck. You hear?"

He nodded, feeling like he was losing control of his own life.

Glass shivered. "I don't like this conversation, Captain. I like you. Don't curse this ship talkin' about the Dark Lord. He belongs with the dead." At that, he disappeared into the fog, bootsteps muffled.

Cassian stood there, dumbfounded. Alone, he felt like he was suffocating. Like the fog was reaching tendrils down his throat and squeezing his lungs, ripping the air right out of him. But he didn't want to return to his room. He'd rather sleep out on the deck without a blanket or comfort than go back in there. If he had to stay up the rest of the night, he would.

He stuffed the dragon into a pouch on his belt, but he didn't put the knife away. Men would likely think him odd walking around with the blade, but he didn't care. He'd go down and clean cannons and weapons. Forget about being captain, he just wanted to be normal and do something he was used to doing. Didn't matter if he'd just cleaned the cannons a few days ago. He'd do it again. Then again. He'd do it all night before he returned to his room.

Freedom. That's all he needed.

Grave of Seas

Torment sailed without stopping. Cassian kept the crew working and eating. When men needed to sleep, he gave it to them. When they needed water, he gave them liquor. Kept the edge off when they were tired. Sailing wasn't easy work—never was—but he was pushing them hard to cross the Warón Sea in a matter of days.

They chased the wind, and on the second day, they found it. Men cheered when the headwind grabbed onto the sails and shoved the ship forward. Cassian didn't join the men in their celebration. He couldn't get over the haunting feeling that he was chasing a dream he'd never catch. That didn't stop him from giving everything he had, and on the fourth day, he decided that if he lived through this, he might pick up carving wooden figurines as a side hustle rather than just a hobby. The infectious anticipation of the coin bled through the men. A heist always got them excited, but this was a promise for something more than any of them dared believe was obtainable in their lifetime. More coin than any of them had ever seen or would ever see. Cassian believed them—needed to—so he shared drinks and talked about their future. He wanted them to believe he was just as blindly excited.

It felt too easy. Get the egg and get out. Return to King Jair and get paid. New life. Nothing came that simple. The longer he went, the more stressed he got. A feeling gnawed at his chest, digging out a hole and burying itself so deep that it hurt when he breathed. Doubt. The coin no longer called to him as it had when his boots walked on land. Out here, the distance made it hard to keep his goals straight. They could take a sharp turn left and head up through the Merrél Sea and go find a new life on the outskirts of Eiyrăl. Water was colder up there, but there were also fewer pirates. And that meant fewer problems. They could hide out there for a few summers, trading goods with the cities like Razan, and maybe even live amongst the landwalkers for a while. Then they could return to these waters once the political turmoil settled and the Queens were at peace. The solution was obvious, simple, and one he should have ordered from day one. Now, less than six days as captain, he had the crew on a suicide heist.

Out by the Grave, the water changed. No longer the bright blue they were used to seeing, but a dark gray that reflected silver when the sun hit it just right. Waves lapped lazily against the bow, and the sails struggled to keep the ship alive in the water. His clothes didn't ruffle like they should, his eyes didn't burn from the harsh salt kicked up by the wind when the ship got going fast. They were dead in the water and had been for most of the morning.

When they tried to paddle, the water resisted. Losing wind in the Grave was as bad as dragging a dagger right across their throats. Water worked differently out here. It was heavy, unforgiving, and home to the Tsu'ran. If they didn't get some movement, they risked being dragged to the depths below by the very creatures they worshipped. The Tsu'ran spared no one.

"Captain." Elliot rushed up, heaving for air. He'd been in the crow's nest for most of their travel. His tunic hung loosely over his shoulders—too big, but they'd not been prepared for his arrival when he snuck on board—and the belt latched around his waist kept it in place as best it could. "I see a ship west of us."

Fantastic—they'd hopefully just found *Dread Deep*. Bad timing, though, because *Torment* was dead in the water. "How close?" Cassian asked.

"Still very far away. I don't think they see us. They're angling closer into the Grave."

Cassian took a double-take. "Further in? That's madness."

Elliot bared his hands. "That's what I saw." As more of an afterthought, he said, "Captain."

Half the crew still did that. Drove him mad. It was another chip at his carefully crafted courage. "They should keep to the outskirts of the Grave. Safer for them." Too many unknowns lurked in the heart of the Grave. Stories passed from generation to generation of pirates all promised the same thing: trouble came to those who sailed the Grave. Cassian tapped his chin, leaning against the railing. Staring west, he tried to see what Elliot saw, but the other ship wasn't visible from the deck. Elliot had a spyglass. Still, just on the horizon, he could see a speck. Likely the other ship, and if they didn't g et *Torment* moving, they'd be spotted. *Dread Deep* would turn around and cover enough space to lose them for good if they remained in their current condition.

"You see the number of masts?" Cassian asked.

"Three, Captain."

"Normal," he mumbled. "Sails?"

"Full wind."

That didn't make any sense. Cassian glared hard at the speck, willing the answers, but none came. He peered over the railing, trying to figure out why they weren't moving. Not a black spot—the water would be the color of midnight. Perhaps they were in a dead zone. Wind moved in channels across these waters, but they usually caught that early enough to change direction. A slight shift in the wind, losing speed, gaining speed—all signs they looked for. He glanced up at the white ribbons tied to the masts, which they used to identify wind direction. They were lifeless. It was like someone snapped their fingers and stopped the wind without warning. They'd sailed these parts before and never come across this problem. Everything about their situation was abnormal. Wind channels shifted, but they didn't just die like this. Cassian knocked on the wood quietly. Bad luck was what this was.

Jules ran up behind Elliot, followed by Bennett. Bennett was Glass's age but looked as young as eighteen. The sun and he were getting along just fine. He was a quiet seaman who spent most of his time mumbling on about old tales lost to most. Few ever asked how he knew some of them. When they did, they were met with stories longer than getting an answer was worth. Bennett was a talker. A boring one. But he was exceptional at his work.

"Captain," Bennett greeted him. "Got any idea?"

Cassian jerked his scarred thumb in Elliot's direction. "We got eyes on *Dread Deep*. That's why we're here. Why don't we turn this ship around, see if we can paddle our way to some wind? I'm thinking it might be just a stone's throw—"

Suddenly, Cassian was thrown forward, slamming against the railing. The men stumbled, latching onto the wheel or sprawling across the floor. The wood groaned, protesting, and the sails strained sideways. A deafening howl bubbled up around them. Cassian dropped to the deck, covering his ears. The sound shredded every thread of thought, growing in pitch until the only thing he could hear was a scream. It didn't fluctuate, didn't waver, and he hunkered further into himself, shrinking from the sound.

And then it stopped. He regained his composure, blinking and disoriented. The creak of the ship swaying met him first, rocking his unsettled stomach into a sloshy mess. Jules sat up, one finger deep into his ear and wiggling his finger in it, as if he had water stuck inside, grimacing. Elliot rubbed his head, and Bennett looked around, confused. The rest of the crew gaped at one another from the main deck. Ryl crawled up the stairs to the quarterdeck. Cassian firmly held onto the railing, dragging himself up until he leaned over. As he did, his head swam and his vision narrowed until he was certain he'd black out and fall over the edge of the ship. As the wave passed, he forced air in and out as slow as he could.

Movement. Fast movement. It slithered just below the surface of the water, too quick to make out details, but massive. Cassian gawked, heart thundering, and watched as the girth of the beast slipped underneath the ship, tail and all.

"Jules," he gasped. The word slurred, caught in his throat by ice-cold terror. "Check the other side."

The sailor numbly nodded and scrambled to his feet, tripping over himself in the process. Jules peered over the railing, stilling.

"I don't—" Jules stopped, sounding like he was choking.

The ship lurched violently. Cassian's knees buckled from the sudden force, and Bennett's head slammed into a spoke on the wheel. Elliot screamed, lunging for Jules as he tipped overboard. Everyone rushed to the railing, Elliot still grabbing onto the ghost of what remained. Glass shoved the young boy out of the way, forcing himself up by Cassian, who smashed up against Ryl. Jules's head resurfaced, spitting water. He looked up and shot his hand straight up, waving madly.

"Hey!" Jules screamed.

An answer died on Cassian's lips as the surrounding area distorted with the movement of the beast. Glass's hand snatched onto Cassian's tunic, hauling him back away from the edge, but not before he saw massive, webbed claws break the surface of the water, silver and blue and covered in scales, and swipe down on Jules. A scream was cut short, and the ship swayed. All thoughts of retrieving their man overboard dissipated as Cassian and the others looked for any sign of the crewman.

"Get the ropes!" Cassian frantically ordered. Glass opened and closed his mouth in disbelief. The rest of the crew was similarly in shock. "Get the ropes!" They needed to try and get Jules out of the water if he resurfaced.

Elliot bolted down the steps, and Cassian turned his attention back to the water, waiting. No movement. Nothing. Not even a splash. Numbness molded into pure shock, hollowing Cassian out and making him weak. In all his summers sailing, he'd never seen anything like it. Sure, the stories of lurking beasts existed, and one would be mad not to believe them, but he couldn't shake the sensation that the *Torment* crew was more vulnerable than most. Sailing deeper into the Grave was a death wish.

The boy returned shortly with a bundle of rope in his hands. Still no sign of the poor man. Jules was gone. Cassian shook his head and turned away, dragging a hand over his face. The Grave was home to the strange and restless. Losing Jules made this real, treacherous, and reckless. He'd promised these men coin and a path forward after the Queens. Now, he doubted he was capable of leading them out of the Grave. He could have just brought everyone to their end.

"Life Eater," Bennett mumbled, sounding as dead as Cassian felt. "Never thought I'd ever see one."

Ryl's jaw went back and forth like he was chewing on words. "How can you be so certain? Ain't no one ever seen one. Could be a Krakí."

"No tentacles," Cassian cut in before anyone could argue. "I saw claws—webbed ones." He shivered, tasting poignant fear on his tongue. "That was a Life Eater. Stories match up with it. Blue and silver, too. Just like they say." His voice shook with unfiltered terror, and he swallowed the emotion back down.

The memory of Jules's terrified face flashed across Cassian's mind, and he flinched. He'd seen men die, but not like this. This was different, cruel, and beyond their control. They were in the Grave now, home of the Vore beasts. Cassian credited his survival at sea to being merciless. When men died, he didn't dream of them at night. He didn't even remember half their names. He didn't spend a moment of regret for their lost lives. But this . . . The Life Eater unnerved him, tore him right out of his comfort zone. Man-against-man, he could control, predict, and win. Man against the leviathan beast, he was as dead as Jules. No control, no predictability.

The silence swallowed the fierce cry of death. Cassian had no words to cut the quiet. Based on the looks these men gave him, they all felt the same. This was real, and they might not make it out of this alive.

A breeze tickled Cassian's cheek, cool. The sails flapped, coming to life. Just like that, the wind flourished, the sea satisfied with the fresh blood. Cassian hardly reacted. Glass took the wheel, business as usual, and asked, "What do you want to do?"

Bennett and Elliot gawked. Half the crew stood on the main deck, awaiting orders. Cassian wanted to turn around, get out of this mess, and sail to the Ashen Sea north of the Grave, where beasts didn't lurk in the waters. Jules was dead because of him. Because he'd had a wild idea of getting rich. He'd killed men before—innocent men on their knees. Spilled their blood all over the ship they called home, and then set fire to it. He'd done terrible things, crimes that would have him executed at the hands of any king or queen. But this was different. Cassian knew Jules personally, spent his life aboard *Torment* with the man. And now he felt *responsible*. The blood on his hands burned, unseen to anyone else.

They'd made it this far. Sailed to the Grave for a chance to steal a dragon egg. Jules came because he believed in the mission. The rest of the crew did, too—it was the only reason they were here. Whether they liked him personally as captain or not, they knew the outcome—if they were successful—was becoming rich. No sane pirate would pass that up. And they knew that such a reward came with risks.

Cassian opened his mouth, then closed it again. He needed to say something about Jules, but didn't know the right words. It was not often a man went overboard and was eaten by a Life Eater. What they'd all witnessed confirmed that these tales were real. These stories weren't fantastical ideas meant to keep men respectful aboard their ships. They were warnings. Cassian was sure none of them had ever borne witness to such a thing before, or they'd surely have told the tale. Jules's soul would be chained to the Tsu'ran for eternity now, restless, and bound to travel these waters. Everyone knew it. Nobody would talk about it.

No, Cassian realized, he didn't want to say anything. If he did, it made him look weak. They needed to keep their focus on *Dread Deep*. Move on. Men could grieve in private, but not here. Not when work still needed to be done. The sooner they got out of this area, the better. Frankly, the sooner they got out of the Grave, the safer they'd be. The egg was the only thing keeping him going.

He cleared his throat. "Get this ship turned around and behind *Dread Deep*. We'll stay behind until night, then crawl closer. We can get a group of men together to board and find the egg. I'll be going, so decide amongst yourselves. I need two other men."

They didn't move. Maybe they'd expected a statement about Jules or the Life Eater they'd witnessed. Frustration ripped through him. "Get on with it," he snapped. "We're wasting time. We get one chance at this. If we screw up now, it's our heads. Jules would want us to continue." That was the best he had. He gestured at Glass. "Watch the wheel. I'll be back."

Cassian didn't wait for an answer. He needed a drink and a moment to collect himself before tonight. Tonight, they followed through with the rest of the plan. Board a rowboat and paddle to *Dread Deep*. He needed the crew to swallow their fear and get a move on. He should be afraid—no, he was—but he couldn't let them see that. The cold, gripping terror threatened to capsize this plan and ruin their payday.

What these men needed was to get on with their duties and forget what they'd seen. They all needed that. Coin would make it all worth it. Once the crew saw the 45,000 Krye, they'd laugh this off and clank mugs together, spouting about Jules's bravery. By the sea, there'd probably be a sea shanty or two about the lad. He hoped there would be. That would be a fitting tribute.

Twisted Luck

Cassian sat hunkered in the rowboat with Glass and Elliot. Plenty of men wanted to go, simply because the dragon egg excited everyone. But only three would go. *Torment* sat behind a small island, hidden, but ready to sail for *Dread Deep* in case things went wrong, which would only happen if the three took too long to return. Cassian, Elliot, and Glass would row their way back to *Torment* after they secured the egg, using the dense fog that lay across the water to shield their approach and departure from *Dread Deep*. If the fog dispersed, they'd have bigger problems.

They needed to keep a low profile when they snuck aboard *Dread Deep*, which was anchored a league north of the small island. The ship hadn't moved all afternoon and into the evening. Cassian couldn't worry about clumsy men knocking into the wrong pirate when they got frazzled. Not everyone was cut out for sneaking around. Bennett was a close choice, but Cassian chose Elliot because of his size. Smaller, leaner—he could crawl into a tight space if needed. But there was more—there always was. He wanted to see Elliot succeed at something big like this.

Glass was as quiet as a feline on the prowl, and Cassian had extensive experience as a thief as a boy. He had to be stealthy, or else he'd risk waking the owners of the jewels he stole. His father used to take him because he could crawl into the narrow spaces and wiggle himself through the bars of closed dungeons. It wasn't common knowledge that dungeons often had hordes of valuables stored in the weapons room, but they were. When prisoners were brought in, they were stripped of everything they owned, dropped into drawers or piles to be sorted later.

Cassian always had a sack on these outings. He'd fill it as full as he could without making any noise and sneak back out before the soldier on duty finished his rounds. Father was always pleased. Never proud, just satisfied with the items. He'd bark at Cassian to keep up and sling the sack over his shoulder, not saying a word unless someone passed by. Then he'd talk to Cassian about odd things boys his age should be doing—studying, playing with others, and so on—and when the stranger passed, he'd let the conversation fall mid-sentence.

Cassian's mother was no better. She'd bring him along on shoplifting jobs so that she could use him as bait. He'd ask questions, play dumb, and earn the attention of shop owners while his mother snuck around and plucked the bagged coin or items off the shelves. It always worked. Cassian made sure of it because if he failed, he was beaten. He'd had more bruises than he could count. Fresh ones on old ones, welts, and lacerations. A whip was kept in their home, propped up over the stove to keep the leather warm, so that if Cassian needed to be taught anything, the hot bite of the leather was ready. A few scars still decorated his skin from that. One along the base of his jaw when he tried to fight off the whipping. Once he was grown, Cassian told anyone who asked that it was a scar from a knife brawl. They didn't need to know the truth. He didn't want anyone's pity.

"Keep an eye on the water," Glass mumbled. "Check for black spots." Not that they could distinguish the water's shades at night. They rowed in the dark to keep any prying eye from *Dread Deep* from seeing their approach. A bit of a way to go, but they were gaining ground. The concerns of being seen were outweighed by what lurked beneath.

Glass dropped the paddles in, grunted, and pushed them forward. The light from the moon reflected a gleam of sweat off his brow.

"You want to switch?" Cassian asked. He was eager to keep the momentum of the heist moving, so that no one could focus on Jules and what happened to him. Few pirates ever concerned themselves with the past, only on what lay ahead instead. Still, everyone knew Jules personally, so this was different. The crew considered Jules a friend. Cassian hoped no one brought him up—mentioning him was not only inviting the Grave's attention . . . it was like shoving a blade into Cassian's chest.

Glass shook his head. "One tired man is better than two." An old saying amongst pirates when they were preparing to do something dangerous. He nodded and peered over the edge again, spying the sea beneath the rolling fog. The dark water looked nearly black under the moon's glow and the current didn't move like it should have. He dipped his fingers in, curious as to how it felt, and found it warmer than he was used to. Another anomaly of this cursed place.

"You think they know?" Elliot whispered. "The Tsu'ran?"

"They know we're here," Cassian replied softly. "The Tsu'ran have been around for as long as this world. They know everything that happens, everyone who enters and leaves. It's their choice what they will do to us, not our own."

The boy tightened into a smaller ball on the other side. Knees pressed against each other, arms crossed, and chin tucked into his chest. "I don't like it."

"You're not supposed to," Glass muttered. "We're here to get a job done."

"No," the kid said. "I mean, why would this ship go so far into the Grave? Don't you think that's strange?"

Cassian wished he had his dragon to carve, to keep his mind settled. "Everything about this is odd," he admitted. "A ship coming from Eiyrăl takes the longest route through the seas by cutting into the Grave? Who does that?"

"Someone who doesn't want to be caught," Glass observed, wiping his brow with his arm. "Or maybe it's not their choice."

"What they're doing is more risky than announcing to the world they've got a dragon egg," Cassian remarked and shook his head, displeased. "I just want to get this over with."

"I think we all feel the same," Glass replied.

Elliot leaned forward. He was the only one keeping an eye on *Dread Deep*. Cassian and Glass's backs were facing it. "I don't see any lights," the boy said.

Cassian twisted in his spot, making the boat wobble. Sure enough, the ship was dark. It hadn't moved in half a day, and now there wasn't any commotion aboard. An icy chill grabbed his spine, and he tensed. Every muscle strained from the movement. Facing the two, he knew *Torment* was waiting for them from just behind the island. They could make this work.

Glass stopped rowing to get a good look, too. "That ain't right," the man mumbled. "You think it's the dead coming aboard? If they ain't got the right stuff, those spirits will cause all sorts of problems."

"Maybe it's the wind," Elliot offered. "Or because of the storm coming?"

Cassian stuck a finger in his mouth before he pulled it out and raised it. A breeze tickled the skin, cool. On the horizon and fast approaching was a storm. The occasional rumble rolled through the sea, warning them of what was to come. "Keep going," Cassian ordered, not addressing the questions.

Slowly, Glass resumed his rowing, shaking his head. "I don't know, Captain—"

"Skip the pleasantries," Cassian interrupted. "It's just us here." He twisted in his seat to observe *Dread Deep*, which was only two bloodlines away. Bloodlines were used to measure distance—it marked the distance of how far a bleeding pirate could swim before he died. A lantern popped up, a sun in the dark, and raced across the main deck to the wheel. The lantern swung violently, ducking below the railing before reappearing. Then a man screamed, and the lantern dropped.

Cassian swallowed, tongue dry. That wasn't a spotter talking about the approaching rowboat. Chaos was erupting on the ship. Another lantern went out, a scream met his ears, and shouts followed. The ship was under attack. The rowboat came to a stop again. The three men watched as more lanterns were extinguished. A horrifying screech came next, startling Cassian. He knew that sound. A Tsu'ran's call. The Tsu'ran wanted payment. Nobody traveled these parts for free.

"I think we need to—" Glass stopped.

The water rippled, tossing the rowboat to the side. Each man grabbed hold of the sides, scrambling to balance the weight and keep the dinghy upright. Elliot yelled, Glass started rowing harder, and Cassian watched the ripple travel toward the island before disappearing in the fog. Bile rose. Krakí or Life Eater, he couldn't tell. The Grave was home to all sorts of creatures, and the only thing he could do was hope he and his men didn't become targets.

"We should turn around," Glass insisted.

"No, we'd never make it back." The answer came before Cassian thought everything through. They were so close to getting the egg, to getting the freedom they deserved. If they turned around now, they would lose everything. King Jair would slaughter him and the crew before the Queens found them. Turning back meant failing. Damned either way. Stay and risk getting killed. Flee and certainly be slaughtered. "We need to try," Cassian finished. "The Tsu'ran must be here for the *Dread Deep* crew. Not us."

"You've lost your damn mind," Glass replied. He spun around, facing Cassian, seething like a wild animal. "You're going to let our crew die?"

"We need that egg," Cassian insisted, trying to stave off the growing wrath boiling inside him "That's our only chance—"

"There are a hundred different chances!" Glass screamed. "We can go anywhere, be anyone. We don't need this egg to do it."

"The coin," Cassian hissed. "*45,000 Krye*. We could buy a ship. Be someone new. The Queens would never know."

"With what crew?" Glass switched positions and started rowing back toward *Torment.* "I'm not doing this. Let's get out of here before some Life Eater destroys our ship. Then we got nothing left. Is that what you want?"

All his life, Cassian had been told why he was wrong. All his damn life, he'd been told what to do and how to do it. He was sick of it. Sick of being undermined and disrespected. Dirty blood, fraud, sea beggar—he'd heard every insult a pirate could spit—and now his one friend was turning his back on him. The Queens made him captain, and he needed to embrace that. This was his heist, his plan. Nobody would ruin that now. He'd wanted the crew to speak up, share their opinions, but he'd not wanted his crew to refuse him.

Cassian unsheathed his dagger, metal shimmering under the dark night. Glass's mouth went wide, and his rowing stopped again. "You're mad—"

Cassian slammed the pommel against the side of Glass's head. The seaman released the paddles, collapsing in his spot. "Grab them," Cassian ordered. Elliot didn't protest, doing as he was told. Cassian tucked the blade back into his boot and traded places. Hauling up Glass's body was far easier said than done. They called it dead weight for a reason. He tucked the man in the corner of the rowboat, keeping his head up. When Glass awoke, he'd hate Cassian for it, but he was done trying to justify why he needed this to work. They were nearly at *Dread Deep.* He wasn't going to turn back now.

Elliot handed him the paddles, his jaw agape. Cassian rowed hard, gaining as much speed as he could in this lifeless water. "Spit it out, boy," he said in between breaths.

"Why?"

Cassian's lungs burned, but the commotion grew louder. "We can't help the *Torment* against that beast. Our only escape is forward. We were hired for a job. I intend to finish it." A partial lie. Nobody needed to know King Jair's threat, or his desperation to be someone other than the dirty-blooded pirate who always took orders and never gave them. In the six days he'd been captain, he'd learned one thing: titles earned respect. He intended to be the best thief the seas had ever seen, and it started with this egg. The Crown of Gods was next.

Elliot's fingers dug into the wood. "We've never done—"

"I don't care what's been done or not." Cassian was half-tempted to smash this paddle into Elliot's head to knock him out, too. But he needed another hand in case things went awry. "Tsu'ran, Krakí, sea-ravaged illnesses—I don't care. We need the egg. We'll leverage the Tsu'ran to our advantage. The crew won't ever see us coming when they're too busy defending themselves."

Elliot looked more like a child than a young man. "And what if they catch us?"

"Then do yourself a favor and don't be seen by the Tsu'ran." The presence of the ship loomed ahead. "Stories say they love the sound of screaming. It whips them in a frenzy. You keep your mouth shut, no matter what you see or what they say, and they'll not take one glance in your direction. You open your mouth and start squeaking, you'll have five of them on you before you make it five steps. They aren't there for you, and they'll leave you alone if you don't intervene on why they're there, but if you catch their eye, don't give them a reason to approach."

Tsu'ran were shapeshifters, hunters, and protectors. They targeted their victims, sought payment by collecting souls, and were strategic about their assaults. They didn't take just anyone, which was something he'd learned many summers ago. If *Dread Deep* earned the Tsu'ran's attention, it was because they either disrespected their territory or refused to acknowledge one of the dozen signs the creatures gave. Their territory, their rules. It was common knowledge they would take on any form most desired by their prey, a way to lure them in. Few came in contact with a Tsu'ran and lived to talk about it. The creatures never let a victim go without a reason.

Under the moonlight, Elliot looked pale. "Keep it down," Cassian ordered. "I don't want vomit in this boat. And if you throw up in the sea, you'll defile their territory. These aren't our waters anymore."

Elliot nodded, face twisted in what must be severe nausea.

More screams. Elliot pressed his hand against his mouth. It occurred to Cassian then that the boy probably hadn't ever seen a real battle. Whenever they docked a ship to carry out the Queens' orders, Elliot stayed behind. This would be his first time looking Death in the face. He hoped the kid could stomach it. He didn't have time to be a babysitter.

"One other thing," Cassian said. The rowboat hit the side of the ship, and he dragged the paddles in and laid them parallel. Then he grabbed some rope to secure them to *Dread Deep*, slipping it through the iron cleats scattered along the ship for docking. Close enough. "They love to talk. If you find yourself in the presence of one, keep them talking. Make something up, tell them stories, anything. Keep a watch on their eyes. They change colors—yellow means you've pissed them off. A little trick to tell if they're in a rage or not. Ready?"

As the last word left his lips, a body smashed into the water to their right. The woman didn't struggle as she sank beneath the surface. That was his answer. Cassian turned and reached for the anchor chain, pulling himself up.

The Cursed Heist

Slime covered the anchor chain, leaving a blackened sludge all over Cassian's hands. His boots slipped off more than once, and his fingers hurt from how hard he was holding onto the metal. Ascending the side of a ship was not new to Cassian, but the Tsu'ran had left their mark everywhere, making the simple task precarious. He checked four times to ensure Elliot followed, which he did, albeit much slower. Glass was still passed out in the rowboat, but he'd wake soon. Once he did, he'd know what happened. If Cassian returned with the egg, they'd have a good laugh about it. If he failed, Glass would never forgive him. He was still annoyed at the crewman's behavior, and when this was all over, he'd make sure Glass knew just how pissed he was about being challenged on this. This heist, if successful, would change their lives.

Shouts and clashing metal met Cassian's ears. Adrenaline surged through him, turning his blood hot. Only one chance to get this right. He didn't know where they'd keep the egg. Maybe stored with the rest of the valuables being transported in the hold. Depended on how much they were carrying, though, which he wouldn't know until he was faced with it. Until then, it was a guessing game. For all he knew, the egg could be stored in a cannon or the captain's cabin.

Another ear-splitting screech. The crew was putting up a fight, but it would do nothing but drag out their deaths. Nobody ever won against a Tsu'ran. If the crew lasted this long, it was because the creatures were toying with their prey. Better for him.

Cassian hauled himself over the railing, legs and arms on fire. A body lay next to him, colorless and with its eyes gouged out. Tsu'ran were clean killers. They didn't tear arms off or slash. They got their victim close before revealing their true form. He'd only seen the carnage from the Tsu'ran one other time—when he was thirteen. This attack echoed that memory.

Shoving himself back from the railing and behind a cargo box, he waited for Elliot to ensure the kid was safely aboard. He studied the cargo box, confused. Odd place to put one, but he didn't have time to ponder. When the boy flopped over, he inhaled sharply and pushed himself against the railing. Cassian brought his finger to his lips.

All around, Tsu'ran and crew engaged. One Tsu'ran for every third man—but numbers didn't matter against these creatures. He spotted one wandering by, flashing him a thin smile in the form of a woman with webbed hands and gills along her neck. Cassian hesitated, confused. Her scaly skin glittered green under the moon, and she had yellow orbs for eyes. She wore no clothes, bare and beautiful, with black hair cascading down her back. Along her spine, horns curved downward. The Tsu'ran woman let out a laugh that sounded like shattered glass and continued her way down the steps to the main deck, targeting a man who was fighting with everything he had.

Cassian forced air in, suddenly doubting everything he'd learned about the sea creatures. Three of her fingers shifted and elongated into tentacles, wrapping around the man's throat until he stilled. Her other hand poked at his clothes like a curious animal before one of her finger-tentacles forced its slimy way into the man's mouth and down his throat. In the same breath, she dug her two fingers into his eyes, plucking them out and popping them into her mouth. She dropped his corpse, dragging her tongue over a tentacle. Blood coated her lips.

Cassian patted Elliot, getting the boy's attention, and pointed at the hatch that led below. Elliot nodded frantically, and Cassian got up to cross. They were desperately close. No more had he taken three steps when a Tsu'ran stepped in front of him. This one was quite similar to the one he'd just seen, except with purple-colored orbs. The Tsu'ran's eye color could tell him everything. Right now, she was calm. Pointed ears stuck out between strands of her dark hair, and when she spoke, she revealed pointed teeth.

"You don't belong here," she hissed. Her voice sounded like a chorus of people speaking all at once—harsh and coarse compared to her elegant features.

Elliot continued past, hugging the railing as he went, face twisted in utter terror.

"You've been busy," Cassian replied as calmly as he could. The more confident he appeared, the less the creature would want to mess with him, or so he hoped. Easier said than done. When he met the otherworldly gaze of the Tsu'ran, every part of him shook with untempered fear. The emotion wiggled itself into the darkest corners of his mind, split his logic apart, and made his knees weak. He swallowed and dropped his gaze. The fear instantly left his body.

"You don't belong here," she repeated. Water seeped from her pores, pooling at her webbed feet.

"I am leaving," he said firmly. "Just grabbing my things."

Tentacles teased his neck and jaw, cold and slick. He suppressed a yelp, his heart ramming against his ribcage. She was toying with him, trying to induce her rage and devour him. "Why don't you look at me?" Another tentacle twisted his right hand. "Ah, a captain. But I ate this ship's captain. So where do you belong?"

"Just leaving," he wheezed as the tentacles tightened. His head was forced forward, so he looked the other way. "Wrong ship."

She giggled. The sound shattered the last bit of control he had. Every instinct burned in him to struggle, scream, shout, and he fought against it with everything he had. The Tsu'ran's influence bled into him with crushing force.

And then a scream erupted. A woman's. Another victim of *Dread Deep*. The Tsu'ran stopped, tentacles retreating and letting him go. Purple shifted to yellow, and Cassian collapsed, slamming hard into the deck. He wheezed, repulsed and terrified, and didn't look back as he crawled to the hatch that led to the lower decks. Yanking it open, he halfway dropped himself into the entrance, grasping a metal railing to keep himself from hitting the bottom. His ribs smashed into the ladder with air-stealing force, and it felt like his arm was going to be torn out of its place, but he reached up and closed the hatch behind him.

He sat there for a long moment, head pressed against the cold metal of the ladder, regaining his composure. The Tsu'ran dug up every bit of fear he'd ever suppressed, contorted it, and fed it right back to him. Never in his life had he felt anything so chilling and raw. It would take the rest of his life to forget that encounter.

"Cassian?" Elliot's frantic voice brought him back to their reality. "Are you okay?"

He nodded and descended, not wanting to talk about it. Down here, it was much quieter, but the shouts and madness unraveling on the main deck still met them. If anyone was hiding out down here, they didn't make themselves known. Cassian didn't want to wait around long enough to find out.

"Take the gun deck," he told Elliot. "I'll find the hold. If you find it first, come find me. If you've got trouble, get off the ship."

The boy hesitated. "And you?"

"It's not me I'm worried about." The meaning sat between them, unspoken. Cassian didn't have to say more. If needed, he'd leave a trail of bodies off this ship. The Tsu'ran wouldn't stay forever, just until they ate their fill. Elliot, on the other hand, wouldn't hold up for long in a sword-to-sword combat with another pirate. And if a Tsu'ran got to him, it was over. The creature had left Cassian tarnished and raw. It would leave nothing of the boy but an eyeless shell.

Quietly, Elliot left, making his way down the hall. Cassian watched him go, questioning his decision to bring him into this. He shouldn't have brought Elliot along, but he didn't have time for regrets now. Hesitation and regrets got a man killed faster than any disease. Cassian went the opposite direction, in search of a hatch that would take him further down. A few steps, and then he paused, listening.

A creak caught his attention. The hall was short, opening into another artillery space that held weapons, ropes, and all other needed items in an attack or defense. The hairs along his arms stood on end. He was too vulnerable, so he unclasped the sheath to his sword and laid a hand on the hilt. The Tsu'ran weren't down here yet—he'd know because there'd be blood everywhere—but that didn't mean men weren't protecting what they knew the ship had.

A thump echoed from the main deck. Another body. The ship was huge for a three-masted schooner. Not a White Horn ship. He could tell by the lower decks alone. White Horns were all built the same, constructed with wood from the southern country—the grains and coloring were lighter, more distinct. Dark wood made up this ship, marked by the occasional white and silver grains. Unique. It was either a royal ship or from a specific region with which he was unfamiliar. If he lived to see dawn, he'd take time to study it more.

A few boxes sat in the corner. There were a handful of livestock coops stuffed with chickens and a four-legged creature he'd never seen before. It was long, had paws, whiskers, and bolted left and right, trying to hide from Cassian's view unsuccessfully. The strong stench of rotten eggs and wet soil met his nose. Ventilation was poor, and they'd probably been down here for a while based on the stomach-churning stench. He approached and opened a small barrel. Feed. The animals clucked and squeaked. He'd kill the crew alone for not taking proper care of these animals. No wonder the ship was under attack—bad luck brought on by the disrespect of the animals. Cassian stuck his hand in, grabbed a handful of feed, and tossed it into each coop. Straw needed refreshing too, but he couldn't do that now. He was already short on time.

Nothing valuable was likely here, but one couldn't be too sure, so he pulled the top off a box. A few nails gave, poorly secured, and he found exactly what he anticipated: cannonballs, rope, and steel bars for forging weapons. The steel was probably part of a delivery, though that didn't explain why it was here. Maybe there hadn't been room in the cargo hold. He wedged the lids between the boxes and the wall to keep them from moving and opened another one. It didn't give as easily, and he kicked the box. The jolt dislodged the nails and the lid came off. A chicken clucked.

Straw. So much of it. Cassian grabbed clumps of it and threw it on the floor. Something had been in here and now it wasn't. The egg, perhaps? It felt reckless to leave a dragon egg in a box in the weapons area, but the crate was the right size. Well, he didn't know how big a dragon egg was. Hadn't ever thought about that until now.

Empty. He straightened. Time to find the hold. He didn't know how much time he had, but he knew he needed to move faster.

Thunder cracked, catching him off-guard. His nerves were frayed, and his heart lodged into his throat. Out on the rowboat, he'd not hesitated to follow through. Now, stuck on *Dread Deep* with the Tsu'ran infesting it and a half-ass plan, he doubted everything. He'd wanted to be someone, not dead at the bottom of the sea, his soul chained to the Tsu'ran for eternity.

"Arin, is that you?" A woman stepped around the corner, a bloody gash down the side of her face. They stared at each other, mutually stunned. "Who are you?" she hissed.

"Sam," Cassian lied. "Been working below. You stayin' safe down here?" He slurred, trying to play it off, but she didn't buy it. The captain's mark was about as obvious as him yelling at the top of his lungs.

"Why are you here?" she demanded. The sword in her hand gestured above. "Did you send those gods-forsaken things to our ship?"

"As much of a compliment as that is, no, I didn't send them." Cassian drummed his fingers on the hilt of his sword. "Bad timing. Best we go our separate ways, yeah?"

She didn't move. The audacity of this woman. He'd paint the walls with her blood if that's what she wanted. Unsheathing his sword, he motioned at her. "Well, go on, then. This what you want?"

More thunder. The portholes along the starboard side flashed white, lighting the sky. He saw *Torment* in the distance, still dark, but moving toward them. The fog had dispersed, and lightning flashed across the sky, illuminating the ship. Irritation surged through him. *Torment* was supposed to stay behind the island. It hadn't been that long since they'd left for *Dread Deep*. What was the *Torment* crew thinking? Cassian would have a word with the men aboard when he returned. If not for the Tsu'ran, spotters would have identified *Torment* and blown their cover. A few raindrops pelted the window, promising a wet row back to his ship.

She lunged. Just as he anticipated a low swing, she switched directions, aiming straight for his head. Cassian ducked, impressed, and kicked out. She jumped and drove the curved blade of her saber down. The tip nicked his shoulder, drawing blood with a sting. He hissed, annoyed, and lashed out. His sword slammed into hers, and she stumbled back from the force. Both hands on the hilt, she locked her legs into place and pushed back.

Cassian slid the weapon down to the handguard and kicked her knee. As he did, he grabbed her weapon and tore it free from her. Without hesitation, he drove both blades through her torso. The woman wheezed a curse, and she fumbled for the weapons, unwilling to accept her fate.

Cassian let go, and she took several steps back. Slick, bloody hands tried to yank the weapons out, but her strength was already waning. She looked between him and the weapons, coughing up blood. She collapsed, convulsing before going still. He took a firm hold of his blade, placed a boot against her, and pulled. It gave with a sickening squelch, and he wiped the metal along her pants. Satisfied, he continued his search.

The shouting was lessening on the main deck. The Tsu'ran were either waiting for others to show themselves or finishing off their choice of souls for the evening. He hoped it was the latter—if he was a religious man, he'd have prayed for it. The Grave was dangerous . . . Sometimes, the Tsu'ran or the beasts that lurked below didn't need a reason to attack. They just did.

He found a small open hatch from where the woman had come. She'd been below, possibly guarding something. Keeping his sword at the ready, he swung around and lowered himself down. The iron ladder hooks nailed into the wood support beam gave some from his weight, so he was careful not to distribute all of himself onto one hook at a time. At the bottom, he stopped. It was dark, save for a single lantern tucked in the corner, barely burning, but enough for him to see his surroundings.

The hold space was narrow, far more so than on *Torment*, and crates were stacked on top of one another to his right. To port, sacks hung on hooks—some full, others empty. The crews' belongings, as if some slept in here. Before him, on the ground, he spied a red leather satchel with engravings in the Old Tongue. Sigils he couldn't decipher and didn't care to.

It was open. He caught the faint glimmer of silver. Cassian approached, kneeling before the lantern. It was stifling down here, and sweat rolled down the side of his face. He dabbed at his brow with his sleeve, feeling the ship rock underneath. The storm was picking up. They'd be stuck here all night at this rate. Elliot and he could hide out in here until dawn, though it wasn't ideal. If any of the crew of *Dread Deep* remained, they'd be a problem once the Tsu'ran left.

He stuck his hand into the satchel, instantly meeting a hard and textured surface that burned. Surprised, he pulled his hand back. "By the sea," he mumbled, lifting the satchel's flap instead. He froze.

An egg. No. A dragon egg. It was so easy that he checked over his shoulder, anticipating this to be a trap. When there was no one else, he concluded that they'd hidden the egg and kept a few crewmembers with the satchel for protection. Scaly texture, silver, and large. He touched it again, prepared to find it too hot, but it was far more manageable. As his hand glided over the egg's surface, the world ceased. His body turned flush, like he'd come down with a fever, and he felt nauseous. A headache tore through him, threatening to rip his head wide open. He coughed, feeling the fire of bile drench his throat. Forcing it down, he took the egg from the pouch and raised it, seeing it fully.

The egg was heavier than expected, like he'd just picked up chains. He didn't have to ask to know it wasn't fake or dead. Life hummed within it in a way he'd never experienced before. His arms buzzed with the heat, filling his core and making it hard to breathe. So many stories about distant Dragon Riders filled his thoughts, faint compared to the loud hum that accompanied his splitting headache. He hardly knew enough of the stories to quote them, as he'd spent his time ignoring what the bards said and pickpocketing the audience. Once he was grown and aboard *Torment*, no one spoke of Dragon Riders anymore. Stories like that didn't take well to the folks at sea. Cassian worried himself more with the kind of rope he brought aboard than the distant tales of once-dead eras.

And now, the past and present converged. Cassian didn't know how to act. Deep within himself, he felt the stir of familiarity, like an old friend had come to greet him. The sensation came from out of nowhere, startling him, but he didn't shy away from it. The warmth from the feeling burrowed into the darkest places of him.

The ship swayed violently, knocking him to the side. His shoulder struck the crates hard, and the egg flew from his grip and whacked him in the jaw. Teeth clattered, the small cut the woman had given him flared, angry, and he blinked, momentarily disoriented. Either they'd just come to the greatest storm in history or—

"Cassian!" Elliot's anxious voice shattered the spell, and he rushed to the hatch.

"What?" he answered back.

"Something just hit the ship!"

Not a storm. Dread sank into his bones, sucking the heat right out of the room. "We . . . We need to go." He sheathed his sword and snatched the pouch up, stuffing the egg inside. Then he tied the leather strings to securely keep it shut, and slung it over his shoulder. King Jair just might get his egg, after all. And he might live to see the coin promised to him.

"But—"

"I got it," Cassian finished, climbing up. "Where are the Tsu'ran?"

Elliot was shaking his head as he pulled himself out of the cramped room with the crews' belongings. It was far cooler up here, and Cassian was relieved to inhale the robust odor of the chickens. "They just left."

Cassian paused. "Left?"

"Yeah. They just stopped everything and left."

Twin peals of thunder cracked, back-to-back. "And the crew?"

"Some are still alive. I heard them gathering on the main deck. They're confused, asking questions—"

"Never mind. I don't care," Cassian interrupted. "We need to get off the ship before the remaining crew go searching. Come on." He started his way back to where he'd killed the woman. Her body lay in the same place, blood staining the wood. He avoided stepping over her—bad luck—and ran to the ladder to the main deck. He stopped with one hand on the metal. Elliot came up behind him.

"You said they're on the main deck," Cassian said. Reality sank in, harsh. "They'll see us."

The ship rocked again, and Cassian almost slammed his head into the metal but caught himself. The sudden jolt wasn't natural. None of this was. Without waiting for a response, he started climbing. Damn if they saw. *Dread Deep* was going to be at the bottom of this sea. Something bigger was out there, and it was hungry.

Cassian shoved the hatch open, crawling out as fast as his body allowed. Rain soaked him, and lightning lit up the sky. Someone ran by, not even sparing him a moment's glance. Elliot followed up the ladder, and they bolted for the railings. The ship swayed again, threatening to take him right off his feet. He swung his leg over the edge of the ship and ran right into Glass.

"You're awake," Cassian observed. "We can talk later. Move."

"You're a wretched pile of shit, did you know that?" Glass replied. They'd use the anchor chain to descend with. The rowboat rocked violently beneath them, slamming into *Dread Deep*. Rowing back to *Torment* in this weather would be perilous, but less so than facing whatever was attacking the *Dread Deep*. Lightning streaked across the blackened sky, illuminating Glass in a horrid display of atmospheric fury that made him look a decade older. A bellowing crack of thunder followed. "What's going on?"

Cassian wanted to apologize for how the entire night was going, but he couldn't get the next words out fast enough. "I don't know, but it's big, and I don't want to be on this ship when it goes down."

Tentacles of the Damned

Rain made the iron chain hanging on the side of the hull slippery. Cassian halfway fell, legs akimbo, and his hands grasped for anything to keep himself from smashing into the dark water below. Elliot's boot kicked Cassian in the head as the boy slipped as well. Glass cursed Cassian's name a dozen different times for being knocked out cold, a giant welt already on the side of the older man's head from the pommel of the blade. The waves were growing in ferocity, shoving the rowboat into the hull of the *Dread Deep*. Lightning lit the sky up, and thunder followed, the sound deafening.

Cassian fell into the rowboat, landing on his back, narrowly missing the seat. The rowboat wobbled, threatening to flip over before settling. A quick check confirmed the dragon egg was still intact. All he could think was that if they survived this, he'd be done with heists for a while. Maybe forever. This was the worst experience of his life. He wasn't even sure he'd try and find the Crown of Gods anymore.

Elliot dropped in next to him with a grunt. Cassian turned to tell the boy *nice work* when Glass smacked him hard with a quick flick of the wrist. Pain blossomed across Cassian's face, and his vision blurred.

"Give me a break," Cassian snapped and rubbed the area, finding it bruised already. As captain, he should reprimand Glass for that, but he couldn't bring himself to say anything. Glass was the closest thing to a friend he had, which meant he could get away with far more than Cassian should allow as captain.

"Just don't do that in front of the crew, yeah?" Cassian half-joked. His voice faltered, his body tired from the long night. Bones ached. Welts he didn't remember getting bloomed in odd places, including the top of his foot. He just wanted a drink.

"That's just to get you started," Glass rumbled. "I'm going to leave you to the dead after I'm done with you." He picked up the paddles and stuck them in the water.

Cassian pointed at the pouch. "But I got the egg." Countless summers of working together meant he could read Glass's crappy sense of humor.

That earned the faintest of smiles. Glass undid the ropes, tossing them at Elliot to manage. The boy fumbled but picked them up and started looping them around his arm and hand. They were already putting space between themselves and *Dread Deep*. Waves kept the rowboat unsteady. Water pooled at the bottom from rain. Cassian reached over and checked the egg for the second time, relieved it was still there. The sudden urge to protect it at all costs was greater than anything he'd ever felt before.

"Faster," Cassian begged.

Glass groaned. "I'm going as fast as I can."

Cassian peered over the edge, expecting a Tsu'ran to reach up and snatch him. He kept his arms close, his knees tucked together. Now that he had the egg, he felt exposed, a waiting target. He might as well hold it above his head and offer it to the highest bidder. He may as well be a Nighthunter. He'd never met one, but knew the assassins worked for anyone and did anything. No head was off limits. Whoever paid the highest coin earned their business.

He scoffed, feeling lightheaded. Maybe that's what he'd do with this. Screw King Jair. He could take this and see who'd pay the highest price. 45,000 Krye was fantastic—more than he could ever need—but he could probably get more. He bet Junok would pay twice that. That family was bizarre, to say the least. They had their hands in all sorts of ritualistic magic—energy, if he was trying to recall his drunk lessons with the stranger. He'd heard from an old friend that they'd mastered ancient ceremonial practices. The kind of stuff that brought the dead back and controlled souls. The kind of stuff Cassian wasn't paid to care about.

"You daydreaming?" Glass asked through a grunt. "Can I ask you to do that once we get to safety?"

Torment was still a way out, but they'd put enough distance between them and *Dread Deep* for Cassian to slump his shoulders. He shook his head. "I want enough liquor to knock me out."

Glass laughed. "You and me both—"

The water rippled, shoving the boat sideways. Cassian's heart dropped. At once, he grabbed a paddle, halting Glass. "Stop."

The beast took a wide turn from *Dread Deep* and started heading straight for *Torment*. Without the fog and the lightning illuminating the sky, the impending carnage was impossible to miss.

Glass paled. Elliot mumbled something about this being the worst day of his life. Why the leviathan changed its taste in targets, Cassian couldn't answer, but the beast gained speed, passing the small rowboat as it went. The rowboat rocked, turning sideways, but the three men didn't try to correct the small boat's direction. Horns stuck out from the water before slipping underneath again. It wasn't a Krakí. No tentacles or suckers to latch onto ships. It was something bigger. A Life Eater. A full-grown Life Eater could swallow a city whole. No ship stood a chance.

They watched as it approached *Torment* before sinking further below the surface. A single splash of water, a bloodline away, was the last thing Cassian saw. Lightning kept the sky bright. They sat there, letting the waves slosh them around. Watching. All they could do was watch in horror. The rowboat sat between the two massive ships—stuck between the place they were trying to go and the place they'd fled. Rain pelted the men. Cassian's clothes stuck to his skin. Water dripped freely from his brow and carved a path down his face. The bottom of the rowboat had a small pool of water gathering from the torrential rain.

Two giant claws reached up, cradling the bow and the stern of *Torment*. Dark purple skin glittered from rain and moon, webbed claws as black as midnight. The beast hesitated, but only for a moment.

Wood splintered, the masts buckled, and *Torment* succumbed to the Grave.

Nothing quite felt right. Cassian wanted to scream, curse, cry—all of it—but not a sound escaped him. Cassian gaped, watching as his entire life was taken in an instant. He could almost hear the screams of the crew as they were taken into the jaws. Massive waves broke out, and more claws reached upward, shredding the sails.

Torment was gone. Splintered wood floated. The beast's guttural roar cut through the water, paralyzing Cassian in utter terror. Waves from the destruction met their small boat, shoving it back toward *Dread Deep*.

"Wow," Glass whispered. His voice was hollow.

The lives they knew were over. Cassian had been captain for six days and managed to call Death down on his entire crew. Well, almost. Elliot and Glass were alive for the moment, but if they hated him and wanted nothing to do with him after tonight, he didn't blame them. If the roles were reversed, he'd get as far from this all as possible.

Fewer crew. More coin. It sounded terrible, but it was the truth. The greedy thought echoed in his mind, even as he struggled to grasp that he was the worst captain the sea had ever seen. Split three ways, he'd never have to worry about a crew again. He could find a small house next to the water and live out the rest of his life in peace. Nobody would ever sail for him now. He'd be Cassian, the only captain in Vore history to not go down with his ship. Nobody would respect him after word got around about that.

Here he was, worried about his status and future, when they were still floating in the Grave in a storm. *Torment* was gone, and *Dread Deep* was in rough shape. The Life Eater didn't reveal itself again, satisfied. Stories did hardly any justice to the mass of such a beast. Few ever traveled through the Grave and lived to tell about it, and now he knew why. It was sheer luck that kept Cassian and the two other White Horns alive, nothing else.

So many men died tonight. Men who stood by his side despite everything. The Queens didn't need to hunt the White Horns—Cassian had killed them off just fine. The sound of retching forced his attention back. Elliot was throwing up, spitting bile and half-digested fish into the water and across the side of the small boat. The rancid fumes made Cassian want to gag, so he pinched his nose and looked away until the rain washed away the remains. Out of sight, out of mind. Damn kid would need to get better at keeping his nerves together.

When Elliot was done using the sea as a personal bucket, Cassian said, "Get yourself together, kid." The boy wiped at his mouth, heaving, and glared at him. "Their territory. Their rules. Let's not disrespect them."

"Easy for you to say," Elliot snapped. "We're in this mess because of you."

"Hey," Glass warned the boy. "Last I heard, you snuck on to prove your point. Feeling brave yet?"

Cassian raised his brow. Glass had a point. Impossible for Elliot to sit here and accuse him of anything when he'd betrayed his father's wishes to prove how tough he really was. Cassian leaned forward. "You wishing you would've stayed with your father?"

The boy shrugged. "I don't know." A weak response. Cassian slapped him. "Hey," Elliot muttered, rubbing his cheek.

"Do you regret coming out here?" Cassian demanded. All his frustrations were bubbling over. He didn't care how it made him look. Elliot was determined to make a coward out of himself, and he didn't have the tolerance for it. Cowardice would get the kid killed as sure as a Life Eater attack. "Or would you've preferred to have been on that ship?"

Elliot opened his mouth, then closed it. Rain turned everything into a sloppy mess. Cassian's hair was plastered to his face, clothes a second skin, and water pooled in his boots, wiggling its way between his toes. The warmth of the egg seeped into his back, offering a small bit of redemption in this disaster.

"No," Elliot whispered. "Not at all."

The right answer. Cassian nodded. "Good. Because if you were on that ship, you'd be in the stomach of the Life Eater. And if you keep that pathetic attitude, I'll leave you for dead myself. Pray to your Gods in private for forgiveness, if you believe in that. Consider ourselves lucky. More coin for us. We have a second chance at life." Or another opportunity to die. It was a matter of perspective.

Cassian couldn't mope about *Torment* or the lost crew. The guilt would eat him alive, but he would focus on the next steps. That's all he knew to do. Surviving and self-preservation were separated by a thin line that blurred more than anyone dared admit. He'd not come all this way to lose it all to grief and doubt. They'd gotten the egg. Now they needed to get out of this rowboat and into a proper ship. They'd never make it back to shore in this.

"*Dread Deep*," Cassian said. The others looked to him. "Not much crew remains, yeah?"

"Right," Elliot agreed. "At least from what I saw."

"We head back." Cassian gestured at Glass. "We need a ship. This is the best option we've got."

"The more you talk, the less I'm certain you're all right in the head." Glass started rowing back to *Dread Deep*, which wasn't far. "They'll want the egg."

"And we tell them Jair's price," Cassian countered. "I'm willing to wager they'll work with us if we tell them we'll get 45,000 Krye, maybe more. After everything they've seen tonight, they'll want to get a cut out of this and leave their losses behind. We need more than three men running a ship."

Elliot scratched his face. "You're telling me we snuck aboard, stole a dragon egg, left to return to *Torment,* and now we're going to return to *Dread Deep* to make a deal with whoever remains?"

"When you add the Tsu'ran and the Life Eater, it sounds almost logical," Cassian added. "We can't be picky with our choices. Food and water are aboard. Fresh clothes, too. And a cot. We've got cramped space, no defense, and no resources in this dinghy. We won't see a single coin if we stay here." Stuck in the dinghy, they weren't likely to see tomorrow night either. They were too far into the Grave to get out safely. Something would come for them before they made it a league.

Glass cleared his throat. "Are we really going to cut them in?"

Cassian snorted. "Of course not. We just need to get to shore. Then we'll leave them behind."

It was the best plan they had—the only one. If this failed, Cassian wasn't sure what to do. He didn't know who remained of the *Dread Deep* crew, but he hoped they were practical sailors who could see reason. If not, it would be a long trip back to civilization.

Prisoners of Destiny

Climbing back aboard *Dread Deep* wasn't ideal, but it was the only choice they had. *Torment* was gone. The crew was dead. And the only thing left was to get out of the Grave before the Tsu'ran came back, or something bigger crawled out from the depths of this nightmare.

Cassian felt numb as he returned to the anchor chain slick with rain. Survivors would be slim, and they would be looking for a fight. He wouldn't blame them. He just hoped he could talk them into a higher payout with the egg, get them on his side, and get out of this disaster.

Once they docked, Cassian, Elliot, and Glass would flee and take the egg with them. He wouldn't split the coin with strangers. And Cassian wouldn't let this egg out of sight because the remaining crew of *Dread Deep* could do the same thing and trick the three White Horns and run.

Nobody played fair at sea.

"Watch your backs," Cassian told the other two as he climbed. The rain had let up just enough to make everything a slippery mess. Thunder rolled, and lightning still turned the dark sky into a light show. *Dread Deep* rocked, gray waves battered the hull and drenched the men as they ascended. Muscles strained against the force, and twice he stopped and held on for dear life as the ship heeled too far over. Again, he checked the egg. Warmth radiated from it like it was his own personal sun.

Rounding the railing, he saw the mess still strewn about the main deck. A growing pile of dead crew sat in the center. Bloodless, damned, and limp, their souls bound to the Tsu'ran now for an eternity. No harsher outcome than that. If any soul got lucky, they might be reborn into a Tsu'ran. Cassian kept one hand tightly around the leather strap across his shoulder, watching for the remaining crew of *Dread Deep* to reveal themselves as Elliot and Glass clambered back onboard. A woman and man dragged a body out of the captain's cabin, only seeing the three interlopers after dropping the dead onto the pile. They took a double-take, as if wondering whether they should fight. Cassian didn't blame them because he felt the same. This entire day was a disaster.

The man opened his mouth, then closed it. Cassian didn't waste any time and asked, "Who else is alive?"

"Um." The woman appeared to struggle for the right response and faced the other *Dread Deep* shipmate. "Two more. That's it. Wait." She faced Cassian again and narrowed her gaze. "Who are you?"

"Long story," Cassian replied, stepping forward. Elliot and Glass followed. "Can we talk?"

The man shoved the woman aside. "By the grace of Greve, who do you think you are?" He pointed at Cassian's hand. "I see that mark. You don't belong here."

They had no idea how true that was. In all the commotion, they'd not noticed the three sneak on board to steal the egg, or slip back off the ship, or even the complete destruction of the *Torment*. Cassian mustered a charming smile. "If you get the last of your crew, we can talk, and I'm more than happy to tell you the truth. Until then, we're just throwing insults and wasting precious time, which I don't think anyone has the energy for after the day we've all had."

Silence passed, marked by the two exchanging looks. Cassian hoped they chose right. Sailing this ship with fewer than five crew would be impossible. And he was willing to wager that the *Dread Deep* crew knew that, too. Without helping each other, everybody was stranded in the Grave.

"Captain's cabin. Go," the man told them. "I'll get the others." He paused, studying the pile of dead. "Well, whoever is left of our crew."

Good enough. Cassian surveyed the dead, noting the captain. Gray hair intertwined with gold rings and interlocking crescent moons on his hand with a circle above them. He'd not seen that tattoo before, but knew it had to be a captain's mark. The *Dread Deep* had lost their captain—bad luck, but he couldn't imagine how much worse this night could get. The pile of the Tsu'ran's victims was significant. *Dread Deep* was practically a floating graveyard.

Cassian jerked his chin in the direction of the captain's cabin. Glass and Elliot followed without a word. Cassian was soaked to the bone and tired of it. He wanted warmth, dry clothes, and a drink. Seaman's Water would do. He hoped *Dread Deep* carried some. He grimaced. All those supplies he'd brought on *Torment* were now sinking to the bottom of the Grave or in the stomach of the beast. He'd spent a lot of Krye on all that. Krye he'd never see again.

Inside, the quarters were much cozier than on *Torment*. A plush chair sat to the side of a large table. Gold-plated quills were bundled up and lying in an open box nailed to the counter with more ink than a man would know what to do with. Opening a few of the drawers, Cassian found piles of fresh parchment, untouched by the salt, and more rolled up and sealed with a purple wax stamp. He picked it up and studied the crest. The same as on the captain's hand. A royal ship.

It explained the grand interior. Even the ceiling was decorated with molding in the shape of waves. A bit ostentatious for his liking, but he supposed it was perfect for a ship that managed to avoid the hand of Death for as long as it had. *The nicer the ship, the crueler the destruction.* He'd heard that once. All this investment in a beautiful ship only meant so much, but it would mean nothing if it sat at the bottom of the sea. It's why he liked more practical decor, not all this wasted gold and unnecessary design.

"They're going to kill us," Elliot mumbled.

"Nonsense." Cassian dropped the scroll back into the drawer and closed it. He opened a few more, in search of liquor. "They're just as confused as we are. Four men couldn't possibly sail this ship. They'll see benefit in us just as we do with them."

Glass nodded, arms crossed. The welt Cassian had given him was red and angry, glistening from the rain, and probably hurt worse than a stab wound. Cassian would apologize for that later, choosing instead to investigate his surroundings. He opened the next drawer and snorted. A few smaller bottles of liquor were tucked away—captain's private collection, he presumed. All his now. He popped the cork out and took a sip. The burn was immediate, searing a hole right into his stomach. No flavor. This was just meant to get a man drunk. It would work.

"Don't you think . . .?" Elliot stopped when the door opened and four entered. Crewmembers of *Dread Deep*, including the man and woman Cassian had already spoken to. They were all battered and soaked, but no serious injuries that he could see. They'd likely hidden for most of the attack. Smartest ones here.

"Make yourself at home," one remarked coldly, shutting the door with enough force to shake the room. Cassian took another drink. Attitudes didn't get pirates far at sea. It only put targets on their backs.

"Thanks," Cassian replied once he swallowed. "Anybody else want some?"

Everyone stared. Cassian's generosity wasn't earning respect by the looks of it. These weren't real pirates. They didn't act like it. Too caught up in the nuances of liquor and who owned what. Glass motioned with his hand, and he passed the small bottle over. The crewman took a swig and inhaled sharply. Cassian raised his brow and said, "Strong, right?"

"Take the dead right out of the Grave," Glass remarked, taking another drink. Glass handed the bottle back to Cassian, who offered it to Elliot. The boy shook his head. Too young to appreciate a good drink when it was needed. In time, he'd learn.

"So," Cassian said, moving the bottle as he spoke. "We've got a little bit of a predicament here, yeah?" Another drink. The liquor went straight to his head. After tonight, it was the best feeling. "You need more men to sail this ship, and we need a ship. So why don't we work together and get out of the Grave?"

"Rot at the bottom of the sea," the woman spat. Dark hair clung to her ebony skin, soaked. "You're not one of us. Why are you here anyway?"

They didn't know. Cassian hesitated, debating between telling him the leather satchel swung over his shoulder was theirs and not saying anything about it at all. Someone on this ship must have known about the egg. He knew the woman he killed did, but who else? It was possible that anyone who knew about this precious cargo was dead, and the remaining crew was clueless. It'd make sense. It felt reckless to let too many people know about such a valuable item. Clever, actually. Cassian hadn't thought of that. But if he didn't tell them, then he didn't have any leverage over them.

"You were carrying a high-prized item—"

"Were?" one man asked.

Cassian pulled off the satchel, undoing the knot that kept it closed. The four shipmates leaned forward. Glass and Elliot did, too. They'd not seen it either. He revealed the dragon egg, unperturbed by all the chaos aboard. Glances were exchanged, expletives were uttered, and Glass asked for the liquor. Cassian handed the bottle to him, then dropped his fingers to tie the flap close again. The leather was cold from the rain against his calloused skin. Once the knot was secure, Cassian slung the satchel back over his shoulder. He'd sleep with this if he had to.

"You were carrying this. Stashed on your ship was a dragon egg. You didn't know?" Cassian couldn't hide the surprise in his voice.

The remaining *Dread Deep* crew shook their heads. "We knew we were carrying a few expensive weapons, boxed up, but not that," the woman said. "Is it real?"

"It's real," Cassian confirmed. The warmth seeping from the egg was unbelievable. It fought off the chill clinging to his bones. "Who was in charge of the cargo?"

"Rehl," one said. "He's dead."

"You sailed the outskirts of the Grave on countless occasions, taking the longest route possible, and you never stopped to ask questions about why?"

"Figured it was the weapons," another man answered. "They're the nicest in the world. Made with krusin steel—"

"No pirate cares about steel," Cassian interrupted. A sword was a sword. "Who do you serve?"

"What do you mean?" the same man asked.

Cassian grabbed the other bottle and tore the cork out. "Are you all dull? Who do you report to?"

The woman crossed her arms. "We serve the king of Kalic."

Ah, so Cassian was right. Kalic was a northern city in the country of Eiyrặl. "So what's a royal crew sailing through the Grave for? Why didn't your king hire pirates to do this job?" The *Dread Deep* crew gawked like he spoke gibberish. "You lot aren't pirates. Not with your ridiculous silk attire and gold-encrusted royal ship. Who but a royal would waste all this coin on frills and crown molding? Pirates know these waters better. We don't need all this"—he motioned at the gold and over-the-top decorations—"to get the job done."

"We took payment." Another man stepped forward. "We serve the king. He tasked us with a duty. That is what we'll do. It's not our job to ask why he wants things done a certain way."

"Not even curious about what you're transporting?" Cassian asked, not hiding his disdain. These people were why he couldn't pledge fealty to any landwalker. Mindless and spineless. Didn't ask questions or challenge choices, just listened and obeyed. By the grace of the sea, he would be surprised if they had any real knowledge of the Grave.

Cassian raised his hand before any could start an argument. "Why don't we start over? Names. I'm Cassian." He took a drink. The fire lit his stomach up.

The woman snorted. "All right. I'm Ali."

"Bauer," the tall one said.

"Sanser."

"Edward," the last replied. Elliot and Glass stated their names, too.

"Good." Cassian pointed at Bauer. "Were you first mate?"

"Aye." Bauer frowned. "How'd you know?"

"Spend as long at sea as I have, and you just have an instinct for that stuff." Cassian scratched his chin, coming close to the old scar. "And the rest of you. Crew, not passengers?"

They all nodded. It was obvious. They all looked at each other before answering. Only the crew would do that. First mates and captains held more authority, possessed more confidence, and didn't hesitate to answer. These three were looking for approval before opening their mouths. Made them easier to manipulate. Convincing Bauer might be a problem.

"I've got an offer for you all," Cassian said. No time like the present. "We've been tasked with getting this egg to a particular buyer who's willing to pay a hefty fee. Prior to tonight, I was splitting that payment fifteen ways. Now, it's looking like seven." A pause. The four slowly nodded, understanding. "That seems pretty fair, don't you think?"

"If I want my head in a bucket," Sanser remarked. "Our duty is to the king, not you."

"Last I checked, that egg is ours," Ali added. "I'm not seeing how this benefits us at all."

"Coin," Cassian insisted. "How much is your king paying you for these travels?"

"Enough," Ali remarked and crossed her arms.

"You White Horns are all scum," Edward mumbled. "Always in everyone's business." Cassian would've gouged his eyes out with the broken edge of the liquor bottle if not for the fact that he needed every member here to safely sail this ship. "Coin is all you care about. We're serving a purpose. And what? You lot show up wherever and however you please and disrupt everything, believing there aren't consequences?"

"My heart." Cassian placed a hand against his chest, feigning offense. "How will I ever recover from that insult?" He took a drink, sloshing the liquid around in his mouth until everything went numb, then swallowed. "Let's get something clear, and let's do it fast." Pointing at the four, he said, "We're currently dead in the Grave. I don't know if it's ignorance or foolishness, but none of you seem worried about that. We sit here any longer, and we'll be arguing at the bottom of the sea, serving the Tsu'ran."

Bauer scoffed. "That isn't true."

Glass rubbed his hands over his face. A sign he was speechless.

Cassian narrowed his gaze on the dim-witted *Dread Deep* seaman. "What?"

Bauer shrugged. "The dead are dead. That's where they stay."

Sanser raised his brow. "Well, the Guardians of Death—"

"Can we not?" Ali snapped, the only one with a sense of urgency. Cassian would keep his eye on her—she might prove worthy of his respect. "You're saying we need to get out of the Grave?"

Cassian nodded. "Aye."

"Well, then I think that's settled." Ali pointed at her crew. "Bicker all you want. I don't care. My faith is in the Gods, not Guardians or Tsu'ran. What I care about is getting out of here before those forsaken creatures come back."

"Did you pray?" The question slipped out before Cassian could help himself. The majority of pirates didn't pray—even more proof these swabbies didn't belong on these waters. The buzz was turning his thoughts into sludge. Just enough to take the edge off but not make him useless.

The woman glared. "Excuse me?"

"Did you pray? Ask Eazon to spare you all some luck and with a snap"—he snapped his fingers—"everything would just work out?" Disgust stained each word black. "If the Gods were real, would they've allowed your crew to be slaughtered? Or do they only protect those who worship them?" Cassian shrugged. "Selfish bastards, if you ask me. But nobody ever asks a pirate what they think of the landwalker deities, do they?"

She opened and closed her fists, jaw set like cooled iron. Elliot started to say something, but Cassian slapped his arm, silencing the boy. Not his battle. And he didn't want Elliot involved. The kid had already dragged himself into a mess.

"It's people like you that make me despise pirates," she whispered. "You're all so self-absorbed. The Gods don't meddle with our problems, but you don't ask questions to know that, do you?" Her tone challenged all the control he could muster. The little chance of giving Ali any respect evaporated. He hated her and her ignorance. "You know nothing, appreciate nothing, and you're too stubborn to realize when you're not welcome."

"And yet, here we are," Cassian replied, flashing a smile. "Are we all in agreement to get out of the Grave?"

Everyone nodded, including Ali, although her motions were slower. Good. One step closer to freedom.

"Let's get her turned around," Glass said. "We can use these waves to our advantage. Grab some wind. Give ourselves a chance before—"

The door opened. The wood creaked, terribly loud in the silence that filled the captain's cabin. In the entryway, lit by lightning, stood a Tsu'ran. A ghastly blister against the skin of the soaked ship that still had the pile of dead in the center of the main deck. Horns jutted from her head in between slick, wet black hair. Blue orbs shimmered, gills fluctuated, and she smiled wide, revealing a row of sharpened teeth.

"Parley."

Tormenting the Restless

Nobody spoke in the presence of the Tsu'ran. Cassian wet his lips, tried to say something snarky, and failed. Nothing came to mind. Impossible when he was facing a creature that nightmares were made of. She tilted her head as if reading his mind, and hummed. The sound was silky compared to her gravel-like and otherworldly voice. But underneath the tune, Cassian felt the curved edge of a claw trace down his spine.

"You carry something precious," she finally said, breaking the long silence.

Cassian believed himself capable of handling just about anything. He prided himself on his flexibility, adaptability, and tough hand. Pirate life wasn't easy—far from it—and he'd be lying if he said he didn't at times wish for a more peaceful path. Landwalkers worried about what they'd eat for supper. Pirates worried their own crew might stab them in the back while they slept. He'd spent summers learning that trust could get a man killed. Expect the unexpected, and he'd never be underprepared for what came his way.

But now he was standing in a room with four crewmembers from Kalic, *Torment's* remaining crew, and a Tsu'ran in the middle of the Grave. And he couldn't forget the dragon egg in the satchel over his shoulder. There wasn't enough Seaman's Water in all the bars of Greve's Point to handle this night.

He cleared his throat, flush. The heat radiating from the satchel was unbearable. He wiped a thin layer of sweat from his brow. The egg's temperature climbed, but he refused to put it down. Anyone here could take it and run, and he wouldn't let that happen. This egg wouldn't leave his sight until he personally gave it to King Jair.

She passed a scornful smile, cold underneath the greenish skin and strange curves of her cheekbones. A blend of woman and creature. "Are you all right, White Horn?"

"Me?" Cassian said. Others turned to him as he nonchalantly wiped sweat off his brow. "I'm fine. What do you want?" He took the liquor back from Glass and took a swig.

"Hm." She took a step forward, and everyone stepped back. The Tsu'ran stopped and raised her bony brow. "What do you intend to do with that egg?"

"None of your business," Cassian snapped.

"It is my business."

"What is this? Why are you here?" Cassian demanded. Another gulp. The faster he drank, the better off he'd be. "Your kind don't interact with us. You're nothing but a—"

She crossed her arms. He stopped, feeling the rest of what he was going to say get lodged in his throat. Cassian choked, fighting for air. Lungs burned, his thoughts scrambled, and he leaned over. He coughed and gasped, feeling like a fish out of water. Not a single soul approached to help.

And then it stopped. Cassian filled his aching lungs, wheezing. Muscles in his back strained, and all his strength disappeared instantly. He hunched over, feeling more ill than ever before. His feet hurt, the light blinded him, and he just wanted to sit down and lay his head against the wall. But he was in the presence of something beyond his understanding.

"What are you doing to me?" Cassian rasped.

"Are you ready to have a conversation?"

Forget appearing brave and in control. He sank to the floor, kicking his legs out and pulling the egg around to sit in his lap. Glass looked appalled, raising his hand and then dropping it again, and the Tsu'ran smiled, revealing her pointed teeth. "Better?" she asked.

Cassian nodded. The fight was gone. It took everything to keep his head up. The Tsu'ran were powerful. He knew they could harvest energy, but he'd never been on the receiving end of it. Out here, they simply referred to it as magic. Those who conquered *manipulating* energy and the waters were Sea Masters. Few ever earned that title because few ever lived long enough for it. Too many things went wrong for those who called upon forces beyond their understanding. Ships didn't carry books on energy or what it meant. All Cassian knew was that those who did use it, generally landwalkers, were messing with something that got men killed. It was bad luck to mess with those things out at sea. The waves carried their own type of magic, one that shouldn't be interfered with by the restless souls who sought more than what they needed.

"Where is the egg going?" the Tsu'ran demanded.

"Barnăl," Ali answered. She didn't sound so brave anymore.

"Saveen," Cassian countered.

The Tsu'ran raised her chin. "For what purposes?"

Nobody answered. Elliot cleared his throat. "Coin."

Thunder rumbled. This time, it was further away. The swaying ship settled some, silencing the storm sloshing around in Cassian's stomach. He swallowed the acidic taste of bile—the kind that creeps up from anxiety.

"You seek to bring the egg to Creitón," the Tsu'ran accused them all. "You seek to change destiny and challenge the ways of Gods."

"We don't wish to upset anything," Bauer quickly replied. His composure shook like that of a beaten boy who'd stolen from the wrong merchant. His voice, once deep and booming, was frail and hardly audible. "We were tasked with a job."

The Tsu'ran scoffed. "And yet, none of you understand the significance of your decisions." She was so disappointed that it saturated the cabin in a stifling stillness.

"We didn't know—" Bauer tried to speak, but the Tsu'ran raised a bony hand.

"Do not seek my sympathy for your ignorance," she hissed. "You have already altered destiny once. This egg should never have ended up on this ship." She shot Cassian a glare that could have resurrected the dead. There was meaning in it that was lost to him. "Do you intend to do the same again? Are you all Gods?"

Cassian raised his hand, drawing the attention to himself. Gods—all everyone did was pray and beg for these unseen deities to save them, to right the wrongs of men. When in reality, man had to correct their own mistakes. He told himself this, even as he tried to shake the memories of the encounters with the man in the alley, and the other in the captain's cabin on *Torment*. "Why does any of this matter to you? Why do you care about dragons and the affairs of landwalkers? Isn't it your sole concern to destroy ships that sail in the Grave?"

"I am not responsible for the ill-advised who travel this region," the Tsu'ran replied, so clearly disgusted by his question that she spat each word. "If you were king, would you let your enemy call your city their home?" The question went unanswered. "My kind have lived in these waters for centuries. We've seen empires rise, only to be destroyed. We've watched great tribes try to master these waters, only to be crushed by the sea. We are judgment, the keepers of balance, and it is our right to know when you carry a force as powerful as a dragon egg."

"I still don't understand," Cassian confessed.

"Of course you don't," the Tsu'ran said. "Dragons are the bridge between realms. They are the masters of both life-giving and death, harbingers of destruction and rebirth. As we *keep* the balance, they *enforce* the balance." She took a step forward, and the others retreated. Elliot knocked the table and looked like he wanted to melt into the wood for it. "You don't feel it, do you?" she asked the room.

This time, her voice was full of pity. Cassian didn't think the Tsu'ran were capable of anything but rage. Everyone shook their heads.

"The shift," the Tsu'ran said quietly. "The energies of the realms have moved. Change is upon us." She raised her chin. "The age of dragons has returned."

Cassian shook his head, which took far more effort than he was willing to admit. The cloaked man had said the same to him. Too many strange things were happening at once for his liking. He was paid for a job, not to solve life's mysteries. The longer he stayed on *Dread Deep*, the crazier his life became. All he wanted was to leave.

"Listen," Cassian said, hoping he sounded as confident as he wanted to be. "I'm not here to get a story from something that wants to eat my eyeballs. I've got a date with the king, and I intend to keep it. Your faith is not my concern—"

The Tsu'ran appeared before him instantly. Her skin rippled like water, dripping onto his own with a frigid touch that made his toes curl and heart stop. Now, Glass stepped forward, but she waved her hand, and he watched in horror as everyone else dropped to the floor with a nasty thump. The Tsu'ran's eyes turned yellow, and he shoved himself into the wall, clutching the egg with everything he had, begging to disappear.

Tentacles slithered over his jaw, tracing the scar. "I don't like you," she whispered.

"The feeling's mutual."

A small tentacle eased its way closer to his lips, reeking of rotten fish. "This ship has crossed far too many times in our territory. We don't want it here any longer."

He wanted to close his eyes. As fierce and terrifying as she was, he was more tired than he'd been in his whole life. "Then why don't you end us like the rest of the crew?"

The tentacle pried the corner of his mouth open, teasing, before retreating. Cassian gagged. The taste of sour slime coated his tongue. This creature was toying with him.

"Certain sea laws of our kind forbid it," she whispered. "I am bound to them, as you are."

All she did was talk in riddles. "Are we done here?"

"No." She sat on top of him, pinning him in place, and let her tentacles explore his arms and shoulders. He shuddered, keeping a firm grip on the egg. "I can't take that from you, though I wish I could."

"Is it part of your laws?"

"Yes." The egg kept him alive. He understood now. She leaned forward, too close for comfort. Cassian tensed as she inhaled next to his neck. "You've been marked." The statement was said with so much surprise that it startled him.

"Excuse me?"

"Marked." She straightened. The blue color in her eyes shifted to gray. Unnatural. "He's marked you."

She moved off him, never quite looking away, but moving as one does when they're uncertain. He should have felt relieved not to be killed or have his soul committed to serve her kind, but all he felt was terror. She looked *horrified*.

"What's going on? Who's marked me?" Cassian demanded and leaned forward, but she raised her hand. Tentacles shrunk and twisted, returning to webbed fingers.

"Pray," she insisted, nearing the door. "Pray for redemption and courage. You'll need it. Your soul is unclean—marked by *him*." A glance at the unconscious crew. "You must leave our waters. This ship is not welcome here." At that, she left, leaving the door open as she went. The rain had lightened into a drizzle. Lazy flashes filled the sky, followed by the low rumble of thunder.

Cassian looked between where she'd been and the egg. It burned in his hand, but he didn't let it go, certain that if he did, the Tsu'ran would return and snatch it from him and take his life. And he still needed answers. He nudged Elliot's face with his boot. The boy hardly reacted, but his nostrils flared. They were alive. He had thought so, but wanted to make sure of it.

Marked. He didn't know what that meant. All he knew was that it scared him. Was he sick? Did he have the Mad Man's Sickness? He sniffed himself. Besides the salt and sweat, he didn't smell sour—the kind of stench that comes when one is ill. Cassian inspected his arms, setting the satchel between his legs and yanking up his shirt, checking for any blackened spots indicating his impending demise. Nothing.

He pulled his wet boots off, peeling back the old leather like seaweed clinging to wood. No signs. Just wrinkled skin from sitting in a pocket of wet leather for too long. The sheath strapped to his calf was loose, having slipped a bit during the night's chaos, so he tightened it like a tourniquet. He stuffed his feet back in the soggy boots. If they were sailing out of here tonight, he couldn't leave these boots out to dry. Footrot was tomorrow's problem.

Sweat dripped into the corner of his eyes, burning. Cassian wiped at it, but found his hands were trembling fiercely. His fingers and toes tingled, going numb, and when he tried to stand, he found he couldn't. At once, his body locked up and his chest tightened. From fear or an illness, he didn't know. His head swam violently, muscles spasmed, and he couldn't get a full breath of air. Ribs refused to expand, his back locked into place, a sharp cramping pain holding him hostage. His hands fumbled, and he clawed at his neck, certain he was being strangled to death, but he felt nothing. Only the bulging veins in his neck as he strained for air. His breathing became loud gasps, and his vision narrowed.

He was frozen in place because terror consumed him. The emotion ravaged his senses, tearing apart the summers of confidence he'd built at sea. Cassian knew that now, recognized the fluttering of his heart and the way his mind went blank. It was the same sensation he'd had when his parents sold him into the hands of pirates.

Cassian grappled for the leather straps of the satchel, frantic to feel the egg. He yanked hard enough to snap the leather strapping and stuck his hand inside. Warmth engulfed his fingers as he laid them against the egg, seeping up his arm and through his entire body. By all the seas, it was amazing. His muscles relaxed, his chest loosened, and he leaned over, holding the egg against him. All he needed was some time to collect himself. To convince himself that everything he'd done so far would be worth it in the end when he got the payout.

Every decision Cassian had made since becoming captain had brought ill fortune. Bad luck followed fake captains—that's what the pirates said when anyone became captain without the proper steps. Cassian believed it now. His days had been filled with nothing but one disaster after the next. If he lived through this and got his payout from King Jair, he would take a break from heists.

His breathing slowed, finally becoming manageable. Cassian wanted to do the right thing—do the job he was paid to do—but he wasn't sure it was a good idea anymore. The harder he fought to make this heist work, the more damning his reality became. One problem after the next. *Torment* was gone, his crew dead, now he was being told he was marked by a demon from his nightmares.

A creeping thought crawled into the back of his mind, threatening to consume him if he didn't do something. *What if it wasn't a dream?*

He peeled himself off the floor, keeping the egg close. No, it couldn't be real. This nightmare of a man hadn't been real. Gods weren't real. They couldn't be. If they were, then Cassian would have to face the reality that his life wasn't as simple as he wanted it to be. That there were deities who could destroy cities and end wars with a flick of their wrists. He stepped over the bodies of the unconscious crew, hardly seeing them anymore. The fatigue gripping him was otherworldly, strangling him from the inside out, but he couldn't sit here any longer. He needed to find more liquor. A lot of it. Anything to get his mind off the dark and unforgiving place it was going.

The White Horn Promise

Cassian dug the dagger into the edge of the table. When he was satisfied with the damage, he pulled it out, then did it again. And again. Over and over, he burrowed the metal into the surface, chipping away at the layer of wood until he was halfway through the table. The egg sat in front of him. To his left, a half-empty bottle of Seaman's Water. He'd found it in the crew's quarters, along with ten other bottles and some other liquor he didn't recognize. Fang's Revenge. The creamy liquid had a pinkish color, so he avoided it. Royal liquor. Never quite did the trick like the rotgut he drank. He'd also found a small bundle of ground coffee that smelled divine.

The storm was nearly gone. As quickly as the Tsu'ran left, so, too, did the storm. The night was still on them, but based on Cassian's tired eyes and the shifting of the sky, he knew a bit of time had passed since he left the unconscious crew in the captain's cabin. Waves had settled, and the ship hardly swayed. The crew still hadn't woken when he found the liquor, so he made himself comfortable in the galley. Yes, *Dread Deep* had a galley—a proper one, not the cramped spaces found on White Horn ships with barrels for counters. Not that it was much, but far more than he'd ever seen on any other ship he'd been on. Must be a royal specialty. Cabinets were locked to keep from flying open, barrels were sealed and nailed to the ground to keep from rolling and deter pests, and boxes were stacked on the far side, full of fruits. He'd taken one look and decided against gorging himself. He wasn't here to eat. Should have—his stomach grumbled at the thought of food—but he couldn't bring himself to pick any fruit up. What he wanted was hot stew and fresh bread.

It had taken all his strength to make it to this part of the ship. When he opened the hatch to the deck below, he'd practically fallen because it was too much work. Each step was like pulling a dozen steeds. By the time he'd entered the galley, his head pulsated with agonizing force and his lungs hurt. Whatever the Tsu'ran had done was enough to cripple him. Terrifying. She'd not so much as lifted a finger at him, and he'd become nothing more than a sack of flour. An ugly, wet sack of flour that reeked of sea, sweat, and Seaman's Water.

In all his summers, he'd never seen magic at work. *Energy*. Landwalkers would bash him for using the wrong term. Whatever. It was black magic to him. Maybe Dark Energy, like that stranger said. He wasn't an expert in that stuff, though. Didn't want to be either. The Tsu'ran were creatures of the Grave, bidders for the Gods, and starved for souls. It's why they took the ships that traveled too close. The Grave was named so for a reason; the region was believed to be a home for the supernatural and traveled only by those with a death wish. Landwalkers thought differently, believed Gods were all-knowing, gave second chances to the wronged, blessed babies, and wanted to help the less fortunate where they could. Pirates didn't believe in that. Never had. The Red Queens were the only group of pirates Cassian knew who mixed their faith in the Red Goddess with their work at sea.

He took another swig. The tattoo on his hand was a terrible reminder of every mistake he'd made in the last six days. He didn't want to be captain anymore. He wanted out of all this. Wanted to turn back time to before Ricard was killed and be a simple seaman. At the time, he'd loathed it, but now, he missed the simplicity of his old life.

Maybe this plan of his wasn't a good idea. Maybe he should toss the egg into the sea and leave. Forget the coin, the king, everything. So much of his life had been up-ended. Too fast. Too harsh. He felt like a fraud. A murdering fraud. He'd lost *Torment* to a Life Eater. The more he reflected on the handful of days he'd carried the title, the more he was convinced he didn't deserve to wear it. To take the life of someone didn't bother him—he'd killed his first man at fourteen. But this was different. The crew on *Torment* had put their faith in him, and he was supposed to do right by them. A strange sensation clung to the back of his throat because of that. *Guilt.* Being captain meant carrying the responsibility of men's lives. Men he knew personally. Men agreed to this heist because they believed in him. These weren't strangers aboard *Torment*. They were his family.

Remorse wasn't something he quite knew how to handle. Regret didn't have room aboard the ship Cassian called his life. Those two emotions wrestled with each other, tugging at places he didn't know existed. Guilt reared its head, so hideous that he flinched in his chair, swallowing bile. He rubbed his face, desperate to claw those feelings out and toss them in a pit. He was a pirate—a damn good one—and that meant he needed to act like it. Thinking about the dead crew wouldn't get him anywhere. Nowhere good, at least. If he wanted to have a night alone with his pity, he could, but not here. Not aboard *Dread Deep*.

"You leave some for us?"

The voice startled him. Bauer stood in the entryway, looking like he'd crawled out of a pile of shit. Dark circles made his eyes appear sunken, his skin was sickly pale, and his clothes were mismatched. If Cassian didn't know better, he'd say the man had one too many and passed out sideways on the main deck overnight. But he hadn't. He'd been a victim of whatever spell the Tsu'ran stirred up. The woman-beast manipulated energy and shattered all sense of confidence of everyone on this ship. They might make it back to shore alive, but he doubted anyone would ever be the same.

"There's plenty to go around," Cassian replied. "It's your ship. You should know that."

"I know," Bauer said. Floorboards creaked as he approached and sat across from him. The chair groaned from the weight.

Cassian pulled the drink closer. "I'm not sharing this one."

"I didn't ask you to," Bauer replied.

"Good," Cassian spat and took another drink. No amount of liquor could make tonight forgettable. "And the others?"

"Slowly coming around," Bauer answered. He sounded as confused as Cassian felt.

Bauer didn't move. He was the last man Cassian wanted to spend any time with. The dagger in his right hand wavered, torn between continuing its ambush on the table or ambushing Bauer. Slicing his throat clean open would give Cassian a place to put his wrath.

The Gods, if they were truly real, would be appalled at Cassian's morals.

Bauer raised his brow and motioned at the egg. "You intend to sell it."

"You were going to sell it too," he replied coolly. "Don't think we're any different."

The crewman shrugged and leaned back. "We were fulfilling a pre-determined arrangement. Coin's already been exchanged." Bauer's smug manner only fanned the flames of Cassian's ugly temper. "You were making a deal. In that regard, we're different."

"Whatever helps you sleep." Cassian took another drink. The bottle was almost empty. He needed more, but he didn't want to get up and leave the egg with Bauer. Taking it with him to get more liquor might leave the wrong impression, not that he cared about making a good one.

Bauer shook his head. "It doesn't matter."

Cassian silently begged the man wouldn't continue.

"King will have our heads for this, anyway," Bauer mumbled.

Cassian bit his tongue, restraining himself from saying something sarcastic. A time and place existed for those comments, and he could sense now was not it. Glass would be proud of him.

"We told you who we work for," Bauer said. "Truth is, we're buying our way to freedom."

Damn. Now he had Cassian's attention. Anything to keep his thoughts from returning to his own failure. "Okay."

"We're not soldiers. We're prisoners. King knew how dangerous this was when he started these deliveries with *Dread Deep*. Didn't want to waste soldiers if ships went down carrying whatever it was being sold or traded. Well, like tonight." Bauer drilled the drink in Cassian's hand with a famished gaze, like he'd not tasted anything in a decade. "One more sail and we'd be free. Or so they told us."

"And you're prisoners, how?" In theory, it sounded great. "You're sailing across the world. You can go anywhere you want. Yet, you return to him?"

Bauer tapped his head. "Up here. Energy Harvester chained us. Keeps us from acting on those instincts. No matter how much I want to, I won't act on it. My body freezes. The only thing I can do is work this ship, sail between ports, and return."

Energy Harvester. Bauer was a landwalker. "You're telling me you can't go anywhere because of magic?"

"Energy," Bauer corrected. "Respect the proper term, please."

The dagger dug deeper into the wood. "Okay. Energy. So how does that work?" Cassian asked.

"A ritual. One that's been forbidden across most of the Vore World. They call it the Krisár ritual. The Harvester drank my blood during his recital of texts, then he carved a sigil in my back, branding me." Bauer said it like he was talking about supper, not his fate.

Cassian waved the bottle. "Why does that matter?"

"Bonds us," he explained. "He's always in my head. Even when he's not there. He can find me anywhere at any time."

"For all of you?"

He nodded.

Cassian couldn't believe his ears. No wonder this ship turned out the way it did. It was cursed with these people on it. That kind of magic wasn't meant for the sea. "Can I see?" Curiosity had a stronger hold on him than fear. He wanted to make sure this man wasn't lying.

Bauer shrugged and twisted in his chair. He pulled up his shirt, displaying scarred skin and a blackened mark on the top of his back. Two lines intertwined, met with a crescent moon over them. He'd never seen such a mark. "Is that Old Tongue?" Cassian asked.

"The language of Gods," Bauer said, turning around. The sliver of peace they'd had moments prior was gone, replaced by a stifling unease that turned the air sour. "Some believe if you know the language well enough, you can channel energy through it. After what I've seen, I think they're right."

Cassian twirled the dagger where it was. "You speak of this like you're okay with it. But that scar looks new."

That forced a strained smile. "I've been paying my sentence off for a decade."

Blood drained from his head, no doubt paling him. A hollowness blossomed in Cassian's chest, turning his limbs cold. Slowly, he slid the liquor bottle over. Bauer took it without a word, taking a large drink. "Then how does that scar look the way it does?" Cassian asked.

"A gift," he replied. "If you're into twisted ones. Every tenth day, the scab reopens, and it's like a fresh cut all over again. Keeps the skin from healing. I've gotten used to the feeling now."

Bauer slid the bottle back. Cassian took it gratefully. "So if this man can sense you all, wouldn't he know what happened tonight?"

"I'm afraid so." Now he sounded meek, a horrible contrast to his large build. "Once the king knows . . . well, I don't know what will happen."

Cassian slowly nodded, curious. "How do you become a prisoner like this? What did you do to earn such a screwed-up fate?"

Bauer scoffed. "Random choice. Soldiers walk the dungeon hall and pick whoever they think the king might approve. I got lucky." He shrugged, but grief flashed across those sunken eyes. Bauer hated his life. Prisoners. Cassian was gobsmacked. The poor fools were bound to serve until they were released from whatever horrors were inflicted by a Krisár ritual. He'd never heard of such a thing. Everyone was a prisoner of something, he supposed. Cassian was imprisoned by the sea, unable to break the habits he'd been raised with. Glass, Elliot, Ricard, Jules, the old captain on Greve's Point he'd given Krye, too. Some prisons were self-inflicted. Others were imposed. The self-inflicted prisons were far worse, he'd concluded. Anyone could convince themselves of just about anything, and that was dangerous.

"Do you think the Tsu'ran will return?" Bauer asked. His voice trembled just slightly.

Cassian grimaced. No, they wouldn't. The creature told him he was marked, practically ran out the door once she realized it, too. Told him he needed to pray. To whom? The very Gods who ignored him? Who let *Torment* be destroyed and the crew aboard be killed by the Life Eater? If Gods were real, then why did they let so many horrible things happen to Cassian? Landwalker religion. That's what it was.

"No," Cassian finally said. "She was pretty satisfied with her threat. Just wants us to leave."

"Then we should get on that," Bauer replied like the men shared a brotherhood. He reached for the egg. Possessiveness consumed Cassian, so powerful that it blinded his logic and turned him into a savage animal. The next part happened before Cassian could think it through. He drove the dagger through Bauer's hand, burrowing it into the wood and pinning the man's hand in place. It happened so fast that the crewman didn't cry out, even as blood leaked out from the torn muscle and skin. Bone had broken, too. Cassian had heard the crunch, felt the jarring snap as the blade cut through the bones like brittle branches. Cassian pulled the egg closer to him, staring at his deed.

"Have you lost your mind?" Bauer roared. The chair squealed as he got up. He hunched over the blade and attempted to yank it out without causing more damage. "I'm going to kill you. No. I'm tossing you overboard to the Tsu'ran. Let them have their way with you." The last bit was said in a whisper so low that if not for the silence, the words would have sunk into the floorboards, never to be heard.

Cassian laughed, hollow. The Tsu'ran didn't even want him. They wouldn't come close to this ship after what the Tsu'ran had told him. Marked like some animal for slaughter. That's how it felt. The egg was warm, sucking out the cold sensation crawling through his body. He'd just stabbed Bauer for trying to just touch the egg. He blinked, disoriented at how fast he'd just acted. How wildly he'd acted. Cassian was reckless, but he was calculative about even the most life-threatening decisions. What he'd just done didn't feel like him. It felt like someone else had just possessed him—like someone else was sailing the ship that was Cassian's body.

But he didn't want anyone to steal the egg, that much was true. Coin was coin, and he intended to get the payout. Damn the rest of the crew. He wanted out. The Krye would give him that. People like Bauer threatened his freedom.

"Long night," Cassian whispered, trying to convince himself that what he'd just done was acceptable. It wasn't. When he killed or harmed someone, he knew exactly what he was doing—he was in *control*. But not now. Now he felt as untamed as the landwalkers believed pirates were. "Sorry."

"You lying swab." Bauer yanked the blade out and clutched his hand close to his chest, surveying the clean entry and exit. He'd be unable to do most of the work on the ship now, maybe forever. Tendons and muscles wouldn't obey. He'd be best manning the wheel. He raised the bloody dagger at Cassian, nostrils flaring and veins bulging, skin hot like a cannon ready to fire. "I've had one screwed up night. You're really pissing me off."

"Why don't we call it a night, yeah?" Cassian suggested. His muscles were tight enough to tear if he moved the wrong way. "Call this a mistake and just go on our way?"

"You just stabbed my hand clear through," Bauer snapped, "and you want to call it a night?" He gestured at the egg with the knife. "That isn't yours. It never was."

"I know." No, he didn't. He wanted it. It was his.

"So hand it over," Bauer said.

"No."

"I think I'll cut your tongue out first." Bauer shook his head, glaring. "You talk too much."

Cassian scoffed. "You're the one who talked this entire time. I didn't ask for your pitiful story." Before Bauer could lunge across the table, Cassian added, "Okay, how about this. You need to bandage that up, and I need to collect myself. Why don't you do that, and I'll keep the egg for the night. Tomorrow, we can work out who watches the egg and when. Set a schedule. Get everyone together and figure that out. That way no one feels left out. Sound good?"

It sounded terrible. Cassian wouldn't let anyone watch the egg. He didn't trust them, not even Elliot. But that was tomorrow's problem. Tonight, he was just trying to stay awake. The liquor had worsened the headache and the fatigue. If Bauer didn't leave him alone, Cassian would drive a blade into his heart next.

The dagger wavered. Prisoner or not, Bauer wasn't a fighter. He just wanted to do a job. Cassian saw right through the man's bravado the moment his shoulders slumped. No real pirate would have let this confrontation slide for a night. They'd have ended up in a brawl or with one of them dead. That was the culture of pirates. Problems hardly ever went unresolved. If trouble existed between crewmembers, they could settle it with bloodshed.

Bauer tossed the dagger on the table with a clank. Blood splattered, and the weapon slid to the edge of the table before it fell to the floor as the ship swayed slightly, landing next to Cassian's boot. The crewman glared, jaw set, before he hissed, "Dawn is fast approaching, pirate. I sure hope the dead drag you into the Afterlife before then."

Bauer left the galley, cursing all the way. Bloody drops followed him. Cassian sat, stunned at the turn of events. His hands felt foreign to him. He felt like a bystander in his own body, like someone had just possessed him to stab Bauer. He didn't like that sensation—like he wasn't in control of his own actions. All this for an egg. He downed the rest of the liquor and set the bottle aside. In the silence that followed, his eyes burned from exhaustion. Holding the egg felt like he was trying to wrestle a Firóle, a giant serpent of the ancient era. Slowly, he leaned down and pressed his ear against the eggshell. He listened.

Thump, thump.

Cassian jumped back. A heartbeat. He didn't imagine that. Couldn't have. He leaned down again, and again, he heard the heartbeat. Strong, bold, and loud. So loud that he expected the awakened crew to come storming in and asking what that noise was. The dragon's pulse raced with his own, booming like cannons until it was all he could hear.

He shook his head. He needed to find a cot and lie down, reign in his impulses. If he killed the remaining crew on this ship, *Dread Deep* would never make it out of the Grave. Everything could be dealt with once he slept off whatever the Tsu'ran did to ravage his body and mind. Cassian wanted to stay awake, but his thoughts were turning to sludge—sour sludge that frayed his patience and made it hard to focus on anything but how hard it was to keep his eyes open. A stewing pot of impatience and irritation was all he was. Useless.

The dagger on the ground was bloody, but he didn't care. He swooped it up and stuffed it back in its sheath, feeling the cool blood squish against the fabric of his pants. As he stood, he knew the ship needed to move. The Tsu'ran had warned him. The remaining shipmates were all just as desperate to get out of here. The need to leave these waters made his stomach twist and his hands itch for a job to do on *Dread Deep* to keep busy. Clean cannons, sharpen weapons, feed the animals aboard. Anything. Yet, he couldn't bring himself to care enough to put forth the effort. He was marked, after all—whatever that meant. The sea demons weren't coming for him or this ship. Damn them all. The fight in him was gone. Maybe he had come down with Mad Man's Sickness, and this was how it started. Hallucinations and black rotten pieces of flesh would come next. Maybe he'd see that dead man from his nightmares again. Perhaps he was wrong—what if that was some landwalker God?

He stopped himself. His thoughts were spiraling. Cassian needed privacy. Silence. Sleep. When he awoke, he could deal with things more clearly.

Dragon's Blood

Muscles ached like he was fighting a ravaging fever. Cassian shifted in his place on the cot, shivering. The thin blanket provided was worthless—better suited to a small woman or a child, not one of his stature—but he still tucked it around himself regardless. When that didn't work, he curled up in a fetal position, arms tucked into his chest. His skin was icy to the touch, and sweat soaked through the straw mattress. He felt like he'd been trampled by a steed, and every time his head shifted, he was greeted by the brutal throb of the worst headache of his life. The Tsu'ran keelhauled his mind, stripped him of his pride, and left him useless. The crew would seek him out eventually, but he'd be unable to help sail in this condition.

Liquor had made his stomach worse. Nausea threatened him every time he so much as twitched. He swallowed the rising bile. There was no bucket or chamber pot in the cabin as far as he could tell, and he couldn't bring himself to search for one. Maybe this sickness would pass by dawn, and he'd not have to tell anyone. Maybe he just needed some rest.

Sounds in the dark. A crack, silence, then another. The dead were coming for him. For once, Cassian wasn't afraid. All he wanted was peace and sleep. If this was how Death came, then so be it. Or he was hallucinating from the fever and would be dead by the morning. He turned over, back facing the narrow room. He didn't want to see how he died. He just wanted the suffering to finally end.

Consciousness came and went without warning, yet another battle where he couldn't defend himself. His body was in control, his mind a mere bystander to his wants and needs. Thoughts moved as slow as crawlers on the sea floor, and instincts took to the shadows. An enemy could march in here and end him where he lay, and he'd never be able to defend himself. Cassian gulped in air, stilled, and slept restlessly.

Scratching. Clicking. Muffled sounds welcomed Cassian back to the present. He blinked, groggy, feeling slightly better. Still felt like shit, but it was manageable. His mind worked a bit faster. The blanket covering him shifted.

He froze. More scratching. In the dark, it sounded to his ailing mind like the dead were peeling their way through the floorboards, opening a pit to drag him through. The lantern hanging to his left didn't give much light from this angle. Facing the wall, he was left to make conclusions he didn't want to make. The Tsu'ran. They were back. Or whoever marked him had finally come to take their prize. Maybe it was the man from the captain's cabin dream, after all.

That forced air in. Heart hammering, he mustered the courage to turn over so that he could see what the noises were. Maybe rats. Ships were prone to such things; especially if the food source remained open to the air. Occasionally, rats even ate rats when food got slim. The weak were cornered and killed by their brethren, their carcasses found scattered around the lower decks. Cassian recalled finding a group of them munching away on one of their own in the crew's quarters. Bloody snouts with greasy gray fur, they turned their black orbs right at him, as if challenging him to come closer. He was only fourteen at the time, but it scared him. Took him a few nights to go back there, and when he did, he found the body picked clean of all blood and muscle.

Every now and then, he still dreamed of those rats. Could feel them crawling over with their scaly claws, poking at him with cold snouts and whiskers. Cassian shuddered. That's what it had to be. Rats. *Dread Deep* was infested with them.

He should get up, go get some coffee to sober himself up, and try and help where he could. Coffee was a staple on ships. Kept the crew going after heavy nights of drinking. Sometimes the liquor was awful—didn't get men drunk or taste good—and it caused more problems than good. Ships kept coffee aboard, stored away in small boxes, ready to be used whenever they needed to sharpen their senses. He could use some now. The coffee on *Dread Deep* was probably the kind that kings drank. This was not a pirate ship. Just an expensive attempt to look like one. A good ship, though. Cassian wouldn't deny that. Sturdy, strong, and big. Any pirate would pay a good fee for one like this.

Something tugged at the blanket. Cassian went rigid. That wasn't a rat, unless it was the biggest one he'd ever come across. A thump, scratch, and squeak. What the—

The blanket was ripped off, leaving him vulnerable and shivering. He shoved himself back, no longer brave enough to ignore whatever godforsaken rat chose him to be its next meal. Feet tucked up underneath him, he grabbed the dagger to his right. He'd gut the damn thing and feed it to the creatures of the sea. Dagger in hand, he scooched over and reached for the lantern. No way he'd trek across the room without it. Rats hid under the cots, and when they wanted to, they raced out and attacked the toes.

He stole a glance toward where his blanket lay in a heap on the floor. A red tail slithered underneath, larger than any rat he'd ever heard of. Cassian gasped, hand smashing into the lantern and knocking it right off the hook.

It crashed to the floor, spilling oil. He lunged for it. Flames flickered, fighting for life. One leaped to the oil on the floor, dancing. Great. Now he'd set the ship on fire. Cassian patted his hand against the flame frantically, skin searing. Oil splattered all over the place, and flames clung to his skin. Panic set in. Heat bubbled up. Cassian cursed every name he could think of, smashing his hand against the wood until the flames were quenched. Once they died, he cradled his hand. Already, he could feel the harsh blisters gnawing their way over the palm and fingers.

He sat there with the lantern to his right. A red tail? Preposterous. Tired. That's what he was. He was hallucinating, feverish, and just needed to go back to bed. Damn the crew and helping them sail. *Dread Deep* moved—he could feel it in the floorboards—and they'd not come for his help, and he didn't want to offer. He wanted—no, *needed*—the silence. His head felt like it would split in two, like one wrong move might cause his heart to give out. He was more alert, but he felt strange. Skin prickled where it shouldn't, his ears picked up a hum that he'd not heard before, and his fingers buzzed with anticipation.

The silhouette of the satchel hanging from its place on the wall was still there, which meant the egg would be, too. He felt absurd. Cassian was usually so much more put together. Nothing ever got under his skin, ever troubled him. Now, he was a disaster. Everything startled him, he was unable to control his emotions, and he didn't know what he wanted anymore.

More sleep would help with that. Cassian grabbed the lantern and set it upright. The light swept over the bottom of the cot, revealing a fiery eye and ruby-colored scales. He gasped and scrambled backward.

A squeak followed, childlike and playful. He kept the lantern close, squinting into the dark where the creature hid. The dagger in his hand was all he had. The door was to his right. He could bolt for it and go find help. Or he could face this like a damn pirate and move on with his night. Too many strange things were happening at once. All he needed was a day to himself. A break.

The creature snorted. Cassian raised his blade, hand shaking, but he kept it aimed at where he thought the beast was sitting. The lantern's flame was weakened from the fall, flickering relentlessly. It would go out soon. Too much oil was spilled, which meant he needed to get this over with while he could still see.

"Well, come on," Cassian demanded. "Too scared?"

Silence. Cassian didn't sound as bold as he wanted to be. His damp clothes reeked of stale sweat, his tongue was sour, and crusties clung to his eyes and lips. Nothing about this screamed *pirate captain*. He should be sleeping off this sickness, not shouting at vermin in the darkness. Maybe he was losing his mind.

The wood creaked, responding to the weight of the creature. Something dragged, probably its tail, and he immediately knew from the sound that it approached him. Blade held steady, he waited, readying himself. He'd kill it and then throw it overboard, go back to bed, and not think about it again. Too many problems and not enough headspace for it.

"Come on," Cassian whispered. "Don't be a coward."

At the edge of where the light reached, a foot appeared. Black talons and red scales. The tiny foot connected to a body, complemented by leathery red wings tucked close. Small bulbous horns jutted out along the spine and neck, stretching down to the tail. At the end was a stub of tiny horns. A mace, of sorts. Narrow horns decorated the jaw, curving down. The nostrils flared. A forked tongue flicked out of the tiny maw.

A dragon. He was staring at a dragon.

Cassian looked at the satchel, unable to see as clearly as he needed to. The bulge of the egg seemed diminished. Cassian studied an object on the ground below the satchel. A piece of an eggshell. He didn't need to crawl to it to know that. Every part of his being knew what'd happened. The dragon that he'd been carrying around finally hatched. The timing couldn't be worse.

"Shoo." Cassian waved his blade, trembling. "Go." He was supposed to get a payout, not have the dragon hatch. No matter how brave he wanted to be, he couldn't be. Cassian wanted to reverse time, return to Greve's Point before he met King Jair. He would have never gone into Shade's Pub if this was how his life was going to go.

The dragon took a step forward. Cassian pressed himself against the wall. The baby was no longer than his forearm. Cute, if not for the horrifying reality setting in. "Don't," he warned. "I'm not your friend or your mother. Get back." He didn't know how this worked. Did dragons imprint? It didn't matter. He was infuriated. The Krye. All the coin he'd been promised was as good as gone. King Jair wanted an egg, not a baby dragon. Maybe he'd still pay, though. By the sea, Cassian hoped so.

This could still work. It would just be a little more complicated.

The beast took another step forward. Too close. Cassian was nervous, so he scooted to the left, closer to the eggshells. The dragon watched him. The slit pupil contracted, dilated, then the baby tilted its head, curious. How'd Cassian know it was curious? He didn't know. Didn't care. Maybe his mind was making things up to try and make sense of this madness.

He picked up the eggshells. Cold to the touch. He tossed the piece at the dragon. The creature squeaked, excited, and picked up the shell between its teeth. It tossed it into the air, then threw it at Cassian. He slapped the shell out of the way.

The dragon jumped at him. Cassian yelped and pulled himself to his feet, scrambling before it could reach him. Shoved against his cot, he raised his dagger higher. "You're screwing things up for me. Did you know that?"

The baby chuffed at him.

Agitation burned as hot as the blisters. Everything was going wrong. Why did everything he tried to do go so horribly awry? He wasn't good at anything. A captain of seven days, a dead crew, and now a failed heist because the stupid dragon hatched. How could he explain this to King Jair? The crazed king would slit his throat before he got a sentence of explanation in.

He slumped down. Dragon or not, he needed to rest. Strength was a luxury, and it was quickly seeping out of his bones as the reality of his predicament settled in on him like a fog on a coastal city. His life was ruined. Might as well take a moment to collect himself, and if the dragon decided to eat him, well, so much the better.

Cassian was in the presence of a real, living dragon. All the stories he'd heard from drunks weren't just tall tales. He recalled hearing about Dragon Rider fights, the wars that ended because Dragon Riders became involved. The Hil War, a pirate-driven war, ended because the Dragon Riders struck a deal, providing pirates with what was now called Greve's Point. Those stories felt more real now than the ship Cassian sat on.

Dragons were real. He was looking at one—a hatchling. He knew the beast would eventually be large—too big to be in this room, or even this ship. If stories proved true, the dragon would be large enough to crush a city. Cassian was stunned. A breathing dragon would change everything. It would not disrupt just his deal with King Jair; it would change the world.

The dragon nudged the blanket, then flared its wings as it teetered. Cassian shook his head, suppressing a laugh. Damn thing *was* cute, he'd give it that. The carving he'd been working on was probably in the belly of a fish by now. Who knew? Now that he was looking at the real thing, he could see that some of his details were off. The proportion of the body with the wings, and how long the snout of the carving was versus what he saw now. The creature investigated its surroundings, sniffing the floor and then his boots. It pulled away and shook its head.

"That bad, huh?" The dragon tilted its head. Did it understand him? "Hello."

It made a pitiful attempt at a roar, but the sound was more akin to a rat being strangled to death. It hopped on the cot. Cassian set the lantern down on the bedside table—if one could call a shelf that—and tucked the dagger back into its sheath still strapped around his calf. Unnecessary. He bared his hands. "Harmless. See?"

In response, the creature flared its wings and dipped its head. Its own way of displaying it meant no harm, or so he hoped. Cassian knew little about dragons. He knew they liked meat and could blow fire. To some extent, he believed they could communicate, or else the Dragon Riders would never have thrived. But his knowledge was slim and built from drunken stories. Even then, he'd shaken them off. Here he was, acting like he knew what this dragon was saying. Damn it, he *did*. He might not know *how* he knew, but he *knew*.

The dragon observed him with its fiery eyes. It took another step forward, obviously cautious not to scare him off again. Cassian didn't move. The scales looked soft to the touch. How long had this little one been in that egg? Dragons hadn't been around in centuries, so he could only assume the little creature had been in there for just as long. He didn't know why it hatched now. Maybe all the commotion got it interested, or maybe it was scared. The Tsu'ran's influence reached beyond the dead. And they'd known about the egg. She'd said dragons enforced balance, whatever that meant.

Another step. Cassian offered his uninjured hand, palm upward. He waited.

The dragon blew hot air onto his skin. The warmth tickled, and Cassian almost pulled his hand away from the overwhelming thrill that threatened to make him scream. He was going to touch a dragon. The crew would lose their minds. Probably wouldn't believe him either.

"Come on," Cassian urged. "I won't do anything."

Hesitation. And then it pressed its soft snout against his hand. A chill clutched his spine with a bone-gripping hold and yanked him to the floor. Cassian coughed, splintered wood piercing his blistered hand, and tried to move, but couldn't. He shook, muscles twisting and frantic, vision blackening, and groaned. His head was being split into two again. An all-knowing presence shoved itself into areas of his mind that he'd never explored, excavating every aspect of him and leaving it out for display. Emotions he'd stomped out resurfaced—agony, betrayal, rejection—and memories...from the grandest moments to the smallest . . . stampeded through his mind. He felt and saw everything at once. Tears burned a path down his cheeks like rivulets of lava. Where the dragon touched, his hand went numb.

More memories. So much more. *He was isolated in darkness, quietly observing a world beyond his own, aware of everything. Stuffed in the dragon egg, cramped and suspended by a membrane that kept him safe. Carried and exchanged. Felt countless hands hold him before being returned to his place in a chest. Heard the greatest dragon roars an era had ever seen, never quite capable of responding in his state. Muffled voices, yells, a fall.*

He was disoriented and alarmed at the rising threat in the world that promised to keep him safe. Then he was shuffled to another place, passed to more hands. And then nothing.

No. Not he. *She. She'd* been placed into a small room in the Kalic palace, forgotten about for centuries. A souvenir for rulers long dead. Polished only to impress the royal guests. She'd slept, submitting herself into a state of slumber reserved for long waits. For she did wait. And when hands once more picked her up, she was awakened from that sleep, eager to see the world that once believed in her. She wanted to hatch. The waiting was no longer pleasant. Her wings were cramped, her legs suspended in the membrane that protected her. Nobody felt right, though. Nobody responded to her calls. Her lifeforce.

Cassian's body had responded to the dragon's summons. Her energy had seeped into him, warming him and altering his mind and body, preparing him for what was to come. His body wasn't used to how her lifeforce—the energy that made up who the dragon was—squirmed in his unfamiliar body, making him ill. But she couldn't wait any longer.

His mind stretched beyond what he thought possible. Terror filled him. He was everywhere and nowhere, on land and at sea. Hundreds of voices screamed at him. Others whispered, tempting. Every emotion rushed him, suffocating him from the inside out. When he tried to grab his mind and reel it back in, he couldn't. Something prevented him. A barrier. *She* did.

The presence blossomed, cocooning him instantly. The weightlessness dissipated, replaced by the grounding sensation of home. The ship swayed underneath, gentle, and his muscles contracted every so often, no longer a fretful seizure. His ribs hurt with each inhalation, expanding beyond their comfort, but he didn't care. It felt like he'd not breathed in centuries.

His hands were bundled into tight fists, knuckles white. He couldn't find the ability to move, though he wanted to. He'd give anything to peel himself off this floor and lie on the soft cot, but he couldn't find the strength. The dragon's fiery eyes came back into view. The presence in his head grew so loud that it felt like he couldn't hear himself think. He blinked. Drool oozed from his mouth, pooling beneath him.

She nudged his arm as if sensing his wants. When he didn't move, she licked his cheek. Cassian's body still wasn't his own. The gnawing headache turned the liquor in his stomach into a sloshy mess. The throbbing around his eyes felt like he'd taken a dagger and carved his name into skin. The numbness in his hand faded, leaving in place a dull ache that was quickly overshadowed by the other pains. Every part of him hurt, even his toes. Moving was impossible.

The dragon blew hot air on his face. Now she was persistent. He moaned a response. She didn't move. Instead, she walked over and curled up against his chest. Warmth radiated over him, soothing his muscles. Everything he wanted to say and do vanished into blissful blackness.

PART 2

"The birth of a hero is forged in betrayal."
~The Vorelian Scrolls

Silver is the Color of Dread

Cassian groaned. He could hear the swells splash against the ship, feel them as his body lulled in response to the sway. His back was locked into place, having fallen asleep on the floor on his stomach. Strength returned, and he opened and closed his hands, remembering the burn. Blinking, he cleared his foggy vision to see the red splotches along his right hand. He stared, recalling the blisters he'd both felt and seen the night before. Where were they now? The healing skin appeared to be days old already. Had he slept that long? Impossible. The crew would have broken down his door and hauled him off the floor.

A mark on his left hand caught his attention. Just above the thumb. A dark crescent-shaped burn that left his skin puckered and discolored. He touched it. No pain. A bit tender, but nothing serious. He wasn't sure how or when he'd done—

Memories crashed around him like a torrential rain, drenching him in every emotion he'd forgotten. *Torment's* demise, the Life Eater, the Tsu'ran, her warning, being on *Dread Deep*, and the dragon.

"Shit." He sat up fast, head swaying violently. His vision went in and out. Everything still hurt. His head pulsed like its own heartbeat, swelling and contracting in a frenzy. He held his head in his hands, wanting to squeeze the sensation out. He wondered if he'd ever have a day without a splitting headache again. His mind swayed like a ship on a violent sea, and his stomach clenched, nauseous from the sensation. He opened and closed his hands again. They were fine, save for the strange mark at the base of his thumb on his left hand. Cassian scratched at the raised dark pinkish mark, confused. He surveyed the skin on his right where the burn had been from last night. Gone. Where blisters should have been, red skin puckered but painless. It looked like his hand had been healing for days already.

Skittering. Talons against wood. A small burp. Cassian twisted and saw the dragon sitting before him, on her haunches. Behind, half of his leather boot was destroyed. "You're kidding." Annoyance flared fiercely. He liked those boots. They were actually his, not stolen. Paid for them and everything. It was the left boot, which was a small relief. The sheath to his dagger tucked into the right boot. How would he explain away a half-chewed boot? Leather pieces littered the floor. The dragon tried to eat them before spitting them back out.

You're awake.

The voice was sudden, female and soft. It pierced his mind and made his headache worse, like fingers had just sunk into his head and shredded his thoughts. Cassian whipped his head around in search of it. The door was closed. It was just the two of them. He opened his mouth, certain he was hallucinating again, when the dragon stepped forward.

I'm hungry.

"Is that you in my head?" The question came out in an unfiltered shock. Cassian's voice shook, squeaked, and adrenaline surged through him at the rate of a man charging toward his death. The presence in his head shifted, cautious and curious, but familiar. The same as last night. The one whose memories he'd experienced. "No," he whispered. "No, no, no—"

The dragon approached. Fear and uncertainty pulsed through his veins, making him want to get up and run. These were not his emotions. They were hers bleeding into his mind. She was scared because of his reaction—scrambling back and saying no. The pain of rejection in her eyes. Cassian knew what rejection felt like. He didn't need to be in the dragon's head to grasp that. Her head dipped, her wings drooped, and she stepped backward. Never in his life had he felt so horrible for his behavior. Never had he thought he'd feel this much wrenching guilt for anything. The sensation gutted him from the inside out, turned his innards into dust, and shredded his heart into a thousand pieces. The feelings were foreign, instant. He felt like a parent staring at their hurt child, and he didn't understand how to process the suddenness of the remorse that wiggled through his chest. He wanted to soothe the dragon's heartache, tell her it would be all right. He'd make it so. But the words didn't come out right away, couldn't. They were lodged in his throat, stuck behind the building rage that suffocated the guilt in one fiery sweep. This was not how his life was supposed to go.

Knocking broke the spell. "Cassian. Are you in there?"

Glass. Cassian gaped. How could he tell him the egg hatched and now the dragon was talking to him *in his head*? No matter. He just would. Cassian needed another person, someone he could confess to. They'd figure out a plan, get out of this, and find a way to get coin for this creature. Anyone would pay a pretty amount of coin for a living dragon. Probably more. That thought bolstered his confidence, and he stood. Not three steps into crossing the room, the flaps of wings were followed by talons on his back. Cassian yelped, turned around, and clawed at the dragon clinging to his back. His foot slammed into the wall, toes bending abruptly.

"Cassian?" The door groaned as Glass tried to open it, but it wouldn't budge. "Locked doors?" he grumbled. "Wretched royal ship."

"Yea—"

You can't. The utter terror in her voice forced him to pause. When he stopped fighting, she loosened her grip on his tunic. The fabric of his shirt was shredded. He could feel the draft along his shoulders. Another thing destroyed.

She looked at him. In that gaze, he saw a hundred different unsaid things. Things no creature as small and new to this world should feel. She was freshly hatched, but she carried herself as if she'd watched a hundred wars and a thousand rebirths. Cassian blinked, shaken by his volatile emotions. He didn't understand. One moment, he didn't think twice about still selling the dragon. The next, he felt like he was looking at an old friend, hoping to never be parted. The pulsing headache lessened as her presence shifted once more, settling into place like she'd always been th ere.

Your eyes.

Cassian blinked, confused. "My—what?"

"Are you okay?" Glass asked.

"No—yes." The dragon clung to him like a bird on a branch while he searched for a mirror or a shard of glass stuffed somewhere. They were left to help see sea spirits. Then again, this wasn't a true pirate ship. He couldn't recall the last time he slept on a cot and not a hammock. This ship was built for transporting passengers comfortably.

Cassian searched the chests at the foot of each cot, the dead's belongings. He saw a belt that looked nice. He'd come back to it. His was getting pretty worn out, and where the sword sheath sat, the leather strained to hold now. In the back of one chest, he found a small round mirror. The item was common on most ships. Anyone who knew the sea knew they were required aboard.

When the dead started talking, sometimes the only way anyone could see them was through the reflection of a mirror. Having a mirror in hand helped men and women move about the ship at night when the voices got too loud. They'd use it to check for restless spirits around corners, in rooms, and in storage areas. If a soul was pacing, they'd leave and come back another time. Any ship that didn't have mirrors was damned. Stumble on a room full of the restless dead and nobody would stand a chance. The living would all go mad.

Cassian raised it to his face, watching the color drain as he beheld silver eyes. Not the amber color he'd had—the hue that revealed a heritage in Creitón. No. The man who stared back at him was a stranger. He brought the mirror closer. The silver was bright, almost metallic. It contrasted against his olive skin the way a jewel stands atop a crown—proud. He blinked. Still there. Rubbed his eyes as hard as he dared. Same color.

Paralyzing panic bubbled up within him. He couldn't show himself. Not like this. The crew would think he was cursed and sacrifice him. Probably stab him where he stood and gouge his eyes out while he bled out. He didn't know what was happening to him. If he didn't have answers, the crew would make their own. And they never ended well.

"Are you dead?" Glass asked.

"What? No," Cassian called back. He couldn't go out there. "I'm . . . I don't know what happened. I'm ill. I can't get up. I think that Tsu'ran did something to me." It was more than that. His life was falling apart. Was this what the Tsu'ran meant when she told him he was marked? The changes he was experiencing, the illness—all of it made his knees weak. She'd gotten into his head. If he prayed like she demanded he should, he'd beg whatever deity that listened to go back in time and turn this all around. Before Ricard was killed.

"You feelin' okay? You sound strange."

"Huh?" Cassian drew his eyelids apart in the mirror. "I'm fine. I mean, I will be fine. I just need some sleep."

"You been sleeping for a day."

None of this looked good for him. "I have?"

"Yeah. Hey, why don't I bring you coffee—"

"No," Cassian interrupted. The dragon's talons dug into his skin, and he hissed. "I'm going back to sleep."

"The crew—"

"Damn them." Now, his temper flared. He didn't care how he sounded anymore. "Give me some time, okay?" They'd manage. A nice headwind would make even the smallest crews work with a little bit of effort. Based on the movement of the ship beneath his feet, he was willing to bet they'd done just fine without him. Good.

"Uh, okay." Steps retreated. Cassian tossed the mirror onto the pile of possessions he'd made.

He needed to figure out what to say and what to do. He couldn't stay here forever, but he would buy his time as long as he could. "These aren't going away, are they?"

The dragon nudged his arm, the way a small child would if they knew they were in trouble. "Don't look at me like that." He kicked the pile away from him, not wanting to see his reflection in the mirror that sat on top. It only served as a sour reminder that his life was ruined.

He'd made jokes about that already—cruel and sick jokes that he didn't laugh at—but this one hit differently. This made him lightheaded, his heart fluttery, and icy-cold panic shoved a hand into the deepest parts of his soul and ripped it out. No half-eaten boot or hatched egg would matter once the crew saw him. No story he told would change how they viewed him. That he'd cursed them and this ship, that he was trying to take the coin all for himself. Pirates only ever cared about one thing: surviving. And he knew this crew of prisoners lived by the same mantra. No one sailed these waters for the view. At this point, it was about living another day. Bauer proved that with his story of enslavement, forced through blood and dark practices to be a carrier for the king's orders. Ali, Sanser, and Edward were all the same. They'd kill Cassian before they let his mistakes ruin their chance at surviving.

He rubbed his face, more out of sheer desperation to claw an answer out of his skin than anything else. Anger made his blood hot, and he punched the wall. Wood protested but remained in place. His knuckles felt tender, so he did it again. And again. He did it until wood turned red and his knuckles were a bloody pulp. He did it until he couldn't see anymore and sank to the floor. His hand was numb, and blood pooled between his fingers and trickled to the floorboards. How could he ever get himself out of this mess?

All he had ever wanted was freedom. All he had ever needed was to prove to everyone that he was more than just a dirty-blood pirate. Now, he was the dirty-blood pirate who'd ruined everyone's chance at seeing another day. Elliot and Glass would have to buy or barter their way onto another ship, which usually meant the first season or two was full of fights, arguments, and distasteful remarks. Nothing pleasant about proving oneself with a new crew. Sometimes, men and women ended up dead because of it. The remaining *Dread Deep* crew would either gut him and toss him overboard or—

He stopped. Panic turned to horror. The kind that made limbs slow and the world tilt.

They could keep him as a prisoner, as leverage for their own freedom. They'd bring him back to Kalic, force him into some sort of deal because this was their egg, after all. Or more likely, they'd take him to the king of Barnạl, who was originally promised the dragon egg. He'd never see King Jair again, not until the man hunted him down himself or sent a Nighthunter to slit his throat in the middle of the night. Regardless, the *Dread Deep* crew would try and hand him over to fulfill their original duties to which they'd been bound—delivering the egg to Barnạl. Ultimately, the crew could take Cassian and the dragon anywhere to sell for a lot of coin if they chose. But if they continued to Barnạl to drop off the small dragon, maybe they'd even be freed from their service for that kind of honest work once they returned to Kalic with Cassian in chains.

A life of servitude. Pirates lived to serve the sea, but they were willing participants. Pirates loved it. Cassian did. Now, he'd be forced into a role without say, likely bound through the same dark practices done to Bauer and the rest of the crew because the Kalic king would blame him for the dragon hatching. He'd be punished for it. Kalic would make an example out of him, turn him into something he wasn't willing to be—a prisoner.

The dragon made a coughing sound. She tilted her head. Boots approached.

"Cassian?" Glass had returned. He didn't know how long he'd sat here.

More boots, these quicker. "Open the door," Bauer demanded. He tried the door, but it was locked. "Come on. Get this opened for us."

The dragon blinked, watching him intently. She wanted him to act like he'd done earlier. Her presence in his head urged him, poking him like an incessant child. A clever one older than her age.

He coughed as violently as he could muster. His chest hurt from the motions. A metallic stench filled his nose as his bloody knuckles came close. "Yeah?" Cassian croaked.

"Don't play with me," Bauer snapped. "You were just fine last night. Everyone knows what you did."

He grimaced. Not his proudest moment. Stabbing a man's hand with little provocation didn't usually settle well amongst men and women isolated on a ship. If the crew knew of the Seven Sea Laws, they could enact a settlement. Bauer and Cassian would have to end this with their weapon of choice. They'd go until someone dropped dead. Pitiful against what possibly lay ahead of him, but he couldn't stop thinking about every possible outcome.

More hard pounding. "Open up!"

Glass usually had his back. Always had. He waited, hoping to hear the man vouch for him, but he didn't. Maybe he still blamed Cassian for the fate of the *Torment*. Perhaps the four remaining shipmates of *Dread Deep* were far more dangerous than he originally thought.

Cassian coughed again. "I'm just—"

"Stop with the lies," Bauer interrupted. "I don't believe a word out of your slimy mouth. You goin' to tell me the egg is missing too?"

After the way he'd held it last night, no one would believe him, but he didn't have any other options. "Well, funny story actually—"

The pounding intensified. Bauer was going to break down the door. Cassian's instincts took over. He grabbed the dragon, small enough still to be easily picked up, and stuffed her under the bed. She went limp in his arms, letting him do as he pleased. He shoved her far enough back that he hoped—no, now he prayed like he'd been warned to do—that no one would come looking.

"Don't follow. Don't come out," Cassian whispered. She was his key to freedom. If he could get out of this mess, he could get her to King Jair and hope the man would still be pleased. He paused, wrestling with the foreign feelings clawing for another chance to be acknowledged. Cassian had a soft spot for the dragon already, but he didn't know why. No. He didn't want to know why. He'd been hired to do a job, not worry about his emotions.

She tilted her head. *Bad*. She'd read his thoughts. He hesitated. Had she heard everything?

She snorted. A yes.

First impressions weren't his strong suit. She'd understand one day. "Stay here." He stood and grabbed the satchel. A few egg fragments were scattered, so he stuffed those inside. Then he grabbed some of the dead crew's clothes and stuffed those inside, bundling them up tight. Half the eggshell was still intact, so he twisted it so that it lay on top. Then he tied the broken leather twine together, hoping it appeared like it had last night—untouched. They'd be too busy with him to worry about the details.

The door gave, and he stood there with a lopsided grin as Bauer and Glass entered. Behind, Elliot. They stopped halfway through the entryway.

"See?" Cassian lifted the satchel. "Untouched. Just fine." He gestured at the *Dread Deep* seaman. "How's that hand?"

"Your eyes," Bauer stated, hardly above a whisper.

Cassian cleared his throat. "Excuse me?"

"Your eyes."

"What's wrong with them?" Cassian asked. He was doing everything he could to remain calm. "I've been sleeping." He staged a cough. "Feelin' a bit down, but I supposed after last night, maybe I caught something."

They narrowed their gaze, unmoving.

Cassian swallowed. "Is something wrong? Is the ship all right?"

Bad. The dragon's voice echoed in his head, and he flinched, not expecting it.

Bauer approached, slower this time, like he wasn't sure if Cassian would combust into flames or not. He snatched the satchel with his good hand, the other wrapped and hanging limply with a dried blood stain. Bauer raised it, peeking in to see the top of the silver dragon egg, then handed it to Glass. The crewman took it without a word, barely even looking away from the piece of entertainment. Cassian shrugged, hoping to convey that he was sorry. Sorry for everything. For the day Captain Ricard died, and for everything afterward.

Bauer punched Cassian, who stumbled into the wall, head spinning, and grappled onto anything to keep himself upright. Bauer pummeled him with sickening speed, fists flying and striking every part of Cassian's exposed body. Cassian didn't try to stop him, couldn't. For once, he felt he deserved the attack.

Burdened for the Wicked

Dungeons on ships weren't meant for comfort. They were narrow, generally no more than two paces to each wall, and offered a small bucket one could piss, crap in, or sit on. Dungeons were on the lowest deck of the ship, where mold went wild if the walls weren't scrubbed regularly. *Dread Deep* was in far better condition than *Torment* had been, which he was grateful for. The dungeon space on the previous ship could guarantee a fatal malady. The rancid aroma of bodily fluids had seeped into the wood over many summers and never left. More prisoners, more fluids. A nasty place. On *Dread Deep,* it was obvious they didn't carry prisoners often; either that or the crew was the best cleaners on the seas.

The bucket probably hadn't ever been used. It sure didn't look like it had. Cassian wasn't complaining. Sitting on a clean one was better than a rotten one covered in—well, he didn't want to think about it.

He'd been sitting there for most of the day. His guess, anyway. Light was low and there weren't any portholes to give him help. This part of the ship was below the waterline. Noises had a different tune to them, and the floor didn't move like it did on the upper decks.

Cassian couldn't recall much after Bauer attacked him. He knew he was dragged down here by one of the others, but what they said was lost to him. The crewman had an impressive throw, and the welt on the side of his head proved it. The bruise was nasty, and any sudden movements pissed it off. Now he couldn't tell if the headache was from whatever was happening inside of him or the assault. At least it hadn't been his teeth or nose. His smile was half the barter's game when he was working with women. And broken noses were just a bloody mess.

Cassian pulled the iron bars. Sturdy. The lock on the door was new. Not a single sign of tarnish or age. Perhaps he was the first prisoner ever on this ship. He looked at the other cells. Spaced evenly enough to keep any prisoner from reaching out to the other. If one inmate had something to help the other, they could slip their hands through the bars and pass that item on. Older ships hadn't figured that out. This ship was new, then.

His knuckles had stopped bleeding, but the bruising and swelling were brutal. He tried to open and close his hand and found the act agonizing, so he stopped. Blood seeped from the beginnings of scabs. His belt hung on a hook in front of him, too far to try and grab. The hook was large, curved in such a way that not even a dramatic list of the ship could loosen the item from its hold. His muscles still ached from last night, and the damp touch of sweat coated his skin. Whether from the unforgiving humidity down here or his body reacting to *energy*, he wasn't sure. Not sure it mattered either. Either way, he was miserable.

Warmth brushed across his mind. He stood, instantly recognizing the feeling. "Not the greatest time," he mumbled. She couldn't help him. Full size and blowing fire, perhaps, but not when she was so small and fragile.

You're in trouble. Her statements were short, but her mind was vast. Like she was still figuring out how to talk, but knew enough to understand the basic language.

"You didn't stay where you were supposed to. You were safest under the bed." He kept his voice low, afraid someone might walk in. The only time he'd felt this much warmth from her was when she shared the same room with him. It meant she was likely nearby.

Her presence grew. She was trying to tell him something. Her persistence didn't waver, and he finally saw an image in his head that wasn't his own. It was stuffed into his head the way a cook stuffs a bird for roasting. The image was of him opening and closing his mouth, but nothing came out. He frowned, unsure, and she did it again. This time, she showed him nodding.

"Do I look like that?"

Annoyance flared. He winced, not realizing her little mind was capable of such a strong emotion already. "Sorry."

The image flashed again in his head. Now, this version of himself pointed at his head.

Cassian raised his brow. "Ah." *Like this?*

The dragon's excitement bled across his mind, and he felt pride bubble up. His own. He'd learned something new. *So, I can talk to you like this? Without sound?* The questions traveled across his mind and found their home in hers. He could feel them settle into her thoughts with ease like he'd done this a hundred times already. Their minds were linked, bound by an energy he didn't quite understand yet.

Yes.

Handy. He liked that. Nobody would ever know he was talking to her. A strange sensation burrowed itself in his heart. Well, it'd been there, but he'd not been able to sense it as clearly as he did now. In this silence, he couldn't shake the sensation. Affection. He liked her. She needed protection. The crew on this ship didn't understand her like he did. That she was curious about the world, afraid of the rocking ship and people, and trying to stay alive. She didn't want to be here.

He shook his head and immediately regretted it. Too much. The goal was King Jair. He couldn't get attached. Not now.

Agony shot through him. So sudden that he stumbled back, striking the bars. He grabbed at his body, checking for a stab wound or anything that could have caused that, but nothing was new. Nothing—

The dragon. That was *her* anguish.

Metal groaned as the door swung open. Bauer walked in, holding the dragon by her feet, like a farmer carrying a chicken for slaughter. Her wings stretched out, and she didn't fight back. Couldn't. Her mouth was tied shut with rope. Behind, Elliot trailed, head bowed.

"Close the door, son," Bauer ordered Elliot. The boy did as he was told. Bauer stopped in front of Cassian. The injured hand was holding a knife, but clumsily. He didn't have a good grip on it. His fingers weren't working like they should have been. Bauer waved the dagger in the dragon's direction. "You got yourself a fan."

The terror seeping from the dragon hardly let Cassian think straight. It made his limbs jittery, and his heart race. "Seems you got one yourself," Cassian bit back and shot Elliot a glare. Whether Elliot's service to Bauer had been forced or not, he didn't care. He'd protected Traz's son as much as he could, but now he was obeying orders from this worthless man.

Bauer leered. "Just showing him how a ship should really be run. Your trick with the satchel was clever. Not sure what you intended on doing once we got curious and looked."

"Nothing." The truth. "Just thought I'd screw with you all a bit more."

"Charming." Bauer raised the baby dragon higher. "You know what this means?"

"That you're a miserable asshole?" Cassian's voice remained steady, even as his thoughts were a scrambled mess from her panicked cries. *Easy,* he insisted. He needed the dragon to settle so that he could get his thoughts in order.

"Close. Means you've got yourself a pet."

Cassian was unsure what that meant.

"Your eyes?" Bauer pointed the blade at him. "For whatever horrifying reason, this dragon thought you were its Rider. Hatched for you. Now you're bonded. Sweet, isn't it?"

Bauer didn't wait for a reply. He threw the dragon against the opposite wall. Cassian yelled and slammed himself against the bars. The action was so impulsive that he didn't even realize what he'd done until afterward. Bauer and Elliot were staring at him. A burning agony seared down his back and arms, overshadowing every other discomfort. The dragon yelped, helpless as she slid to the floor. Her wings bent at an odd angle, and she shook herself to correct them, but in the motion, Bauer swooped down and grabbed her by the front leg. She squealed, but the sound was muffled by her tie. With the tip of his dagger, he poked the dragon. Scales bent, too new and malleable. Cassian stuck his hand as far out as he could, wrestling with the bars with no success. When prying at her scales didn't satisfy Bauer's sadism, he stuck the blade into the tip of her tail. She shuddered and thrashed.

Elliot stood there, a statue. "Do something," Cassian demanded—*pleaded*.

"Think carefully before you do anything," Bauer warned Elliot. He lowered the bloody blade to the dragon's foot, gesturing at the little clawed toes. "Think I might take one for myself. What do you think?"

The panic in Cassian's chest wasn't hers. It was his. He believed Bauer's cruel declaration. The wild gleam in those ugly eyes was akin to that of a starved animal's, a promised payback for what Cassian had done to his hand. Summers of chained servitude could make anyone go mad. But add desperation and a bloody history, and that made anyone unstable. Elliot slinked back toward the door, hands twisting in a nervous habit. The boy took on the appearance of someone who'd just witnessed the dead pacing the hall. Too much of a weakling to act, but too afraid to even walk out. A sense of betrayal as thick and hot as melted iron seeped into Cassian's veins. He hated the kid for being so cowardly and soft.

"What do you want?" Cassian asked.

Bauer raised his brow. "What do I want? I want my crew back. I want this dragon back in her egg. I want everything like it was before you showed up."

"Well, I can't turn back time, but maybe we can make a deal." He was begging—pathetic. His hands shook, and his chest tightened. This dragon was being thrown into a war she hardly understood—one he didn't even grasp—and it was unfair. All of it. She didn't deserve this. He couldn't fathom watching her suffer.

Is it true? Am I your Rider?

She blinked. *Yes.*

She chose him. She trusted he'd keep her safe, and he'd done nothing but make her first day a nightmare. *I'm nobody.*

Affection poured into his mind from her. The purity of it was crippling. Cassian hadn't ever felt that before. His entire life was one rejection after the next. Parents sold him, used him, and abandoned him when he was no use. Pirates weren't lovable, barely friend-worthy. He'd spent his life dealing with one betrayal after another, worried that he'd be stabbed in the back or be forced to kill someone he thought he trusted. Living his life with the same philosophy of violence and distrust for the sake of his own survival. And here this creature was, trusting he'd protect her because she saw the best in him. It was nauseating, empowering, and paralyzing all at the same time.

"I don't care about deals. There's nothing I want from you." Bauer raised his dagger. "Actually"—he pointed at the foot—"why don't I take a souvenir for all these troubles?"

"No," Cassian begged. "Don't."

Bauer raised a brow. "And why is that?"

Because he couldn't bear to watch, couldn't bear to *feel* that torture. "You're making a mistake."

Bauer scoffed. "Why?"

Cassian's voice shook, no matter how hard he tried to keep it steady. "Because you can still sell her—"

"Her?"

Damn. "Sell her," he repeated. "They'd pay high coin for her."

"Is that so?" The question wasn't what Cassian wanted to hear. It reeked of malice. "And what of you?" Bauer pressed.

"What do you mean?" Cassian asked.

Bauer wagged his dagger. "The Rider bond, pirate. What of it?"

Cassian cleared his throat. It was suffocatingly hot in here. His head felt like it was going to explode. "It doesn't matter."

"Then you shouldn't mind me taking a souvenir," Bauer remarked and dropped to the floor, pinning the dragon between his legs, and laying her front foot out. She thrashed and fought, but she was too small to make an impression. Her wings were crumpled, her other legs smashed against her body. Bauer leaned over, separating a forefinger. His hand engulfed it, easily keeping the foot still. The dragon's mind was unreadable, coated in icy terror that burned a hole right through Cassian's resolve.

And then Bauer attacked. His dagger broke through the young scales. They snapped. Blood flowed, and he started to saw. She screamed. The rope did little to muffle the sound. It ripped apart every layer Cassian had so carefully constructed around his life. Every lie he'd told himself, every promise he'd failed. He'd wanted freedom, wanted off this ship, wanted away from it all. But as he sank to his knees, mouth agape, hot tears carved their way down his cheeks, uninvited. He couldn't handle her pain, her desperation, her fear. This was all too much. The sound was worse than anything he'd ever heard. No dying man made him feel this way. No strangled cry gave him this much anguish. Guilt crushed him, buried everything he'd ever known, and left him raw and vulnerable. The black tendrils of the sensation wrapped around his soul and stayed. He'd never forget it. No matter what happened.

Bauer twisted the forefinger, ripping the last bit of tendon apart. Blood as red as her scales saturated the wood and his hands. The blade glared, mocking as the crewman wiped it across his pants, careless of the stain it would leave. The monstrous pride never wavered as he held up his prize: talon, scales, and bone.

"That'll make a good necklace. Don't you think?"

Cassian would kill him. He would slowly saw each of the bastard's fingers off until he had nothing but stubs. Then he'd force them down his throat until the man choked. When he was suffocating, he'd rip them out and then proceed to carve his way to Bauer's heart. Then he'd tear it out and stuff that down his throat.

Cassian seethed. The dragon stopped fighting. She lay there, broken. A day into this life, and she'd found herself in the hands of a monster. Elliot stood there, green. A coward. He could have intervened. He bore responsibility, as surely as Bauer did.

Bauer stood, shoving the dragon away like she stank. She limped away, head bowed and wings tucked close to her body, and not stopping until she found a dark corner of the room. Cassian couldn't even watch, too ashamed. She'd hatched for *him*. He didn't know entirely what it all meant, but he knew enough to know he should have done more. That she'd relied on him to protect her, and he'd failed. Again.

He tucked the talon into his pocket. "I'm not going to sell her," Bauer said softly. "That would be too kind. I'm going to sell both of you. Barnǎl will be pleased. He wanted a Dragon Rider."

With that, he left. Elliot stood frozen, staring into the shadows where the tiny dragon had crawled. The boy opened his mouth, then shook his head. A tear rolled down his cheek, which Cassian found repulsive. No sympathy would be spared for the boy, not when he'd done nothing to prevent Bauer's cruelty. Forgiveness wasn't granted to traitors.

"I'm sorry," Elliot finally wheezed. He sounded like he'd been the one stabbed and beaten.

"Get out of here," Cassian hissed, "you wretched coward."

Restless Waters

Cassian's life was a disaster. His decisions had all failed, and he'd managed to lose everything he'd ever worked for—respect, a title, and a ship. All in a matter of days. Glass and Elliot turned on him without a second thought. Pirates were nothing but thieves. It was true. But they were traitors, too. Anything to live another day. If it meant stabbing their captain in the back—for that's who he was, short-term—to ensure a fatty meal and good drink, then that's what happened. Loyalty didn't exist out here.

"Hello?" Cassian's voice cracked, weak. As weak as he felt. Put him in a room with men and women of all ages, and he could talk himself into anything they wanted him to be. Put him in a room by himself, and he realized he was nobody. Cassian had spent his whole life trying to be somebody he wasn't. He'd sailed these waters, lived the life of a pirate and loved it, but he wasn't born for this legacy. He wanted to stand for something more than just being a thief.

Being a pirate meant working for the right price. His sole purpose had been to be a Queens' Bidder, steal, and enforce a law he wasn't sure he believed in anymore. For a long while, it worked. Convincing himself this life was the right life for him meant he didn't have to challenge the ideas that stirred deep within him—wants and needs denied to him as a child. He was raised by landwalkers, not the sea. At ten, this world became all he knew.

No response. He didn't blame the dragon. If the roles were switched, he'd do the same. Not even a hint of how she felt brushed his mind. It was like she'd shut herself completely off from him. The feeling was isolating. Left with only his thoughts, he realized the constant presence of her brought him peace. Company. Now, without it, he hated the silence.

He wanted to be someone. He needed to. Purpose was what he'd always craved. A higher calling that wasn't defined by the next heist or kill. Up to this point, he'd convinced himself that was it, but he was wrong. Stuck here, stripped of everything he thought he wanted, he didn't want any of it.

What he wanted was to get off this boat. Take the dragon and run. Get as far from it all as they could and find somewhere quiet. He wasn't sure where that was yet, but he knew it wasn't here. She needed time to heal, recuperate, and make her choice. The dragon was clever, he'd gathered that much, and she deserved to decide how she wanted to live her life. Cassian wouldn't force her into anything. In less than a day, the two of them together had done nothing but ruin each of their lives.

A sneeze. The sound jolted him from his thoughts. He strained to get a better look, but the angle gave him no mercy. "Are you there?"

Silence. Then, softly, the clack of little talons against the wood filled the room. The relief he felt was indescribable, and he shoved his face against the bars to get a better look.

There she was. Hardly as feisty as he knew she was, limping out from the shadows. Her tail dragged behind her, her wings hung to her sides, and her head remained low. The stubs for horns along her jaw were bloodied from where she'd touched the wound. It didn't appear to be bleeding anymore, which was a relief, but her mismatched foot was swollen compared to the others.

Guilt morphed into need. "Come here," Cassian insisted. "I'm sorry." And he meant it. He was sorry for everything he'd put her through.

Squeezing through the bars was no problem for her small size. She passed right through, the tips of her wings scraping the iron, and crawled into his lap, tucking herself into a tight ball. Tail wrapped around, hanging over his boot, and her snout was stuffed into the crook between his leg and her arm. She took several large breaths before quieting down. As she did, Cassian rested a hand on her shoulder. Colder than he was used to.

"It's all right," he mumbled. Admittedly, he wasn't sure if that was to himself or her. "It's going to be all right."

Slowly, her mind blossomed within his. The hums, vastness, warmth—it dusted away the isolation and settled all around them. He smiled, relieved. The sensation of her company—of this bond, as Bauer called it—gave him peace. He wasn't sure what to call this yet. Friendship was premature. Loyalty was extreme. Trust was foreign. But commitment. Now that was a possible word choice. She'd come back to him because she chose him. He still didn't know exactly what that meant, and he wasn't sure he ever would, but having her here was all he needed for the moment. This small gesture gave him hope that he'd not utterly destroyed everything. At least not yet.

"A name," he muttered. "Surely you must have one?" He grazed his fingers gently over her scales. He didn't know if it helped her, but it gave his mind something to focus on.

No, she answered.

"Do you want one?" It wasn't right to keep calling her *she* and *creature* if she wanted a name. Everyone wanted one.

Her mind prodded his, curious. The sensation was odd, like being poked, and he grimaced. The strangeness made him want to wiggle and stretch, but he forced himself to remain where he was. Curiosity washed over him, not of his own mind, and he understood.

"I don't know what to call you," he admitted. "Names are personal. They embody everything we want to be. Take Bauer. His name is grungy, and he's nothing but a slimy barnacle. He's got nothing to offer, and if you don't scrape him off, he might turn into something ugly. Well, he is. But you know what I mean." He laughed at his joke. "Anyway, you want a name that gives you power."

She snorted, hot air blowing over his leg. The little one understood, but she still had so much growing to do before she would be able to make such decisions. It was up to him to give her something good.

"Are you familiar with the Old Tongue?" When she didn't answer, he said, "Me either. I mean, I know a little, but just from pirate tales and the odd word here and there. Good language though. Everything has a sense of strength behind it, even an insult." Cassian leaned his back against the iron bars. "There's this story about a ship that sailed to the edge of the world. They called her *Paradise*. When the crew arrived, they didn't find a drop-off or some wall that so many old stories speak of. Wild thoughts, by the way, this belief that there's a wall or drop-off. They found the water looked like glass. Not even the ship made waves. For several days, they sat there, dead in the water, until a seawoman fell overboard. Some versions say she was pushed. Others say she jumped willingly after hearing voices. Regardless, when that happened, their world tilted, and they found themselves in a lake that belonged to the realm of the dead. The Soul Realm."

Her breathing slowed further.

"They returned by accident, or so the story goes. Tricked the dead into granting passage back to the living. They returned to the same spot, one woman down and spooked. They sailed their way back to land, only to find that an entire moon had passed since they'd set off. Time didn't work the same in the Soul Realm. Not sure how accurate that story is, but I've never heard of another ship accidentally crossing like that either, so it could be fake. Probably is, now that I tell you this. It sounds crazy, but I'm also sitting in this cell with a dragon in my lap. That sounds pretty wild too, doesn't it?"

She snored.

"I know. Boring. Stories are for drunks and lonely nights." Cassian sighed. "I could name you after a great historical figure—no, that's terrible. Forget I brought it up. You'd go the rest of your life telling me how horrible that is."

Here he was, talking about their future when he wasn't sure what tomorrow would bring or what he was doing. Bonded. The word echoed over and over in his head, chipping away at his pride and leaving him raw. Reborn. Given a second chance. Terrified. Too many emotions to process at once. But he knew she needed reassurance, and he wanted to give that. She was owed that much.

He racked his mind. Put on the spot, he couldn't think of anything. "I'm trying too hard," he told her. "And you don't care because you're asleep. Seems like a big deal to give you a name, and you're just snoring through it. Should I wait?" He didn't want to. Cassian was anxious to give her something to look forward to—an identity, a purpose. So far, he'd given her every reason to hate him, and he wanted to soften that impression by giving her a powerful name.

"No, no." He shook his head. "I know what my problem is. I'm thinking in terms of historical figures. I'm thinking of kings and queens, or tales of heroes. It doesn't feel right because that's not you. You're not the shadow of someone else's fame. I don't want anyone to think of you as a replacement, holding onto someone long dead. And I certainly don't want anyone to compare you against anyone else."

Cassian's back was sore from the bars digging in. He shifted, and she gave the smallest huffs. He stilled, deciding he'd remain in place if she was comfortable. Little dragons were just like any other newborn—tired, hungry, and vulnerable. He needed to remember that. Hard to do that when he pictured this massive beast biting the heads of men or burning cities to the ground. That's the stories he'd heard in those pubs. Not defenseless dragons no longer than his arm with soft scales and gentle squeaks. This changed his entire impression.

"A ship." Cassian already felt right about this direction. "We name our ships based on what they symbolize. *Torment* was named so because the Queens' Bidders crewed her. We were what ships feared. I'm assuming this ship has its name because it's supposed to make an impression. Frankly,

I think it's a terrible name. What's *Dread Deep* even mean?" She didn't reply, not that he expected her to, but he still waited to be sure. "Probably something the king made up and thought it sounded clever. It does, I'll give him that. Anyway, that's what I'm thinking. You will symbolize something grand, bold."

He leaned his head back, letting his fingers move slowly over her scales. Her breathing was steady, warmth seeped through him, and despite their circumstances, he was at peace. After everything, she'd made her way back to him, and that showed something—loyalty. Not a currency he was used to in these waters.

"The red sun," he mumbled, liking the feeling it gave. "Your eyes are fiery, your scales are red—it's good, right? Well, I wouldn't call you the red sun. It would sound pretty bad. But let me think . . ." He thought hard on it, trying to recall the basic Old Tongue words for that. "Ser . . . Sah . . . I think *san* is sun. Red? Starts with—oh, wait. It's *yila*. Yes, I know that. I saw it on the side of a ship once. One of the Su'rüles had it—they're always clever with their names. So, that would mean I would call you San'yila. That's how it works, right?"

Cassian wasn't sure. He wasn't an expert in reading or writing in Old Tongue. Skills like that hadn't seemed important. Now he wished he'd learned, though. He dreaded calling her the wrong name, but he was almost certain it was the right words. Regardless, he loved the sound of it.

"San'yila," he whispered. A smile stretched across his face. It was perfect. He knew he was getting attached already. Their bond was wiggling deeper into his soul, shifting priorities and forcing him to look at the world differently. More than that, he had nothing else left. The remaining *Torment* crew wasn't defending him. They weren't down here giving him food or asking how they'd get out of this mess. The king's crew seemed to think selling him and San'yila would work in their favor. They'd not mentioned bringing him back to Kalic, and he wasn't going to offer.

Cassian knew he could get the two of them out of this. He wasn't sure how yet, but he was certain he could get off this ship. Several dinghies were always attached. Surely one would still be available. If he could get out of here, they could make a run for it. Worry about food later. Cassian wouldn't have time to go perusing the galley for food and water. They'd have to rely on the fish that swam too close. Most rowboats had a few resources for catching and prepping fish on board—in case of emergencies, if the crew had to flee without warning. That would do. Water would be a bit harder. If he could snatch a waterskin on the way out, that would be ideal. Drinking salt water would kill him, San'yila too. Well, he assumed. He didn't know much about dragons.

That's what they would do. Cassian nodded. "We've got part of a plan." It might not be clean, but it was the best they had.

No Dreams are Peaceful

San'yila's squeak tore Cassian out of a dead sleep. His head slammed into cold metal, and his shoulders ached from being slouched over in the confined space. His back protested as he straightened. Everything hurt. Even his fingers. His tongue tasted of dirt—gritty and salty—and he blinked, eyes dry like he'd rubbed sand into them. The dungeon was no place to sleep, though he couldn't recall when he'd finally dozed off. Likely somewhere between telling San'yila another fantastical story and listening for bootsteps. Halfway through the night, he'd sworn, by the creak of wooden floorboards, he'd heard someone approaching. He'd waited, and then nothing. Later, the same.

In his situation, he couldn't tell if it was the dead screwing with him or if some of the crew was watching him. Likely the latter. Not often a Dragon Rider stumbled aboard. The title felt wrong somehow. He wasn't sure what to call himself, but that wasn't it. He was nothing more than a dirty pirate with a bad streak of luck. One problem after another. Locked away under *Dread Deep's* main deck was just another.

The dragon's presence washed over him. Foreign but growing more familiar to him—admittedly, more comfortable than it had been before. He liked the way her mind felt. Peaceful, even if she was young and confused. He was, too.

Hungry. The little word echoed through his head like rippling waves. He shrugged.

"Sorry, little one." His stomach grumbled. "We're stuck at the moment."

She tilted her head, clearly unsatisfied. *Hungry,* she said again. More persistent.

A quick glance at the door confirmed they weren't going anywhere. "I've got nothing for you. You're not eating my boot if that's what you're asking. Don't forget, you tried and failed at that." Cassian's voice slurred from exhaustion. He felt like he could sleep for another three days.

San'yila rocked on her feet, careful not to press too hard on the injured one. He watched, bothered, but didn't say much. Eventually, the others would have to come back. Hopefully with food.

You failed me.

He straightened. "Huh?"

San'yila watched him with one fiery eye. *You failed me.* Her voice grew harsher, meaner. A hard contrast to the little one he was speaking to prior to falling asleep.

"I know," he said. "I'm sorry."

Are you?

Panic wiggled, making him squirm. "What's—"

She snapped at him, flashing incisors too large for her narrow snout. Cassian slid backward, trying to avoid her, and felt hot fingers reach through the bars and wrap around his throat. He gasped. He tried pushing away—he thrashed, but the hand tightened and shoved him back in place. The iron bars cracked his head with agonizing force.

"Now, now, that's no way to greet an old friend, is it?" Hot breath tickled his ear. Cassian didn't have to twist his head to know who it was—to recognize that voice. It was the man from his dream.

"Let me go," Cassian wheezed.

"And ruin the fun? I think not." The man loosened his grip just enough for Cassian to get a full breath. "You've got an interesting head. Did you know that?"

"I—" Cassian frowned, startled by the statement. "I don't understand."

"So easy to read. So easy to manipulate. One little dragon has you all worked up, doesn't it?"

Cassian fumbled to find the right response. "What's this about?" he demanded sharply.

"Rushed?" the man asked slowly. Too slow, as if he savored the word. "Need to be somewhere?"

"Not at all. Just a bit over all of this," Cassian snapped.

The grip tightened again. In the single act, a dozen warnings and threats flooded Cassian's head. He wanted to run, dig a hole to the bottom of the ship, and swim as far from this man. Whoever this man was, he didn't belong on a ship. He carried himself like Time waited on him, and it made Cassian afraid of him.

"I once heard a man say he wanted to be more than just crew," the man whispered, his voice sending a chill down Cassian's spine. "When he dreamed, he dreamed of traveling the world, finding a small place next to the coast to call his, and friendship. But he also dreamed of something bigger. He wanted people to love him, to want him. Do you feel wanted yet, Cassian?"

Terror didn't begin to describe how he felt. His heart rammed hard enough against his ribs to make them ache. Every muscle turned to stone, locking him in place. He'd tried to write it off as a dream before, but it wasn't. This was real. All of it.

"Very good," the stranger complimented him. "You're learning."

He could read Cassian's mind. "Who are you?" His voice croaked, sounding as helpless as he felt. As brave as he wanted to be, he couldn't do it. His voice shook.

"Does it matter?"

"Yes," he answered without hesitation. The dragon to his left hadn't moved. She didn't even flinch when Cassian attempted to rip the man's hand off him. The man's other hand snaked through the bars and stilled him with a blade pressed against his jaw. The blade nicked him, drawing a warm trail of crimson that oozed down his neck to his collar. "Let me go."

"No." The answer was so simple, it hurt. "You want to know who I am, but you don't even know who you are. Doesn't that make it trivial?"

"I know who I am," Cassian replied, wheezing. This man had an iron grip on him.

"No, you don't. You never have. And now, the world expects you to have all the answers."

Cassian's fight drained. He didn't know what to say to that.

He could practically hear the smile in the stranger's response. "Imagine this. A Dragon Rider with nothing to lose because he never had anything to give. Sounds pitiful, doesn't it? My heart hurts just mentioning it."

"What do you want?"

"What do I want?" The frigid blade trailed up toward his ear. "I want what everyone wants, Cassian. Peace. Purpose. Friendship."

The man was mocking him. This visitor didn't want any of that. He had what he wanted; he could do anything. Instead, he threw Cassian's words right back at him.

"You don't think a man like me wants—*craves*—friendship?" He sounded genuinely surprised. "Don't we all want companionship?" He twisted Cassian's head to the dragon, who still hadn't moved. "Isn't that what you want from her? What she seeks from you?"

Cassian's heart thundered so loud he couldn't even think straight. *Thud, thud, thud.* It picked up speed. He couldn't breathe. His lungs burned, ready to burst. Hands tightened around his throat, cutting him off from the air. Heat rushed his face, and panic turned his gestures frantic. He would—

Cassian shot up, gasping. He frantically looked around. His head felt like he'd slammed it into the metal bars, and his mouth was drier than the Hazar

Desert. The brig door slammed open, and Elliot marched in, paler than the dead, followed by Sanser. No sign of the man who'd been here. Everything the man had said was still crystal clear to him, and he could feel his lungs on fire. He was being followed. Whoever this man was wanted Cassian's attention. San'yila dipped her head and crawled back behind him. He wished he could protect her like she wanted him to.

When he touched his chin, he found his fingers came away slick with blood.

"Knock yourself out?" Sanser chuckled, but it was strained. "Actually, I don't care. Elliot."

The boy approached and lifted a bundle of keys. He already had the right one in his hand, inserting it into the lock. He didn't twist, though. Cassian glared, begging the kid to meet him in the eyes. To face his destiny.

"Don't do anything foolish," Sanser warned, agitated. "We've got guests." Behind, another person entered. If Cassian had anything to throw up, he would have.

The Red Queen hardly reacted to the scene—a dragon and Cassian in the dungeon cell. His russet-colored skin was covered in black tattoos, silver and gold rings decorated his fingers, and his shaggy black hair framed a scarred and war-lived face. The sword strapped to his hip was sheathed in leather that was nicer than anything Cassian had ever seen before. Slick, freshly polished, and clothes that declared a lifestyle of adventurous sails rather than battle. This wasn't a lower-ranked Queen.

"As promised," Sanser whispered, standing to the side. He looked half the man he'd been the night before.

"Hm." The Queen surveyed the two like he was choosing livestock to buy. Nostrils flared, and he planted his hands on his hips. "You lied to us," the Red Queen hissed, turning to Sanser.

Elliot's hand still clung to the inserted key. That boyish gaze finally met Cassian's, fearful. This wasn't normal. The crew of *Dread Deep* had not expected this. The crushing reality of whoever tormented Cassian vanished instantly as a new threat took precedence.

Sanser licked his lips and said, "We didn't—"

The Queen's movements were smooth, too fast to anticipate. He reached over, unleashing a dagger tucked in the sleeve, and drove it into Sanser's throat. The man fumbled, mouth opening and closing like a fish out of water. He stumbled into the wall. The Queen kept the dagger jammed into flesh and bone while Sanser squirmed, close enough to court Death. The Queen pinned Sanser against the wall while blood poured from the wound, draining down his shirt and onto the floor. And then he went still. With a quick flick, the Queen yanked the blade free and wiped it against Sanser's sleeve before tucking it back into the sheath fastened to his forearm.

San'yila shoved herself into Cassian's back, looking like she'd crawl her way through the floor. *Bad.* The word echoed between their bond, haunting and final.

Stay close, Cassian ordered the dragon.

"Come on, boy, open it up." The pirate crossed his arms, sounding gruff. "So you're the one they're hiding."

"Uh." Cassian wasn't sure what he meant. "Been down here for a day, I think."

"We've been chatting with them for quite some time, trying to figure out why you all are in our territory," the Red Queen replied. "*Dread Deep* is a royal ship. She's not welcome here."

Elliot opened the door of the dungeon, the metal hinges screeching. He stepped away from the small cell and tucked his chin to his chest, wiping blood on his pants frantically like it burned his skin. The boy clearly wanted to disappear. The floor creaked under Elliot's movements, which made him freeze as if he expected the Red Queen to turn the blade on him. The boy wanted to be tough, had snuck aboard *Torment* to follow Cassian, and now he was nothing but a spineless fool next to the room's entrance, taking up space in the long room. The Red Queen eyed Elliot for a moment, perhaps debating on killing him, too. Between them, the body of Sanser lay sprawled, a warning.

Slowly, Cassian stood, taking San'yila into his arms. Scales scraped against skin, and her talons sank into his shirt as she fought to be as close to him as possible. He winced. He was a walking wound at this point.

"Not my ship," Cassian replied. For once, he was relieved not to be the captain.

The Queen waved at the crumpled body and said, "We're here for one reason: *that*." He pointed at San'yila, then dragged his hideous gaze to Cassian's. "Just so happens you're a part of that deal now. Come."

The Red Queen approached the door without slowing, snatching Cassian's belt and sword in the process from the hook. The echo of boots and groaning wood muted all other sounds, including Cassian's thundering heart, which was racing so fast that he was lightheaded. Glad to be out of the dungeon, Cassian walked but slowed long enough to make sure Elliot, who was still shoved up against the wall, met his gaze—a small stain against the room's new bloody decoration. The son-of-a-bitch was a coward, and Cassian would never forgive him.

Elliot mouthed the word *bad*. Cassian faltered, startled by the warning.

"Coming?" the Red Queen asked. His proud attitude suggested that hesitation was not an option.

"Yeah," Cassian muttered. He wished that he had a weapon. The best he had was a punch and a kick, but that didn't get anyone far when the Queens were involved. The pirate's tattoos were symbols of family ties and Queen culture, accentuated by prestigious ink declaring him as a high-titled commander—a sun across his collarbone, surrounded by Old Tongue sigils. Queens were structured that way. A clan as large as theirs made it a kingdom at sea.

The pirate didn't say much as they strode to the main deck. Elliot trailed close behind Cassian, a shadow to their heavy footsteps. The boy was even more mewling and subservient than usual, forcing Cassian to rethink his judgment. Something was going on. Something big. This didn't involve Elliot and Glass anymore. This didn't affect just the few aboard. They were dealing with power-hungry Queens.

Him. He was the problem. San'yila, too. Dragons and Riders weren't supposed to exist. Not anymore. None of this was supposed to happen, and now nobody knew how to handle it. The man from his vision was right. Cassian didn't know who he was, not anymore.

"Up we go, mate," the Red Queen ordered and motioned for Cassian to go first. A sure sign he didn't trust Elliot.

Without argument, Cassian urged San'yila to hold on and climbed the ladder. He was hungry and weak, and the exertion took everything he had. The hatch was open, letting the sun warm his features. Cassian averted his gaze, momentarily blinded by the glare, before he pulled himself off the ladder. He blinked furiously, catching the faces of a dozen Queens even before his eyes had adjusted to the light.

Their ship was tied to *Dread Deep*. Four masts, red sails, and cherry-red wood. It was the nicest ship he'd ever seen. A snarling creature was carved across the bow, a menacing figurehead. Its forked tongue stretched out, incisors sharpened to a point roughly the size of a man, and black paint where the eyes were. Along the hull, written in elegant red, was *Salvation*.

It didn't feel like it one bit.

Standing to the side, guarded by a few Queens, was the remaining crew. Glass, Ali, Edward, and Bauer. They hardly looked Cassian's way. Bauer already had a streak of red rolling down his cheek. The black eye blossoming was confirmation this had all been a struggle. Elliot was the only one uninjured—either because he'd been a coward or clever, Cassian couldn't say. Ali looked like she'd been dragged through shit. Her face was covered in grime, her tunic was shredded, and her jaw was locked in a hostile scowl.

A man flashing silver teeth stepped forward, dressed in a fine-knitted cloak that likely hadn't ever seen the sun. He presented himself with his hand resting on the intricately carved hilt of his sword, resembling a woman reaching outward. His dark, leathery skin was covered in red ink along his neck and hands. Captain.

The coat was just for show, a cultural tradition of the Queens when they displayed their wealth and power. Not that they needed to. Their ships alone were enough to make the bravest pirate sweat.

The captain halted before Cassian, smug, but his gaze wandered to the dragon in his arms before snapping back. "So, you're the little secret."

Cassian didn't know what he was talking about. He cleared his throat. "I'm sorry?"

"Your crew denied your existence," the captain replied, sea tongue so thick that the words moved like sludge. "Said it was just them before we wanted to have a look around. Then they got real nervous. Isn't that right?" He looked over his shoulder to Bauer. "Dirty thief." The captain shook his head. "Are you injured?"

"What? No," Cassian said.

"Your dragon?"

"Beside the toe she's missing, she's quite fine," Cassian snapped.

"She?" The captain raised his brow. "Does she have a name?"

Cassian's mouth was dry. "What's this all about?" he asked.

The captain's smile cracked. "And her name?"

A small thing, but to Cassian, it felt like the captain was trying to take the last thing he had left. "It doesn't matter. What do you want?"

"Cassian." The name rolled off the captain's tongue like acid. "That's what they call you. It is your current name, yes?" Numbly, Cassian nodded. Pirates changed their names occasionally, usually because they were on the run from a bounty. "I'm trying to be polite. You are the captain of *Torment*, yes? Ah, well, were."

The jab stung. "You bilge-sucking maggot," Cassian hissed. The insult embodied every emotion he felt—resentment, sorrow, terror. He wanted to carve his name in the captain's skull and string him up on the bow of the ship.

The captain wagged his finger. "I'd be careful what I say next," he scolded. "A dragon doesn't protect you from me."

Cassian clenched his jaw. Men were willing to pay a fortune to get their hands on this egg, and now it'd hatched into a *living* dragon. Yet this man didn't even flinch. Bizarre was an understatement. Cassian held a piece of history in his hands, and the pirate appeared bored. Either he was mad or he'd already seen things beyond this world that Cassian couldn't imagine.

San'yila urged him to comply. The mental nudge was soft, a tilt in the other direction that made him rethink everything he'd said. He swallowed. "Her name is San'yila. She's several days old."

The pirate grinned, wild. "The red sun. Clever. You will be coming with us now."

"Hold up," Bauer intruded, stepping forward before the Red Queen behind him tightened her grip and hauled him back. She was a burly woman, one Cassian wouldn't want to cross. Bauer hardly put up a fight. "You just wanted to see. You got what you wanted, now leave us."

"I don't think so," a man bit back, stepping forward from the crowd. He wore the standard tunic and pants but had a red sash cinched around his waist underneath a dark leather belt. The pirate stopped before the captain and whispered something in his ear, then backed away, hardly sparing Cassian a second glance.

"Hm." The captain grabbed a coin pouch from his belt and tossed it, letting it land between the remaining *Dread Deep* crew with a loud clunk. "We don't need that anymore."

"What?" Bauer screamed, pointing at Cassian. "We had a deal. We shook on it!"

The captain did a quick jerk with his chin, and at once, others descended on him. Cassian stiffened, only concerned that nobody would rip San'yila out of his arms. Hands gripped his arms tenaciously and pushed him forward. He twisted in his spot, hearing the captain bark orders that gouged out the last bit of strength he had.

"We're done here," the captain declared.

Metal sang against scabbards. Elliot's ear-piercing yelp drove a dagger right into Cassian's heart. He turned in time to watch five blades slice across exposed throats. Blood spurted, thrilled for the release, and washed across the main deck. The Queens let go of the dead, letting the bodies flop against the floor and spasm before going still. In unison, they cleaned their blades and sheathed them, like they'd executed choreographed massacres a hundred times before.

Glass's body lay crumpled next to the railing. He was one of the toughest men Cassian knew. Maybe he'd not seen clearly toward the end, but Cassian didn't want him dead. Glass was a damn good pirate, and one of the only friends he had. Glass raised him, gave him a safe place, and taught him everything he knew, and with a pathetic gesture, the captain took it all away. Elliot had been witless, arrogant, and had so much to learn. He didn't wish the boy dead. He'd have settled this by a quick word and then slapped him on the shoulder and poured him a heavy drink. They learned their lessons by brute force. Conversation hardly settled anything.

And now Elliot would never learn. Glass would never talk about wild stories or share his outrageous theories. Dead. Enraged didn't begin to describe how Cassian felt.

The red-sashed pirate stepped forward then, amber eyes drilling into Cassian with the heat of the sun. A warning. Cassian understood. This was a test, and he needed to pass to stay alive, not say something that got him in trouble.

"The necklace," Cassian managed to say. The captain turned to him, brow raised. "Off the man next to the railing. Can you get it for me?" Glass wore that everywhere. He didn't recall a time when the pirate hadn't worn it, and now he wanted to honor Glass, the life he'd had, by holding onto it. After everything, he couldn't let that necklace sink to the bottom of the sea.

The captain chewed on a decision for too long before stating, "You heard him. Get the necklace. Check the supplies, take the boots, you know what to do. Let's get going." One of the Queens retrieved the necklace from Glass, then approached Cassian. The blood-soaked silver was slick as it plopped into his hand. "All yours."

Cassian nodded, unable to say anything, the words lodged in his throat, angry and anguished. The weight of the necklace finalized it. His entire life was over. Everything he'd known no longer existed. The last two people on the sea who knew him were dead.

"Go on," the captain snapped. "Unless you want to stay here when we set it on fire."

He didn't. He couldn't live with watching Elliot and Glass burn.

Cassian didn't believe in destiny, not like the landwalkers did. He found the idea of believing things happened for a reason obnoxious and believed only by those who didn't want to take accountability for their actions. Kings were cruel and blamed the hand of fate. Torturers felt worthy—proved that it was what Destiny wanted. Fools who put their faith in the Gods placed their hopes in Destiny solving all their problems.

For Cassian, he'd always believed that the only way to solve a problem was to face it head-on or outrun it. As he stepped aboard *Salvation*, he hashed out what it meant to be a pirate. Pirates were survivors, flexible, handled high-stress situations well, and never went a day without a drink or two. Scavengers, thieves, but more than anything, they were explorers. They sailed the Vore World, saw things that no landwalker would ever see, and sought adventure.

He wanted to be all of that. Cassian wanted to be the adventurer who embraced these changes, but he couldn't. Wouldn't. The pirate he had been wouldn't be boarding *Salvation*. That man would die in the flames that took *Dread Deep*. The man in place was not afraid of the Queens. The world had taken everything from him, and when he was down, continued to kick and insult him. He was sick of it. Sick of being the victim. Cassian was raised to be a merciless thief—the boy who killed his first man and laughed—not this pathetic coward he'd become in such a short time.

The crackle of flames snapped him back to reality. Queens rushed around, pulling docking lines and calling orders. Few hesitated long enough to look at the dragon before returning to their tasks. After being a crewman for so long, he felt strange standing there and not offering a helping hand.

The red-sashed pirate appeared to his left. Dark hair tossed in the breeze picking up. He motioned ahead and said, "Captain will see you in there."

Long Live Brutality

"Thirsty?" the captain asked, sitting down in a bright red leather chair across from Cassian. They were in the captain's cabin. Dark wood sucked up the light that spilled in from the windows on either side of the room. The desk was a hunk of blackened wood carved to look like a woman lying on her side. Along her spine, red gems shimmered. The desk wrapped around the captain like a cocoon. All the cabinets and drawers had gold handles carved to look like waves in motion. A room this highly decorated meant *Salvation* never expected to sink.

The captain popped open a bottle of clear liquor and poured himself a glass, then proceeded to pour the second glass without waiting for Cassian's response. He stuffed the cork into the bottle and leaned back. Jewels clanked against one another, and his sword scraped against the chair. Cassian grimaced. Some people treated weapons like they cost nothing. It was probably one of twelve the captain owned.

"We're heading out of the Grave," the captain added. "Finicky place, ain't it?" He chuckled at his own remark. Cassian didn't join in—he didn't see the humor.

San'yila nudged Cassian's hand, wanting to investigate the cabin. He tightened his grip on her. *Not yet.*

Her mind flared in question.

I don't trust him, she stated.

She was antsy, much like any child would be. Not even the clear threat their situation held could prolong the inevitable curiosity. Annoyed, he pinned her with both hands in his lap. San'yila snorted.

The captain smiled. "Damn near Gods to many," he commented. "Here's to the dragons, the original rulers of this world. Do you know much about them?"

The singular drink mocked Cassian. He could use five of those right now, but instead, he was trying to keep San'yila from doing something regrettable. "I've heard a few things here and there," he replied. The priority was learning what the Queens wanted with him. This crew obviously knew that another Queen had killed Ricard and then declared Cassian as captain of *Torment*, which was now at the bottom of the Grave. Politics wasn't his skill, and he wasn't about to insert himself into it.

Behind them, the ship he'd called home for only a few days burned. The smoke would be seen for leagues, marking Queen territory and challenging anyone who thought themselves courageous enough to traverse this region. Flames snapped wood, forcing the once majestic ship to its knees, until nothing was left. It would sink to the bottom and join the others, young and old. *Dread Deep* was beautiful. Two ships destroyed in a matter of days. What a waste. Pirates didn't think about the consequences of that. Feasible wood for other builds, a ship to be used by a crew who lost their own—these were the things Cassian was forcing himself to think about instead of the taboos of keeping the dead from getting lost on their way to the Afterlife.

"Why aren't you surprised about the dragon?" Cassian pressed. He wanted answers. "Ask anyone and they would be in shock about San'yila, even me, yet you sit here as if you have a fleet of them back from wherever you come from. So, why is that?"

The captain took a sip and motioned to the untouched glass on the table. San'yila hadn't moved, but Cassian was parched, desperate to wash down the sour taste of his dead comrades. The bloody necklace was tucked in a pocket, staining through the fabric. Cassian would have to peel the metal out once it dried. Blood had a terrible way of gluing itself to fabric.

"We are more than just pirates, us Queens. We are protectors of the sea," the captain responded quietly, as if he spoke about a long-time lover. He raised his chin, proud. "Higher-ranked Queens get privileges that others would cut their arm off for. I work closely with the inner circle."

"And?" Cassian insisted. He must have appeared broken, face drawn by lack of sleep and terror, because the captain regarded him with a tilt of his head. San'yila wiggled in his grip, drinking up his nerves in such a way that he couldn't suppress his aggravation. Her mind pressed into his own, like a child poking their parent, begging to be released so she could explore.

The captain passed a strained smile, the kind reserved for irritation. Cassian saw right through it and pleaded with the dragon that she be still. She relented, albeit begrudgingly. They weren't here for drinks and a chat. There was something more to this interview; he could sense it as well as a pirate senses the shifting winds for an oncoming storm, but he'd been unsure how the conversation would proceed. Now he knew.

"You're a valuable item to us," the captain said. "You offer us leverage. So let me make this easy for you. If you refuse to join our ranks, I'll kill the dragon and then you—once you get a real good feeling of what it's like to sever such a divine bond. It is madness from what I hear. Join, and we'll ensure you are revered and well taken care of, provided with everything you need and then some." He bared his hands. "It's not a hard decision, is it? You've got nothing. You're a captain to no one, owe no one anything, and now you're at a crossroads."

"Leverage for what?" Cassian asked. Nothing about the question made him feel good. His stomach twisted with nausea, threatening to release bile all over the blackened desk.

"A war is stirring," the captain answered. "Deals aren't being honored, and it's caused some shifts in our ranks—"

"Like murdering your ruler?" Cassian interrupted. He didn't know how the Red Queens managed to do that. There were hundreds, if not thousands, of Red Queens all over the world. Surely someone would have had a problem with the murder of their ruler, Zinfel.

"A slight adjustment," the captain corrected. "Politics on land require a more assertive hand to ensure we keep our territories. Those who reign on land find themselves greedy for the water. They will not have it."

Cassian shook his head. "I'm not here for your war. I'm not here to clean up the Queens' political mess. I've got enough problems. I don't need this on top of it all."

"You seem to think you have a choice. May I remind you—"

"Yeah, I know." San'yila tensed in his lap, sensing Cassian's spiraling temper. "So far, you've taken me out of one dungeon and put me into another. You're cryptic about your answers, and you won't even spare me information that's relevant. The Queens live for war. Your people thrive on it, seek it out. Don't speak to me like this is a terrible misfortune that's befallen you. I've got half a suspicion that you sought it out."

The captain didn't reply. The lack of response pissed Cassian off. He was tired of being treated like he didn't have a say over his own life.

"Am I—are we—supposed to be your prisoner for the rest of our lives?" Cassian growled. Agitation devoured the terror blossoming in his stomach. "Is that how this works? Give me a good threat and a reason to live and now you'll suddenly spare me? And I am supposed to fall to my knees, grateful for the mercy you didn't spare for those of *Dread Deep*? Am I really to believe you have honor after what you just did?" He leaned forward, emboldened by the slight eyebrow raise betraying surprise the captain gave. "You aren't going to kill me. You won't. No, better yet, you can't. You're part of the inner circle. You've shared that much, so I know that you're beholden to laws that forbid you to act without the circle's approval. I'm a big enough prize that you could be promoted, maybe earn the hand of another respected Queen, or pay off a debt you owe. So, which is it, Captain? Or do you want me to sit here and act like I don't know a damn thing about your kind?"

The captain's lip twitched. "What do you *think* you know?"

Finally, a decent conversation. As a White Horn, he was no fool to the laws the Queens lived by. "Queens abide by the Seven Sea Laws," Cassian explained. "However, those of the inner circle abide by nine—the two intended to represent respect and loyalty. Queens act as family units. Your name gets you farther than anything else. Based on that cloak I saw you wearing earlier and your red tattoos, I'd say you're part of an inner circle family, perhaps a brother or cousin. Queens are protective of their information. What goes on amongst you all is unknown to the rest of the world, unless someone talks, which I know has happened at some point, or else the rest of us who live and die on the water wouldn't have the information we do have about you." He tilted his head, recalling as much as he could, satisfied to see the captain didn't move or try to interrupt.

"You mentioned deals," Cassian continued. "I'm assuming you mean with someone in Caster or Junok, maybe both. They are two of the major ports of the Vore World. So I would assume that your problems are coming from one or both of those royal families. Ah, another thing: Queens don't get their hands dirty with thievery or petty crimes. Your finances come from running the imports and exports of cities. Although I heard a rumor you also make personal runs for certain landwalkers, depending on the pay, and I'll be frank, I believe that. Your ships would be perfect to make those runs—nobody willingly comes within a league of a Queen unless it's by accident."

The captain nodded. The previous annoyance that flooded his sun-aged face drained as satisfaction blossomed, softening his features. For just the slightest moment, the captain seemed impressed that Cassian knew so much about the Red Queens. He'd learned everything from Ricard. Cassian's earliest summers at sea were spent listening to Ricard speak about the Red

Queens, their values, and their dynamics. Ricard didn't know everything, but he shared what he did know.

"But here's something I can't quite figure out," Cassian continued and leaned back, kicking his old boots up. San'yila sank into his lap more, never taking a fiery eye off the captain. She was wary, studying the man who sat across from them. In a matter of a couple of days, Cassian felt like he knew so much about the dragon already. "If you're part of the inner circle, then why are you out by the Hil Islands captaining a lesser-ranked group of Red Queens? You've got a debt you're paying off? Trying to impress someone? Or—"

"Am I calling upon the dead to create black spots in the sea?" the captain interjected with a snort. His fingers intertwined, rings rubbing against each other like he wanted to strangle Cassian and was fighting the urge not to. Cassian fought to hide his surprise. Beyond the captain's cabin, men shouted orders, oblivious to the standoff occurring between the captain and Cassian. The ship rocked in response to the waves crashing against *Salvation's* hull.

They sat staring at one another for what seemed like an eternity. Cassian swallowed. "So those are your mischief?" he asked. "Do you have a Soul Speaker aboard? Is that how you're doing it?"

The captain laughed, cold and hollow. "The Queens' business is just that—ours. I didn't invite you in to tell you my plans or what we were doing. We aren't deaf to the stories you foul-smelling barnacles spread. We know what you say about us."

Cassian bit his lip hard enough to taste blood. "So, you aren't responsible for the black spots?"

The captain looked to the window and spat, "No."

All this time, Cassian wanted to believe it was the Red Queens, that they were the ones harming the waters, opening gateways to the dead realm, and encouraging the damnation of ships. It felt easy to place the blame on the worshippers of the Red Goddess—they were wild and untamed. "Then . . . what's happening?" Cassian mumbled.

"Do you really think we have that answer?" The captain sounded stunned. "And if we did, do you think I'd share it with you?"

Cassian hated how dismissive the captain was to him. "Perhaps."

"Well, we don't," the captain snapped. He motioned at Cassian with his drink. "Let's get something straight. You will have a choice to make. I was going to wait until we arrived back at port, but I'm feeling sympathetic and think you should have some more time to think things over before you open that sour mouth of yours."

Cassian raised one eyebrow. "I'm flattered."

"Don't be," the captain replied, curling his lip. "I'd cut that tongue right out of your mouth if it were up to me." The captain leaned forward and topped his drink off. He spared a glance at the untouched second glass, like he debated on taking it for himself. Cassian was tempted by the liquor, but he refused to let go of San'yila. "Let me tell you how this is going to go. Depending on your attitude, I might just give you a nice bed tonight, so don't be a fool, yeah?"

"Go on," Cassian permitted.

The captain set the bottle aside with a loud clap against the wood. "*Salvation* has rules you need to follow." With each rule, he raised a finger. "Respect is earned. Keep your mouth shut and listen to what the crew has to say, and they might just let you have some food. Titles don't matter here. Dragon Rider or not, if you treat my men poorly, I will tie you to the anchor and drop you to the bottom of the sea. I'll let the Tsu'ran have their way with you and your ungrateful tongue. Don't be a barnacle either. If I or any of the men catch you sitting around when you should be manning the deck, I'll stuff you into a coop and let you sleep with the livestock. And if you drink the last bottle of Seaman's Water and you don't tell anyone, then any of these men can declare the second law and fight you to the death. I won't stop them. Am I clear?"

Cassian's temper got the better of him. "You can't kill me. I don't think Kinson would be all too pleased to learn you killed the *Dragon Rider*." Those words made his mouth sour. Pirate was better. A pirate with a bad streak of luck who'd just wanted a fresh start and a hefty payday.

"I'll whip you," the captain replied without hesitation. "And then I'll tie you to the anchor and drop you. She wants you alive, but she didn't say in what condition." He flashed a smile, revealing a silver tooth. "How's that sound?"

Horrible. And Cassian didn't doubt the captain's determination to see it happen.

"You will be a Queen," he continued. Nothing about his declaration was kind or generous. "Kinson will want you to become one. A Dragon Rider with the Red Queen name would make us unstoppable. Not even the landwalkers would stand in our way." The captain tapped his finger against the wood with a fierceness that could leave a mark. "Question is, how do you want to go about it? Do you want to embrace this change, be inducted, and earn the respect of our men and women by doing all the right things? Or do you want us to break your mind and turn you into one of our puppets? We've got a few of them. Wouldn't be lonely." The captain drank, dragging out the next part like he had all the time in the world. "You will meet the Serulic family, and you will address our leader by her rightful title: Viv'an. Kinson has been aggressive in her decisions—a warm welcome to all those who thought the Queens were becoming passive. She does not take well to those like you with a loose tongue and poor sense. Do not think you can win her over with charm and laughter either. She is deaf to those things. Kinson will give you the same speech. She'll tell you your choices, but you will only have the day to decide, if that. The Serulic family isn't fond of waiting, never have been."

"They sound wonderful," Cassian remarked.

The captain snorted and shook his head. "It's that attitude that will get you killed. Be careful with it. If it was my brother who'd found you, he'd have strung you up and skinned you already." Cassian's stomach dropped. San'yila shoved her snout into his leg, sensing his anxiety. "They will test you, and if you fail . . ." The captain dragged out the last word and shrugged. "Well, I don't care."

Cassian licked his lips. "What do you mean *test me*?" He wanted to squirm in his seat, but he kept himself as still as he could, hoping to look brave.

"Exactly as it sounds. A test. Everyone who is brought to the Queens is tested. It's our way to test your will, see if you're strong enough to even be a part of our crew." The captain took a drink. He acted like they were chatting about supper. "You will have to harvest energy."

Nausea moved through Cassian's body like a howling storm. His blood chilled, turning his limbs cold and forcing a sweat to his brow. He swallowed, tasting bile. "What?" he asked.

The savage twitch of his lip betrayed what he was doing. He wanted to scare Cassian, stomp all over his self-assurance, and it was working. "You are bonded to a dragon—an ancient beast that once ruled this world. Your body and mind changes with that bond, granting you abilities that many would pay a lot of coin to have. You must harness energy to prove you are worthy of the Queens' respect. Is that a problem?"

"Well, yeah." Cassian's voice shook. The boldness he had prior was gone, shriveled up and left like the dead who dried in the sun. "I can't."

"Can't what?" the captain whispered, but based on the wicked glimmer in his eyes, he already knew the answer.

"Harvest energy," Cassian confessed, hardly audible. "I've never done it, don't know where to begin, don't know what I'm doing—I don't even know what *energy* is." He recalled what the stranger had told him in the alley, but that didn't do him much good if he didn't know where to begin.

"Hm." The captain drank. "Consider it luck that I told you then. You've got some time to prepare."

"How am I supposed to do that?" Cassian didn't try to hide his nerves.

The captain shrugged. "Not my problem." The ship listed. A scroll on the counter rolled to the other side. "Water's getting choppy. Good sign that we're out of the Grave. Don't think you're not going to be put to work. I'll have you sharpen the weapons with Red. Good guy, so don't piss him off. If he doesn't like you, no one does. Consider it a trust exercise. You do that right, and I'll let you sleep on something soft tonight. If not, you can sleep on the floor with the bones of our last prisoner." The captain flashed an all-knowing smile and added, "We like to keep little reminders around here."

Standing, the captain downed the rest of his drink, grabbed Cassian's, and did the same, then took the glasses and bottle and put them in a drawer and locked it. "Keep your dragon close. I don't want it distracting the crew. A few of us like exotic meats, too, so best you don't get too close with anyone."

"Her," Cassian reminded. He stood, anxious to get out of this place. Six days aboard a Red Queens ship. The goal was to stay alive, but none of that would matter if he couldn't pass the test coming to him. "What's your name?"

"They call me Captain Black," he answered. "Best you don't find out why."

The Pirate with the Crooked Grin

Whetstone against steel. The finer grit of the smooth edge was used to make a sword or dagger cut like a razor. Cassian carefully dragged the stone over the blade's edge. One slip-up, and he'd lose a finger. It might still remain attached by bone, but it would be ruined for any sort of use for several moons, and the nerve damage might be permanent. Nobody ever talked about how the most mundane tasks could end up creating the most dire situations. Men crippled themselves building things, cut fingers and toes off while sharpening weapons, and died slipping on the rigging and falling to their deaths while climbing to the crow's nest. He'd seen his fair share of reckless and patient pirates alike climb the ropes, only to misplace a foot, have a rope snap, or a bad wind tear through. Snapping necks was common business at sea.

Cassian set the blade aside and picked up a new one. He flipped the whetstone over to the coarse side, careful not to press too hard. The rhythmic grating sound drowned out the smashing waves against the ship. It drowned out his thoughts too, which he needed. He'd tried to take dried bread offered to him earlier, only to immediately cough up bile and half-chewed remnants. Not wanting to give himself a bad name, he swallowed it down and gave the rest to San'yila, who was munching on one of the freshly caught fish. The pungent fragrance of the sea made his head spin, but he couldn't leave her. So he sat on the far end of the table to do his weapon work. He wasn't seasick, far from it, he was nauseous from nerves. Nobody ever boarded a Queens' ship and lived to tell about it.

The whetstone was too dry. He stopped, leaned over, and grabbed more oil. Glass's necklace—now hanging against his chest—swayed with his motions. After Captain Black's icy welcome, he'd rinsed the silver and put it on. The weight was comforting. He rubbed the coarse end of the whetstone with his hand, then wiped his fingers on the rag to his left. Satisfied, he returned to the work, intent on making sure he did the finest work possible. No assurance that being a good swabbie would keep him alive or in good graces, but it was the only thing he had control over.

Once the metal was smoothed out, he switched sides and continued to work out the final adjustments. The blade was old, but clearly well-loved. The edges were already fairly sharp before he got his hands on it, but Whrel, one of *Salvation's* crewmembers, told him it didn't matter—a task was done when it was due. Part of the ship's rules. Cassian understood. Captain Ricard was the same. Cassian simply nodded and continued his job. He needed to pick his battles, and that wasn't one he wanted to fight.

"I think that blade is done," Red commented, sitting across from him, chewing on something he'd plucked from a pouch on his belt. The narrow table between them had more gashes in the wood than the tables in the pubs at Greve's Point, where drunken pirates gouged holes into the wood on dares. The red-sashed pirate didn't flinch when San'yila arrived, and he'd hardly spoken since they started their work. Not a soul had come into the room either, leaving him alone with Red. Cassian had observed him quietly for some time, making sure he sharpened the sword like the Queens preferred.

"I know," Cassian said. "Just wanted to have another look. Make sure it was perfect."

"You do that for every sword, and we'll be here all night," Red remarked, clearly annoyed.

Cassian ignored him, taking the rag over the metal for a final polish. The oil gave it a menacing gleam. The grip's leather was aged, cracked, and would need replacing before the next summer, but sometimes the well-used items were the optimal ones. He wouldn't judge that. If it were up to him, he'd wear the same boots for the rest of his life, but most fell apart fairly quickly after the sea water got ahold of them. Salt destroyed almost anything.

Cassian grabbed the plain and cracked sheath and stuffed the weapon back inside before snapping the clasp closed. "Should we oil the sheaths as well?" he asked.

"No," Red answered without hesitation as if he'd expected the question.

Cassian hesitated, confused. "Why?"

Red didn't slow his work as he said, "Because we'll be here all night."

Cassian gaped. "So, you want me to skip this part of the maintenance because you'll be stuck with me longer?" he asked. "Do your stuff. I don't care how long it takes. I need to not look like a fool to the crew." He grabbed another rag from the pile to their right and dipped it into the oil. With far more force than he wanted, he scrubbed the sheath down.

"You know, we have leather oil," Red calmly pointed out.

That was it. Cassian wanted to stab him. He bit his cheek hard enough that he felt the delicate skin break and tasted blood. "You seemed to believe it wasn't important, so I assumed you didn't have any," Cassian remarked, pissed.

Red shrugged and flipped the sword he worked on over. "Huh. Should have asked."

"You're impossible," Cassian said, exasperated. He wanted to scream but chose to set the rag down and leaned back instead. "Where's the leather oil?"

The pirate pointed with the whetstone to the other bottle on the table.

Anger and humiliation fought for a place in Cassian's head, but in the end, he snatched up the bottle and grabbed a new rag.

"We're running low on those," Red commented.

"Of course you are," Cassian bit back without slowing his work. He dumped some leather oil onto the new rag and began re-oiling the sheath, damn whatever Red said about *running low* with these rags.

A crunch made Cassian cringe. San'yila was chewing on the fish's head. Blood and tissue dripped from her small jaw, her eyes half-masked, and a hum filled his head. He could taste the fish and shuddered. The dragon didn't even notice.

Could you be . . . He tried to find the right word. *More private about that?*

She blinked, unsure what he meant.

I can taste your supper. It's disgusting.

She snorted. For such a young thing, she had a lot of spunk. *Delicious,* she proudly corrected.

Cassian shook his head and returned to the sheath. Red watched.

"What?" Cassian asked, annoyed. He set the weapon aside and grabbed the next one. When he pulled the sword out, he grimaced. This blade should have been melted down three summers ago because it was well past its prime. The edges were nicked, the metal blotchy and gray, the pommel claw broken off. Whoever owned this one couldn't find the courage to let it go. Perhaps a family heirloom. He'd try to do his best and make it worthy of a name.

Red raised his brow, still chewing. "I find you two interesting, that's all."

"Hm." He took the coarse edge of the whetstone and started his work at smoothing out the edges. "Not the worst thing I've heard today."

"What is the worst thing you've heard?"

Cassian slowed his work. "Why do you care?"

Red didn't hesitate. "Man to man. That's all this is. I can't imagine things have been easy for you after"—he gestured to San'yila—"you know."

"Yeah, you could say that." Two days ago, Cassian didn't want her. She was a payday. An egg with a price attached to it. Now, he couldn't fathom being separated from her. Things were changing too fast.

Red raised his brow. "You don't like me, do you?"

"You're not particularly my favorite," Cassian answered.

"Why?"

"You're a Queen," Cassian replied. "I don't like the Queens."

Red nodded. He didn't appear to be offended. "But you, as a White Horn, serve the Queens and perhaps, just perhaps, wish to be one. Funny business, sea work is. Don't you think?"

Cassian didn't reply. Couldn't. Red was arrogant and smug, and he wasn't in the greatest mood to deal with that right now. His life had been turned upside down, and the pirate wanted to make friends. It wasn't a good time for that.

"So, what is it? The worst thing you've heard today?" Red was determined to break Cassian's carefully crafted façade—but Cassian didn't want the Red Queens to know how nervous he was. He'd spent his whole life learning to be cruel, but Red's demeanor fractured the tough exterior with far too much ease. The pirate across the table unsettled him more than he liked to admit, and he didn't quite know why yet.

"Meeting your captain was quite possibly the worst thing. Hearing what he had to say, all that," Cassian answered quietly, keeping his voice steady. Disrespectful, but he didn't care what this man thought of him. He wasn't here to impress anyone. Manners were never Cassian's strength. He focused his attention on a nasty chip. It wouldn't be smoothed out, but he could soften the edges.

"And what did he have to say?" Red asked, raising a single eyebrow.

"I'm not telling you that," Cassian snapped. He didn't want to blather on about his life to a stranger. And he certainly didn't trust Red. "We're not friends."

Red shrugged. "Didn't say we were." He sheathed the weapon and set it aside, then picked up the next one. "Sometimes it's nice to just chat. Don't you think?"

He reminded Cassian of Glass. Too much so. Glass had earned his place in Cassian's inner circle, where only several people were ever allowed in. Glass could ask anything, and if his friend needed anything, he would have helped. Now, all he had left was some old necklace Glass wore religiously. The whetstone in Cassian's hand slowed as he asked, "What's your motive here?"

That got Red's attention. His gaze hardened with a fierceness that hadn't been there a moment ago, but his voice remained steady. "Not everything is malicious. Not everyone is out to get you." The pirate's motions with the whetstone were quick, too fast for Cassian's comfort as he worked. "You all are the same. Constantly wondering who else is going to screw you over."

"What?" Cassian stopped what he was doing, staring. "All of us? What, you mean the White Horns? A bit of a broad brush to paint us with, if you ask me. I could do the same for the Queens. You all are a bunch of ego-driven madmen with nasty attitudes."

San'yila sneezed. He checked on her. The fish was nearly gone.

Red raised a hand, signifying defeat. "I meant no disrespect."

"Sounded like it to me." Cassian dragged the whetstone down the blade. The metal sang loudly. "But let's pretend I didn't hear that. So what's really got you all warm and fuzzy with me?"

Now, Red chuckled. He was relaxed—too relaxed—like nothing in the world bothered him. "All right," Red said. The pirate prepped the blade by cleaning it with his rag before dousing the whetstone in oil. His motions were precise, tense, but his face remained stoically devoid of emotion. "What's your plan after all this?" Cassian frowned at the question. Red motioned with the stone to their surroundings. "Surely you must believe there's another side? An end to all this?"

Red was strange. He spoke too philosophically, was too concerned with Cassian's well-being, but he couldn't say it was unfamiliar or unwelcome. Glass had been the same to some degree. Just not as well-dressed or clever. "If you think the Afterlife is the other side, then yes, I do," Cassian said. Red raised his brow in question, and Cassian pursed his lips, annoyed that he had to explain himself. "I've got a feeling that unless a miracle drops from the sky or I become the luckiest man alive, I've got a cordial invite to dine with Death." He shrugged. "It's fine, I guess."

No, it wasn't. None of this was. But he didn't know what else to say. He couldn't tell the pirate he planned on finding a way out, or that he'd kill a dozen men to take a small ship out of the Queens' territory. He wouldn't go down without a fight—he just needed to know what he was working with first before plans were made.

Silence blossomed between them, cold and ugly. Cassian shot San'yila a glare when her mind poked his with the incessance of a fly swarming a carcass. She had no manners. The dragon crawled closer to him. She wanted in his lap to sleep.

Really? he asked. *Now?*

She blinked up at him, reeking of fish.

Fine. He set the whetstone down and reached down. She was dead weight in his hold and made a small squeak of triumph when she contacted his lap. Warmth seeped through, and she tucked herself in a tight ball, wrapping her tail around her body, but it still hung over the edge of his leg. He readjusted her wing, so that it wouldn't get caught if he moved, and then returned to his work.

The pirate across from him still didn't speak, persistent even in his silence. The intensity that festered between them was stifling. Cassian's skin itched, his mind prickled, and he progressively grew more unsettled in his seat. Even the necklace felt like it weighed as much as five steeds around his neck. He wanted to move, shift, stand, pace—all of it—but couldn't with San'yila in his lap.

The metal kissed Cassian's hand, slicing skin clean open. He dropped the whetstone and hissed. Grabbing the nearest rag, he pressed it against the cut to staunch the bleeding. The oil made the wound sting, but he pressed harder. Damn the pain. Damn it all.

Red slowed, feigning surprise that Cassian saw right through.

"What is it?" Cassian pressed. "Don't play a fool with me. You're obviously clever, and you've got something you want to say, so do it. Do you want to kill me? Tell me what a dirty-blooded pirate I am? Or are you here to mock me like your horrible captain and think it's funny? Come on now, don't be shy. I'm ready for it. I've had a real shit few days, so nothing you say will surprise m e."

San'yila retracted from his thoughts, nervous.

Red set the whetstone down and leaned back. He crossed his arms and studied Cassian like he was unsure of what to say. Maybe deciding if he should cut Cassian's tongue out. Queens seemed to be the tongue-cutting type from his experience.

"You're not meant to be here," Red observed dryly.

Cassian scoffed. "You think?"

"You've made some really bad decisions, but that doesn't mean you're a bad person." Red raised his hand before Cassian could tell him to stuff his foot up where the sun didn't shine. "She hatched for you for a reason, didn't she?"

"What's this about?" Cassian demanded. Too many people were trying to tell him how his life was going or would go, and it was really starting to gnaw at his patience.

"We all have a choice about who we want to be," Red quietly replied. "Do you want to hear your choices?"

Cassian frowned and said, "Not from you." This wasn't any pirate he'd ever met. "Who are you?"

"Bear with me." Red raised a hand apologetically. "I get ahead of myself sometimes." He leaned forward and picked up the whetstone to continue his work, but Cassian didn't move. None of this felt right, but he couldn't get up and walk away no matter how hard he tried. Red's presence had Cassian by the throat, even though he'd hardly said anything insightful.

"When I was about your age, I didn't think the world could touch me. Actually, I was certain I could do no wrong. I had it all together, caused trouble but never got caught, and always managed to talk myself out of all my problems. You know, the nasty crewmate, the captain with a bad temper, and the slimy thieves who snuck aboard and thought they could pocket a few extra Krye when no one was looking. I figured out pretty quickly I could convince anyone of anything, good or bad. Kings would pay a fortune to have my tongue working for them."

Arrogant fool, Cassian thought.

"I managed to wiggle the crew out of some precarious situations. Captain had a penchant for getting us into situations we couldn't pay our way out of, so used my skills instead. It worked, for a while. Then word got around that I was the captain's puppet. Our ship got away with one too many things, and it caught up with us."

Red tapped the wood of the table to an unknown tune and said, "I wanted to be what *others* needed me to be, not who *I* needed to be. Big difference." Whetstone scraped against the dull edge of the blade.

"And?" Cassian snorted. "That's the best you've got? Telling me how to live my life through some mistakes you made? I'm not being what anyone needs me to be—I am who I am. This is me. I'm just trying to stay alive."

"Prey will adapt to any situation to stay alive." The insult was clear. Cassian's blood boiled. Everyone wanted a say in his life, especially now that a dragon was in his lap.

"I don't need or want your opinion," Cassian snapped. He checked the bleeding on his palm. Still going, so he wrapped the rag as tight as he could and tied a knot to keep it in place. He picked up the whetstone and returned to the blade. Stabbing Red wasn't an option, so he opted to take his wrath out on the weapon.

"Your two choices are simple." Red spoke like he'd not been told off. "You can continue as you are, embrace the way of the Queens, and live a long and hard life full of political contention for use of you and your dragon—it will happen. You know how we are. Pirates dread change, but Queens despise things we can't control. You are that. We've got enough unknowns to deal with. Last thing anyone needs is a pirate flying around and defying all laws made to obey the sea."

Obey the sea. Old talk. Cassian had not heard that phrase in a long time. A traditional phrase that showed respect for the waters the pirates sailed. Many still believed they were guests aboard the ships, allowed to sail because the sea granted it. Cassian was no exception to that philosophy.

"And you know they won't let that happen," Red stated. Cassian waited for him to continue, unsure he wanted to hear what Red would say but too curious to say otherwise. The way the pirate spoke—the confidence and certainty—was unlike anything he'd ever heard before. Cassian's anger chipped away as fast as it solidified, and he didn't have any strength left to argue. Words seeped into the deepest parts of him, sinking their claws in and holding tight. He knew Red was right.

"They will chain you to their ways, break you into submission. San'yila will have no choice but to follow. You are her Rider, her everything," Red said. He sounded troubled. Each word carried with it a resolve that made Cassian freeze. "The Queens will turn you into a weapon for their control. They'll make you wish you were dead." Red shook his head and ran his fingers along the metal to check the evenness. "No life is worth living like that, bound to someone else's needs."

Red worked a little while longer, taking the smooth edge of the whetstone and finishing the one side of the dagger before flipping it over. He reached over and oiled the stone in his hand, leveling the coarse surface into the oil and sloshing around twice.

Cassian's mouth was dry. "Or?"

"Hm?" Red swept the whetstone in long motions down the blade, working with the care of a blacksmith. The pirate had done this a hundred times.

"Or?" Cassian repeated, louder. Something about the way Red spoke made him rethink his decisions.

"Or you leave it all behind. Flee. Get out of here. Sail to land and start anew."

"You just say that because you want me out of your way," Cassian said. "Or you're trying to trap me into a betrayal of the Queens."

Red snorted. "And why would I want that?"

Cassian didn't have a proper answer. "Because I threaten whatever political hold the Serulic family has on the Queens."

"A good theory," the pirate complimented him. "But no. Under their control, you'd strengthen them immensely. You know that. They want you, and they'll do anything to have you."

Nothing about that response gave Cassian peace. "So I stay and be forced to serve through some dark ritual"—he could only think of Bauer and the crew of *Dread Deep*—"or I flee, not that I know how, and start a life on land." Cassian shook his head. The audacity. "And what? Sell fish? What about San'yila? She won't be this size forever."

"You head north. Go until you find a cause you can stand behind."

Cassian laughed, uncomfortable. "What's that supposed to mean?" He cleared his throat and added, "Captain Black would kill you if he knew what you were telling me."

"I'm sure you're familiar with all the stories of the dead," Red said softer, ignoring the comment. Either he was completely mad or wasn't afraid of the captain, or maybe he doubted Cassian would ever rat him out. "I'm also sure you're aware of the political tensions in the countries, which have caused major upset in some of our trades. There are plenty of causes to fight for out there now. Things that would give you purpose and a second chance at a life you want."

Cassian froze. The pirate spoke like he knew him personally, which was unnerving. They didn't know each other, and Cassian preferred it that way, but Red acted like they were old friends. Cassian's wrapped hand wavered over an uneven edge.

"It's not like your current life is heading anywhere promising," Red commented. "Leaving all this behind would give you that second chance."

Cassian was overthinking. He forced air in and returned to the grinding of stone against metal to try and still his racing thoughts. "You're awfully committed to seeing me out of your way."

"Hm." Red snorted. "We all have choices we want to make, and choices we have to make. I like to consider myself open to the different opportunities out there."

Too much. Cassian didn't like how comfortable Red was with him, and that made him suspicious. Red's confidence made him arrogant, a fool to life, and it would get him killed. Caution was the pirate's slang for staying alive. One never jumped aboard with a bunch of strangers out at sea—they could be cannibals. It'd happened before. Red seemed to believe he could go anywhere without consequences.

Cassian returned to his work, suddenly eager to be done and as far from Red as he could be. Nothing about this conversation gave him peace. If it were Glass talking, the advice would have been welcome. But this conversation did the opposite. Cassian was uncomfortable with the idea that a Red Queen would want to help—no Queen ever helped, unless they were out to gain something. Red could be setting Cassian up, to trick him, which felt more likely than the idea that Red simply wanted to help. Cassian was wary of the Red Queens, and he had every right to be. They'd done nothing but destroy his life.

Maybe Red was high on whatever seaweed the *Salvation* crew picked up. Some seaweed contained elements that made a man hallucinate or giddy. Others were poisonous. He wasn't much of a chewer—never had been, which made him an oddity amongst the majority of pirates in the Vore

World. He'd watched a man seize and cough up blood after eating the wrong seaweed once. The Dead's Hand. That's what they called it.

San'yila settled, and her breathing slowed. At least someone was relaxed.

Red flashed a smug look that made Cassian want to reach across the table and slit his throat with the blade he sharpened. Instead, he sat there, swallowing a response he knew would get him killed or whipped, fixing his gaze to the sword in front of him.

"Sooner or later, Cassian, you will have to decide who you want to be."

Queens' Gate

Working aboard *Salvation* wasn't easy. Cassian spent most of his time looking over his shoulder and sleeping with one eye open. He didn't trust the crew, not with San'yila. They eyed her like a meal. Maybe to the Queens, she was. The only privacy he got was when he was stuffed in a private room that hardly fit the cot he used, like he was now. The Queens had done that because nobody wanted him in the crew's quarters. But he didn't mind. It gave him and San'yila a safe place to ponder, and he often did it while holding Glass's necklace.

He worked with Red for the six hard days they sailed. That wasn't intentional—he couldn't stand the arrogance and smug attitude—but it always seemed like he found himself next to the pirate. Cleaning duties, Red was there. Feeding the livestock, he showed up. Working the main deck, Red was next to him, tying ropes and dropping the anchor. Out of all the men or women it could have been, it was always him. Cassian tried to swap places with another pirate when they checked the rigging, only to be shoved forward and barked at. He was twenty, but to these men, he might as well have been a boy because that's how he felt. The more he tried to avoid Red, the more the pirate seemed to appear. He didn't even need to say anything, but every time Red was around, he was reminded of their discussion from the first day. Cassian needed to get out of here.

Red got under his skin like a parasite, wiggling and scraping against muscle and bone, making his motions abrupt and his replies sharp. Cassian rubbed his neck more times than he could count, and he knew it was a nervous habit. When he did sleep, it didn't feel rested. He woke up exhausted. On the third day, he fell asleep eating, only to be awakened by San'yila pouncing on him just before another Red Queen walked in. She might be young, but she learned fast. They needed to play the good pirate by obeying commands and keeping their guard up to stay alive.

The dragon stayed close. Too close. Cassian took a sheet and wrapped it around himself, making a pouch for her to sit in while he worked. Before that, she followed him around on the main deck while they were tightening ropes for the oncoming storm, nearly getting stepped on. Captain Black tore him a new one and gave Cassian a black eye for that. It was healing now, but the first night, it swelled shut, and he was shoved into the galley to help prepare meals for the crew with the youngest shipmate, a twelve-year-old boy with an attitude that would have earned Cassian a black-out beating at that age. After that, he got the sheet from his cot and used it to swaddle San'yila. It earned him looks to have a dragon strapped to his chest, but it was the best idea he had. She was out of the way, and that meant he wouldn't get mauled.

Rain or sun, she snuggled in that make-shift pouch, clinging to his clothes and occasionally burping rancid fish. He didn't like the way the others looked at her, but he kept his head down and worked. Yanking and climbing rigging were far more complicated than they needed to be with her bulk strapped to him, but he made it work.

She prodded his mind with questions often—too many to count. As the days went by, her mind matured. She grew fast. Despite her small form, her presence aged. She learned by observing and asking questions about what Cassian did. Her sentences became longer, more complex, and more precise. She understood emotions, wants, and needs. Most importantly, she understood danger and when Cassian needed her to stay quiet. Like when a brute the size of a mountain slapped the dried fish from Cassian's hand and wanted to start a fight simply *because*. The Queens were proud, but that didn't mean they were civil. The Seven Sea Laws permitted fights to the death to settle disputes if needed—Arian had stayed true to that and was now rotting. Cassian, no matter how badly he wanted to cut the wretched bilge-drinking fool's tongue out and give him to the crows, remained seated and quiet as others encouraged the fight. The brute slapped his head, pushed him around, and even spilled old ale over him, but Cassian kept his mouth shut. San'yila turned to dead weight in her pouch.

And Red was always there, watching from the corner of a room or always within earshot. It shouldn't surprise Cassian that he was around—the ship was only so big—but it unnerved him. The only privacy he got was in the small cabin assigned to him, but even that felt like it had eyes stuffed into the walls.

He knew he was sailing into a trap. A prison. Nothing about this would go the way he wanted, but he would try and bend the hand of fate in his favor. Cassian didn't want to die or be enslaved to a bloodthirsty cause. Serving the Queens against his will was out of the question. He'd die before that happened. San'yila or not, being forced to serve a cause he didn't support was crueler than any death.

Nobody outside of the Queens had ever seen their home territory. Stories about secret islands traveled through the countless ships at sea, regardless of rank or clan. Many were laughed off; others thought the Queens were rulers over the beasts that traversed these waters. Hard to doubt a claim like that when the Queens had ruled these waters for centuries. They probably held a deal with the Tsu'ran.

Cassian shuddered. Even the memory of the slimy creatures made his skin crawl. Nothing about them was safe or normal. Having spoken to one, seen the way she treated him—told he was marked—it unsettled him. Another mystery he didn't fully understand. Red would probably have the answer to that. Red thought he knew everything.

"You're summoned!" a man yelled. Pounding following.

Cassian dropped the necklace, the pendant striking his chest with the sharp edge of the skull. San'yila lay across his chest, sleeping, but the sound woke her. "Sorry," Cassian mumbled to the little dragon. He should have been sleeping, too. He'd worked through the night and been told to rest in their final stretch to the Queens' territory. He hadn't been able to shut his mind off, though. And the meal he'd brought back with him—a sad collection of dried fish skin and stale water—sat untouched. Anxiety ripped through him like a maelstrom. They were approaching Queens' Gate, home of the most powerful pirates in the world.

"Coming," Cassian called before the pirate on the other side could throw an insult. He sat up, taking San'yila in his arms as he did so. He didn't need the sheet in his cabin, so he let her crawl onto his shoulder when he stood. Talons pierced skin, and he winced. "Easy."

She snorted and shook her head, smacking him in the cheek. Small scales scraped the skin, and he pulled his head back. Those were new. She was heavier than a few days ago. All she did was eat and sleep. And annoy him.

She blew hot air into his ear, and he recoiled. "Hey!"

San'yila tilted her head, blinking with one fiery eye. She'd heard his thoughts.

Cassian reached down and picked up a piece of dried fish skin and offered it to her. "Truce?" She took it. "All right, then."

The distraction didn't ease his nerves. If he could have thrown up, he would have, but he had hardly anything to empty from his stomach. Cassian forced air into his lungs, only to find them protesting. He rubbed his chest. He couldn't stay in here. They'd break the door down and drag him out. He couldn't fight his way off the ship—he'd lose that fight. One man against two dozen Red Queens would earn him a proper whipping and cracked ribs . . . if he was lucky. They'd deliver him to Kinson barely alive. The only thing he could do was walk off this ship with his head held high and hope he could get out of the Queens' territory before they chained him to their cause.

We'll find a way, he told San'yila. *We have to.*

He'd made his decision already, but now he felt the weight of that promise. The realization slapped him as hard as a crashing wave does when stirred up with the help of a fearless storm. He nodded, confident they could make a plan. In the days following the loss of the *Torment* crew to the Life Eater, he'd had to accept that if the choice was there, if he could have tried to save them at the risk of his own life, he wouldn't have.

He needed out of here. And he needed to do it fast. A new life awaited him. One that wouldn't be tied up with pirate politics or this savage crew. As much as he loved the sea, he loved staying alive more. And now it wasn't just about him. The dragon on his shoulder, who continued to believe the best of him, deserved a chance at life—at purpose. Two things he'd never been granted. Not by choice, anyway. It was either run or become enslaved to the Red Queens.

If he was going to die, then he would go down with a fight. He'd take the Red Queen ruler with him, too. But if he lived through this, he would run, find a small alcove or quiet mountainside, and give San'yila a proper upbringing. One that didn't include having toes cut or being afraid.

"You coming out or am I coming in?" the Red Queen called, slamming his fist into the door again.

"Easy now, sweetheart. I'm getting dressed," Cassian replied. Sarcasm slipped out before he could stop it, and he grimaced. *Stay alive.* Easier said than done when he had a mouth like that.

Cassian opened the door to the brute who towered above him, whose arms were crossed. They stood there, dancing between a fist fight and moving onto the deck. Cassian's muscles were tense, his blood hot, while his thoughts lingered on the approaching doom if he didn't find a way out. Survival instinct won.

"We're expected," the brute stated. He eyed Cassian like he was a piece of rotten meat. "Coward." With that insult, the Red Queen walked down the hall, too narrow for his wide shoulders.

Cassian waited before following, wanting to put enough space between them so that he'd see a punch coming. San'yila nudged the side of his head, sensing his hesitation.

We'll find a way, she echoed.

Now, with the looming reality ahead, he was too terrified to believe her.

They made their way to the main deck. The hot sun blistered his skin, an abrupt welcome after the darkness of his cabin. He blinked and rubbed his eyes, forcing them to submit to the change in light. All around, pirates stood at the ready, hands over their chests as the *Salvation* rolled into Queens' Gate. Cassian stammered, dumbfounded by what he saw.

Ahead, hundreds of ships lined up. They floated next to each other, palaces of the sea, with their flags raised. Ships twice the size of the one he was on now marked the port's mouth—a challenge to anyone who dared to seek entry. For as far as the eye could see, Queen ships sat in wait. A fleet that could crush an entire country stood at the ready. His knees weakened. Stories spoke of the expansiveness of the Queens, but the tales hadn't done their numbers justice. The Queens could have the Vore World if they wanted.

Impressive didn't even come close to describing what he saw. Cassian felt like a wounded seal cornered by predatory whales. He motioned to the endless sea of ships. "This . . .?" Nothing else came out.

The brute slapped his shoulder, hard enough to make him stumble. San'yila's talons broke fabric and dug into his shoulder to keep herself upright. Wetness seeped across his skin, and he saw red spread across the tattered fabric of his shirt. San'yila's regret poked at his mind.

Don't, he said before she could apologize.

"Fleet's a beauty, ain't she?" the brute said.

Cassian nodded, choosing not to reply. Nothing would compete with the mass expansiveness of the Queens' armada. The White Horns were impressive—stories as old as the Vorelian Empire spoke of the rose-crested pirates who spared not even their children's blood. But this was different. Final. Resolute. Domination.

Salvation sailed forward, entering the wide valley of ships. Men and women stood aboard the ships, arms crossed. Some held baskets, others with nets full of freshly-caught fish, while a handful crossed their arms and stood with their chins high. Children dressed in brown leather and covered in red paint stood wide-eyed and curious. Captains saluted, and crews nodded to one another. As they sailed deeper into the harborage, Cassian realized each ship was connected. Gangways and docking lines kept them tethered to one another. A floating city, tucked up behind the Grave and unreachable by the rest of the world.

A number of pirates crossed their arms over their chests in an unfamiliar gesture, although Cassian gathered it might be one of respect. He leaned over to the nearest pirate, a woman dressed in leather and beads. His face must have had the question written all over it.

"*Salvation* is an honorary ship," she told him without looking his way.

Ahead, on the horizon, he saw land. An island. He didn't even know an island existed behind the Grave—nobody ever crossed far enough to know of it. And if they had, they never made it back to tell others.

Cassian searched each ship, finding small market stands with ribbons tied to the ropes. Several children hopped ships, cradling items close to their chests and laughing before being scolded by parents. Young men covered in tattoos and body paint watched, neither impressed nor interested.

"Is this normal?" Cassian mumbled.

"Not every ship earns this greeting," the brute answered.

"No." Cassian waved at the fleet. "Do they always stay like this?"

The brute shrugged. "Preparations."

"For?"

The brute flashed him a cold smile. "Too many questions, White Horn."

As much as Cassian dreaded Red, he wished he was standing next to him now. He craned his neck in search of the pirate, finding him ten paces away, hands planted on his hips. Red nodded at Cassian, then pointed ahead. Cassian's eyes followed the gesture.

The island was approaching. He could see a small village set up close to the shore. He expected grand palaces and homes made of stone, but there weren't any such dwellings. Only huts and tents nestled close to each other, which appeared tattered and worn. If the Queens owned this territory, he didn't understand why they'd not taken it upon themselves to build something more . . . permanent.

Unless they didn't plan on staying.

Settled right on the coast, just beyond the village, was a table with chairs. A woman sat drinking and watching the oncoming ship. A bundle of dreadlocked hair streaked with red sat atop her head. Her tawny skin was covered in tattoos unique to the Queens, and she wore a necklace adorned with a dozen differently-sized bones. Cassian stood, paralyzed. Kinson Serulic. The leader of the Red Queens. The woman who would determine his destiny.

"Perfect timing," the brute said. "She's ready to talk."

"How—" Cassian stopped. "How did she know to expect us today?"

Boots came up from behind. "The Queens have ways," Captain Black said, halting beside him. The captain must have sensed his question. "You live through today, we might just show you how it's done."

By the Gods. Terror burrowed into Cassian's heart, malicious and agonizing. He wouldn't make it out of here.

We'll find a way, the dragon insisted. Her presence startled him. He'd been so caught up in the surroundings that he'd nearly forgotten about her. He glanced over at her, and she tilted her head, mildly offended.

He didn't know what to say.

"Remember what I said?" Captain Black asked.

Cassian laughed, hollow. "How could I forget?" Today, he'd be tested to prove his worth as a Queen. Today, he'd either die a coward or be branded a Queen.

His thoughts raced. Hundreds of ships, all heavily occupied by the looks of it. How would he get out of here? Sure, he could take a rowboat, but only if he could get access to one and could slip away without being seen. The fleet of ships surrounded most of the island, so unless he managed to sneak aboard one of them as a stowaway, he didn't see how any of this would work. He should have jumped off *Salvation* when he had the chance.

Captain Black grinned. "All right, slow her down and let's grab the dinghy! Just one. We ain't staying long." He looked back at Cassian. "But I'll stay long enough to watch the show."

The terror Cassian had felt earlier solidified and dropped into the pit of his stomach. Only one option would keep him alive: Joining the Queens.

The crew got to work, furling the sails and dropping the anchor, which wouldn't fall far before it struck the sandy shelf. The water was too shallow to continue the rest of the way aboard the ship, so they would have to row. He could almost feel the anchor strike the bottom in his bones as the chain stopped and men called a successful landing. The ship slowed to a crawl.

Red approached. "Captain—"

"Just the man I want to see," Black said. "You'll take him to shore with me."

Cassian followed the red sash pirate to the boat prepared for them. Not that there was much to prepare. It was lowered into the water next to a rope they'd descend with. As tough as Cassian tried to act, he couldn't stop the shake in his hands or his racing heart that threatened to run off without him. San'yila nudged his head again with her warm and soft snout.

I know what you're going to say, he told her, *and I'm not so sure anymore that I believe it.*

Red stopped next to the railing and motioned to Cassian. "After you."

Cassian tried to say something snarky, but his tongue weighed as much as iron. Red grabbed him before he could swing over the side and descend. He squeezed Cassian's shoulder and whispered, "Your mind is the most powerful weapon you have. Use it." He gestured ahead. "Go."

Daughter of the Red Goddess

Boots sank into sand, the sun blistered the back of his neck, and Queens surrounded him. Many of the Queens and their families stood on the beach watching as Captain Black, Red, and Cassian rowed ashore. Children covered in white and red body paint and bones piercing their septums waved. Pregnant women cradled their swollen bellies, wearing precious little fabric to cover their bodies. Men with scarred branding crossed their arms and stood beside the table where Kinson waited. Guards. Servants. He didn't know what the Queens called their soldiers, but he didn't need to ask to know that the extra show of force was because of him. A White Horn in Queens' Gate was unheard of. And if it had ever happened, no White Horn ever lived to tell about it.

Despite the hundreds of ships and the countless Queens surveying the scene, Cassian could have heard a fish burp from the depths below. Red walked on his left, the captain on his right. Cassian might not like either of them, but now he felt like they were all he had.

San'yila's anxiety bled into his own. His heart quickened, and his stomach twisted in knots. His once-steady hands trembled as they neared the table. The little dragon was overwhelmed by the number of people. He wanted to comfort her, but he couldn't even settle his own racing thoughts.

You're— He stopped himself. It would be cruel to tell her to stop. To scold her. The abrupt realization of that stomped out everything else, and he blinked. When had he become so soft?

They stopped before the table. A small collection of sliced bread and cheese lay on a serving board. No fish. For once, fish wasn't involved. Cassian spent so many days eating all types of cooked and raw fish that to *not* see it was surprising. Kinson sat with a cup wrapped in her bony hands, each finger tattooed with a red line that ran to her nailbeds. Closer, he could see a tattoo of a red crown encircling her head. Her eyes were deep set, framed by sharp creases earned by years of harsh sun and harsher expressions. The bridge of her nose was encrusted with bony stud piercings that looked alarmingly like teeth preparing to clamp shut on her fleshy lump of a nose. To insert those must have been excruciating. She smiled, revealing red teeth. Whether dyed that color or from what she ate, he didn't know. She was brutally beautiful.

"You." In that one word, Cassian heard disgust, thrill, and bitterness. Everything the Queens stood for and fought for was packed in that single statement. Cassian defied all of it. "Please, sit." Her accent was thicker than anything he'd ever heard before.

He hesitated, trying to determine whether he would be stabbed by one of her guards before he made it to the chair. Before he could formulate a self-defense strategy, Red pushed him forward. Kinson chuckled and took a sip of her tea. Cassian didn't like the sound of her voice.

As he settled into the chair, he felt ever smaller. Everything he'd worked for and wanted to be was leagues beyond his reach. He was officially in Red Queen territory—how would he ever get out of this? For the first time in his life, Cassian didn't feel the awe he'd once held for witnessing such an impressive fleet of ships. He felt cornered, like prey, and angry. Angry that his entire life had been one mistake after the next; one unlucky change after another. He didn't want to die, and he didn't want to serve the Queens. The tattoo on his hand, the rose, was his pride. He'd been —he *still was* a White Horn captain.

Kinson's amber eyes flashed behind him. "You are dismissed."

The retreating sound of boots met his ears. Red and Captain Black were gone. No turning back. If this was what Destiny wanted for him, he would kill her with his bare hands, or die trying. Something inside him snapped as he stared at her in her finery. She wanted to enslave him. His fear melted into the rage he'd so carefully curated his whole life. He'd be damned to the Grave before he'd show her an instant of respect.

Kinson set her cup down—dainty and out of place next to the fierce nature of her appearance. "You are hungry, yes?"

"No," Cassian said.

The guards stiffened. In all his life at sea, he'd never seen a pirate act as a bodyguard before. Such duties were often left for landwalkers, where their queens and kings sat on plush thrones and ate too many grapes. One pirate took a step forward, but the Red Queen ruler raised her hand. "It be quite a'right," Kinson assured the man. "He don' be knowin' our traditions well yet, but he will, yeah. He will." Her gaze never wavered from Cassian's. "You will address me as Viv'an." A challenge. A dare to see if he would submit.

Agitation blinded him. "I will not." Each word was said with so much disdain that he shook.

She raised her brow, amused. "Thirsty?"

"No."

"Hm." She wasn't perturbed, picking up a slice of cheese and bread from the wooden plate. "Shame, yeah. I wanted to give you a proper Queen's welcome."

Cassian scoffed. "Cheese and bread will not make me respect you." She paused at his audacity. "How'd you do it? How'd you successfully kill Zinfel and not have an uprising?"

Now she frowned.

"Don't pretend you don't know what I'm talking about." The guards didn't move, but he knew they waited for Kinson to give an order. A slight breeze brought with it the promise of the sea—salty and alluring. So close, and yet out of reach. With sand beneath his feet, he itched to return to the water. "You killed Zinfel for her place," Cassian added. "Your family had been planning that for a long while, hadn't you?"

San'yila jumped off his shoulder and into his lap with a huff. She didn't like any of this. She tucked herself as small as she could against him. Without thought, he rested a hand on her warm scales. The scar above his thumb began to itch profusely.

"You heard," Kinson applauded. Her lip curled upward for just a moment before dropping. She looked like a child earning their first gift—thrilled that Cassian had said what he did. "Either you're from *Torment* or word travels fast." It wasn't a question, and she didn't wait for him to give her a proper answer. Maybe she didn't need one. Kinson picked up her tea again, slowly wrapping her fingers around the small cup. "A change was needed. Despite the, oh, political shift for us, the people are happy. That true, Deliro?" She peered around her shoulder to the largest man covered in Queen markings. Deliro nodded curtly. "Yeah. Happy."

Cassian eyed Deliro, unconvinced by his weak response. Perhaps the Queens had a different way of showing their satisfaction. "Why?" he asked. His shoulders and back ached from how tensely he sat in the chair, ready to jump and run at the slightest threat. "Zinfel was loyal to the crews. We had a system. And then one of your ships shows up threatening us and executing our captain because of his loyalty to Zinfel."

Kinson shook her head. "You think you know what loyalty means, but you don', and you need to be taught." She took a slow drink. The heartbeats that passed between them stretched as long as a season. Cassian bit his cheek, feigning patience, when he wanted to grab all the cheese in front of him and stuff it down her throat.

Finally, Kinson lowered her tea and said, "You see, the Red Queens have served these waters for centuries. Loyalty to keep us that way, yeah. We haven' changed our ways because of respect. Duties, White Horn. Obligations, accountability, pride. Keeps the Queens as strong as we are."

"Loyalty to your traditions," Cassian pointed out. The corner of her lip twitched.

"Humor me." She set her cup down again and picked up a slice of cheese. "What do the White Horns stand for?"

"You know that answer already," Cassian replied. "The White Horns serve you."

"Yeah?" Kinson asked, one eyebrow going up. "Huh." She sounded genuinely surprised.

Cassian's guard slipped. "What?"

"You sit across from me, and you speak like my crew came for your ship because of opportunity." She leaned forward. "I sent them. I asked them to hunt *Torment* down because your captain was workin' against the Queens' interests." Kinson drummed her fingers against the arm of the chair, lips pinched. "You speak as if you don' know the Queens."

Ricard wouldn't have done that. Cassian was bewildered and speechless. He wanted to tell her she was wrong but couldn't. He didn't have proof, nothing to declare Ricard's innocence. Not that she could prove her claims either.

He didn't have to ask.

"Captain Ricard was aidin' Zinfel with some, oh, politically disruptive practices, yeah," Kinson continued slowly. "They didn't align with our traditions, or our current needs." She threw the word back at him. "That be why my family did what they did."

"How honorable of you," Cassian spat. He didn't hide the cynicism that dripped from his voice. "I almost respect you."

Kinson didn't flinch at the hostility. She was fierce. "The Red Queens do more than just point fingers and tell ships where to go, yeah. We have our ears everywhere, land and water. We got men and women who serve councils, their identities kept quiet. We smuggle goods that cost more than any kingdom. The world thrives because of our services, because of our ships. Landwalkers are a necessity, not somethin' to be dismissed. They have an impressive influence on the economy, White Horn."

Cassian opened his mouth, but she continued.

"A war approaches us. Our hand will be forced more than it already has. A prophecy speaking of a new era is here, and we must act on it or risk being left behind. You familiar with our old beliefs?"

He wasn't. He knew she knew that. The Queens kept their culture a secret.

"They be calling it the Díanzon Prophecy. A King of Monsters lives amongst us, yeah, as strong as a God and as violent as the sea. He will bring war to our waters, bring cities to their knees, and destroy centuries of hard work for a twisted definition of peace. He will take our Goddess, raise her from her peaceful slumber, and steal her heart. If he does, there will be no sea to call home and no land that is safe enough for any pirate to walk. The King of Monsters will submerge the world into total darkness, feeding false promises of a new beginnin' when there is none. Only war. Our responsibility is to keep that from happenin'."

Cassian licked his lips, suddenly thirsty. He wanted to ask for the tea now, but he was too proud to break down in front of this woman. He'd made a promise to himself to remain strong, but what Kinson told him shattered his confidence.

"How can you believe in such a thing?" Cassian asked, mouth agape. He knew politics amongst the landwalkers were tense, but basing an entire political strategy on a prophecy? Those were just legends told by bards on a drunken night.

Kinson slapped her hand on the table, making him jump and causing San'yila to dig her talons into his legs to keep herself in place. The Red Queen ruler leaned forward. "You blind, White Horn? Look around you!" She raised her voice. He knew people were staring. "You feel it in the waters?

You taste the change on the wind? They speak of fallin' kingdoms in Sorréle. They tell of a man who can wield fire and who drinks the blood of his enemies. Men and women alike fear him, yeah. Some even say the Gods don' know what to do with him. *They fear him*. We must prepare."

Cassian scoffed. "Gods don't fear. If you even believe in that stuff, which I don't."

Kinson shook her head. She looked to pity him in that instant, and he regretted his words. "Gods fear, White Horn. And if you ever thought otherwise, then you're prayin' to the wrong ones."

Cassian swallowed the little bit of spit in his mouth. The gulp was audible in the terrible silence, and it made him cringe. "So, this is what you want with me? To make me a servant to your cause because you believe some madman is running around in Sorréle?"

"We don' just believe, we *know*," Kinson corrected. She shook her head. "Morei Geral, former king of Geral. Only recently lost his title. We believe this marks the start of the end." She motioned at his empty cup. "Thirsty?"

By the restless sea, he was. He could have drunk fifteen cups right now and still been thirsty. Nerves do horrible things to the body. "I'm fine," he lied.

"Okay," she said, and motioned to the guard behind. From a pouch, he pulled free a small dark bottle and handed it to her. She popped the cap and poured it into her tea. "A little somethin' stronger."

Intentional. Cassian rubbed his fingers along San'yila's back, just where her wings met her shoulders, distracting himself. He wanted five of those bottles of liquor and a big bowl of stew, but he refused to give Kinson any impression that he was comfortable or trusting enough to accept her hospitality.

Her statement about this Morei Geral hung over his head, festering. Cassian didn't care much for the landwalker politics, but he did find it interesting that the Red Queens were so worried about a single ex-king. There'd been plenty of empires that rose and fell in the past while pirates sailed, yet this one bothered them.

"Tell me more about this Morei," Cassian said. "What about him makes him different from any other power-hungry king?"

"The prophecy," she replied. "Never have the sun and stars lined up as they have. Makes us believe he is the King of Monsters. He will come for our waters, for our people."

"And why would he do that?" Cassian pressed. "Landwalkers don't know the waters like we do."

"Because he seeks to make the sea his."

"Then kill him." Seemed fairly straightforward. One man against a fleet of Queens felt like a pretty obvious win.

She took a large drink before pouring more liquor into her cup. "You are foolish. The King of Monsters can't be stopped like that. He controls fire, yeah. If the rumors are true, he's far more dangerous than we would know how to handle. The Gods can' kill him, so how could we? No." She shook her head. "Our only way is to prove our value and retain the rights to the sea. We do that with you."

All the blood shunted from his body, turning his shaky limbs frigid. He knew he paled—he could feel the blood drain from his cheeks. San'yila nudged his hand. Her presence shoved itself deeper into his head, aggressive and unlike her.

Strange energy is here.

He blinked, confused. *What?*

She snorted, peering over the chair behind him. Cassian didn't want to be a parent right now. He needed San'yila to behave. His life was being traded around like he didn't have a say, and it was starting to really piss him off. *Not now, San'yila.*

The dragon leaned to get a better look at the source of what had disturbed her. He kept a firm grip on her to keep her from slipping off.

Kinson smiled, but it was cold. "He's quite cute, yeah."

"She," Cassian corrected again.

"Ah, she." The daughter of the Red Goddess leaned back, crossing her legs. She looked like she'd gotten exactly what she wanted—a Dragon Rider before her—which scared him more than talks of Gods and prophecies. "You'll carry the Queens' message once she's old enough to fly. You'll see Morei for yourself when he finds his next throne. The prophecy says he will, so I'm sure it's just a matter of time, yeah."

All of this was going too far. "I am not your puppet," Cassian snapped. Kinson tilted her head. "I did not come here willingly to serve you or your cause. You speak to me as if you and your people want nothing but peace, but you're slaughtering crews and burning ships in the name of your family. You fear a man who likely wants nothing to do with you—he's probably got bigger issues than worrying about a cluster of pirates hiding out behind the Grave. And now you want me to champion your cause? How bloody honorable."

Kinson shifted her finger. At once, the guards were on him. Cassian kicked out, tucking San'yila against his chest. Hands grabbed and pulled, ripping him out of his chair. He needed to defend himself, but he was too busy trying to keep San'yila safe. He resorted to kicks and rolls. The dragon squeaked and snorted. Her mind went wild with fear, and he tried to tell her not to worry, but he couldn't get the plea out fast enough. A boot met his jaw and stilled his frenzied struggle. Hands shoved themselves between his arms, latching onto San'yila. She screamed. A horrifying high-pitch sound that shattered all Cassian's reasoning. He couldn't let them have her.

"Let go of her," Cassian hissed.

Adrenaline surged. He kneed the pirate closest to him, then yanked the dragon free and stood. Arms wrapped around him with brute force, tackling him to the ground. Cassian hoped San'yila kept her wings tucked because he never had a chance to shield her from the fall. He kicked again, hearing a grunt as his boot landed true in the guard's crotch. Sand went into his nose, ears, clothes, every exposed hole and crevice, and he slammed into the table, knocking everything to the ground.

He ducked to avoid a swing, only to feel metal burrow into his shoulder. Stunned, he stumbled and tried to move, but the blade wanted to go with. Too deep. A tingling sensation raced down his right arm, angry and agonizing. Blood seeped and with one final tug, the weapon was pulled free. His knees were kicked in, forcing him to the ground. The hot sand burned right through the fabric against his knees.

San'yila clawed at his chest, trying to get away. Maybe he should have let her go at the start, but he'd been so focused on keeping her close that he'd not considered that letting her go might have kept her safer than he could. His head swam, and he blinked up as Kinson approached. She gestured at the pirate closest to him.

The pirate ripped San'yila out of Cassian's hands. The dragon slashed, fought, and flapped. His heart shriveled up into half its size, hating what he saw. She'd already felt enough agony because of him, because of what he'd done. He'd made a promise to protect her after what Bauer did, and he'd already failed her. Again.

San'yila wanted to see him as something more than he'd been his whole life, but she was wrong. Every decision he made ended in blood and bad luck. Cassian wasn't a good man, and he surely didn't know how to satisfy the Red Queens without giving them what they wanted.

Hot blood poured down his back. He could feel it ooze and seep until it reached the base of his back. The fiery pain burning his shoulder made it difficult to move. San'yila still struggled, and the pirate attempted to pin her against the ground, calling for rope.

Stop, he told her. Her mind emptied at once, hanging on his every word. *It's not worth it. You will injure yourself.*

She blinked, half her body buried in the sand, wings laid out. *I'm afraid.* Her voice was so small and meek compared to the feisty dragon he'd come to know so well.

Me too, he confessed. Cassian couldn't lie to her. Not about this. *Just don't bite any fingers off, yeah?*

A pirate returned with rope. "That won't be necessary," Cassian told them. "She will behave."

The Queens didn't move, unconvinced.

"Go on. Let her go," Cassian insisted. He pleaded with San'yila to remain calm. *We only have one chance. Keep your head up, little one.*

Cassian didn't know what that chance was yet, but he knew if they continued down this route, they'd be killed before sundown. Maybe they still could get out of here. It just might not be how he originally planned, and they certainly couldn't escape if they were dead.

The pirate pinning the red dragon slowly raised his hands. San'yila did as Cassian advised. She straightened and shook her wings free of sand, dipping her head in submission.

Cassian swallowed the violent impulse that made him want to lunge for the pirate who had dared to touch her. His mind blossomed with the twisted fantasies of how best he'd kill the pirate—how he'd kill all the Red Queens. He hated them before, but now, he would make it his lifelong mission to watch them burn.

Kinson's bony fingers wrapped around his jaw, tugging him back to the present. She leered down at him, rotating his face so she could look at his neck. "The trinket you wear. Is for good luck, yeah? You feel you need it?"

Cassian knew he couldn't do anything to get her fingers off him. Not without getting San'yila harmed in the process. "It belonged to the only man I ever called a friend. And if you try and take it, I will gouge your eyes out with my thumbs." It was the last thing he had of Glass and the life he once took for granted. He would cherish the necklace until his last breath.

Kinson snorted, unbothered. "You've got plenty of space for the Queens' mark. But you need to pass our test first."

"You're a maggot-loving whore," Cassian hissed.

"Mm, I like your attitude. It will serve the Queens well. Yeah, it will." Kinson leaned down, so that they were almost nose to nose. "You seem to think we only want to keep control of *our* waters, White Horn. That's your mistake." She let him go. "Take him."

To Bleed for the Sea

Cassian was dragged and dropped into a pit of sand inside a round tent. Wood fenced him and another man, covered in tattoos and piercings, into what looked like an arena. Bones jutted out from his nose and ears, and he was bald. He leaned in close, practically brushing Cassian's nose with his. The golden ring around his brown irises was startling—he'd never seen anything like it. Cassian couldn't believe this was happening. Fourteen days ago, he was a seaman on *Torment*. Now, he bore the captain's mark for the White Horns, carried the weight of a dead crew, and was bound to a dragon, a creature he had believed to be extinct.

He wanted to be brave. On his knees, he forced himself to stand, only to feel a whip claw its way across his back. The resounding snap filled the tent, and the voices of the crowd went quiet. He blinked back tears, breathless, and kept himself upright. He wouldn't fall now.

San'yila's presence recoiled at the pain. He tried to push her away, burrow into himself, but she refused to leave. The dragon was held by the pirate who'd picked her up. He held her like she was a wild animal, unsure if she'd bite or not. While Cassian would love to see her do just that, he advised her not to.

Give me space, he pleaded. The bald man rubbed his fingers against his large silver and red rings. The look in his eyes was wild. He was clearly a man who'd courted Death and loved the way she felt in his arms.

San'yila made a harsh and high-pitched sound in her throat. *No.*

He glared at her. *San'yila—*

"Ey'kon be a master of his art," Kinson announced, "and his medium is pain." Cassian hardly had time to grasp everything before Kinson was in his face, shoving the bald man aside. She lifted his chin. Muscles tensed as another whip lacerated Cassian's back. The stab wound from earlier throbbed from the whipping, turning his arm into fire, and blood drenched his back. He'd been warned that he would be tested, but he hadn't thought it would be like this. He hadn't anticipated the brutality of a public flogging. This wasn't a test; it was punishment. Already, his mind felt fractured, torn between figuring out what to say to this woman and keeping himself vertical.

Red's presence was impossible to miss—the only pirate in here with a bright red sash tied around his waist. Frustration seared his senses. The pirate was here to mock him with that ever-persistent smug expression, as if he'd known and expected Cassian to end up right where he was.

Kinson's fingers trailed over his jaw. Another whip crack. He leaned forward into her embrace. If not for her, he would've collapsed. His hands latched onto her wrists, holding himself upright. "Prove your worth, and we might just grant you the Queens' mark." She straightened then, peeling his hands off her, and retreated out of the sand pit.

Rage boiled over, fueled by desperation. San'yila struggled in the man's grip, and Cassian shook his head. *Stop,* he begged. *You'll get us both killed.*

Ey'kon stepped forward. Cassian wanted to stay standing, to meet this man at eye level for a proper fisticuffs greeting, but he wasn't granted that. The whipper kicked him in the knee, and he dropped, hissing as the whip dug into his back again, tearing fabric and skin. The dozen onlookers were transfixed, unblinking. Red crossed his arms, expressionless. Cassian didn't know why an audience needed to be present for this torture.

Blood splattered the sand. Cassian's muscles shook, and his body fought to stay upright. Sweat poured off him, burning a salty path down his back where wounds were open. The first tendrils of strangeness teased at the outer edges of his mind, like a growing itch. The sounds and the surrounding world receded at once, turning foggy. He forced air in, tasting iron.

The tendrils grew in numbers and boldness. They encircled his mind, coiling around every thread of thought until he couldn't think properly. San'yila's mind reared back, angry, and the assault on his mind was instant. Ey'kon's head twitched, and his upper lip curled in a snarl fit for a famished beast preparing to feast on Cassian's suffering. A slight shift of his gaze toward the dragon confirmed the fear building in Cassian's chest. San'yila's mind was caught up in the attack.

The tendrils squeezed, encircling his thoughts, bursting each one like they were unwelcome cysts. Every bit of strength drained from him, soaking into the ground as blood and sweat. He fell forward on all fours, heaving. His vision blackened. Emotions popped like boils, oozing out and coating his mind in anger, terror, and desperation. Memories were exploited, down to the most intimate and traumatic moments. He relived being abandoned and bludgeoned, only to find himself drowning in the waters he called home. Cassian struggled to stay conscious above the invasion into his mind, but he felt the sickly cold tendrils wrap themselves around his ankles and yank him under without warning. *Water poured into his lungs, filling the cavity until he couldn't breathe. The darkness of the sea engulfed him, unforgiving, dragging him further than any ship would ever sink to. Bubbles stopped leaving his lips, his motions turned sluggish, and when he blinked, he found he couldn't separate the darkness anymore—*

A blinding light obliterated the scene, shoving him out of the vision like a merciless wind treats a crewless ship.

Cassian gasped, dragging himself up from the sand. He blinked, acutely aware of his surroundings. Yanked from the horrifying illusion of drowning, he dug his fingers into the hot sand, relieved for the ground. Time froze as he grasped at just how real that vision felt. Ey'kon was twisting his thoughts, feeding him terrible nightmares, exploiting his deepest fears. The Energy Harvester had full control over Cassian's head, what he thought, felt—all of it. The tendrils slithering over his entire being were the work of Ey'kon, who harnessed energy to make it possible. The overwhelming terror that surged through Cassian's veins in that instant made him dizzy. He'd never felt this isolated and vulnerable before, never believed he would be a victim to *energy*. Carefully, he studied the small room, aware that everyone watched, unblinking, waiting for the next bit of gruesome entertainment. When Cassian tried to meet anyone's eyes, they averted their gazes—they had no honor. Even at his lowest, these pirates couldn't meet his wide-eyed plea for help. Of course, they wouldn't help anyway. This was his test.

The tendrils returned, tightening around the little bit of freedom Cassian had in his head and constricting it. His thoughts dissipated and the small room vanished, replaced by the illusions fed to him by Ey'kon. The vision of the sea fought to return, to drown him again, but he pushed back with the little mental strength he had, determined to prove his worth. Cassian squeezed his eyes shut, pouring all his attention toward overcoming Ey'kon's control, on wrangling and suffocating the tendrils that swarmed his mind. He would not be a victim. Not to this coward, who couldn't even have a proper sword fight, but instead relied on a whip and twisted energy practices to seek dominance.

Slowly, Cassian curled his fingers around the sand, only to feel the angry slap of the whip strike once more. His concentration fractured, and Ey'kon launched another psychic attack. Cassian's mind was swept away in an instant, dragged under by the next illusion.

The waters of the sea he once adored engulfed him, dragging him under. He tried to push himself to the surface, only to feel icy tentacles wrap around his legs and yank him further down. He didn't have the same strength as before to fight the weight of the water and tentacles. Already, his lungs ached and his vision blurred. He would drown in these waters—in the core of a man's mind he knew nothing about. A harsh reality to his already shattered sense of self. *The waters darkened, and the pressure mounted. He didn't know how long he'd have until his lungs burst and his heart gave out. His eyes felt like they would bulge right out of their sockets, his nostrils burned, and—*

It wasn't real. This was all an illusion. Nothing more.

Cassian spasmed. The water's touch didn't feel like it should have. The bubbles escaping his lips faded. He blinked, the motion slow and agonizing. He sorted through the panic, subjugating the beast of fear into submission so that he could think straight. He opened his mouth, tasting blood. Not salt. Not the sea.

He moved his arms. They scraped against sand, not the cool, soft touch of water. Wounds stung as he tensed and moved. The water turned to dust, and he blinked, gasped, and raised his head to look at Ey'kon. The Harvester faltered and then doubled his efforts in another assault on Cassian's mi nd.

The sea came into view in his mind, drenching him with the unforgivable cold of isolation. He lashed out, shoving the thought away. Again, Ey'kon slashed at Cassian's reality with the visions of drowning, but Cassian squeezed his fingers into the sand, reaffirming what was real, and where he was . . . in a room surrounded by Red Queens on an island, not in the sea. He focused on the torment—the agony that drenched his back and turned his shoulder numb—pulling him back to his painful reality. He was injured, maybe even abandoned, but not alone and helpless like the Harvester wanted him to believe.

He was Cassian. He was a White Horn captain. He was a pirate. Forged to withstand the brutal winds of these merciless waters, born to stand against the rains of sorrow, and carved into a man who didn't give up so easily. He'd seen Death, yes. Ey'kon wasn't the only man to share her embrace, and he wouldn't be the last. Death was cold, but she never wandered too far from those who learned to love the hum of the song she sang.

He was a Dragon Rider.

The burning white light he'd seen earlier bubbled underneath the surface, just within reach. Cassian reached for it, much as he would do to uncover buried treasure. His fingers sank into wisps of bluish mist, thick at first, but slowly, it dissipated. Ey'kon's ire burrowed teeth into his spine, threatening to overwhelm the thin thread of logic that Cassian had. His head felt like it would split in half—being at war in his mind with this Energy Harvester was more excruciating than the whipping.

San'yila's presence was stuffed aside, barred from entry. He refused to let her in, would be damned if she would be exposed to this monster of a man. The dragon's screams were distant echoes, and he couldn't decipher if they were only in his head, another cruel trick by Ey'kon, or for the audience to hear.

The mist parted, clearing to reveal the bright white light. He stuffed his hands into it and felt the frigid buzz of life fuel his veins. His blood turned hot, his heart skipped, and the energy soaked him to his core.

Ey'kon tilted his head. In that instant, the Energy Harvester's persistence to seize control faltered. The sliver of hesitation was all Cassian needed to bathe himself in the newfound strength and take back control of his mind and body.

Cassian forced his legs underneath him, one at a time. He dragged his left leg up, boot sinking into the sand. Another whip's lash bit his skin, but he didn't waver. Cassian harnessed the force that kept him up, the burning white light that stayed alight in his core. He would not be a victim. And he would not let Ey'kon win.

Someone shouted. Cassian couldn't understand the words. The outlines of those who stood and observed this battle of minds blurred. The room came in and out of focus, and the tickle of sweat that rolled down the side of his cheek was lost to the fire that burned within him. The only person he could see was the Harvester.

Cassian would kill him. Yes, that's what he would do.

The emotions of the last decade spilled over, turning his resolve into stone. He stood, seething, silencing the agony that flared in his back. Before he could be interrupted again, he lunged.

Cassian grabbed ahold of Ey'kon, knocking him to the ground. He straddled the Harvester. Ey'kon tried to kick him off, but Cassian tightened his legs around the man. All the hate Cassian had ever felt, all the rejection and agony of his upbringing, poured into the single act of wrapping his hands around the man's throat and squeezing. Cassian's mind went blank, his vision red. Ey'kon would die for ever thinking he could control Cassian. He was his own master. Queens did not control him. Mystical visitors in his dreams did not control him. Destiny did not control him. He would make her bend to his will just as he intended for Ey'kon to do.

Ey'kon released the remaining hold he had on Cassian's mind just as he gasped and gritted his teeth, struggling for breath. The Harvester's hand struggled to find a firm grip on Cassian's neck. Cassian pressed his thumbs into the base of Ey'kon's jaw and wrapped his fingers around the inked neck, ready to suffocate the man. An end as quick as dragging a blade across his throat would be too kind for the torture Ey'kon had and was willing to put Cassian through. And then there was the pain he'd put on San'yila.

Hands from behind ripped Cassian off the Harvester with bruising force. A multitude of faces met his, but he couldn't place them. Sounds didn't reach him like they should have, and his hands shook with blinding rage. Breaths came in short bursts, and the hot splash of blood soaked his skin. He lashed out with a hand, but it met nothing but air. A dragon moved in front of him, cautious, as if unsure of whether the sand she stepped on would hold her. San'yila. He reached for her, only to watch another pirate yank her by the wings. She tried to claw her way out of the man's grip, but she was useless when being held in that fashion. The offending Red Queen was lost from view as another stepped in front of the scene. Cassian blinked, horrified.

And then the whip lacerated his shoulder with searing agony. The whipper stood over him, not hesitating in his assault. Cassian was kicked next, and he could hear at least one of them crack. He tried to move, but he was forced onto his stomach by several pirates, and his hands were bound behind him. Sand pressed into his cheek. He fought hard to free himself from the restraints, grunting and huffing until enough sand coated his tongue to choke him. The whip responded, harsh and unforgiving. Over and over.

The excruciating pain obliterated his concentration on the energy that had given him life. He returned to himself, feeling every injury, every bit of fatigue and disappointment. Cassian wheezed, tasting blood. A cut along his lip burned where sand met it. He couldn't recall where or how he got it.

Cassian lay in the pit, beaten and bloodied. Little more than a corpse with a dying breath. The exhaustion that rose to claim him once and for all was unlike anything he'd ever felt before. Slumber cradled him like a lover after a long night of ecstasy—a feeling Cassian hadn't had in many summers. Slowly, slumber coaxed him to relax, telling him his ordeal was over. The fighting, worries, running, none of it mattered anymore. The insufferable torture floated further and further away, and his thoughts turned to sludge. This wasn't exhaustion, he realized, this was Death coming to have him for herself.

Next to him, a warm little body curled up along his side and pressed a snout against his cheek.

Branded to Serve

Muscles ached, strained, and protested from the lack of movement. Cassian's hands tingled, going numb, and his toes were exposed, devoid of the boots he'd grown accustomed to. The cool air against them brought more life back into him than ice water after a drunken night. He blinked, groggy, and tried to move his neck. He couldn't.

His arms were stretched out, his face pressed against something solid. The necklace lay heavy against his chest. He inhaled deeply. Wood. The moist fragrance of wood filled his nostrils. He blinked again. More feeling returned, and with it, the nasty memories of the Red Queens' test. The intense memory of the sensation of drowning reared its ugly head, making him anxious. He tried to move his arm, only to find it refused to obey. Again, he tried and again, he couldn't get his arm to move.

Cassian was tied down. Voices echoed overhead. His ears refused to listen at first. It took everything in him to turn his attention to the sound.

"Another day," a woman said. "The ink looks good."

"Hm. I need to do another pass through," another woman observed. Pricks along his upper arm jolted him to full awareness. He yanked his arm, but that did no good. Nothing moved.

"Ah, you're awake," the first woman stated, far too cheerful. "Don't move. You'll ruin your neck piece."

"Wha . . ." Cassian slurred. His tongue was so dry.

Warmth engulfed his mind, so sudden and jarring that he felt flush. *You are hurt.* San'yila's voice radiated through his entire being, harnessing more affection for him than he'd ever felt in his life.

"Don't move," the second woman ordered. Her voice was gravely and hung over him like a thick blanket. "Your back is healing nicely. We can't risk you opening those wounds."

He couldn't move even if he wanted to. The ropes that kept him down were so tight that he'd have rashes where it dug into flesh.

What happened? Retreating back to the safety of San'yila's presence was more welcoming than the outside world.

The dragon's mind poked his own with the gentle touch of a mother. *You nearly died.* She flashed images in his head, relaying what she could without words. The dragon still had much to learn when it came to speaking, but she'd improved so much already. He saw himself whipped and kicked after trying to strangle Ey'kon. He'd been dragged to another tent afterward, treated with herbs and healing rituals before he'd been tied as he was now.

How long have I been unconscious?

San'yila hesitated. *Three days.*

Shock rippled through him. He lay immobile, feeling the pricks of needles pierce his skin. Over and over, dot after dot, the women worked. They were marking him. The Queens never intended for him to die. They needed him to serve for their cause.

I'm sorry, he told San'yila.

She didn't grasp his meaning. *For what?*

For all of it, he confessed. *For putting you in this mess. For all the troubles. For everything that'll happen next.* Because once they saw him healed enough, they'd force both of them into servitude. She'd be raised a servant to the

Queens, he'd be imprisoned to a cause he wanted nothing to do with. The Queens had stripped him of everything, and now they were all he had left.

In a soft voice that dusted off the cobwebs of emotions he'd not felt in many summers, she said, *I'd rather be chained to this world with you than alone.*

A sharper sensation pierced the skin close to where the stab wound was. He flinched, pissed, and started to struggle. The pain radiated down his back and into his core, hideous.

"We'll have to put him out," a woman said. "He's moving too much."

Someone cursed, and the sound of rummaging met his ears. Cassian panicked. He didn't want to embrace slumber again. He wanted water, to move, to get away from it all. In one yank, he tried to get himself free, but all he did was flop like a fish out of water.

"By the grace of the Red Goddess, you are a squirmer. Man up!" A woman's hand reached around and pried his face out from the wood, turning it so that he could see the glow of a lantern. Next to it was San'yila. The red dragon was in a cage.

"Wha—" Cassian's throat felt like he'd swallowed swords. Each word strained and hurt to say, but he needed to speak. His lips smacked, cracked and dry. "What . . . is she—"

"Shush," the second woman ordered. A sour-smelling bottle was pressed against his lips and tilted, forcing a warm bitter liquid onto his tongue. "Drink. Don't make this harder on yourself."

Cassian didn't want to, but the angle made it impossible to ignore. He blew out, forcing the liquid down his chin and coating the wood he lay against. The acidic taste on his tongue made him gag, which only caused his bruised ribs to protest.

San'yila urged him to obey as the woman smacked his face like a scolding mother. He didn't want to. Cassian sealed his lips shut, fighting the woman's insistence. He tried to shift his head, but that didn't work. A leather strap around the crown of his head strained against his movement.

You must, San'yila pleaded. Her fiery eye met his own from across the small room.

What? Why? His thoughts were clearer, accompanied by the adrenaline.

It will keep the peace.

He stopped fighting. San'yila's response tore him right out of his prideful place and sat him in front of reality that he refused to acknowledge. If he fought, the women would have to seek out the aid of those who wouldn't be so kind. Less trouble, fewer problems. The dragon knew that and was trying to warn him.

The older woman leaned down, meeting his gaze with bright blue and kind eyes. Red ink dotted her cheeks, curving upward. "Are you ready?" She seemed to sense the change in his attitude.

Cassian nodded. Well, the best he could.

She brought the bottle back, and this time, he let the liquid burn a path down his throat. His gag reflexes wanted to refuse the drink, but he stilled the reaction. So many summers at sea made him an expert at such an act. This bitter-tasting drink was tame compared to Seaman's Water. As the liquid sloshed and settled in his stomach, he felt the effects almost immediately. His mind wandered without his permission, and he blinked slower than usual. The woman set the drink aside and ran her hand over the side of his head like a proud mother, then proceeded to twist his head back down so that he could stare at the dirt. He didn't fight it.

The first cheerful woman patted his head like he was an animal. "Sleep well, Dragon Rider."

The sound of tapping lulled him back to the present world. Cassian blinked, aching and sore, and shifted his head. The leather strap was gone, giving his neck freedom to move. With it came the tender touch of inked skin—the same feeling he'd had after his hand was done to hold the captain's mark. He'd been on land for a handful of days, and all he wanted was to get back to the sea. Out there, the troubles felt further away. Here, where his boots sank into sand and he could grasp vegetation, the world wanted him. If he could disappear, he would never have to worry about being wanted again.

"The Queens made you their symbol," a voice quietly said. Cassian swallowed, and his throat croaked from the action, dry.

"What do you want?" Cassian asked. A chat with Red couldn't come at a worse time. He wanted to be alone with San'yila.

The dragon stirred, sensing his needs. She was still here, locked in a cage that shouldn't house her. If he could get out of these restraints, he'd release her and destroy those bars. A dragon shouldn't be imprisoned. People could put other people behind bars, but a dragon should be beyond the reach of man. One day, she'd be too big to control—or to subdue.

"You overexerted yourself," Red said. "You have almost no knowledge about energy harvesting, don't you?"

"And you're the supposed expert?" Cassian remarked. "Are you here to tell me how to lay here, strapped to this bloody table, too? Am I doing it right?"

Red didn't flinch. He never did. "I have found the sea is no place for proper energy training. Pirates find that process tiring—boring, even. Tough love, right?" He laughed at his own joke. Cassian didn't find the humor. Not with his current position. "What do you know about harvesting energy?"

Cassian didn't reply. Pride kept his tongue locked. San'yila urged him to listen.

Why?

He is different from the others, the dragon replied slowly. *He doesn't feel like the rest.*

Cassian scrunched his face, confused. The motion hurt. *What? You can feel people?*

San'yila snorted, the sound loud in the silence that loomed between the two men. *You can't?*

A drink would have been nice to take the edge off. "Well, go on then. I'm listening."

"Hm." Red drummed his fingers again. Cassian couldn't see him and wasn't sure where he sat. At this angle, he could only see the cage that San'yila was housed in and the lantern that flickered lazily, unperturbed by the mounting tension.

"Energy is everywhere. The wood you lay on, the sand you step on, and the waters you sail on are all a part of a system beyond this world. Each possesses a lifeforce—a soul, some might say. A core energy source that connects you with the rest of the world. You drew from your own when you went up against Ey'kon. A risky thing to do when you don't know your boundaries."

When Red didn't continue, Cassian whispered, "The light . . . I could feel it."

"Precisely," Red answered. "You found your lifeforce and drew too much from it. Harvesters die that way all the time. You should consider yourself lucky."

Something unnerved Cassian about Red. The pirate possessed an air about him that challenged the way Cassian perceived the world. Pirates were smug, but Red had enough arrogance to fuel a kingdom. Pirates usually didn't settle well with that attitude—it was beaten out of them by their leaders. If he'd walked around with that persona while Ricard captained *Torment*, he'd have had his face stuffed in a bucket of rotten fish and told to clean the daily catch for a summer, shoved in the smallest room aboard. The Queens were proud, but Red was beyond even their power-hungry and self-absorbed impressions.

"Thanks," Cassian mumbled. "I sure feel lucky."

"Lifeforces, for the most part, are made up of Light Energy. An energy that has been tampered with, impure. That makes it far more malleable for Harvesters to use. Manipulating is the correct term for that, by the way. The world tarnishes the energy's purity—our very existence changes the energy's makeup. Make sense?"

"Sure." It didn't. "So, what's magic?"

"Imbecile," Red muttered.

"Magic is an imbecile?" Cassian asked, not hiding the cynicism. "Good to know. Thanks."

San'yila fluffed her wings. He knew enough to know she was annoyed by his behavior.

"Magic is energy. The term *magic* is improper, used by the uneducated. A way to explain away the impossible," Red said. "If you harvest *energy* and call it *magic*, you will look like an *imbecile*."

Cassian cracked a half-smile, unable to forget the cloaked man he'd met at the ally in Greve's Point. That man had also said something similar. "You mention most of the world is made of Light Energy. Then what else is there?"

Red scoffed, dismissive. "Dark Energy—"

"Clever name," Cassian remarked dryly. "I'll have to compliment the creative who did that next time I meet them."

"Sarcasm will not solve all your problems," Red stated.

"But it will solve some," Cassian pointed out.

"True." A chair creaked, and Red came into view. He faced the dragon. "Dark Energy is volatile, wild, and will get you killed faster than that tongue of yours. It is pure energy, bound to the countless dead who wander the God's Realm—"

"What?"

"The living realm. Our realm," Red explained. "Dark Energy embodies the most powerful elements of this realm—fire, water, the metals in the ground, and wind. These elements are pure Dark Energy. Easy to assume that such everyday interactions with necessities like water or fire are mundane, but they aren't. To the non-Energy Harvester, you can't hear Dark Energy's call. But you will come to hear this call, Dragon Rider, and when the day comes, you must understand the dangers of listening. Dark Energy is a living, breathing energy separate from lifeforces that seeks out what serves her purpose. Chain yourself to her, and you will fracture your mind and go mad. Only a few have ever conquered Dark Energy, but none live long to bask in that triumph. Eventually, she will always take the soul of her host."

"A parasite," Cassian acknowledged. Nothing else could accurately describe Dark Energy as Red explained it. All this time, he'd sailed on waters that housed the restless dead. It was apparent—the voices at night, the lost souls reliving their final moments, even the black spots—but he'd never considered what it could all mean beyond unsettled ghosts and curses. The water he loved wasn't as innocent as he wanted it to be. He shivered, freezing. "Can you harvest Dark Energy?"

Red turned to glare. "You've not listened to a word I said—"

"It was just a question," Cassian snapped. "You seemed to know so much about it."

"What I've told you is only a sliver of the complex relationship energy has with Mother—" Red stopped, face twisting. The shift in his demeanor was sudden, taking on the appearance of a stranger. "I am only trying to help you. You are a young Rider. The last thing you need is to fail to understand a concept so mundane and get yourself killed."

Cassian didn't know what to say.

Ask about the feelings I have, San'yila prompted. *About how people feel different.*

Ask him yourself, he bit back. He didn't want to be the messenger.

San'yila tilted her head. *No.*

Why?

She didn't answer. Odd. He knew she could communicate with others if she wanted. He stared at her, hard enough that Red looked between the two, sensing the telepathic conversation. Cassian relented. "She wants to know why you *feel* different than the others." The statement sounded strange on his tongue. Cassian was a man who spoke of sails and ships, not things he couldn't pick up and touch.

Red raised his brow. "She says I feel different? Do you mean my lifeforce?" The pirate turned to the dragon, expectant. He was incredibly comfortable with a creature that hadn't been seen in centuries.

Yes, she answered. Cassian relayed that.

"A story for another time," Red answered, a small smile painting his lips. "But she is right. You would do well to practice *feeling* your surroundings as she has. It might save your life one day. Wouldn't want an enemy to sneak up on you while you're neck deep in a drink, no?"

Cassian hated that answer almost as much as he hated his situation. "I have no choice, do I?"

Red's smile fell, and he laced his fingers together. "If you wish to stay alive long enough, you will have to make a sacrifice."

The answer lay before them, bare and grotesque, and Cassian wanted to melt into the table. As alluring as a woman in a brothel who wore nothing but lace, and as hideous as the hag who cursed the name of men while dragging her short dagger through the belly of a crow. He knew Red was right, knew the answer well before he ever stood face to face with Ey'kon, but accepting it was more than just a nod. He had to embrace the entire meaning, play a character that nobody doubted, be the man—the Dragon Rider—they expected him to be.

Join the Red Queens. Embrace their culture, the ways of life, their motives. Lure them in, build their trust, and then when their backs were turned, flee to freedom. But he couldn't while San'yila was young. He needed her to grow. When she was large enough, they could fly out of here. No crew or ship would be needed. He knew it wouldn't keep him safe forever. The Red Queens probably already anticipated Cassian's wild escape plan before he even thought of it. But if he could delay the inevitable—another horrific whipping—long enough for San'yila to grow into a dragon large enough to fly, he might just live to tell about his time with the Red Queens. If the Red Goddess worshippers anticipated his escape, then he would have to outsmart them at their own game.

Cassian risked being chained to servitude, much as Bauer and the crew of *Dread Deep* were. But if he could feign acceptance and play his role right, he could delay that decision, maybe even avoid it entirely. He and the Red Queens would be watching each other, calculating every move. Predators stuffed in a small space, waiting for the other to lash out first.

"Why are you helping us?" Cassian asked.

The pirate fiddled with the pommel of his sword, averting his gaze. "You are a Dragon Rider now, Cassian. Whatever I might think of you doesn't matter. Keeping you alive for the greater good is the only thing that matters."

Once more, the answer was vague. "I don't understand."

"One day, you will." Red retreated from view. "I will do my part, but I expect you to do yours. The Queens are merciless, but they reward loyalty. Give them a little show, and you just might live long enough to see the other side of the world."

PART 3

"Even the Gods fear the Dragon Rider."
~ The Vorelian Scrolls

The Sun of the Wicked

Three moons later

Cassian downed the tea—sweet and pink—and set the cup down. "I don't need anymore," he said before Felah could say otherwise. The woman fed him and the rest of the Red Queens who had come ashore. She was always cooking, prepping, and going on about how important it was to eat. In the three moons since the day he'd been tested, beaten, and whipped, he'd watched Felah cook more food than he'd seen in his entire life. She was everyone's mother and had earned her name from the Old Tongue. It was a respectful reference to a woman who cared for a community. Or, in this case, pirates. Cassian had met her within several days of his ordeal—he'd been shoved into her care while he continued to heal from his wounds.

The elderly woman patted his shoulder, topping off the cup without hesitation. "Nonsense." Her accent was thick, and for the first moon, he spent more time than he wanted to admit asking her to repeat herself. "I have tea. You drink tea."

Cassian picked up a cracker and smeared the berry jam across it. Bread didn't last long out here. "I can't argue with you, Felah."

The woman began mashing leaves in a bowl to create a paste for cooking. "You learn fast, boy."

He chuckled as warmly as if she were his real mother. "Anybody feed Captain Nibbs yet?" The behemoth sea turtle lived on the west side of the island. Since arriving at Queens' Gate, he'd learned that Captain Nibbs had earned a reputation for being greedy and expectant for food. Nearly every day, the sea turtle waited by a broken tree for someone to bring a meal. The Red Queens said he'd been around for decades, and he showed up wherever the Red Queens moved. Captain Nibbs recognized them as much as they recognized him.

The first time Cassian brought food—fruits and wide leaves plucked for their sweet taste—the turtle practically took his finger off in its zeal for the snack. Felah had laughed and scolded Captain Nibbs for being rude. In time, Felah promised, Captain Nibbs would warm up to Cassian. And he had recently, now far gentler when he took the food. It was a highlight of Cassian's day when he could visit the sea turtle.

Felah checked the drying leaves on a nearby table, which would be used for creating rope. "No need," she said. "Cui took her son over there a bit ago."

Cassian silently cursed. He'd see Captain Nibbs another time, then. "Do you still need help with basket weaving?" he offered.

Felah swatted at him and shook her head. "Nah. Why don't ye help with constructing the ships? Ye a strong man."

Because he would end up in a fight, that's why. Cassian kept to himself when he could or opted for Felah's nurturing company to keep his temper in check. Stuck with a group of Red Queens who treated him exactly as they saw him—a dirty-blooded White Horn—he risked ruining the delicate peace he'd managed to make in the past season. Cassian had picked several fights in the first days he was on this forsaken island. Earned himself a new black eye and a threat of more whipping for his behavior. But after he kicked in the teeth of a slimy Queen who tossed an insult in San'yila's direction, Cassian was finally left alone.

Every day had become predictable. He woke to the horn that was blown at first light, dressed, and then sought Felah out or kept to himself. When he was alone with San'yila, he often helped her learn more about her wings and explored the island with her. They even greeted Captain Nibbs, who, in all his bulk, fled until he realized she wouldn't eat him. She was still young and saw the best in both their situation and Cassian himself. He loved it—her optimism kept him sane. Pouring his attention into her growth and development helped keep him preoccupied and allowed him to forget that they were essentially captives.

He did just about anything Felah asked. He learned to knead bread, weave, sew, and helped children learn to read and write. Felah was more than just a mother, she was a teacher. The youngest came her way whenever they didn't have chores to do, and she quickly put Cassian to work entertaining them. He read out loud, helped them practice wood carving, and told them stories. In return, Felah told him everything and anything about the Red Queens, which he loved. He'd learned more about the Queens from her than anyone else on the island.

When Felah learned he had a knack for wood carving, she had him work on a few different pieces for her. A raven, a Krakí, and a ship. The statuettes were now placed strategically around her home. He appreciated the gesture. Felah was one of the only people who seemed to really enjoy his company, and he enjoyed hers as well. They seemed to find comfort in having each other around.

Life hadn't been easy. He flexed his hand. The captain's mark he'd been given as a White Horn glared up at him, faded from the sun—a memory of a life he once had. That and the compass on his right forearm were two of the only tattoo pieces he had from his previous life. The Queens spared covering those, whether from kindness, as a cruel reminder, or to mock him, he wasn't sure. Anyway, he was glad to have them. He'd gotten the compass at sixteen when he'd officially been considered a full member of *Torment's* crew. A rite of passage, some would say. He'd had other pieces done, but they were small—some done on drunk nights—but the compass was his first symbolic mark. The beginning of his journey as a pirate and young man. Maybe the Red Queens knew it. He liked to tell himself that.

Red was right. They'd made a symbol out of him. The Queens' tattoo artists had covered his skin in pictorial stories of their oceanic victories—a way to send their message without having to be there en masse. Landwalkers couldn't deny the influence of the Queens now. Not with Cassian carrying their story and declaring control and dominance. When the whip wounds healed, they marked him there, too. Sigils in the Old Tongue that meant *war*, *savagery*, and *strength* decorated his lower back.

A colorful Krakí wrapped around his left forearm, tentacles tightening around his knuckles and elbow. A Life Eater, a serpent-like creature with a blocky head and scales of a dragon, squeezed his upper right arm, talons sinking into the skin to keep a strong hold. Tattoos that took on the appearance of fierce waves cut through his chest, and the largest piece was on his back; a woman holding a sun, feathered wings teasing his shoulders. The Red Goddess. She hid some of the scars, but not all. Underneath his collarbone, an anchor rested, bold against the other, more narrative pieces.

At first, Cassian had been angry. His skin was used for their personal propaganda. A weapon, tool, bargaining chip—it was all the same to him. As the days slipped by and the wounds of his whipping healed, he realized being inked by the Queens was a passive attempt at controlling him. He couldn't argue. If he did, they'd chain him to Ey'kon as a servant, no longer in control of his thoughts or actions. Ey'kon was a master Harvester, had countless summers of experience and exposure in dark rituals forbidden by most landwalkers. Cassian, still in his infancy of harvesting, didn't stand a chance against him.

The Harvester hated him. Dragon Rider or not, Ey'kon would drain him of all his blood and string him up for the dead if he had his way. Their confrontation during his test left a bitter taste in Cassian's mouth. Ey'kon was too smug for his own good, and the brutal encounter between them had left the Harvester with something to prove. Ey'kon was itching to assert himself, and glared at Cassian whenever he had the chance. Cassian kept his distance whenever he could.

In private, when the lanterns were extinguished and the other people slept, Cassian tried to find that burning white light of his lifeforce again, the same white light he'd grasped onto the day he nearly killed Ey'kon three moons ago.

With San'yila's help and a great deal of practice, he'd found it. The dragon guided him, offering advice from her own exposure to her lifeforce. Harnessing and controlling her energy was a skill she naturally acquired as she grew older. Despite her young age, she seemed to know much more about the energy that made up lifeforces than he did. Twice, she'd scolded him about his mishandling of his own lifeforce. Like a hungry and tired child, Cassian would snap at her, only to apologize later because he knew she was right.

In the first moon, the exertion to control the energy made him sweat. It took everything in him to keep his concentration. This wasn't wood carving, this was wrangling an energy he knew little about. The concentration slipped away if he blinked or breathed irregularly. He'd spent most nights retching in the bushes because of the intense strain on his body from the practice.

By the second moon, he could scoop up a ball of energy sourced from plants, seeing the work through his mind's eye. With San'yila's guidance, he managed to break it into two smaller burning white balls of light. He'd toss them in the air, manipulating the energy to change shapes, like that of a bird or serpent. Then, when he understood that, he turned the ball of energy onto the plants, shaking leaves and making them bend to his will.

By the third moon, he'd finally learned to strengthen his concentration in almost any situation, working it like a muscle until he was comfortable enough to reach for his lifeforce during the day with commotion. While Felah would chat, he would turn his attention to anything else in their vicinity, focusing on the lifeforce while following whatever the woman said.

When he got comfortable with one object, he added another, engaging with Felah all the while without breaking concentration or tiring.

In return, he helped San'yila learn how to fly. Not that she needed help, but he aided her by keeping her company on her hops and early attempts at stretching her wings, gave her advice about wind, and dusting sand off her snout when she crashed.

The stronger he became, the more likely he could get San'yila and himself out of here alive. If he revealed to Ey'kon or anyone that he trained in secret to harvest energy, he'd be bound to Ey'kon with a dark ritual or beaten to a bloody pulp. Or both.

You bore me, San'yila grumbled. Her presence was a welcome, if somewhat cranky, comfort in this strange new normal.

And you're so much more interesting, Cassian snorted. Felah looked at him from her mashing.

San'yila snapped her jaws closed. The visual image passed across their mental link as clear as if he stood before her. She lay just outside the tent, since she was too big to enter now. He couldn't believe how fast she'd grown in these first three moons on the island. For her sake, he was glad for the consistency and stability. The notion of raising her on the waters and on the run terrified him. No matter what became of him on this island, he'd at least given San'yila a fighting chance by giving her a place to mature so that she could finally defend herself.

Not that he knew much about dragons. His knowledge was still slim—laughable even. To call himself a Dragon Rider felt like an insult to the Dragon Riders of old. He wasn't even sure what it meant to be one, beyond being a weapon for someone else's war.

"Ye prayer today, ye do it?" Felah asked, breaking the spell of reverie.

He studied the half-eaten cracker still in his hand. "Always, Felah. Always." A lie. He didn't. The Queens gave their thanks to the Red Goddess every morning. He'd been sourly wrong about just how ingrained the deity was with the Queens. She was not just their religion; she was their identity.

Everything they did, they sought the approval of a Goddess who didn't answer. Ships were blessed before they set sail. Men courted women with the approval and blessing of the Red Goddess, and ceremonies were held on every full moon because they believed the veil was thinnest and the deity could hear them. If babies weren't blessed within a certain timeframe, they were sacrificed to the Tsu'ran by being thrown into the sea.

The beads hanging in the entryway danced. Cassian looked up to see Red standing in the doorway. For once, the red sash was missing, and the pirate was snacking on a plump crimson fruit. He flashed a boyish grin. "Morning, Felah."

The woman scoffed. "So, ye have come to make a mess of my hearth, yeah?" She wiped her hands with a rag. "For four days it took me to get the smell out after ye dropped the fish guts all over it."

The pirate took another bite. From behind, San'yila's large red head peeked in. One fiery eye blinked, and the black slit pupil dilated. Horns protruded from her jaw and the top of her head, racing down her back and to the top of her tail. Cassian couldn't believe her size. Had she grown in the past hour? It seemed she was bigger every day.

"But you think of me all the time, don't you?" Red teased.

Felah shook her head, her lips pursed in a thin line, but the tug at the corner of her mouth conveyed her amusement. "Ye need to find a woman your age, Red. Ye games, I'm too old for."

"You know what makes a woman attractive?" Red asked, chewing.

She tilted her head. Cassian picked up a cracker and bit into it.

"Laughter and their smile," Red answered. "You have the best of both."

Felah laughed, bright and embarrassed. Her aged cheeks flushed, and she shook her head. "Ye need something? If it's Captain Nibbs, I'm afraid he's all taken care of today."

"A shame. I like that turtle." Without hesitation, Red pointed at Cassian and said, "I want to make sure he's treating you with the respect you deserve, Felah. He is, isn't he?" She rolled her eyes. That seemed to please the pirate.

"I'm here for you. Come with me." Red's unwavering gaze didn't break from Cassian.

The salty flavor from the cracker died on Cassian's tongue. "Me?"

"Yes."

He swallowed. "Why?"

Red raised his brow. "Nervous?"

San'yila snorted, breaking the awkwardness. Cassian cleared his throat. "No. I just—well, I've not been summoned before." He stood, practically knocking the chair over. "What's this about?"

Red took another bite and chewed slowly. Despite the presence of a dragon right behind him, he showed no discomfort. When she was younger, the Red Queens had no issue handling her like she was a chicken ready for slaughter, but as she grew, the same pirates who'd yanked her around hesitated when they got close to the red dragon. A single swipe from her talons could kill a man, and everyone knew it. No matter how bold the men and women acted, they kept a boundary with San'yila now. Cassian still didn't know if it was fear or respect, likely both.

"Viv'an summons you for the meeting of the families. I told her I'd personally fetch the Dragon Rider." Red ate the last of the fruit, then tossed the core to the side. "Coming?"

Nerves squelched Cassian's appetite and confidence, strangling them until all that was left was the same hollow feeling he'd had when he first arrived. Kinson hadn't seen him in at least two moons. Cassian thought he was safe, that he'd appeased her enough to keep her from breathing down his neck. He'd grown too accustomed to this prison.

"Sure." Cassian didn't sound as brave as he wanted to be.

Cassian stepped out of the small home with Red close behind him. The sun greeted him with a hot kiss, searing his skin with the late morning heat. A shadow stretched across the sand, moving as San'yila approached. The surrounding pirates retreated. The dragon's red leathery wings fluttered, scales glittered, and talons sank into the ground. All but the one that Bauer stole from her when she was only a day old. Her front foot only had three talons left—the nub of the stolen one was marked by a scar. Small scales tried to grow in place, but never quite reached, leaving lumpy flesh and a pinkish scar. Everyone earned their scars, even dragons.

Do not worry for me, San'yila scolded gently. *We have moved beyond this. That scar was my very first lesson about the cruelty of weak-hearted men.*

Cassian raised his hand in defeat. *I feel guilty*, he replied. No matter how much he tried, he couldn't forget. Most nights when he couldn't sleep, he relived those first few days with the dragon. He'd never felt so much horror, and even after all this time, the same icy panic crawled through his limbs. Not even the day he'd been abandoned by his parents or when the remaining crew of *Torment* were killed could come close to the emotions he felt when he failed to protect the fledgling dragon. The bond he and San'yila shared, that she gifted to him, redefined his purpose and priorities.

He wasn't just Cassian the thief and dirty pirate. He was *more*. What precisely that *more* was, he was still trying to figure out.

San'yila dipped her head, and he dragged a hand over the crest of her head where the protective scales were smallest. Warmth seeped into his veins, and an energy carved a path up his arm, seeping into his blood and burrowing into his core. At first, he'd not been sure how to handle the overwhelming sensation of *life*. As San'yila grew, her lifeforce became stronger, harder to ignore. Every time he touched her, the energy made itself known, like an old friend catching up after a long stretch of silence. But now, he craved it the way the desert yearns for the rains after a long drought.

You grow bigger every day, he observed. Cassian lowered his hand just underneath her jaw, where scales gave way to a soft crimson skin. He scratched. San'yila hummed.

And you become more anxious to run every day, she countered gently.

Cassian scoffed. "Lead the way," he told Red.

They fell into step, side by side. The dragon followed. Queens still stopped and watched as they passed, although many had grown accustomed to their presence. It was hard to ignore Cassian, let alone a dragon. His silver eyes were beacons for attention—a blatant display of otherworldliness, and what some would call divine intervention. Many no longer stared when they spoke to him, although the occasional child gawked a bit too long. Queens who sailed in without having met him yet were always taken aback. A few words were exchanged, and the pirates would go about their way, only looking when they thought Cassian wasn't paying attention.

Red was quiet, an abnormality for the usually preachy man. "What's on your mind?" Cassian asked. The walk was short, but the silence made it feel like an eternity. Cassian didn't want to spend the entire time worrying about what Kinson would say to him. He spent enough nights thinking about his situation.

"Nothing."

Curt, annoying, and vague. Cassian didn't like it. "Do you know something I don't?"

Red raised a single eyebrow. "About?"

"Don't play coy with me. This—" He motioned ahead. "Am I walking into some death trap? Do I need to know something?"

Easy, San'yila advised, but she sounded strained. She was worried, too.

"The whole world doesn't revolve around you," Red replied coolly. "I've got other things on my mind. Walking you to meet Kinson does not excite me like you think it should."

Cassian stopped and faced the pirate. "What's on your mind?"

"Stalling will not help or resolve what lies ahead," Red told him.

Cassian crossed his arms. "I'm not stalling. I'm trying to figure out why you were chatting with Felah all friendly-like and barely spare me a word. Did I look at someone the wrong way? Did I take something of yours? What is it?"

Red took a single step forward. Cassian's anxiety molded into fast-spreading frustration. Cassian didn't know how else to cope with his nerves—violence came easy for him and was far more comfortable than the jumpiness that bubbled within his stomach from the summoning. San'yila stopped, snout hovering close enough that he could practically taste the air she breathed—humid and hot.

"You're picking a fight with the wrong person," Red whispered.

Cassian wanted to slap him. "And who should I be picking a fight with?"

Red poked him in the chest with bruising force, narrowly missing the pendant hanging from his neck. "Yourself." Red kept walking, not checking to see if Cassian followed.

Cassian rubbed where Red poked, the skin tender and still sore from a recent date with the tattoo needles. Agitation simmered, but instead of crafting a retort, he chewed on everything he wanted to say and do. He needed a place to put his feelings—a face to punch, a neck to strangle, anything. Instead, he swallowed everything back down.

The meeting of families lay ahead. Cassian forced air in and looked to the sky, where he'd yet to venture. What did the families want with him? The question was comical, if not cruel, to ponder. He knew what they wanted. He'd always known. And now, he would have to face the tune of a song he dreaded.

Prophecies and War

Cassian hated politics. He also despised men and women who thought they were special because of some title given to them. Council, kings, queens, Lords, Ladies, chancellors—the list went on. Respect was earned. Under the right conditions, it could be taken. Kings and queens thought they didn't have to work for it. Universally, they were lazy fools with an inflated impression of themselves. Kinson was no different. Same with Ey'kon, Raryl, Zilac, Hezil, and Ash, members of the inner circle and war council. He would have given a finger to be with Felah rather than here.

Few times had Cassian ever felt like bait, but now was one of those times. He felt strung up, fattened, and ready to be fed whole to a Firóle. Kinson didn't want him sitting at this table because she valued his opinion. He was here because they wanted something from him. Or maybe Kinson had him here as a show of her power.

Easy, San'yila advised. Her head rested next to his chair, large enough to crush it if she so pleased. At this angle, he could see the individual scales that decorated the crest of her head. Horns were sharpened, catching the light from the sun that was allowed in. When she'd hatched, her head had been far more narrow. Now her head was wide, bulky, and menacing. She could bite a man's leg off. He wondered how large she would become. Based on her appetite, he knew she wasn't slowing down any time soon.

The dragon snorted. Ash startled to his left. Cassian glared, tempted to kick him. This big, bad pirate was as jumpy as a child when it came to San'yila.

The round table held all six families. Kinson was the only female, the one chosen to lead. Ey'kon represented one of the families of the inner circle, too. That thought soured his mood immensely. He knew the Harvester influenced Kinson, but now he knew, because Ey'kon had a seat at the table, that he also had a direct say on what the Red Queens did, which included how they treated Cassian. He was both an Energy Harvester and a Red Queen family member of the inner circle. Kinson might be the leader, but no decisions were finalized until the inner circle, the war council, supported them. Put Ey'kon on a ship, and he'd be the most dangerous person: a Sea Master. Few ever sailed for long as a Sea Master—an Energy Harvester and captain. Power like that came with an insatiable thirst for more. Perhaps that's why Ey'kon stayed on land. Or maybe he was hoping to wiggle his way further into Kinson's vision of the future.

In that regard, Cassian found the man clever. But in all other accounts, he wanted to cut his tongue out and leave him for the Tsu'ran. The Harvester didn't hide his disdain either. They couldn't look at each other without one or both glaring in challenge. Ey'kon's pride was hurt, even after three moons, and Cassian wanted to finish what he started. But now, knowing Ey'kon represented one of the six families, he was worried that the Harvester had something crueler planned.

He envies you, San'yila said. Her voice was like the cool breeze on a hot day. *His heart does not belong here, but he feels he has no choice. A pity.*

I would still kill him, Cassian commented.

I never said you shouldn't, she mused.

Kinson stood, resting her hands on the scratched and aged table. The thick slab must have weighed as much as a small ship, given its width. Drinks were in front of some of the attendees, but not Cassian. He wasn't afforded that luxury. The Red Queen leader's teeth were stained red with berries harvested along the coast of Creitón, a reflection of her rule and influence in the Red Queens' culture, and beads hung from her shoulders and her hair. Leather left little to the imagination, hugging only the groin and breasts, displaying a world of red tattoos. Cassian had learned that Kinson loved to flaunt her body. As the daughter of the Red Goddess, her body was a sign of power. She could have and do anything she wanted, and the roughest and cruelest Queen would bow to her. The men fell silent at her movement. Even Ey'kon, unlikable as he was, was just a puppet on a string, awaiting her commands.

The men at this table were some of the toughest and most menacing pirates Cassian had ever seen. The inner circle of the Queens represented the strongest families of the seas. They would stop at nothing to ensure their lineage and faith in the Red Goddess continued to thrive for centuries to come.

"Thank you for arriving on short notice," Kinson said, her eyes sweeping across the guests at her table. She looked petite next to the mass of these men, but she held enough authority to command an army. Bangles clattered as she shifted. "Recent report states there are more black spots. A fifth one was spotted south of the Nighthunter Federation. As of now, there's no clear source for these marks, but they continue to destroy our ships when we get too close. Avoid these at all costs. Don' get within a league of one, yeah, if you can help it. I fear these be growing worse. Spread the word."

Men nodded. Cassian hadn't known there were five, and made a mental note to ask more about it when he could. Nobody at the table revealed any emotion on the matter. If they were as troubled as he felt about the unexplainable event, they didn't let it show.

Kinson pursed her lips. The single act betrayed her exhaustion. She looked like she'd not slept in days. "Zilac has returned with news from Caster. The king has obliterated our ships with Dark Energy."

Ash ran his hands over his face. "Demon King," he muttered.

"Don' call him that," Kinson warned. "Our faith don' acknowledge him by that name."

"But it is a prophecy," Ash countered, gently despite his monstrous size. "The Díanzon Prophecy mentioned his name would change with time."

"The King of Monsters," Zilac added. "His proper name."

Cassian held his tongue. He knew that not all Queens were pirates, and that their ranks had infiltrated every city across the Vore World. Some acted as advisors to rulers, devoid of the standard Queen's mark or sea-inspired tattoos to keep landwalkers from identifying their allegiances. Others managed the business of trade on land, traveling to the deepest parts of the country to exchange high-valued items like relics, secrets, and information. They were the economic powerhouse of the world, driving financial value across land and sea.

In the few moons that Cassian had been here, he'd learned from Felah that half the cities wouldn't be where they were now without the secretive aid of the pirates. Felah lectured him on a lot of topics that no other Queen would share with him, which was another reason he liked her. The Queens aided countries in their development, provided resources for rulers to win wars that were world-changing, and acted as mercenaries for the select few cities that had pledged fealty in private. Or, in the case of Raveer, the royal family had a bloodline tied to the Red Queens. They *were* Queens. Pirates were everywhere and easy to spot, if one knew what to look for.

The startling realization of just how involved the Red Queens were with the world kept him up most nights in the last moon since he'd learned more. Felah told him everything, treating him like a son and spending more time than he cared to admit talking about her people. They funded the Nighthunters, the paid assassins who lived on the panhandle of the country of Diyră, who went after anyone if the bid was right. He'd been a fool to think he'd ever be able to outrun them. Sooner or later, the Queens would have found him. With San'yila, he had much more to worry about. Running would only get him so far with these pirates. He needed an action plan, a destination, and refuge.

Sitting at the council of the Red Queens as a guest was unheard of. No pirate had been granted this right, and Cassian soaked it in. Everything he learned would aid him in his quest for freedom. What he learned here could change the entire dynamics of the sea—White Horns and others would pay a hefty fee to get this kind of insight.

"Your ship?" Kinson cut in.

"Destroyed, Viv'an," the Queen replied. "Watched her go down in flames. The crew jumped ship, and I was pulled out of the water. We barely escaped."

Kinson slammed her hand onto the table. Her nostrils flared, and a vein bulged in her forehead. "You promised this would be easy! You said Caster's defenses would be down. He will expect us now."

Zilac held his hands up in defeat. "My source has never let me down. What happened was not intentional misinformation."

"He's stronger than we expected," Hezil offered. His sea tongue was thick. Cassian's ears were sharp, but he strained to hear the pirate who was covered head to toe in colorful tattoos. "Consider this in our favor. We know his capabilities. We know where Caster stands."

Kinson nodded, seemingly satisfied. "We have to work faster than originally planned." Her eyes flicked to him, too fast to determine anything. "We can' risk any more ships, yeah, too much at stake."

Cassian drummed his fingers on the table, weighing whether or not to speak up. The Krakí's tentacles inked into his arm slithered and moved with his motions, alive. Nobody stared at him like a Dragon Rider. Hardly anyone glanced at San'yila. Whatever these people saw on a day-to-day basis must have been impressive enough to not flinch in the presence of a magnificent creature like the dragon. And now they spoke of prophecies and war like they were mundane occurrences.

Despite living in Queens' Gate for three moons, Cassian had been naïve to believe he'd learned about their ways. He was so wrong. He may never get the opportunity again to ask the questions that boiled on his tongue.

San'yila didn't stop him. She wanted answers, too.

The men and Kinson spoke feverishly about strategy—things he didn't care about. They droned on about the placement of ships, how many they would need versus how many should stay and continue to enforce the Queens' sea, and whether or not they could successfully go after Morei Geral, king of Caster, and not lose an entire fleet of ships. They were afraid, Cassian realized. They hesitated to make any solid decisions.

Cassian's fingers stopped moving, and he slowly raised his hand. It took a moment, but Ey'kon's furious gaze met him with blinding heat. Kinson's glare followed next. She motioned at Cassian impatiently, and the conversation ceased.

"What?" she asked.

Cassian cleared his throat. "I must be missing something, and apologies about that. But you all seem really worked up about this, and I can't help but wonder . . . Why am I here?"

Not the question I would have started with, San'yila observed.

What? You'd have started with what's for supper?

I just ate, she remarked. *But don't think I won't eat you all for acting like mindless barnacles. I am constantly stunned by how you men and women act. Too caught up in the details and losing sight of the big picture. That sea turtle has more intelligence than these pirates.*

He didn't doubt her threat. *At least start with Ey'kon first so I can watch.* In the last several moons, San'yila had taken on a much more otherworldly wisdom. She saw the world differently and made observations that would usually escape Cassian. She saw the world not as it was, but as it could be.

Kinson crossed her arms and tilted her head. She looked like a serpent preparing to strike. "Why?" she asked, but it was not truly a question. She knew. Everything about the way she studied him told Cassian she wanted him here for a reason. "You are our means to an end. You'll be ending this war before it gets any bloodier."

Everyone's gaze was fixed on him. Cassian wanted to sink onto the ground where the dragon lay her head. He wanted to crawl into the Soul Realm and disappear, anything to shake the hungry looks of the Queens Council. His skin prickled with dread, and he forced air in. They wanted to weaponize him.

"Excuse me?" Cassian whispered.

"You're the end. The sword that will strike, yeah, the deal that will bring peace. You'll kill Morei. Yeah?" Kinson asked, disgusted. "You think we brought you here out of the kindness of our hearts? You think we'd let a White Horn call this place home?" The other pirates nodded. Ey'kon looked like he was feasting on Cassian's emotions.

I'll kill them all, San'yila grumbled. A low growl vibrated the table and chairs. Cassian held his hand out to halt her as the power and confidence were torn right out of the room.

Slowly, Cassian stood to meet Kinson on equal ground. He might not be a king, but he wouldn't be treated like an imbecile. Some men started to rise with him, but the woman stopped their progress with a stern look. Cassian licked his lips, finding his mouth was dry. Not from fear, but from anger for these people assuming they knew him.

"If you think I have stayed here because I was comfortable, you're wrong." The response came slowly. "If you think I have stayed because I wanted to support a cause I know nothing about, you're also wrong. You ripped me from my life and dropped me into a world that spits on my kind. Dirty-blooded White Horn, right? I am beneath you all." He didn't wait for their answers. He knew where he stood. "But if you think I will end a war you started, you're wrong. I am not your puppet. And I will never see you as anything more than a slimy and wretched disgrace to the pirate name, *Viv'an*." He threw all his hate into that last word. It would be the first and only time he would ever use it.

The woman raised her chin. "Bold words for someone to say when they bore the Queens' mark."

"Forced on me while I couldn't defend myself," Cassian countered hotly. "How dare you assume I wanted any of this."

Ash stood and grabbed Cassian, shoving him down into his seat. San'yila moved quickly, infuriated. Her blinding temper took his breath away as she stood and forced her snout into the pirate's face. Men leapt up from the table, scrambling for swords and shouting. Other pirates stuck their heads into the tent, faltering the moment they saw San'yila with her talons pressed against Ash's chest, pinning him against the table. All she needed to do was press down, and they'd sink into flesh and crack bone. He'd die instantly.

The thirst to see that happen intoxicated Cassian. He begged her to follow through on her threat, to see the blood spill. Madness would ensue, but it would be because of him. He reveled in that thought, letting a smile slip and a snort escape. Since arriving, his life had been taken away from him. Cassian had been molded in the past season to feign loyalty and swallow his rage. No more. If San'yila acted, he would take his life b ack.

The dragon tilted her head, eying Ash. Her pupils dilated. Her mind was bursting with want. She wanted it too—she wanted to kill him. Her predatory instincts were in full control. San'yila needed just one push to make Cassian's blood fantasy come true. He salivated at the thought.

A single look around the table confirmed what Cassian needed to know. They were afraid of him. Underneath the bold declarations and authority was a group of pirates who feared his potential. Feared what San'yila would do if she grew violent. Their disinterest in her had been a front . . . in truth, it had been an attempt at a power play. They thought if they treated Cassian and San'yila like they were another commodity, treated them like they were mindless servants, then Cassian and San'yila wouldn't question the limits of their own capabilities.

But what if the dragon and her rider called the pirates' bluff? Challenge the Red Queens, and suddenly, they became the most powerful people in the room. That epiphany bubbled in his veins, euphoric.

That's enough, Cassian told her. San'yila's nostrils flared, and she blew hot air on Ash's face before retreating.

Cassian took the silence as an opportunity. "You speak of the Red Goddess as if she condones your actions. Would she? Would she support what you've done to me or San'yila? Or the thousands of lives you've taken? She represented rebirth, not destruction and imprisonment." Ey'kon opened his mouth, but Cassian raised his hand. "The question was rhetorical. You will tell me anything to justify your actions. You think you're all special. You think that you stand before your faith as honorable pirates, but you're no different than the kings and queens who slaughter innocents in the name of peace. In the name of Gods who do not listen to their pleas. You're just as bad as Caster, just as damned as the rest of the world." Cassian's voice shook with violent passion. He'd wanted to say this since the day he awoke, marked to serve the Queens.

"You fear Morei, a man you know nothing about. You fear change. You fear being forgotten about," Cassian continued, laughing, feeling manic. "You think because some king grows more powerful and challenges your status quo that you are forced to act to prove your place. And now you think that dragging me into your problems will resolve everything. What do you hope for? That this king will bow his head in shame and apologize? He will wreak havoc on you all. He will not spare me because I come on the back of a dragon. He will turn his cannons and soldiers on me, shoot San'yila and I out of the sky with fiery cannonballs before we even make it to the ground." He lowered his voice. "And when he's done with me, he will come for you all and leave nothing."

Cassian snapped his mouth closed. Too much. In his rage, he'd spilled far too much and revealed how he really felt. His rant revealed his worry and fear to the pirates at this table, two emotions he'd carefully hidden from the

Red Queens since his arrival. And based on the expressions of everyone in the room, he knew they'd gotten exactly what they wanted: confirmation. Nobody feared him, they feared the dragon. San'yila owned the reputation the day she hatched. The reputation came from centuries of stories passed down to each generation. Now, with her growing bulk, nobody questioned the legitimacy of those old tales of fierce dragons who tore cities apart. One day, that could be San'yila.

Envy. The bitter emotion nearly made him choke. Cassian envied the king of Caster. He wanted to create that much fear of his name, wanted the world to know him. Before all of this, he'd dreamed of disappearing, settling on the coast somewhere. He couldn't get that here, and he might never get that. Not that he ever intended on staying, but he wanted more than just the title of the Queens' Dragon Rider. Now, Cassian wanted to prove *why* San'yila chose him. He didn't want to be a puppet, tasked to solve the Red Queens' political problems, didn't want to end their battles because they failed to plan better. This was *his* destiny, his life, and he wanted—*needed*—to take control of it. He wanted to be the ender of greed, the harbinger of death, and the destroyer of realms.

He wanted to be the most feared Dragon Rider ever to take flight. He wanted the world to chant his name, speak of his stories like how they speak of the Gods and beasts. Cassian deserved that respect. San'yila too. They'd been through too much already, and now these Queens thought they could steal their future because it suited their needs. No. He wouldn't allow it.

A knock on a wooden beam behind broke the tense spell. "A ship has arrived," a young girl said, voice unnaturally loud. If she sensed the brewing fight, she didn't let it show. "They found what we've been looking for."

The Crown of Gods

Pirates gathered outside the tent. A buzz filled the air, charged with a nervous frenzy that made it hard to stand still. Cassian didn't—couldn't—let his thoughts drift too far from the interrupted meeting. These people intended to use San'yila and him like workhorses on a farm. Use them until they dropped dead.

Cassian's attention turned to the chest dropped by a young woman who was hardly inked. Another summer and she would be as covered as the rest of her pirate comrades. The woman's auburn hair shimmered under the sun. Freckles dotted her cheeks and neck. She looked about as old as Elliot had been. The thought knocked the confidence right out of him. So much blood on his hands already. And so much more would be, from the looks of things.

The inner circle families hovered. Ey'kon stood beside Kinson like a well-trained hound, Raryl had his burly arms crossed, displaying the same Kraki tattoo that Cassian had, but faded with the decades of sun, and the others hardly looked away from the chest. Whatever was in here was enough to stop a meeting that had quickly turned hostile. They were only a dozen paces from the tent, but it felt like they'd stepped into another world. Even the breeze teased his clothes with a cautionary touch that seemed to warn of a brewing storm. The skin on the back of Cassian's neck prickled with an unseen presence, and he quickly rubbed it away.

Everyone seemed to forget about Cassian and his outburst, even as the dragon loomed behind him, her growing head casting a large shadow across the men and women. Kinson's hands opened and closed, as if she couldn't figure out what she wanted to do. Cassian and San'yila stayed several steps back. From the corner of his eye, he caught Red's unwavering attention just on the edge of the circle. The pirate was everywhere and nowhere all the time. He wondered if the Queen had been eavesdropping.

The chest was scuffed up, old, and discolored. Grimy black stains covered what were once stunning gold inlays of beasts. The lock was broken, the wood was water-damaged and splintering. This close, his mind hummed with a tingling sensation that whispered to curious thoughts that begged to be heard. The sudden sound made him falter. A quick glance confirmed San'yila was sensing the same. Her mind heard what his did. She blinked.

Dark Energy, she said.

Cassian knew. The more exposure he got to energy, the more he could recognize certain sounds and sensations. Light Energy was bright, impossible to miss in the dingy world around him. To him, the energy was hot, but he'd heard Red describe the sensation as frigid. He didn't know why he perceived it differently. But Dark Energy . . . This was different. Haunting—it called to him. Just as Red had warned. If he focused enough, he could almost hear the hushed voices. What they said was lost to him, too muffled and quick to be deciphered. A chill raced up his arm. The energy radiating from the chest was freezing.

Cassian eyed the prized possession, noting the Old Tongue sigils carved on the chest's sides.

"Cursed, I tell ya," a man remarked, gesturing at the chest. "Shouldn't be here."

"You're just bein' weak," a woman replied, crossing her arms. "Job's done. That's what we were hired for."

The first man waved his hand at her. "Ya fool."

Another woman stepped forward, hands balled into fists. "I don' care what ya say. Damn thing's been nothin' but bad luck."

Cassian observed. The dirt coating the skin of these recently-arrived pirates, their clothes frayed along the edges, told him that this was the crew who'd retrieved the chest. And they were at odds about how to handle their find with each other. Kinson let them hash it out, never once taking her eyes off the chest. In her expression, he saw conflict. Whatever lay within the chest was threatening enough to make even the Red Queen ruler hesitate.

Pirates going about their daily tasks slowed to watch the scene unfold, chatter dying as more people gathered. Nobody seemed to notice, save for Red, who pinched his chin with one hand while the other was wrapped across his chest. A single flick of his finger spurred movement back into the pirates who'd stalled in their duties. A silent order. Cassian hadn't realized the influence Red had until that moment.

The pirates who had wanted to watch the chest open quickly continued on their way, looking dazed, leaving the inner circle in privacy. Red turned his dark gaze to Cassian. At once, Cassian looked away, not liking the stare Red gave him—expectant and disapproving. He turned his attention to Ey'kon. The Harvester's expression remained placid. He was dressed in a fitted white tunic, revealing a red sun along his chest when he shifted: one of the high-ranking Red Queen marks. Meant Ey'kon had once sailed, too. Cassian cleared his throat, hoping someone would speak up about the chest.

Nobody did. Instead, all sound died. Kinson and the rest of the pirates in the small circle seemed paralyzed by the chest's presence. He cleared his throat again, louder, spying Red's unwavering stare from the corner of his eye. A chill washed over him as fiercely as if he stood underneath a waterfall, drenching him in an anxiety that made his fingers twitch. The silence needed to be broken. He couldn't stand it anymore.

"What is it?" Cassian questioned. His voice shattered the silence as if he'd just banged drums. Everyone startled, taking him and San'yila in as if they'd just remembered the two were still there. A few exchanged questioning glances. Cassian knew the looks—they didn't want him here to witness this find.

Kinson's chest rose and fell, coming to life as if she'd just been yanked from a trance. The Red Queen ruler blinked and pushed a few dreadlocks over her shoulder. Then she finally acknowledged Cassian with a threatening glare he couldn't tell was meant to elicit respect or challenge him to a duel. By the restless sea, the Red Queen ruler likely wanted to tell him and San'yila to leave. He and the dragon certainly had no right to be here, as far as she was concerned. He'd already made it clear that he had no intention of going along with her master plan. Perhaps, though, she could use this treasure to persuade him?

But Cassian didn't move; he refused to. Prior to his life being bonded to a dragon, he was fearless and reckless. Now, though, he needed to be more strategic in his thinking. Insecurities and uncertainties clung to his senses much more than he ever dared to admit, fueled by the constant need to protect San'yila. He didn't worry about his safety, but hers.

Three moons had passed since he'd lost touch with the man he'd been before the Queens took him. More and more, he felt like a stranger to himself. The face he knew so well stared back at him in the washing water each morning, but he didn't recognize the silver eyes anymore—they were vacant and submissive. He'd been so focused on keeping San'yila alive that he'd sacrificed everything, even himself. Cassian needed to start reclaiming who he was, and it started today.

The Red Queen crossed her arms and jutted her chin in the direction of the chest. "Somethin' we've sought for many summers, yeah, a relic from the Lirallian Empire."

"He shouldn't be here," Ey'kon hissed, gesturing at Cassian. "Viv'an, I ask that you send him off."

The Red Queen ruler regarded the Harvester. A silent battle warred between the two. The pirates who made up the small circle shrank, clearly made uncomfortable by the standoff. Surrounding Queens on the outskirts of the circle shifted, unsettled, but not Red, who didn't even flinch.

"No," Kinson finally said. "Don' challenge me again in front of my people, Ey'kon. Must I remind you of your place?"

The Harvester licked his lips but didn't reply. Ash, who'd been standing next to Ey'kon, stepped away as if the Harvester might explode into flames, muttering something too softly to be heard. Not even the breeze could break through the wall of tension that encapsulated the small circle of Queen leaders.

Cassian didn't know why Kinson wanted him here. Perhaps this was how she thought to manipulate him—or that he would be influenced by the relic. It wouldn't ever work, but he would worry about that later. Right now, his thoughts were on the relic in the chest, although he loved watching Ey'kon being scolded. Cassian had been looking for the Crown of Gods, a relic that was believed to be forged during the Lirallian Empire by Henry Junok—the madman who committed heinous crimes and was responsible for the Diyrạllian Massacre—before his life went to shit. If the rumors were true, there were three relics from the reign of the Lirallian Empire, all with unique capabilities. The last time he was at Greve's Point with the *Torment* crew, they'd not learned anything about the relic's whereabouts, and he'd admittedly forgotten about it because of everything that had happened. He didn't know a lot, but he knew the relics were supposed to be powerful. At the time, his only concern had been how much coin he could get for it.

"Which one?" he asked, eager to get answers.

Kinson's smile was strained. "I didn't realize you knew the history." She sighed, head sweeping over the other pirates in what could only be described as judgment. "Seems the Dragon Rider is the only one here with a workin' tongue."

Cassian shrugged, but the motion was stiff with Kinson's harsh insult to the surrounding pirates. "Most pirates know about relics. What makes me any different?"

No response. None was needed. Even as the question left his lips, he understood her meaning. He was a Dragon Rider—a relic like this could make him unstoppable if he got out of here. Relics like the ones from the Lirallian Empire were extraordinary, supernatural even, if harnessed correctly. If the relic were in Cassian's hands, he could be a devastating threat to the Red Queens. Or, as Kinson was probably thinking, a threat to the Demon King.

As if to confirm this, Ey'kon shot him a glare. The other pirates, the crew who'd retrieved the chest, didn't move. They had no place in this conversation, but they were why the relic was here in the first place, which kept them pinned in this discussion until the Red Queen ruler dismissed them. The surrounding inner circle members, like Raryl, kept his arms crossed and his lips pinched in a thin line.

"Rül'Cril," Kinson whispered. "The Crown of Gods. It can control the Vore beasts. History says that Henry Junok never used it during his reign, no, never had the chance to before he was executed. Some say the only person who ever tried to use it was the God of Dreams himself, yeah, and it broke his mind when he did."

Zilac scoffed. "Old sea tales," he mumbled in disgust.

Cassian swallowed, ignoring the comment. "The God of . . .?"

"Sekar," Kinson clarified. "He'd mark his victims with dreams and madness. Thought this relic could give him more control, yeah, or so the tales say." She spoke quietly, as if pulled into a memory nobody else was privy to. Cassian didn't know why she would share that with him, but he wished he hadn't heard it, because it opened a maelstrom of horrible concerns and frightful assumptions in his head.

The dream. The man. The journal entries from Ricard. The Tsu'ran said Cassian was marked—the same term Kinson had just used. Cassian's knees weakened. A crippling sensation washed over him, moving through his mind until it seized his logic and snapped it in half. Glass had told him he thought Captain Ricard was marked by the Dark Lord. The Dark Lord was the God of Dreams. Sekar. The man he spoke to said he'd seen Cassian's dreams.

Cassian opened his mouth to ask more about the deity, but snapped his mouth shut. Now was not the time. He was letting his mind go wild with this mention of Sekar, and he needed to chain those worries until they grew out of hand. Cassian's encounters with the strange man on *Torment* and *Dread Deep* were carefully packed away, untouched for this last season, but they resurfaced in an instant. Maybe the Gods were real, and maybe they didn't need prayer to seek out what they wanted. The conversation with the strange man echoed over and over in his head, too loud to ignore. Something about this wasn't right. The sudden rush of clarity caused him to sway.

"Your time is up, Captain. It's time to answer to Destiny."

San'yila's mind washed over him, drowning out the racing thoughts. She cocooned him, much as she had done before when he couldn't sleep, and his restlessness woke her. She filled his mind with promises of a future he still dreamed of, one that gave them the freedom to be whoever they wanted and to soar the distant skies that painted the horizon.

The small crowd of Red Queens still expected a response. What he wanted to do was inquire more about Sekar, to try and wrestle his racing thoughts into submission. The ghost he'd seen in the captain's cabin, the same that had followed him to the dungeon on *Dread Deep* . . . maybe this ghost wasn't actually a ghost at all, but something else—a God, the Dark Lord.

"What do you intend to do with it?" Cassian inquired. It felt like a safe question.

"Master the beasts that once ruled this world," Kinson answered matter-of-factly. "We can' expand our territory without facin' possible threats that we can' handle. This will allow us to have more tools to be successful."

"Harness Life Eaters? Against . . . Morei?" Cassian pressed. He couldn't believe his ears. Ey'kon's cheeks were flush. The Harvester was infuriated that Cassian was even allowed to ask these questions.

"He is one threat, yeah." Kinson's chest rose and fell. Zilac and Hezil nodded simultaneously as if to confirm the ruler's response—too forced and too staged. In that single motion, Cassian knew she wasn't being honest with him. Why would she? "We are in a new era, Cassian. We either be the feared or we be the forgotten, yeah, no place for anything else. Surely you must want a place in the new future? A chance to cleanse your name and prove to the world that you're not just another dirty-blooded pirate?"

Cassian's mouth was dry. This was far bigger than he'd anticipated. Kinson was trying to lure him in, feed him false promises of hope and new beginnings. It was so obvious now. The only person who seemed bothered by that strategy was the Harvester, whose ego was damaged because of Cassian. The Red Queens wanted more, but Cassian had not thought they'd find a weapon so potent that a even God would lose his mind to it. He didn't doubt the relic's power or potential, but he didn't think anyone on this island should hold it. These people were savages, prideful wretches who felt the world owed them something when that was so far from the truth.

Rül'Cril. The Crown of Gods. Ricard had been after that relic before everything fell apart. Three moons ago, Cassian had been a man who'd sailed these waters wanting the coin that came with a prize like that. But then he'd gotten caught up in the hunt for a dragon egg and the promise of 45,000 Krye, enough to buy his own ship and crew, and a reputation that would earn him the respect he always felt he deserved.

It half-amused Cassian to think that King Jair probably had a bounty out for *Torment*, not that Jair would know where to begin looking. Pirates weren't easy to find in the best of circumstances. In this case, the ship itself was in the belly of a Life Eater, and Cassian had been ambushed and taken to the other side of the Grave. Now, covered in the art of the Queens, damned to make an enemy of himself, and starved for a purpose greater than being a mindless tool, he knew what he wanted—*needed*—to do.

Steal the Crown of Gods. He couldn't leave without it. The Red Queens would stop at nothing to master this relic and use it for all the wrong reasons, not that Cassian had any idea how to use a relic like this for *good*. If he left the relic with them, they would ruin his life, hunt him down, and torture him until nothing was left of him. If they didn't make him a mindless puppet now, they eventually would. No matter what, the Crown could not remain in the Red Queens' hands. They were too vicious, and with a relic like that, they would be unstoppable. The fears stretched across his mind like a chasm opening up at the bottom of the sea, swallowing everything whole.

Power was intoxicating, and Cassian admittedly wondered what it would be like to use a relic like that for himself, but nothing could squash the terror burrowing into his chest at the notion of such power in the hands of the ruthless Red Queens. Already, the tensions at sea were escalating because of the Red Queens and the murder of Zinfel. When would the Queens stop in their quest for domination? Once they had the entire world as their own? That would leave nothing for the other pirate clans. The White Horns would become obsolete, landwalker kingdoms would turn into endless resources for the Red Queens to draw on, and every pirate would be expected to join an empire that served only the Queens. If they could turn beasts into mindless weapons, they could do whatever they wanted.

No. Cassian couldn't let them keep the relic. Whatever happened, he needed to get the Crown out of their hands. He wasn't sure what he would do with it, but that was a *tomorrow* problem.

"I'm suddenly feelin' generous. What is it that you want, Dragon Rider?" Kinson asked him, voice too high-pitched. The Red Queen ruler rubbed a hand over her face, looking like she could sleep for a century. Cassian wondered how long the Red Queens had been searching for Rül'Cril. Based on how Kinson's shoulders slumped and the long exhale that dragged out, they must have been searching for far longer than the *Torment* crew had been before Ricard was killed. With a lazy and slow flick of her wrist, she motioned for the pirates to pick up the chest, and they obeyed.

Cassian shook his head. "A good drink, but I can get that at Felah's. Perhaps you need something?"

Kinson studied him with new appreciation, and it was clear how she'd taken his suggestion. She might be tough, but that single act betrayed every-thing she'd kept hidden—the yearning, the want for affection, the physical intimacy all people craved. The pirates treated her differently because she was deemed the daughter of the Red Goddess, given her title, but not him. And for that, he knew she wanted him . . . for nothing else than to feel wanted herself. It was a feeling that Cassian couldn't and wouldn't return. Not after what she'd done to him.

"Be at my home at high sun. I want to speak to you privately."

One problem after the next. Cassian was tired of it. He could hardly speak his mind without setting off a whirlwind of issues. If it wasn't war, it was loyalty. If not trust, it was fear. These people were managing him like a blind man would manage a nest full of razor crabs. They couldn't do anything right, and every word said or action done just pissed him off more.

A part of him wanted to slaughter every pirate on this entire island, let San'yila have her fill. She might not be fully grown, but she was still large enough to cause massive harm and kill plenty who stood in her way. At Cassian's shoulder height, she probably weighed as much as two or three steeds, and she would only get bigger. San'yila was the real threat on this island. But the more logical side of him knew he'd be lucky to get off this island alive without trading his soul for something in return. That didn't mean he didn't dream of slitting the throats of every pirate here, though.

Ey'kon cleared his throat, coming to life. This was the closest Cassian had been to the sadistic Harvester since *the incident*. The animosity that hung between them was stifling. The Harvester's gaze drilled into Cassian, and he imagined Ey'kon would like nothing more than to kill him in front of the other pirates. A long pause blistered, agonizing, before Ey'kon asked, "Do you feel it?"

"Huh?" Cassian bit the inside of his lip to tame his growing worries. He felt the pinch of delicate skin break and he tasted blood. He faked a cough. "Feel what?"

Ash, who'd stood beside him, stepped back quickly, offering more room for the Harvester to lunge if he wanted to. Ey'kon narrowed his gaze and hissed, "The energy."

"Oh," Cassian mumbled, aware that the other pirates huddled close watched. He couldn't tell anyone the truth. He didn't want the Harvester to know so much about him, and he feared what Ey'kon would do to him if he said he did feel the Dark Energy. "No," he lied.

"Probably a good thing," the Harvester remarked and laced his hands together. "Certain power shouldn't be handled."

A loaded reply. Cassian wasn't sure what to make of it. Ey'kon's assertiveness suggested he wanted to prove to every Red Queen on the island that he shouldn't be challenged. Ey'kon wore his arrogance, well, like a crown.

"Agreed," Cassian mumbled, retreating with San'yila away from the crowd. As his boots sank into the sand, her black talons reflected brilliantly under the sun. Such a small detail, but the *realness* of it kept his legs steady.

What do you think of that? Cassian asked, sinking to the sand beside her. He wanted a moment to collect himself, and he couldn't think of a better place than sitting with the dragon.

I think stealing the relic is a mad plan, she replied. *It is a dark object. The energy is unlike anything I've ever felt before.*

But do you agree that it shouldn't stay in their hands?

Silence. *Yes*, she admitted.

The waves lapped the shore lazily. *What if we leave tonight?* Cassian suggested and peered around her shoulder, watching the chest be carried toward Ey'kon's working tent. Of course the Harvester would insist on watching over the chest personally. Power-greedy son-of-a-bitch. It would make Cassian's life easier, though. He could sneak in, kill the Harvester, and take the chest. Convenient and efficient.

If the sky permits, then I say we should.

He eyed her, realizing what that meant. Was she big enough to carry him? She was bulky, larger than him, and growing fast. Her size could kill a man, so there was no doubt of her capability, but he suddenly realized that maybe he might be too big until she grew larger.

San'yila hummed, amused. *Do not fret, little Rider. You underestimate me.*

He rubbed his fingers over her hardened scales, appreciating the much-needed humor. *Little? Is that what you think of me?*

Soon, I will be twice this size, she proudly declared. *Perhaps even bigger. So, yes, you are little.*

Cassian shook his head, refraining from a smile. *It's settled. Tonight, when everyone is asleep, we act.* Cassian patted San'yila's leg to his left. *Tomorrow, when the sun rises, we will be free.*

The Dance for Power

Cassian was at Kinson's private home. A small wooden building with the necessities—a window and chimney—the door painted with a vibrant sun, which indicated her title as Viv'an and honored the Red Goddess. One thing Cassian had quickly learned about the Red Queens was that they loved to paint, whether it meant marking their skin permanently with ink or creating grand illustrations. To them, marking their skin or what they owned conveyed pride in their culture—a way to honor their beliefs with beautiful depictions of war, beauty, strength, and resilience.

As ordered, he'd arrived at high sun and knocked. The day was hardly halfway old, and so much had happened already. The Crown of Gods was at Queens' Gate. Ricard had been after the relic, and Cassian had wanted to continue the search until the egg heist presented itself. If they planned this right, Cassian could sell the Crown to an honest buyer who just wanted an artifact and live comfortably for the rest of his life. He didn't want the Crown for himself, had no intentions of wanting to harness whatever dark forces fueled the relic's capabilities.

Dark Energy, he corrected himself. Cassian knew it, and had felt it. If he didn't listen to the voices, heeding Red's warning, then he would be—should be—fine in handling the Crown. Then again, part of him wondered how irresponsible it would be to sell it. Sure, the coin would promise a future where he didn't want for anything, but there would always be the risk that the Crown ended back up in the Red Queens' hands, which the world couldn't afford. The power that the relic emitted could resurrect a thousand men. Anyone, even someone as untrained in energy harvesting as he was, could feel it. Put it in the hands of someone who knew what they were doing, like Ey'kon, and it would be a weapon of mass destruction.

Put it in the hands of Morei Geral, the prophesied King of Monsters, and the Queens would be left with nothing. Cassian's lip twitched upward. Now there was an angle. He didn't believe in prophecies or legends, but he did believe in power. Morei could give him exactly what he hungered for—revenge on the Red Queens.

San'yila nudged his shoulder. He looked up at her. Affection poured from her bond into him, trying to ease the brewing storm of violence that was always on the horizon with him. Nothing could take away the man Cassian was raised to be, not even a second chance at life. No amount of dreaming or fantasizing about a peaceful life could change that. He was bred and raised to be a thief and a murderer, and to take what he wanted. When the Red Queens tested him by placing him before Ey'kon, he fought with everything he had and nearly killed the Harvester. If the Red Queen ruler believed she could bend Cassian to her will, she was wrong.

The door opened. Kinson appeared, terrifyingly beautiful. Her dreads hung loosely, falling halfway down her back. Leather straps covered her crotch and breasts, revealing the rest of her ebony skin, which was inked in red tattoos. Jewels decorated both hands and forearms, and around her neck was a large amulet in the shape of a sun.

"Ah, Cassian." Her teeth were still stained red. Kinson opened the door wider. "Come in, yeah. Come in."

She stepped aside. Cassian stood at the precipice of the entryway, half certain some of her men waited inside to kill him. He wasn't sure this was such a good idea.

She waved him in. "Please. Let's get on with it. I'm getting new ink shortly."

He blinked. She had so many tattoos that he wasn't sure where she'd put a new one. He searched her skin as discreetly as possible, finding small spaces that could fit a new tattoo, and allowing his curiosity to traverse the curves of her body and the softness of her skin like a man's hands would. It'd been too long since he'd lain with a woman. Now he was starting to see Kinson as something more than a bloodthirsty tyrant with no ability at mercy. Not because she was a good woman, but because Cassian let his mind wander too far from his reach. He saw a young woman take on the fate of the Red Queens with her chin held high and willing to bear the weight of centuries of tradition and pride. For a fleeting moment, Cassian saw Kinson not as she was—harsh, impassioned for her people, and cruel—but as who she once was: determined to prove her place, stubborn, and, to some, kind. He'd seen the way she treated her people. When politics weren't involved, she loved to wander through the huts and tents, offering a helping hand to those who needed it. She was a complicated woman.

San'yila pushed him forward. He stepped inside.

I will be right here, the dragon said.

"Sit," she said as he entered. Kinson closed the door behind her and crossed to the galley, where she poured two cups of tea. "I hope you don' mind. I took the liberty to assume you'd want some tea."

Cassian nodded, struggling to form words. "Yeah, that's fine."

She raised an eyebrow, and he blinked. She wanted formalities. Persistent little fly, she was. He refused.

She set the kettle on the wooden counter and picked up a small bottle with a creamy substance. "Kendell's Milk?"

He hesitated. "In the tea?" Kendell's Milk was a creamy liquor that could knock the burliest man to his knees after one glass. To the landwalkers, it was Kendell's Milk. To most pirates, they called it the Anchor, because it could drag anyone to the bottom of their senses and leave them rambling at the rancid-smelling beakhead of the ship until dawn.

Kinson chuckled and poured a heavy amount into hers. "Yeah. It's a perfect companion for the leaves. My people have drunk this combination for centuries."

Something stronger than tea sounded fitting. "Sure, though I don't need as much as what you just poured into yours." The last thing he needed was to be drunk for whatever conversation would be had. For once, he wanted to be sober.

She didn't listen. The Queen topped off his cup with the same amount and capped the liquor. In the past season, he'd learned the woman loved her liquor. Kinson spent many nights up later than most, drinking away. She stirred both cups and then picked one up to hand to him. Cassian thanked her.

"Sit," she repeated, motioning to one of the thin leather chairs. He reluctantly did so, facing the door and her. He wouldn't die with his back turned. Kinson seemed to notice, hesitating before she settled across from him. From here, he could see San'yila's bulk. Hard to miss so much red.

Kinson took a sip and hummed into her cup. The single act made her look summers younger, and like she didn't have a care in the world. For a moment, she was beautiful. Then she opened her piercing gaze and leaned forward, harnessing the authority she knew so well. "I have been told you have taken to our studies well."

Cassian nodded. "Aye."

"And that you're exceptional with a sword."

The cup's warmth radiated into his hands. "Aye."

"You have anything to say about that?"

Her question confused him. "About my skills?"

She nodded.

He snorted. "Well, what should I say? I'm a pirate. I spent my life defending myself and thinking quickly on my feet."

Kinson took another drink. "You spent the first part of your life on land."

The insult was there, hidden underneath her smile. "You think less of me?"

"You're a man of many hidden talents," she whispered, then motioned at the cup. "Drink."

San'yila urged him. *Be careful what you say. She is a serpent, waiting to strike.*

He raised the cup to his lips, hesitating before taking a drink. *And what do you suggest I do?*

He could practically taste the dragon's cynicism. *Do what you do best—be yourself.*

Wild, reckless, and bold. Cassian was all of those things and more. He would be careful, but he wouldn't bend the knee to this woman. Politics didn't suit him, and he didn't like being told what to do. He took a large drink, the strong taste of the liquor burning the back of his throat. Kinson was right. The tea paired incredibly well with Kendell's Milk. The creamy liquor was a rarity at sea.

"Your tattoos healed well," she added, letting her finger circle the rim of her cup slowly. "Felah tells me your scars need time." She shook her head, her dreads dancing with the motion. "Whips always leave a mark, yeah, no amount of oil or care can ease those."

He nearly scoffed at her ignorance. Or madness. One of the two. It was her order to have him whipped and tested. Now, she acted as if she felt pity for the very scars she placed on him. "It is what it is," Cassian replied, hoping to settle that discussion. "I don't even think about them." Half of them were covered in ink.

Her smile was strained, revealing a hardened woman who knew little of affection but craved it. Perhaps she missed it from her younger summers, before she was consumed by politics and war. "What do you want, Cassian?"

His fingers drummed the cup. "For supper or in life?"

"Both."

Cassian shrugged. "Tonight, I'd love a fatty boar roasted over a fire pit. The skin is incredible when it crisps up. As for life . . ." He tilted his head from side to side. "I'd like the chance to explore and not have to worry about waking up with a blade pressed against my throat." He leaned back, taking the cup with him. San'yila's fiery eyes peeked in the window. She wanted him to be himself. This was it.

Kinson took a sip. "You think you have a blade pressed against your throat?"

"I think you and the others fear my intentions. That's why I'm here, right? After earlier, I'm sure you're all bothered that I have a tongue. The pirate who hatched a dragon, and a dirty-blooded White Horn, no less. That must bother you all to death. The Queens are supposed to have it all—to be the face of the sea. Yet, you are obligated to protect me because you want nothing more than for me to serve you. To end your little war. A Dragon Rider for the Queens—what more power could you have?"

Cassian didn't want to offer the obvious: that the Crown of Gods could be as powerful, if not more powerful, than a Dragon Rider. He didn't know much about the relic beyond what he'd heard—and he hardly knew enough about what it meant to be a Dragon Rider—but he knew enough about the Red Queens to know that they didn't hunt the Crown down just to have a table centerpiece. The Queens would take control of the sea and go after Morei Geral. The Crown of Gods was destructive, and potentially deadly.

You are pushing your luck already, San'yila said. *I didn't tell you to be a fool.*

He took a drink, glad for the burn of the liquor. *And I will not play dead for this woman.*

"This is how feel?" she asked.

He nodded. "More or less."

Kinson raised a brow, whether impressed or annoyed, he couldn't tell. "Any king would have your tongue for speakin' that way, yeah, but I'm relieved."

Cassian faltered, nearly choking on the drink.

"You see, I don' want a puppet. Maybe you thought I did? Maybe you thought I'd stick you under my thumb and force you to do everything I demand?" She asked so sweetly that they could have been talking about a trade, a barter for a precious item in the markets that landwalkers used to sell and buy goods.

"I know what your Harvester can do," Cassian replied, keeping his voice steady. "I know you're hoping to convince me to see things the Queens' way so that you don't have to enforce a bond between me and your Harvester. Probably because you don't want to entrust him with that kind of power over me." When she didn't move, he took a drink. "Am I wrong?"

San'yila wasn't fond of his approach, but she didn't advise against it either. Answers needed to be had.

"No," Kinson relented. "But if you force my hand, yeah, I'll have no choice in the matter but to have Ey'kon bond your soul to his." She leaned forward again. "I want you to be a part of this. Do I have to explain myself?"

He shook his head. "Obey or die. It's clear."

The Red Queen sighed. In it, he could hear her frustrations mounting. "I asked you here today because I have a request. If you succeed, I think we can come to terms with our arrangement. In time, you may even learn to love our culture and ways."

Cassian took a drink.

"One of our ships has gone rogue. *Red Pearl.*" The information surprised him. By now, he would have thought those who challenged the new ways would be dealt with. "I could send a crew out to fetch them, yeah, but it would take three times as long. I want to send you."

A hundred things crossed his mind. He'd anticipated a fight, a snarky remark, a bridge-burning question to fly out of his mouth and get him in trouble. Instead, the only thing he could think of was that he'd never flown on San'yila before. She was large enough for him now, but he'd never pressed the matter. Not until their wild plan to leave. Flight made him a risk, and he didn't want to give the Queens the wrong impression when he was trying to earn enough favoritism to get them off his back. Sure, he'd thought of trying to fly before attempting to leave tonight, but he'd not been brave enough to crawl into the growing gap between San'yila's shoulders that would accommodate him. Cassian was made for sailing the sea, not flying over it.

"You would leave today, after this conversation."

"I—" He stopped, unsure what to say. This day was coming. He'd known it was, but he still wasn't prepared to handle the onslaught of emotions about flying. Fear squirmed in the pit of his stomach. He'd never been higher than the crow's nest. "How do you know I won't just take off and leave?"

Kinson didn't miss a beat. "You are a man of many things, but you won' abandon your word. If you commit to something, you'll follow through. That is how I know."

He wasn't a man of his word. Kinson would sell anyone and anything if it meant getting what she wanted. He was far from a man who fulfilled promises. He was the man who broke them. If needed, he'd abandon an entire crew for his survival. In the days following the loss of the *Torment* crew to the Life Eater, he'd had to accept that if the choice was there, if he could have tried to save them at the risk of his own life, he wouldn't have. Faced with that understanding, he wasn't a coward. Cassian had proven that. He was a man who knew his priorities, and at the time and now, San'yila was the only priority that outranked his own survival.

"And what if I don't?" he challenged, keeping his voice steady. "What if you set me loose and San'yila and I flee across the Vore World? What will you do?"

The smile she flashed was so cruel and wild that he sank into his chair. She knew something he didn't. She stood as gracefully as a dancer and walked around the table, letting her fingers drag across the wood. Cassian wanted to move, but if he did, he'd show fear, and he refused to do that. Not with her. Kinson straddled him, getting so close he could taste the liquor on her breath. She'd been drinking even before their meeting.

I can burn the building down, San'yila offered.

He nearly laughed at the absurdity. *And take me with it? Let's see where this goes.*

The dragon was displeased. She didn't like Kinson's proximity, and as the Red Queen lay her hands across his shoulders, San'yila growled so low that only the bond between them picked it up. He could feel the rumble vibrate his own chest. Kinson tilted her head, and he worried she might have heard.

"You can'," she whispered as sweet as if she spoke to a long-lost lover. "I can find you wherever you go."

He tensed, even as she ran her fingers over the back of his neck. "What?"

"Rül'Cril." Her fingers grazed his neck, tickling the sensitive skin under his ear where the Queens' mark was. "You know that to control a beast directly, all you need is a pinprick of their blood?" Her nails poked him. "Of course, you can use it without, but the effects are less . . . personal. Yeah, personal." She smiled, obviously pleased with the threat in her answer. "Does that satisfy, White Horn?"

Fury and fear fought for a place in his head. Emotions stormed his reasoning, and it took everything in him not to stuff his thumbs into her eyes and rip them out of her skull. Then maybe he'd take her tongue. The Lirallian Empire relic's perfectly-timed arrival was no coincidence.

"What did you do to San'yila?" Cassian demanded, but he remained as still as a statue, keeping his hands from latching around her throat and squeezing the life out of her. He wanted answers first.

Kinson chuckled as she let her fingers trace the anchor tattoo on his exposed chest where the V-neck of his tunic split. The sensation tickled, but not in the pleasurable way that Cassian knew the woman hoped for. It made him seethe. She had lost her mind. "Rül'Cril, White Horn. You don' strike me as someone who needs things explained to them, yeah, you don'. So let me give you a hint: Retrievin' the Crown of Gods was not a coincidence. It was intentional. For San'yila. And it's already done."

Time halted. The world as he knew it—a struggle but reliable and predictable in this past season—tilted, and his head spun. The relic he'd been searching for before Ricard was killed and his life was turned upside down was the same relic the Red Queens were after. And they'd found it. Not to control Life Eaters or Krakí or other beasts that lurked, at least not yet. No. They'd wanted the relic to control Cassian and San'yila. This was how they'd enslave a Dragon Rider to their cause, by binding San'yila to the Crown of Gods and turning her into an instrument.

Torture him. Bludgeon him until he lost teeth and spit blood. Chain him to the bottom of a ship and drag him across the sea. Whip him again until he bled out into the sand. Cassian would have taken any of that before this. Drawing on a power as ancient as that relic wouldn't end well for anyone. This was never San'yila's fight, and now Kinson was using her as leverage. How they managed to get blood from the dragon was a question he was afraid to know the answer to but needed.

Did you know? Cassian asked. *Did you have any idea what they did to you?*

The dragon's mind fluctuated, as if she couldn't figure out if she wanted to withdraw from him completely or wrap his mind in hers. *I was scared,* she finally replied. *When you were unconscious in those first few days, they did many things to me. I figured it was because they were curious, not because they were planning something like this.* San'yila's thoughts faltered, her mind as fragile as dust in the wind. *I let you down. I am sorry.*

This is not your fault. It never was, Cassian snapped too harshly. Anger wrapped its burning fingers around his throat. His vision narrowed, and his breaths grew shallow. San'yila tried to say something, but her words were lost to him.

"Don' look so upset," Kinson mumbled, tightening her hold on him. A hand slid down to the necklace, cradling the pendant between her breasts.

Under different circumstances, he'd have taken her on the table, but he wanted nothing to do with this mad woman. Repulsed was an understatement. He would tie her to the anchor of a ship and drop her to the bottom of the sea. Let the creatures of the waters have their way with her while she drowned. "I be only thinking ahead. Consider yourself lucky that it wasn't the Krisár ritual. Then you'd have nothing left of yourself, or of your dragon."

He knew the Krisár ritual, had learned of it from Bauer and the *Dread Deep* crew. Everyone at sea knew the dark practices of old times. Land-walkers thought they burned all the texts of such cursed practices, but they never accounted for the books at sea. Forbidden rituals still made their rounds on these waters. No king or queen was brave enough to declare war against the pirates who still practiced the old ways. The Krisár ritual bound two souls together in an unequal share of power by the consumption of the victim's blood. A blade of power must be used—one rich in energy—for the ritual to be successful.

Cassian would have no choice but to obey the Red Queens with San'yila unable to fight, bound to their orders with the relic. And if he refused, Kinson would order the Krisár ritual and turn him into a mindless weapon.

He looked away, keeping his hands limp at his side and forcing air in to compose himself. San'yila's warning reached his thoughts, shifting through the red rage. He couldn't kill Kinson. Not yet. The dragon was upset. She wanted to rip the roof off this home and snatch Kinson right out, snap her spine in half and tear her head clean off. The dragon's bloodthirsty violence pulsed in Cassian's veins, synching with his racing heart. But San'yila didn't act, no matter how much he wanted the dragon to do so.

Your life, San'yila quietly told him. *I cannot act. Not yet. Not without the risk of losing you.*

Dutiful as always. For being so young, she was far more stable than Cassian was. She didn't let the discovery blind her like it did with him. He wanted to submerge himself in the darkening thoughts, take his frustrations out with the help of a blade, but he wouldn't act without San'yila.

When we get out of this mess, Cassian replied, never letting his eyes leave the Red Queen ruler, *I will do everything in my power to keep you safe. Damn the Gods, beasts, kings. I don't care what becomes of this world, so long as you are safe.*

The dragon's nostrils flared, and Cassian felt the motion throughout his entire being. He could almost feel the hot air wash over him, despite the wall separating them. *I trust you*, she hummed.

He closed his eyes, wanting to melt into the chair. Trust. A word so foreign in this world. She trusted he would get them away from the Red Queens, cleanse her blood from the Crown, and give her back her freedom. It would become a race against time before they used the relic's abilities against San'yila. He didn't know how the Crown worked, or what it would be like for San'yila when the relic was being used, and he didn't want to find out. The dragon was not even half a summer old and had lived a nightmare. She shouldn't know this kind of agony.

I would not trade our experiences for the world, no matter how cruel, the dragon told him. *I have you, and that's all I need.*

She was so well-spoken, so brave. If Cassian could ask for anything, it was to have a sliver of San'yila's wisdom. He opened his eyes. Kinson wanted something from him. She wouldn't be straddling his lap otherwise.

"You want me, don't you?" Cassian whispered, dragging his hands across her thighs, pressing his fingers hard enough to leave indents in their path. Hot skin met his own, inviting, but he didn't act. Wouldn't. The question was loaded—intentional. He studied her movements, waiting for a reaction, or for her legs to tighten their hold on him.

But Kinson regarded him, unmoving, daring him to continue. And he did, unable to stop himself.

"A Dragon Rider by your side, loyal and forever in your debt. A lover." The last word was sour on his tongue. Far too much resentment oozed from his mouth, unfiltered. "You save my life, offer me a home, a second chance, and in return, you want me to give you the affection you so desperately crave. But it's more than that, isn't it?" Cassian suggested softly, letting the words take their time to fill the small space between them. He opened and closed his hands, feeling the burn of energy come without warning. The edges of his mind frayed from the overwhelming power. San'yila's familiarity came with it. This was her lifeforce that he'd gained access to, so beautifully bright and wild that the sudden intensity made him flush. "Your goal to take over the world starts and ends with me. What better way to know you'll get what you want by keeping me in your bed at night." It wasn't a question.

He latched onto her hips and shoved her off, pushing her up against the table and forcing her to stand. Kinson stumbled but composed herself quickly while Cassian stood. Even with their height difference, the Red Queen carried herself like she was the tallest person in the room. Impressive, if not for her sick games.

"You want respect from me," Cassian hissed, leaning in, "you earn it. Don't you dare think you can gain my trust by spreading your legs and feeding me lies. I know what you really want. I'm here because I didn't have a choice. I stand before you now because I chose to. Nobody here tells me what to do—I will not tolerate it. So you want my loyalty?" Their noses touched. "Then grant me my freedom. Keep me chained here, and I'll be sure to make your life miserable."

San'yila warned him to stop, but her pleas were drowned by the maelstrom of violent rage clamoring against his skull. He'd been beaten and whipped into submission, forced to be someone he wasn't. He wouldn't bow to some woman who was willing to rip his life away. The Red Queens were savages. And now they believed they'd broken him enough to make a loyal servant out of him. They were *wrong*.

"I'll play your little game," he continued. "I'll find the ship and declare the all-powerful rule of the Queens, give them something to fear. But it won't be your name they speak. It'll be mine."

He watched her take it all in as if seeing him for the first time. Kinson didn't flinch or recoil; she kept her chin up and shoulders squared. When he shifted, he felt cool metal poke his arm with feverish delight, waiting to break skin.

"Your temper will get you killed if you don't learn to think like a warrior. Yeah, it'll get you killed," she admonished. "I could kill you right here, but then what? I'd have to deal with your dragon and the mess of it all—if there was anything left after San'yila had her way. We don' stand in a dragon's way, but we'll stand in yours." The blade dropped on the table with a heavy thud. San'yila was infuriated. Her emotions bled into him like wind fanning a raging fire that scorched a vulnerable forest. Her grumbling grew louder, filling the room with low threats that both he and Kinson could hear.

But the Red Queen made no motion to indicate she worried about San'yila. Instead, Kinson stepped away and picked up her drink. She tipped the cup back, downing the rest in one go before she set it down with a loud slap against the table. Her body moved with the arrogance of a ruler who had everything they wanted before she faced him and made her final decree.

"You're expected to see U'shun before your departure. While you've been stewing in your poor attitude, we've worked to ensure you are a proper Dragon Rider. Go. And don' show your face until you have returned successfully from your trip."

Born for the Sky

Cassian was still heated from his exchange with Kinson as he marched to U'shun's hut. Connecting with San'yila's lifeforce gave him a sense of recklessness that he struggled to control, like he was a starved and feral animal. Prior to the confrontation with Kinson, he'd felt slivers of the dragon's lifeforce, but he'd never been immersed in it until now. San'yila gave that to him, hopeful he would compose himself, and to remind him that they were unstoppable. It hadn't worked. It only fanned the flames of his already deteriorating self-control.

He would play the game and do Kinson's bidding, seeking out the *Red Pearl* that sailed west of Queens' Gate. He had to. The options that presented themselves were limited. If he stormed into Ey'kon's hut and slaughtered the Harvester, he would have to deal with several hundred or more pirates. San'yila couldn't defend them against all that, and he couldn't put her in that kind of danger. Killing Kinson would have the same results. They could flee, just as he warned Kinson they might, but based on her confidence with the relic, he couldn't risk calling her bluff and submitting San'yila to the horrors of the Crown of Gods.

And that unnerved him. The Red Queens had too much power already. He needed to get the Crown. He couldn't leave the island without it. No matter what happened, that was his priority. Everything else—murder, revenge—would wait until he knew the Crown was safely out of the Queens' hands.

Cassian rubbed the back of his neck, unsure if the sting came from the scorching sun or his nerves. U'shun hauled a saddle out from behind a door of leaves, and he stuffed his thoughts aside. Straps were folded neatly on top, so that they wouldn't drag. The leather was a pristine and well-oiled reddish-black, iconic of the Queens. The cantel gleamed with gold-engraved sigils of the Old Tongue. Courage, strength, and loyalty. The last one was a mockery. Plenty of space on the rear rigging provided him the ability to tie pouches for travel, hoops carefully spaced for him to tie belongings to. He studied the leather masterpiece, stunned that such a thing could be created in just three moons.

Others watched subtly, save for the children who stared without shame, as U'shun approached. The old leather master hardly ever smiled, and nothing seemed to surprise him. Even now, as he raised the saddle for Cassian to take, he only grunted. Dragon or steed, U'shun didn't care. Old tattoos decorated his exposed skin, faded by time and cracked from many summers in the sun. The Krakí wrapped around his arm, just like Cassian's. Skin as thick as leather shimmered with a fine layer of sweat. He reeked of long days and mu d.

Cassian took hold of the saddle. It was heavy, and his back strained to keep him upright. Muscles injured from the brutal whipping pinched in discomfort. No matter how often he trained, certain movements always stirred up the injury, reminding him of that grueling event.

"What am I—" Cassian started.

"Put it on her," U'shun stated, waving his calloused hand at San'yila.

The nerves flared, visceral and overwhelming, and Cassian's knees grew weak. "On?" He knew this time was coming. When he walked out of Kinson's, he came here per her order, already mentally preparing for their plan to get off this island once and for all. But now, faced with the crushing reality that he'd have to saddle and finally fly with San'yila, he didn't know if he could do it.

Cassian belonged with his boots planted on the hard and sturdy wood of a ship's deck. He drew his gaze upward, watching a blue-feathered bird fly by with ease. Not up there.

"Saddle up." U'shun sounded just as bored as if he'd just worked his fiftieth sword of the day. "Need to check the straps."

Cassian swallowed and the lump of dread scraped the back of his throat. The arrogant and reckless man he'd been in Kinson's was nowhere to be found. He faced San'yila. The dragon's excitement bubbled across their bond, young and innocent. All she knew was the wind beneath her wings. She'd flown before, but never far. She always remained above the island and close enough for Cassian to watch. Now she would have him with her.

This is where we belong, she insisted. *Together. Up there.*

At her statement, his stomach exploded into a merciless storm of nausea that made a cold sweat sprout along his brow. Cassian wiped at it, finding his hand shaking from the motion. *Keep it together*, he told himself. Last thing he needed was to look like an outright fool in front of the curious Red Queens who were gathering at the scene.

I don't know, Cassian confessed, lightheaded. *I don't think I'm ready for this.*

San'yila snorted so loud and abruptly that sand billowed upward. She did not reply. And she didn't have to. Cassian knew that she wouldn't relent until they were both in the air.

The sun was hotter than he remembered. Sweat poured off him. The saddle felt like it weighed as much as the iron anchor for a three-masted ship—too much for him. Still, with some effort, he managed to swing the leather over the gap between San'yila's shoulder blades. The saddle sat, snug and nearly perfect.

U'shun shoved Cassian out of the way and messed with the placement. He grunted, mumbled something, and laid the leather straps against the scales. He said something again and then stepped away. "It will do."

"Will do?" Cassian couldn't believe his ears. "What if it breaks while I'm up there?"

I will catch you, San'yila offered.

Her reassurance didn't put him at ease. *With those talons?*

She tilted her head and blinked, amused.

"Go on." U'shun waved him off like a pestering child. "I have work to do."

Cassian's mouth was dry. The saddle straps were similar to those on a horse's saddle, which he only knew so well because of his early summers on the back of one. His fingers fumbled with the straps. He swung the girth strap under her belly, walking around her until he reached the other side. Metal clasps locked into place. He checked them over, tugging and pulling at different angles. They held. The fit was snug once he tightened them.

How does it feel?

San'yila shifted. *Good.*

He'd hoped she would tell him it was too tight or that she hated it. Anything to drag this out longer. Cassian returned to U'shun's side, who quickly inspected the saddle with a single glance. He didn't even seem to care. With a nod, he reentered his hut and returned moments later with a bundle of items. "For you. Kinson's orders."

He shoved the items at Cassian, who took them. A brand new pair of boots, bracers, and a belt with a sword. The leather bracers were plated with layered metal that would flex, shaped like scales. The boots were made of dark leather and had sigils carved into them—the Queens were religious about the Old Tongue—and freshly polished. They weren't ostentatious, but they were high quality, and they were clearly made for long-term wear. He'd never seen leather look so loved before on a fresh pair of boots. Then again, most of his shopping was off the dead. The belt was beautiful. Matching leather with the Queens' mark on it—a woman holding the sun. Braided leather bordered both ends, and loops were placed strategically around to hold pouches. A sheath with a sword was already in. He set the items down and unclasped the sheath, drawing the blade out.

Along the hilt, just at the base of the blade, shone a detailed engraving of the Krakí. Tentacles wrapped around the metal and hilt, crafted into the head of the beast, which was plated with gold and had rubies for eyes. Old Tongue sigils were etched into the tentacles. The blade itself was extraordinary. Slightly curved, the edges were serrated just enough to tear skin as the blade was yanked out. Along the spine of the weapon, more sigils were inlaid over a slightly darker silver. His jaw went slack. It was the nicest thing he'd ever owned.

"You made this?" Cassian asked, running his hand over the Krakí. The details on it were impressive. He could count the suction cups on each tentacle.

U'shun nodded. His hard exterior cracked, revealing a shadow of a smile and a man who loved his work. "Aye."

"Incredible." All thoughts of the world disappeared. He couldn't recall a time he'd seen such a majestic sword. The iconic curve of the blade marked it as a pirate's weapon—unique to those who sailed the sea. Landwalkers preferred their swords straight. Nothing wrong with those, but they lacked character.

If we wait any longer, the sun will set, San'yila commented. Her wings shook with anticipation. *Let us be off.*

Cassian eyed her. *The sun is still high.*

She snorted. *If you drag this out any longer, the dead will rise.*

Her persistence got under his skin. Cassian wanted to hold this moment for as long as possible. He'd never been given anything so nice before, but he also knew he was wasting time. The dragon was right. And he also risked earning Kinson's attention and ire if he waited any longer to leave. He wanted nothing to do with her.

"Right," Cassian muttered. Quickly, he switched his boots, put the bracers on, and replaced his belt. The cracked and aged leather from his original and worn belt earned a disgusted look from U'shun. "I've had that one for several summers now. I don't want to hear it." He shoved the old belt into the leather master's hands and asked, "You're a blacksmith, too?"

U'shun nodded.

"Here," Cassian offered and tapped the sheathed blade in the old belt. "This one has seen better days. It'll keep you busy."

U'shun shrugged. "I'm just going to melt it down." Little seemed to earn a reaction out of the leather master and blacksmith. Cassian knew U'shun appreciated the praise, but he hardly let it show.

"You are quite charming. No wonder Kinson likes you so much," Cassian remarked dryly and turned to San'yila. Might as well get this over with. He had an audience, after all. Queens had gathered about, sensing what was to come. A tickling sensation clawed his mind. He shook it off. If there was one thing he wanted out of this, it was never to see Ey'kon again.

San'yila wasn't tall yet. She had grown in girth and bulk, but she wasn't so tall that he needed help getting on. She bent slightly for him to latch a firm hand on a horn and, much like mounting a steed, he swung his leg over her lowered wings and settled into the saddle. He didn't let go of the warm horn, afraid he'd betray the shaking in his hands. One breath in, one out. *Just like riding a horse. Except this one can fly.*

Cassian's thighs strained against the new position at first, but the familiarity came back quickly. He'd done this before—not this exactly—but he'd been on a horse. Thirteen summers ago, he had fled a small village with his parents after their criminal activities were exposed by the local bard. They'd stolen horses and fled for two days before finally selling the beasts to a farmer who didn't ask questions about the low price. He held onto that memory as tight as he dared, trying to look anywhere but at the crowd of onlookers.

He and San'yila had a task. Successfully complete the task, and he would keep the peace between himself and Kinson. Fail, and they would be at risk for damning themselves to a life of servitude. He knew—well, theorized—the solution to all his problems. Kill Ey'kon and Kinson, take the Crown, but not during the day with so many awake and wandering about. That would draw too much attention.

San'yila shoved his thoughts aside. *It is time.*

She stepped forward, clearing a space for them to take off. Cassian panicked and tightened his grip on the horn to steady himself. He felt every movement reverberating through his arms and legs. Her muscles flexed and contracted underneath him, and her leathery wings stretched out, catching the slight breeze. His stomach lurched.

I don't know if I can do this, he confessed. The sea lay ahead of them. The dark blue hues looked foreign to him suddenly.

You are ready. Her tone left no room for argument. *I did not give my life to a wingless bird. I gave my life to a man who will help me change the world. To see the world as I do.*

That didn't help. It only made his nausea worse.

San'yila raised her head. The red scales glittered in the sunlight. *Hold on.* Not a single bit of fear or trepidation. He needed her confidence for this.

The dragon lurched forward. One, two, three large and powerful steps, and then she launched herself into the sky. Her great wings beat downward, her hind legs strained, and her talons dug into the sand. If that had been stone, it would have cracked by the sheer force of the launch. Cassian hunkered down, unprepared for the pull that the wind had on him. San'yila flapped, gaining altitude. He dared a look over her shoulder, watching the ground disappear and the pirates grow smaller and smaller. Ants. He closed his eyes, feeling dizzy, and pressed himself against the horn of the saddle, which had a thick aroma of fresh oil, musk, and a hint of sweet spices.

San'yila's excitement oozed into him, melting away the doubt like a flame does to candlewax. Slowly, his stomach settled and his taut muscles loosened just enough to allow him movement. He opened his eyes, staring at the vast horizon of blue. *Beautiful.*

Look around, San'yila pressed. She sounded dreamy. No. She was *happy.* He'd never heard her so satisfied. The sensation blossomed in his chest from their shared link, silencing all other thoughts.

She'd kept close to the island the first few times she'd tested her wings. Cassian would walk along the coast, letting his feet sink into the warm sand and cool lapping water. While he did, San'yila would jump, flop, and do short stints of flight to build her strength. Surrounding wildlife would scatter at her presence, including Captain Nibbs, and San'yila occasionally hunted fish and let loose playful grumbles and growls. But today was a monumental moment for her. San'yila flew as she was born to do. This was her destiny. Not to be bound to an island, poking fun at a sea turtle. Up here, her wings cut through wind and turned the sky into her own kingdom.

Carefully, he straightened his posture. His iron death grip on the horn didn't change, though. He wasn't that comfortable yet. The wind whipped his clothes and hair, threatening to yank him off, but a smile tugged at his lips. He looked behind them. The island that had been his home—his prison—for three moons appeared tiny and insignificant now. The chains of his bondage didn't feel so tight anymore. He rolled his shoulders, allowing himself the pleasure of enjoying this moment. The sensation of freedom burrowed deeper into his bones. Elation bubbled up and over like a pot left unattended. The feeling was so sudden that he boldly took one hand off the horn and raised it to the sky. He yelled as loud as he could.

In response, San'yila let loose an ear-shattering roar, daring the Gods to challenge her. He grinned, proud and free. He was a Dragon Rider.

A Dragon Rider in Blood

The hunt for *Red Pearl* was far more grueling than Cassian anticipated. Once the thrill of being on the back of a dragon was consumed by stress about his predicament—not that he was used to flying, by any means—he turned his attention to searching the sea. Up here, where the clouds hugged the sky and the wind was chillier, he could see for what seemed like forever. Ships dotted the horizon—most of the familiar hues of red he'd grown accustomed to seeing—along with islands that called to be investigated. If not for the pressing threat of the Crown of Gods being used against San'yila, Cassian would have taken a detour to do some exploring.

Red Pearl had been last sighted out by Hil Islands—a two-to-three-day sailing trip. But on the back of a dragon, Cassian realized they were making incredible time. A half-day's trip would get them to Hil Islands, which meant *Red Pearl* would likely still be in the area, based on the report Kinson had given him before he left. If all went well, they'd return to Queens' Gate once the night had taken her place in the sky.

In the moments of peace he found in the sky, Cassian's thoughts returned to the idea that blossomed back at Queens' Gate. Kill Kinson and Ey'kon, and take the Crown. The relic was too dangerous to remain in their hands. If he had to bury it into the sea floor and sink a ship on top of it, he would.

The plan could work. They'd have to be fast and night would be the optimal time to act. He'd have to have everything he needed before taking action, because he wouldn't get a chance to turn back. A clean stab or deep cut of the throat should end Ey'kon without a doubt. Kinson would be more of a problem. Her late-night drinking meant she was up far later than most, but it didn't make the task impossible. He'd have to be on San'yila's back without delay to avoid the onslaught of attacking pirates, and she'd have to fly fast to miss the arrows and cannons.

What about the saddle? he asked. If the plan unraveled as fast as Cassian thought it would, he might not have time to grab the saddle before the Red Queens attacked. Unless they kept it on her, but that would depend on what time they returned. If U'shun was still up, he might try and remove the saddle. Cassian wouldn't be able to argue—that would draw too much attention.

We forget it.

Cassian didn't like that answer. Leaving such a nice piece of leather behind just didn't sit right with him. He eyed the hard scales. One wrong move, and he'd shred his legs open. He rubbed a finger over the edge of one—sharp and merciless. That would tear right through fabric if he caught it right. A bad wind was all they needed for him to accidentally hurt himself. The saddle was used as protection, but also for him to hold on to during her maneuvers. A deep dive would toss him right off if he couldn't grip anything.

I don't know, he finally told her.

Think on it, San'yila insisted. For one so young, she sounded more like a parent coaxing their child into trying something new. He chewed on a response, but chose against saying anything. Saddle or not, the priority was getting the Crown and killing anyone who stood in their way of freedom.

Hil Islands loomed ahead. Vegetation dotted the jagged peaks and flatlands. Blackened rock carved a river to the sea, disappearing into the vivid blue. Birds flew about, some scattering and screeching from the approaching dragon. Sandy beaches decorated most of what he could see. The place was stunning—a piece right out of one of the novels he used to read before he was placed on a ship. He'd seen Hil Islands before, but this was different. Up here, it felt like he was seeing the world for the first time.

And what happens after? San'yila questioned softly. The question hadn't been addressed, but he knew what she meant. What happened after they left Queens' Gate? Neither had brought it up to the other in their growing urgency to flee the Red Queens.

Cassian rubbed the leather along the ridge of the saddle. Her curiosity melted into his mind and dragged a response right out of him. *Morei Geral. He could be our best option. The Queens wouldn't dare come for us, and we would be protected.*

Seek out Morei. The realization was sudden, gutting the original plan from Cassian's head in one sweep and leaving in place a barren landscape that was quickly filled with the new and startling plan. Go to the enemy. The Queens would never expect it. If Cassian could earn the support of Morei Geral, he could gain a menacing ally that would help him crush the Red Queens.

And what if Morei wants to weaponize us? San'yila's voice rolled across his mind like a distant storm. *We wanted to leave the Red Queens, find our own path. That was our goal, and now we speak of this Morei. We don't know him or his intentions. If this is who you wish to seek out, I will not fight you, but I must ask that you think this through. We could be walking into another trap.* San'yila was silent for a long moment, the pause feeling closer to an eternity than a few heartbeats, before she added, *I want the Red Queens to suffer for what they've done to us, but I don't want us to lose our freedom for it. We must be careful.*

Cassian's mood soured, knowing the question was plausible. If the Red Queens were to pay for what they'd done, stealing the two of them away from a life of choice, then he needed Morei Geral or someone equally as powerful backing them up. But the risks were strikingly obvious: they could run from one twisted ruler to another, chain themselves to another mad political plan that left them in bondage yet again.

We don't have to decide right away. The answer was the best he had. *Let's focus on getting out of here. When the day comes, we will choose where to go.*

The dragon hummed in agreement. She wouldn't press it any further, and he appreciated that.

Red Pearl came into view. The small ship wasn't as impressive as some of the ones the Queens owned. His nerves tingled. Kinson had sent him here for this—to make a point and declare the authority of the Queens. Those aboard didn't align with the new political shift. The Red Queen hadn't told him what to do, but he was willing to guess what she wanted.

Cassian forced air in, coming to life. He shifted, muscles already sore from the trip. *Best course of action would be to drop me off. You are too big to land on this one. Hover above, and I'll drop to the main deck.*

San'yila steered right, increasing her altitude. If anyone was looking, they'd likely see her. The red dragon was hard to miss. Even with her moving to get into position, he sensed hesitation from her.

"What is it?" he asked out loud.

Clouds hugged the horizon, toward Creitón. A storm would ravage this region soon. He didn't want to test his comfort of flying like that yet, so the sooner he dealt with those on *Red Pearl*, the better.

They speak of Morei as if he is a curse, the dragon replied. *Are you sure that is where you wish to place your trust?*

Cassian knew what she meant. They knew so little of the mad king, only what the Queens had shared; that he was the King of Monsters and had slaughtered his own citizens. But he was powerful, could harvest Dark Energy, and was exactly what the Queens dreaded. Prophecy or not, Morei Geral was their best bet at finding protection.

More than that, though, the king could offer something more than the life Cassian had been given—one full of empty promises and regret. If so, he would have to accept that his future wouldn't be what he wanted it to be; it would be full of battle, seeking revenge, and so much that he had yet to learn. But Cassian was ready for it.

In this past season, he wondered if his purpose wasn't with the pirates after all, but with the landwalkers. Living on Queens' Gate had been the longest he'd been ashore since he was a child, and while he'd wanted to hate it, he couldn't. Living on land wasn't as terrible as he'd wanted to believe it was. The more he reflected on his life, the more he believed that Destiny was forcing him to make a choice: bury his head in the sand and try to remain at sea with San'yila, or leave this life of piracy behind for a new one; one that was terrifying, new, and entirely his own making.

San'yila heard it all through their bond. *I will follow you wherever you go. I simply want us to have the freedom of choice.*

And we will, he assured. *The Queens want to take control of these countries to leverage their faith in the Red Goddess and commit atrocities to assert their dominion. I can't stand for that. But this Morei might be exactly what we need. If the Queens fear him, he must be opposed to their aims and powerful enough to stop them.*

San'yila hummed her agreement. They might not have all the answers, but they had a possible direction. And that was a good place to start.

The dragon tilted downward into a steep dive. Cassian tightened his hold on the saddle horn. Wind challenged his grip, wanting to rip him clean off. He couldn't imagine flying without a saddle. If he squeezed his legs against scales, his flesh would be torn if San'yila jerked. If he couldn't hold onto anything, he would be as good as dead.

His stomach lurched as he saw men and women scramble on deck, yelling words lost to him. They would be the first to see a Dragon Rider outside the island. He wanted to convince himself that he didn't know how he felt about that, but as their gaping mouths took him in and a few tripped over one another, he realized he already knew the emotion stirring.

He loved it. He loved the immediate reaction he had. Cassian had spent his whole life being told he was the dirty pirate, that he wasn't good enough—betrayed and treated like shit. No longer.

Let them fear us, San'yila rumbled. She drew her wings up, slowing their descent. The jolt was sudden, and he lurched, catching himself with his grip on the horn. She stopped beside the ship. The switch from flight to sitting motionless in the air was jarring, but he let his momentum carry him forward. Cassian swung his leg around and jumped.

His knees bent under his weight as he landed on the main deck. He'd barely missed the railing, and he'd halfway believed he'd miss the jump altogether. For the first attempt, though, it was a good landing.

Cassian had just landed on a ship after jumping off the back of a dragon.

He'd relive that later once a good ale was in his hands. As he straightened, he unclasped the sheath and pulled free his sword. The weapon glimmered under the sun. Behind him, San'yila snarled, the sound reverberating through the wood beneath Cassian's boots, and she began to circle the ship, close enough to intervene if things got out of his control.

The small group of pirates before him didn't react right away. Their delayed response conveyed shock, terror, and all the slivers of emotions one feels in the face of Death. He didn't blame them. They'd maybe heard through the whispers that a Dragon Rider lived amongst the Red Queens, but they'd not been back to Queens' Gate to confirm it. Cassian reveled in this moment. He'd spent three moons hidden away, preparing himself for the day he'd carve a spot in the world with his name. Now, beholding the small group of pirates nearly cowering before him, he knew that moment had come.

"Where's the rest of your crew?" Cassian asked.

The one closest, a man with a silver tooth and a scraggly beard that hung to his mid-chest, shook his head, the spell breaking. "The . . . crew?" His voice rasped like he'd been screaming for days.

Cassian nodded. The *Red Pearl* crew didn't lunge or attack as a group immediately, which he would leverage to his advantage. They stared at him like he was a deity. He blamed the lack of response on shock, but it would wear off quickly, so he would act fast.

"Dead," the woman answered, standing next to the first man who'd spoken. She was older, skin like leather, and hair braided down her back. When she crossed her arms, a laceration stretched across her bicep, red and inflamed. A wound earned from fighting the rest of the now-dead crew. "They were in our way."

Cassian appreciated the candor.

"We heard—" The man who'd first spoken stopped and smacked his cracked lips. "We knew there was . . . We just—I don't—"

"Spit it out," Cassian ordered. "You thought the Red Queens would send one of their own ships? Surely you must have known they'd come for the *Red Pearl* after the mess you made." He paused, watching frightful gazes track the circling dragon. "Or are you surprised that Kinson sent a dragon?" The question came out frigid, as menacing as a winter storm that men and women lost toes and fingers to. Unforgiving.

Silently, they all nodded.

The winds shifted. *Be quick*, San'yila urged. *The storm is coming our way.*

"Let me tell you how this is going to go." Cassian took a step forward. The small crew took a half-step back. His fingers twitched, and his breaths came long and slow. He needed this—this *release*. For three moons, he'd kept his mouth shut and obeyed, but now he could unleash all the pent-up rage he'd been holding in. A smile teased Cassian's lips. They feared him. They didn't deny the power he had—the worth he so rightfully deserved to have. "I'm going to kill you all." Cassian spread his arms wide, letting the declaration fester in the space between them until it turned the air sour. "Queens' orders. Savvy?"

He didn't wait for the crew to reply. Cassian lunged, swinging his sword from the side to catch his first target by surprise. It worked, and the blade sank into the man's arm, nearly cutting through bone. The victim screamed. Cassian yanked the weapon out and kicked him square in the chest with enough force to crack ribs, sending him sprawling. Blood splashed across the main deck. Adrenaline and bloodlust charged Cassian's mind and body, turning his motions into calculated lashes. It felt as if he had been waiting for this fight for an entire season.

An attack from his left forced his attention to turn. Cassian deflected the sword in time, only to feel the starved metal of a blade glide across his shoulder, breaking skin like it was nothing more than warm butter. The cut was shallow, but it was the last push he needed. Cassian had been stewing on his ugly temper for quite some time, and now given the chance to let it free, he didn't hesitate. His mind went blank, his sole intention lay in the downfall of this crew. Everything he felt for the Queens came out, unchecked, maddening—*intoxicating*.

Cassian punched the woman, and her nose popped underneath his fist. Blood spurted from the break, coating his knuckles in hot liquid, and she stumbled. He shoved his elbow back, driving it right into the throat of his other attacker. The man gasped, stunned, and Cassian turned and shoved the blade right through his heart. He pushed the weapon so hard that the man lurched forward, wheezing his final plea. Cassian twisted, feeling muscle and bone give, and yanked the barbed blade out, pulling most of the man's innards along with it. The pirate collapsed in a pitiful pile.

His silver sword now dripped bright red. Cassian turned his attention to the remaining three pirates. The woman clutched her bleeding nose, eyes watering. The first man kept a sword in his hand, but he'd shoved himself against the railing in preparation to jump overboard, a coward. The final pirate faced Cassian—a young man no older than seventeen, perhaps. A man by all accounts, but his freckled face and soft skin told Cassian that he'd not been at sea long. Maybe a stowaway. The young man held his short, curved sword with shaky hands.

The wind picked up, rocking the ship. Wood groaned from the sudden shift and waves splashed along the side, growing restless. Cassian's body reacted with ease to the ship's movements, his core tight and knees locked.

Behind, the looming squall darkened the sky, threatening to unleash a torrent of rain and lightning. They still had time, but not much.

"Come on." Cassian motioned at the swabber. "Let's fight."

The young pirate hesitated. The woman took one step forward, and he shot her a glare. She stopped, obeying. That kind of control didn't come to just anyone. It was because he was a Dragon Rider. They feared him.

"Come on!" Cassian yelled, faking a lunge. The young man stumbled back, nearly falling from the swaying ship. Pathetic. "Don't you want to be remembered for something?"

San'yila didn't tell him to stop, didn't advise on what he should say or how he should act. No. She cheered his bravado. Her own excitement poured into him, turning him wild. He could practically taste her elation on his tongue. If there were a hundred of these pirates, he'd kill them all.

The swabber raised his sword weakly and took a half step forward. He jabbed at Cassian. In one swoop, he disarmed the young man and sent his sword skittering across the deck. "Again!" Cassian demanded, drunk from the wildness of San'yila's primitive impulses that filled him. "Pick it up."

The young pirate nodded and did as he was told. Cassian tracked him, never taking his eyes off the other two pirates, who were too gutless to intervene. When the swabber picked up his sword, Cassian stepped closer and taunted the boy. "Go on."

In one weak swing, the young man swung his sword down. Cassian knocked it aside and latched his hand around his throat. "You came aboard this ship unable to defend yourself," Cassian hissed. "You think you can be a Red Queen? You think you deserve the title of pirate when you can't even hold a sword?" He squeezed. The swabber latched onto his wrist, trying to pull himself free. "You are a disgrace to all pirates. The dead will shame you." Without hesitating, Cassian shoved his sword into the pirate's chest, twisting hard over and over until he felt the tip break through his back.

Blood seeped from the swabber's lips, bright and red. It rolled down his chin and onto Cassian's hand. The young man spasmed, choking, until he fell still. Cassian pulled free his sword and dropped the pathetic excuse of the pirate with a thump.

The woman with the broken nose raised her bloodied hands. "We can make a deal—"

He crossed the small space between them and dragged the blade across her throat before she could react. Blood spurted from her veins, drenching him. She clawed at the wound, and he kicked her in the knee. She collapsed, fighting for her life. It was no use. She'd be dead before he made it to his final victim.

The winds shifted, growing harsher. The air carried the scent of fresh water, promising a torrent of rain. The ship rocked violently. With no one on the wheel, the *Red Pearl* was rogue. Thunder from the approaching storm rolled across the deck, distant but strong.

We are running out of time, San'yila urged.

One more, he reminded her. The man was trying to stand. Cassian crossed and, with his free hand, grabbed the sword from the pirate with far too much ease. He tossed it across the deck and shoved the man against the railing, blade pressed against his throat.

The pirate whimpered. "I'm sorry, mate. We didn't think—"

"I don't really care what you think, *mate*. Faced with death, you'll beg for the five-day-old shit in bilge-rotten water if it meant you could live." He pressed the blade harder. Skin broke, and a thin line of blood trickled down the man's neck. "I want you to carry a message," Cassian hissed. "I want you to tell the world about me, Cassian the Dragon Rider. Put the fear of my name in people's minds. Let them know I don't fear anyone, not even the Gods. I will hunt anyone down who denies me, even kings."

The man nodded, despite the blade against his throat. More skin broke.

"I don't know if you're taking me seriously," Cassian replied, mouth watering with the urge to dig the blade deeper. "Are you?"

He nodded again, fiercer. More blood rolled. "I—I will. I promise!"

"I'm just not convinced." Cassian grabbed the man's hand and turned the blade on it. He splayed his fingers against wood. The pirate opened his mouth to protest, trying to pull free, but anger made him stronger, and he swung the sword down.

The pirate let loose a blood-curdling scream.

A finger flopped to the deck. Cassian kicked it through the crack, sending it to the sea. Blood poured from the hand, and Cassian let go, letting the man clutch the injury close.

"Better get that cleaned and wrapped before the fever comes," Cassian advised, watching the pirate look between his bloody hand and the sea. "If you don't follow through on your word, I will find you in the Afterlife."

The pirate nodded frantically.

Cassian cleaned off the blade with the nearest dead pirate's shirt. Satisfied, he sheathed the weapon. "Get the bodies overboard before the storm hits. The Tsu'ran love the fresh smell of the dead, and they'll come looking."

"Yes, Captain."

The tattoo on his hand. Cassian flashed a crooked grin, sensing San'yila's approach to take him away. He looked back at the broken pirate. "Keep that tongue sharp, and you might just live to see fifty." The mission had been to assert the Red Queens' control, remind *Red Pearl* who was in charge. Cassian should have carved the Red Queens' name into the pirate's stomach, spoken of Kinson's reign, but he hadn't. He wanted the surviving pirate to spread *his* name, not Kinson's. To let the world know he was coming. The sea wouldn't, couldn't, hold him and San'yila forever.

A searing pang cut through Cassian's head, making his knees weak. San'yila wavered, her head shaking, and her wings buckled as if she would fall. Just as quickly, she pulled herself up in time to slow before the *Red Pearl*. Her mind swelled and contracted, like a wave crashing to shore, and her body shook.

The pirate he'd left behind no longer mattered. The pleasant taste of control turned sour, and Cassian quickly pulled himself up on the railing.

One hand on the shroud to keep himself up, he looked right at the dragon, whose wings flapped with strained force.

What did they do to you?

San'yila's breath came out in loud rasps. She appeared to be struggling to keep herself upright. Her head dipped like it weighed more than a hundred men. *We are to return immediately.*

Rül'Cril. They'd done it. They'd stripped them of their freedom once and for all. *They hurt you*, he said.

A warning, she managed. *Let us go. The storm's winds grow fiercer.*

She avoided his inquiry. Cassian sheathed the sword and jumped. He grabbed the horns along her neck, avoiding the flap of her wings. Carefully, so as not to hurt her in the process, he pulled himself up onto the saddle, a scene that he would replay over and over—a pirate grappling to haul himself onto the back of a dragon. He would have enjoyed the memory if not for the brutal reality sinking its teeth into his already frayed self-control.

When he prodded her mind, the pang returned with a vengeance before she shut him out to protect him from the agony, leaving only a sliver of thought for them to communicate. Cassian pressed a hand against her neck, scales slick and hot to the touch. For the first time since she'd hatched, she didn't share her full mind with their bond. The little bit of San'yila's thoughts gifted to him remained vague, marked by relentless torment and a desperate need to keep flying.

As he settled into the saddle, San'yila veered right, back the way they'd come. They'd done what was asked of them, so why would Kinson do this? His thumb grazed the Old Tongue sigil of trust. A wretched lie. The Red Queens had gotten them away long enough to enact whatever twisted plan they'd brewed up. Luring Cassian and San'yila out to deal with the *Red Pearl* had been a ploy, a trick, so that Kinson and Ey'kon could try their hand with the relic. And it worked. Whatever dark ritual was performed to activate the Crown reached the dragon and wreaked havoc on her mind.

Cassian would kill them all. Slit their throats and drench the sand in their blood. He'd been quietly dreaming of it since Captain Black had taken him and San'yila from *Dread Deep*. He'd played their game long enough, obeyed the rules of their culture and expectations to stay alive. But it ended today. Tonight, he and San'yila would take back their lives.

Corrupted Violence

San'yila and Cassian out flew the storm, but only barely. The wind whipped and snapped, the jaws of a monster they couldn't afford to get caught in. Rain battered their backs, lightning streaked the sky, threatening, and thunder cracked. San'yila flew low and fast, and he didn't tell her otherwise. She was the dragon with instinct—he trusted her with everything he had, even if he'd not come to terms with admitting that out loud yet. Announcing trust was like announcing a target on his back. But the dragon knew. He didn't have to ask to know that. They missed the heart of the storm, narrowly avoiding the violent winds and rain.

He laughed the kind of mad laugh that made people hesitate and take several glances. It started in the pit of his stomach and slithered up to his lips, letting loose a torrent of unstable and frightful sounds that would get him locked away as a lunatic, had it been heard by landwalking authorities. Damn the relic, damn everyone who doubted or feared his and San'yila's potential. They'd done it. They'd flown across the Grave, found Hil Islands, and accomplished their mission with a brutality that should make the Queens proud. They'd sent the message that would travel the world: a Dragon Rider lived. He'd heard the rumors from others—that a dragon as black as midnight soared the skies with a Rider who'd fled the country of Sorréle. He scoffed. He didn't believe it until he became a Dragon Rider himself.

San'yila didn't stop him. She was as wild as he, tarnished by the cruel hands of fate and pirates who thought they could control them. Power, he realized, didn't truly come from bloodlines or titles. It was forged from control. The more he controlled, the more powerful he became. He remembered the look in those pirates' eyes, felt their terror carve a path right through his morals, and burrow deep into his sense of purpose. This, he knew, was what it felt like to be unchained. The Queens sent off a quivering and uncertain duo, but the pair that returned had the taste of freedom they so desperately craved.

The island approached. The gray waters of the Grave stared back up, lifeless—a trick. The monsters that lurked beneath the surface waited for their victims, patient in their darkness. He would learn to embody their approach after they figured out how to escape the Queens.

He would kill them, obviously. Only spilling their blood could right this wrong. What they'd done to San'yila was abuse. Monstrous. They thought they could tame him, force him to bend the knee, but they were wrong. What they'd done to her was the last push he needed. If he got himself killed fighting for control over his own life, then so be it. At least he would die a free man.

Ships loomed ahead, stationed in their usual positions: A massive fleet that could bring kingdoms to their knees. The Queens were the true owners of the Vore waters. His and San'yila's approach would elicit thrill and awe in the pirate colony. Queens would stop what they were doing to get a look at him—he loved that. San'yila, a bit smug herself, did too. Behind them, the sun was closing in on the distant clouds, casting long shadows across the world. Night was upon them, and the landscape glittered with the burning hearts of lanterns.

San'yila veered past a cluster of lanterns entering Kinson's small home, aiming for the other side of the town, where she could land on the beach. In the dark, it was hard to confirm without seeing the sun-painted door for himself, but it looked like the one where he'd been earlier. The half-dozen pirates clustered in Kinson's home didn't worry him like they should have. Instead, it just annoyed him that they should meet at the moment when the dragon and Rider were returning triumphant from their errand. Irritation made his blood burn hotter than the sun, kept his senses sharp, and made his fingers twitch. He would storm in there and demand they release the dragon immediately. San'yila would not be a part of whatever war Kinson wanted to have with him. If he had to offer himself up in trade, regardless of what that meant, then so be it.

The Red Queens were cruel. They didn't share the same morals as other pirates, and pirates had few to begin with. Kinson was the embodiment of everything the Queens represented—merciless, heartless, and destructive. They were a prideful people. The moons he'd been here proved that they were far more culturally rich than even the White Horns, but that didn't excuse what they'd done. He understood now how they'd managed to rule the sea for as long as they had. They didn't care who stood in their way.

The dragon landed with a huff, talons gouging sand with the jarring impact. He slid off, feeling his muscles protest after sitting for so long. His back ached, and all he wanted to do was stretch out on the ground, but he turned to San'yila with genuine affection. Their bond, once so strong, suffered from what the Crown of Gods had done to her. She'd kept the majority of her mind shielded from his, sparing him the ongoing agony that she'd wrestled with all the way back to the island. She was utterly exhausted, looking as if she might collapse right here on the shore. San'yila was in no position to put up a fight or fly.

"Rest," he whispered, laying a hand on her shoulder. The scales burned to the touch like she fought a fever. Underneath, muscles shook, and her breaths were strained. *Is this because of the relic?* He'd never seen her so uncomfortable. A dragon was born to fly. The extreme fatigue that San'yila displayed couldn't possibly be from just a flight.

This time, she didn't shy away from the answer. *Yes. My body feels odd. Like I am not fully in control. Each beat of my wings feels like I am fighting against a maelstrom.*

His fingers curled in on themselves. He'd suspected as much, but to hear her confirm it unleashed a level of fury he didn't think himself capable of. Cassian turned and stormed toward Kinson's home. They'd done their part—served the Queens as commanded—and now the woman would relinquish her control on the dragon. If she didn't—

No. It didn't matter. Cassian would kill her. Tonight was the night. His original plans didn't matter. Not now. He'd figure out Morei Geral and his next steps after they left this island in flames. The only thing that did matter was that he shoved the blade strapped to his hip right through Kinson's chest and ripped her still-beating heart out so she'd have to look at it while she died. Whoever stood in his way would meet the same fate. He was done being the victim.

The small town nestled on Queens' Gate lay before him, tucked away from the relentless lapping of waves that dragged the loose sand from the shore away. The homes were dark. The several compact and cozy pubs that many Queens used to catch up were also quiet. This was a portable town. In the little time he'd been here, he'd seen Red Queens tear down and erect huts and tents in new places, following weather patterns and the sea's behavior. The small streets were made by the constant walking of men and women, forged by many seasons of hustle and bustle. The Red Queens had built a life here. Despite their reign at sea, they cherished the stability that land could provide. Vegetables, livestock, a home, the sand beneath their toes, all of it. In that, Cassian had grown to appreciate the quietness one's life could have at land.

Noises from a narrow street to his right caught his attention. Drunken laughter and a glass shattering, fracturing the silence that had filled the area moments prior. Cassian stopped. From the low lights, two silhouettes appeared, stumbling. Kinson's house was still too far away.

"Hey!" one man called, then laughed obnoxiously as he spotted Cassian. "You wanna hang with Stone and me? Name's Beard. Like the beard on my face, you know. You need—"

Stone jabbed Beard in the ribs, cutting him off with a huff. Beard probably wasn't even his name, but Cassian wasn't going to ask. He prayed to the sea that the two drunks would get bored and scamper off like the repulsive critters they were.

"He's drunk!" Stone announced, doubling over into his own inebriated fit, practically collapsing into a stack of barrels. The light of the lantern turned their faces and faded ink across their necks a rusty orange. Young and reckless, just like him, but without the rage. Cassian could see it all over their faces without ever needing to know names. These were the kind of men who caused fights in the pub and then spent the next summer joking about it.

Cassian's luck couldn't be worse. He tried to keep his head down, but they kept shouting at him. The attention was far too risky, so he halted and faced them. "Not tonight, men," Cassian greeted them.

"Oh." Stone squinted at him like he was looking through a porthole and declared, "You're the Dragon Rider!"

Beard slapped Cassian on the shoulder like they were old friends catching up. Cassian slipped out from underneath the grip. "Say, you know how to fly? You think we could get a dragon ride?"

Beard's words were slurred. He probably didn't realize how that sounded. Intrusive, rude, and appalling. Cassian glared at the sot. Nobody had ever asked to ride San'yila, and now that the question sat between them, it festered like an infected wound. A sliver of him tried to write off the drunken statement as ridiculous, but he couldn't. If he and San'yila managed to leave tonight, he wanted the world to know he'd not tolerate such barbaric disrespect.

Cassian punched the man square in the jaw, sending the drunk stumbling back. Stone tried to catch his friend, but the ale slowed his reflexes. Beard fell, and Stone looked from his friend to Cassian and back again, mouth agape.

"You—we—" Stone stammered.

"I didn't come here to be a piece of entertainment," Cassian said. He took one threatening step forward, and Stone scrambled back. The one on his ass didn't look as scared as his friend. "Nobody touches her but me. San'yila is not an object. She is a dragon, and she will burn you to death if you disrespect her boundaries. And if she doesn't finish you off, I will."

The dragon chuckled from their bond. *Why don't you finish them off now?*

Cassian stopped. San'yila was supposed to talk him out of this, tell him that he needed to have more self-control if he was going to get them out of here. That he should keep his head down and continue his march to Kinson's. Instead, she was encouraging him to unsheathe his blade and kill these men before they caused any more trouble. Or maybe he wanted her to tell him to stop. Perhaps he needed the dragon to balance him, to talk him down from being too reckless and impulsive. Or maybe he was just trying to find a reason not to kill these drunks for the thrill of it.

Not a day went by that he mourned the loss of those men who went down on *Torment*. Not anymore. Regret had long left him to the far more alluring embrace of violence and resentment. What happened with *Torment*, no matter how untamed and maddening, brought him to the one thing he would burn the world to protect: San'yila.

Cassian kicked. Beard tried to roll, but was too sluggish. His boot struck ribs with a sickening crack. Cassian kicked again. And again. Stone came to life, clawing at Cassian with stubby fingers that couldn't get a firm hold. Cassian threw his elbow back, feeling it crack the man's nose. Stone yelled, stunned, and retreated, holding onto his face as blood poured down. Too much commotion. Someone was bound to hear, and he didn't want to be here when others came looking. He unsheathed his blade and slashed at the man on the ground. The blade sliced the skin on his leg as clean as slicing butter. The sooner he finished off these men, the better.

Beard, still on the ground, tried to stand, but Cassian kicked again. He took his blade and shoved it into Beard's back. Metal sank with far too much ease, cutting right through muscle and bone like it was nothing. The man collapsed, wheezing, and tried to move again, but it was no use. Cassian twisted the blade, satisfied when the pirate went still. Nobody would question him now.

Blood dripped freely from the blade. Cassian turned—

And found himself face to face with the same man from the captain's cabin, the ghost that Ricard spoke of in his journal entries. The one with the menacing grin and the dark eyes. The same ghost who'd found him in the dungeon of *Dread Deep*. Cassian stumbled back, catching his foot on Beard's body and falling on his ass. Cassian never looked away from the brooding dead eyes, even as his elbow lit up with a fiery pain from striking the ground.

No . . . That wasn't a ghost. That dark gaze gouged a hole right through Cassian's confidence, stripped him of his identity, and left him as nothing more than a wallowing fool who couldn't get a full breath of air.

"Sekar?" Cassian's question came out so weak, it was pitiful. He was sprawled on his ass before a God, one so reviled that half the world wouldn't dare acknowledge him in their prayers. He tried to reach San'yila but found he suddenly couldn't. His mind felt like it was caged, locked away like an animal awaiting slaughter. And the cage was getting smaller, squeezing him from all sides.

The man motioned around them. "Look around you."

Cassian did. Barrels he saw stacked only moments prior were nowhere to be seen. Beard's body was gone, and the bloodied blade used to kill the drunk was now clean of its heinous crime. All that remained was the stranger and Cassian, hunkered down in a narrow street. Not even the lanterns, which had flickered with life previously, burned with the same brightness. A darkness had fallen over the street, one so thick that Cassian couldn't get a full breath of air. He felt as if he were inhaling smoke.

"Illusions are powerful," Sekar continued, "but they can be harmful. We can convince ourselves of anything, can't we?"

Cassian nodded numbly, trying to find his tongue.

"Destiny calls, but you still ignore her." Sekar motioned at their surroundings. "Go. Return to your home."

Cassian's thoughts started to return with more force. The chains confining his mind lifted, and he felt the heat of San'yila's mind return. She slept. The sluggish snores met his mind with crippling reality. Everything he'd just experienced was an illusion, even San'yila's encouragement to kill the drunks. He didn't know what was real anymore. San'yila and he had arrived back on the island, but when had it changed? When had his reality become an illusion?

Cassian glanced about, waiting for another surprise. Upon further inspection, the blade in his hand was still clean. No blood. Everything had felt *so* real. Lanterns flicked lazily as the suffocating darkness lifted. Not a soul to be heard or seen.

"Sheathe your weapon."

Cassian did so without question. Even as the metal slid into the casing, he hated himself for acting like a coward. Obedience wasn't his style. Something was forcing his motions. This wasn't him. Couldn't be.

"You're the one," Cassian blurted out, sounding as desperate as he felt. He started to ramble like a blubbering fool. "You did something to me. Marked me, I don't know. It's you, isn't it? You're the Dark Lord, the one they speak about, the one who messes with people's dreams." When the God didn't reply, Cassian took a step forward. "Tell me. I'm not losing my mind, am I? Are you real?"

"I am real." The answer was as slow as a ship dead in the water. "And I am who you say I am."

Cassian's knees grew weak. He had known the answer, had realized it the moment he turned around and saw the God standing there, but to hear it confirmed made his innards squirm. If he had anything to throw up, he would have.

Instead, Cassian licked his lips, finding his mouth parched. "Was it you in the alley at Greve's Point?" The hooded man who'd told him about the

Guardians of Death and energy constantly tugged at the back of his mind, an incessant itch he'd not been able to rid himself of. But it all suddenly made sense. Sekar had been toying with him all along. And based on the faint quirk of the God's lips, Cassian knew his question was answered.

"Revenge is beautiful," Sekar whispered. "But only when it's done right."

At that, the God dissolved like dust caught in the wind, the fragments of his presence swirling before disappearing altogether. That smug expression never wavered from Sekar's tan complexion, as if he'd just proved a point Cassian couldn't quite grasp. Once the God was gone, Cassian ran his hand through the vacated space. Nothing. Just like that, the deity was gone.

The Gods were real. Why they wanted anything to do with him was a mystery.

The startling truth of that made the world sway. His entire life, he'd cursed the Gods' names and denounced their existence. A tingle crept up the back of his neck, and he rubbed it hard, looking around to confirm he was still alone. No lanterns were lit in the nearby homes.

How long had the Gods watched him? He suddenly felt vulnerable, like his whole life was on display. Cassian wanted to stomp his foot and demand Sekar return and answer his burning questions, but he couldn't bring himself to do so. All the tall tales he'd heard about the Vore Gods felt impossibly real now. Harnessing the sun to dry the seas, ending wars with a single flick of a wrist, starting and ending plagues. Cassian's mind raced.

But Cassian was a nobody. A dirty-blooded pirate with a penchant for finding trouble and with a hand that was comfortably too quick with a sword. Having a God intervene in his life unnerved him, tore up his certainty about every decision he'd ever made.

Cassian swallowed the nauseating truth for why a God would interfere with his life: he was born to be a Dragon Rider. Everyone wanted him, even the Gods. Everyone wanted a say in his and San'yila's life. He wasn't sure what to make of that yet. Or how to handle it.

Shaking, he stepped off the street, turning onto a far more narrow path that led to the quaint and tiny home given to him. He needed a drink so strong that it would take the disturbing thoughts right out of him, help him ease the crippling anxiety that made it difficult to walk and think straight. Cassian and San'yila would leave tonight. They had to, but he needed to collect himself. The night was still young, and he promised himself that once he got a drink or two in him, he'd settle his nerves enough to deal with what had to happen next. Maybe he was doing this all wrong. Perhaps Sekar had shown himself because Cassian was making a mistake.

When he'd climbed off of San'yila's back, he'd been ready to charge into Kinson's home and slaughter her, then Ey'kon, and take the Crown of Gods. Now, as his hands trembled and his chest remained tight, he questioned every decision that had led him to this point.

Slowly, pulled by the need for safety and privacy, he walked back to his tiny hut, ready to lose himself in a bottle.

Drinks for the Gods

Alone in his small lodgings, Cassian downed his second glass of Seaman's Water. Bolstered by the courage liquor could bring, he was certain tonight was the night. San'yila and he would flee once the Harvester, Kinson, and the relic were dealt with. Whether the God wanted him to act or not, Cassian couldn't stay here another day. Not after what they'd done to San'yila.

As the liquor carved a pool of heat into the pit of his stomach, he felt more certain that what Sekar had told him wasn't a threat, but a caution. *Do better. Plan better. Revenge was beautiful, but only when done right.* A Vore God wouldn't tell him that unless he supported Cassian's intentions. He scoffed into his drink. He had spoken to a God. Sea creatures were one thing—pirates knew they were real—but deities were different. The world was getting stranger by the day. Next thing he knew, he would be chatting with Guardians of Death and sharing wine with ghosts.

Cassian swirled the liquor in his glass. He needed to be alert when he acted, but that didn't mean he needed to be entirely sober. Once the night was a little older, he would put his plan in motion. Until then, he would settle the nerves and gather his thoughts.

He needed a little bit more time to collect himself from his encounter with the Dark Lord. The illusion felt as real as a memory, and it made Cassian doubt how he could trust his senses. He could feel the blade sink into that man's back, smell the body odor and ale, and recall how his boot sounded when it met ribs.

The Gods wanted his attention—and they had it. Energy harvesting wasn't just some wild tale for the hopeful—he could harness it, even if he wasn't very good at it yet. And pirates didn't have all the answers—the Queens sought a war with the landwalkers and Morei in their blind faith in the Red Goddess. After these past three moons, everything he thought he had known his whole life was in question. Cassian felt like he was learning everything all over again; the world, politics, survival, and what it meant to be a Dragon Rider. A destiny that he didn't want three moons ago was now his. And after today, he understood that if he didn't take his role seriously, he risked not only himself being manipulated or being weaponized, but he risked San'yila as well.

Cassian took another drink, staring at the clear liquid. His hands were tightly wrapped around the mug. Any tighter and he feared breaking it, but it was the only thing keeping him upright. All he wanted to do was crawl into a fetal position and forget about it all. His life wasn't as simple as he wanted it to be. He'd found purpose, but it wasn't in the form he'd expected or wanted.

San'yila was sprawled in the sand on the shore where he'd left her earlier. The cluster of homes made it difficult for her to rest comfortably next to his place. He knew they'd purposely given him a place several rows of houses deep so that he wasn't always so close to the dragon. They were probably hopeful that would keep him from acting out. He didn't know. At this point, he figured most decisions like that were carved from their need to keep strategic control.

San'yila slept. He prodded her a few times, hoping to find comfort in their chats and tell her what happened, but she didn't stir. He couldn't fault her.

She needed the rest if she were to soar across these waters again. Thunder echoed in the distance—too far away to be bothersome. He was glad for that.

His thoughts wandered. It was hard to believe that only hours ago he'd flown on the back of a dragon and sought out the *Red Pearl*. Without hesitation or moral qualms, he'd killed the crew. Without a second thought, he'd made his mark on the one survivor he'd left behind, so that when the man rowed away from that ship, he'd be one finger down and with a harrowing story to share. Cassian stood by his promise—a guarantee that he would fulfill his word and hunt the man down if his name wasn't carried across the water and winds.

Pirates didn't have time to sympathize with the victims their blades took. What shook him was how and why he'd acted as he had today. Violence came easy for him—too easy, some would say—but he'd always placed the logic on quick thinking and merciless decisions. Today was different. Today, he'd killed because something in him *needed* to. Because he loved the jarring sensation of his sword sinking into the chests and the swiftness of metal gliding across skin. He'd felt unstoppable, powerful—in control. For the first time in many moons, he'd been the one making the decisions, and it bled over into how he killed. This was who he had become.

The tattoos were his story—his promise. He didn't resent them, not anymore. He appreciated what they represented. If he got out of here alive, he would make sure everyone knew what the Queens did to him, what they'd hoped to gain by making him a prisoner to their political game.

And when the time came, it would be he who would bring the Queens to their knees.

He took a drink. The bottle was still over halfway full. When the night was old and the stars vivid, he and San'yila would act. Just a little more time.

A knock. Cassian startled. He held his tongue. He hoped the visitor would go away.

The knock came again, more persistent. "Let a good friend in." It was Red.

Cassian weighed telling him to drown and join the Tsu'ran. He topped his glass off.

"I know you're awake. And I know you're just sitting there," Red added. "Open up, will you?"

Something about the timbre in Red's voice caught his attention. It was kind, soft—more like a friend than an adversary. Cassian eyed his glass, unsure of whether to tell the pirate to go away or continue to ignore him. Yet, he couldn't bring himself to wish Red away. The visit was so unexpected that it made Cassian wonder if Red had something important to say. Curiosity won.

"Okay," Cassian grumbled and stood. He approached the door and un-latched it. Tired hinges squeaked, and there stood Red in his smug and preachy gloriousness. They didn't quite get along, more akin to two bick-ering brothers who didn't like each other but needed one another. Red was dressed plainly and carried no sword. He practically looked like a witless landwalker, not a tough pirate who slept with a dagger in his hand and could order others around with a flick of his wrist. "What do you want?"

Red motioned at the drink still in Cassian's hand. "Can I join?"

Cassian curled his lip up at that. "We're not friends."

"Never said we were. So can I?"

They stood in the doorway, locked in a silent battle of wills. Cassian wanted to slam the door in his face, but he couldn't bring himself to. His arm wouldn't budge, even as his grip on the wood tightened.

"Fine," Cassian huffed. "But don't ever look at me like that again." He stepped out of the way and motioned for the pirate to enter.

"Like what?" Red asked.

"Like you don't know what you're doing," Cassian replied and closed the door. He locked it. "You can't fool me. You're the only one around here who seems to know what's going on, and I don't mean knowing what Kinson knows. You're playing both sides." If the pirate wanted to have a late-night chat, then Cassian intended on getting answers.

Red raised a brow. Cassian motioned for him to sit and grabbed another glass from the counter to his left. The galley was as small as a room on a ship—tight, narrow, and cozy. He settled in and filled the second glass to the brim. Satisfied, he set the bottle down, slid the glass toward Red, and took a large drink of his own.

"What makes you say that?" Red asked and picked up his drink.

Cassian chuckled. "Spare me the 'ignorance is bliss' attitude. I see the way you look at everything, how you never say a word, but you always—and I mean always—manage to be in the right place at the right time. How does that work? Do you do favors for Kinson? Not the public kind either, if you know what I mean." It wasn't uncommon for any captain or ruler to sleep around with those who reported to them.

Red grinned, so damning and uncharacteristically dark that Cassian faltered. As quick as it was there, it was gone in an instant. "Staying alive means bending the rules a bit. Wouldn't you agree?"

"Of course." Breaking them served Cassian better.

"I've learned that if I bend the rules just enough to stir the nest, I can get whatever I want," Red stated casually, taking a long drink. "Nobody ever has to know who did it or why, but I'm always right where I need to be when Kinson comes looking. That's what matters."

"I would say you're exceptionally lucky, then," Cassian replied. "Bend or break the rules enough, and you're bound to get caught."

Red shrugged. "As I told you once, I'm outstanding at talking myself out of almost anything."

The arrogance was back.

"So, you're working behind Kinson's back," Cassian dared to declare.

Red raised a brow. "I never said I was working behind anyone's back."

"Then what do you mean by 'bending the rules?' You can't be the hero here if you're working on stabbing the Queens in the back in the same breath."

Red smiled, clearly amused. "You seem to think I have an end goal in all this. A motive for doing what I do."

"Everyone has a motive," Cassian hissed. "It's what keeps us alive."

Red set the glass down and leaned back in his chair. "What if that motive is just to have some entertainment?"

Cassian curled his hand into a fist, swallowing his temper, which was getting worse by the day. "Then I'd call you a liar. A damn good one, but you don't fool me."

Red shrugged. "Then what do you want?"

Cassian leaned forward and said, "I want your story. The *real* story. I believe you got yourself out of some dangerous situations with that tongue of yours, but I highly doubt the rest. And I also think you're withholding information. So what is it?"

Red took a slow and deliberate breath. "There's a difference between the story and the truth. You are not ready for the latter. But I can tell you my story. Will that suffice?"

"Choke on bilge water," Cassian snapped. He downed the rest of his drink and filled the cup again. He did the same for the unlikeable pirate across from him, who nodded in appreciation. "Do you think I am shallow-minded? A barnacle on the bottom of a ship? Do I look like I wanted to be toyed with, Red? All I want are answers. Is that too hard to ask for?"

That made Red laugh—hearty and full. "Not at all. But the truth of who I am would change everything you know—or wish to believe." Red took a drink.

"After the night I've had, I doubt anything you say could surprise me," Cassian remarked.

"Oh, I'm not so sure about that." The playfulness in Red's voice was back. Proud, smug, overconfident. Cassian was certain the pirate was overqualified for whatever role he served for the Queens. He belonged behind a wheel, manning a ship, to be a captain, to be in Kinson's position. Not taking orders.

Cassian muffled a laugh at his own thoughts. The liquor was going to his head, and now he was starting to see Red in a more positive light because of it. "You're the most arrogant asshole I've ever met. Do you know that?"

Red flashed a charming smile that would have earned him any woman in the world as he said, "You're not the first to tell me that, and you will not be the last."

Cassian motioned at him. "So speak. Tell me your story, if you can't tell me the truth."

Red nodded and looked around the room as if seeing it all for the first time. When his dark eyes returned to Cassian's, they bore the weight of a man who'd seen a hundred lifetimes. "When I first sailed those waters, I did so 900 summers ago. I was on the most feared ship, the *Serpent's Fang*, and our stories were carried well beyond the sea. Landwalkers knew us. Kings begged for a seat with us—anything to earn our loyalty. Nobody wanted us as enemies, and those who earned that title were hunted by yours truly."

Red paused. His story had sucked all the air out of the tiny room.

Cassian blinked, trying to figure out where the joke lay. "You said 900 summers?" The question came out hardly above a whisper, disbelieving. Cassian must have misheard; 900 summers would be impossible unless . . . Unless Red wasn't mortal. He tried to snort, dismiss everything, but Red's stoic demeanor tore it right out of him.

"I have served the Red Queens for all those centuries, returning when I saw fit. A pirate will always be one by blood, no matter their upbringing. The sea calls to us just as the mountains call to the winds. This is our home—it always will be." Red grabbed his glass of Seaman's Water. "When I was at the height of my capabilities, I earned the title of Silver Tongue. That's what landwalkers call it these days, but back then, when the pirate slang was stronger, they called me the Sea's Lover. Don't ask how they landed on that one, but I was so proud of it. I was, what, only twenty-five? Back then, captains and honorary titles weren't given to just anyone—no offense—and one was usually over thirty before they ever saw the captain's cabin. That was the way of things. It was all I knew." Red downed the rest of his glass and Cassian filled it to the brim again.

"My mother was a whore. She took to a ship, hoping to seek passage, but lay with a few too many seamen and fell pregnant with me." He grew somber. "She wasn't sure who the father was—she never figured that part out, and it didn't matter. She didn't want me. When she gave birth, I wasn't even a day old when she took me to the nearest dock and handed me over to the first pirate she saw. Said I was the bastard son of a Queen and to deal with me. Learned that from a letter my mother handed over with me." He shrugged. "I never saw her again."

San'yila stirred. Her presence engulfed Cassian's mind to let him know he wasn't alone, but she remained quiet, listening. Her eerie silence as she listened and Red's seriousness chipped away at Cassian's brewing caustic remarks. The only thing he had left to do was drink, and even that didn't taste quite the same right now.

"The sea became my cocoon, lover, mother—all of it. Everyone was a father to me, but I never stayed long enough with any of them to call them that. When I got bored and acted out, I was beaten. Respect the sea, respect the rules. If I obeyed, I might just live long enough to get my first tattoo." He raised his hand and pulled his sleeve up, revealing a ship's wheel highly faded against his tan skin. Red pulled the sleeve down. "I got that when I was ten."

Red waved his hand as he said, "That was my childhood. Despite what you might think, I wouldn't trade it for the world. It made me who I am." He swept his gaze across the tiny room again, the motion full of yearning. "At that age, I wouldn't have traded anything for my life. It was perfect . . . a pirate's definition of perfect, as I am sure you understand."

Cassian did. Perfection didn't mean friends and drunken sea shanties while manning the wheel of a ship. Perfect meant a place to sleep, food, and a good drink while enjoying the open seas. With that life came rough men and women and the occasional fights, but it was *the* life. Cassian had taken it for granted, and now, he was stuck on an island surrounded by Red Queens who wanted to weaponize him and San'yila. What he wouldn't give to relive just a single moment on *Torment* again, patting Elliot on the back and cracking a joke with Glass.

Red fell quiet. The stillness between them was suffocating. Cassian couldn't get a full breath, fearful that if he interrupted, Red would stop talking. He wanted to challenge the story and throw his drink, but for once, he had nothing to say.

"It was a full moon," Red began. He leaned back, getting comfortable in the chair like a bard preparing to tell a haunting tale. The glimmer in his eyes dimmed. "I remember because the light reflected brilliantly against the water. We'd just said our farewells, swapped shifts, and I was manning the wheel—a proud moment for me." The small smile faltered. "They snuck up on me. Wrapped a chain around my throat and shoved a dagger into my back. My success at such a young age made others resentful of me. And more often than not, resentment makes enemies out of those you trusted." Red drank long and slow. "Men I trusted turned on me, because they were tired of me getting the attention. They tossed me overboard, bleeding out like chum, and went about their ni ght."

Red studied the liquor like he saw it for the first time. "I drowned in the very waters I loved. What greater betrayal is there? Some might call it a beautiful end, but at the time, I found it all horrifying." Red paused, letting the moment rot between them. "Then I was reborn into what I am now—a God."

Red didn't say more, just drank. Cassian's jaw fell slack as he tried to process everything he'd just heard. His mind raced with the budding realization that he might know not just one, but two Gods. That was a reality that was too overwhelming for him to swallow. A short and strained laugh escaped. "You're the most clever storyteller I've ever heard."

Red raised an eyebrow. "Is that so?"

"Obviously," Cassian replied and took another drink. "You want to make an impression, you've made it. Tell me a grand story about learning to survive after being betrayed. The bards would love you and all your symbolism."

San'yila didn't react. Her quietness unsettled him. *What is it? Do you believe him?* Cassian questioned. So much had already happened today. Sekar's face still stained his thoughts, and now he was being told the pirate he'd come to loathe but appreciate was also a deity. He was hard-pressed not to throw his hands in the air and walk out of the home and straight into the sea.

His lifeforce feels different than the others, the dragon observed. *Always has. I just didn't know what to make of it.*

Absurd. Cassian grabbed the bottle and topped off his glass, needing something to do as Red tilted his head, like he'd expected nothing less.

"All right," Cassian said. The bottle hit the wood with a loud snap. "If that's your story, then what do you expect me to do with that? Applaud you?" He clapped his hands dismissively to add to his point. "Tell me, oh great Silver Tongue, if this is your story, then what is the truth? Is this some sort of riddle?"

Red didn't react, didn't even bat an eye at the harshness. "As I said, you are not ready for the truth. Not yet. But you will be soon."

Cassian scoffed and dragged a hand over his face. "So you tell me your story for what? So that I may pray to you at night? Do you want me to get on my knees and beg for your forgiveness?" He wagged his finger, feeling like he was losing his mind. "I already met one God. He's been following me since Greve's Point. I don't need you on my case, too."

"Gods don't work that way, White Horn," Red muttered, brow raised in annoyance. "And if you've met Sekar, then you must be doing something right or horribly wrong. Have his loyalty, and you can go anywhere in the world. He is one of the ancients."

Cassian didn't know what to say. Earlier, he'd been face to face with Sekar, swallowing the reality that a deity had been following him. Now, stuck at this table with Red, who declared himself also a God, he wanted to scream.

His entire life felt like it had been shredded over and over, changing faster than he could understand. Cassian needed a day to gather himself, get his thoughts in order, and ask the right questions. Right now, with his gut full of liquor and his mind full of doubts, he wanted to punch a hole in the wall of this home until his knuckles bled. Underneath the shock, Cassian felt like Destiny was toying with him. Every time he thought he knew what he needed to do, another surprise was shoved into his face, uprooting his confidence. There wasn't enough liquor to get him through tonight.

When he was younger, he dreamed of being swept away from his cruel parents by a kind princess who gave him a soft pillow to lay his head on at night. As he grew older, he realized that such dreams were nothing more than empty hope driven by bitter resentment for what his parents put him through. A desperate need to feel wanted, perhaps, because his parents hadn't wanted him unless he could help turn a profit. And now that he was bonded to a dragon, everyone wanted him, but they wanted him for the wrong reasons.

Cassian lurched out of his chair and punched Red right in the jaw. He rolled back on his chair and went crashing onto the floor. Heated, Cassian kicked him in the ribs as Red tried to stand. The God laughed wildly and Cassian hit him again in the face, narrowly missing his nose. San'yila urged him to stop, but he shoved her pleas aside. He was tired of being lied to, of being played for a fool. Red was no different than the rest of them, God or whatever he was.

Red suddenly dodged a fist and kicked out with renewed viciousness, his boot landing on Cassian's knee and forcing it sideways. Another strike, and Cassian's eye throbbed from a sloppy punch.

"Make it even, yeah?" Red remarked and grabbed his glass, taking a drink and setting it down.

Cassian tried to stand, but his knee protested, locked up and burning. He carefully dragged himself up and tested his weight. His knee screamed, but he forced himself to stand. Red raised his brow, though whether in judgment or because he was pleased that Cassian hadn't backed down remained unclear.

"So what is it?" Cassian rasped. Red tilted his head. "You told me your mighty story of being this grand piece of shit, but what's the truth?" His voice shook, desperate. He *needed* answers. "Do Gods help people at all, or do they make a living screwing with people's lives?" He rubbed the bruise exploding across his face, feeling completely overwhelmed by the utter betrayal that bubbled up in the back of his throat. "You're a God. All this time, you could have helped me. All this time, you could have intervened and done something, helped San'yila and me, anything! But you let us suffer." His voice shook. "What God stands by while people like Ey'kon and Kinson destroy the lives of others?"

Red's jaw was discolored from the fight, but he still managed a weak smile. "Get some rest before you make a fool out of yourself." Red didn't waste any time. He turned and walked out of the home, letting the door close behind him with a thud. Cassian stared after him, confused. The God hadn't bothered to answer his question.

Strength left him, and he slumped to the floor, leaning his back against the wall. If there was ever a time he felt defeated, now was it. San'yila prodded him, concerned, her gentle mind like a cool breeze on a hot day.

I'll be fine, he told her. *I just need to collect myself.*

Cassian closed his eyes. The liquor and short fight caught up with him. His mind held a storm of emotions. The harder he tried to make a life of his choosing, the more Destiny pushed back, it seemed. Before Ricard and finding the dragon egg, all Cassian wanted was a big ship and to be captain. That dream felt leagues beyond his reach now, so innocent and naïve that he nearly choked on the thought alone. Now, he was conversing with Gods and trying to steal a relic from the Red Queens.

His head swam, shutting the thoughts down. What he needed was a chance to rest, just a few moments, before he got up and went to Ey'kon's.

San'yila was anxious to move. She didn't want to wait, but he couldn't move. Not now.

Everything caught up with him, pinning him in place. Sekar, Red, the flight with San'yila, the *Red Pearl*, and the heavy dose of liquor created a paralyzing spell that Cassian couldn't break. He balled his fists up and bounced them off the splintering floor, feeling the rough wood poke his skin. Cassian pressed his lips together, fighting back a scream . . . The kind of gut-wrenching scream that would wake the sleeping Red Queens and draw too much attention.

All he wanted was control over his own life. And now, it seemed, he was doomed to make a decision he wasn't ready to make: continue to bury his head in the sand, hopeful he could retain some sliver of a life he once knew and the man he once was, or embrace a new version of himself, whoever it may be.

The Mad Rider

A roar shattered slumber's peaceful embrace. Cassian jolted awake, slamming his head against the wall. Metal kissed his cheek, sharp and merciless, and meaty fingers dug into his jaw, peeling his head from the wall. Ey'kon.

The Harvester grinned with an edge of madness. "Rise and shine, Rider."

San'yila's thoughts barged into his own, horrifying and unrecognizable. She was on a rampage, and glimpses of her mind flashed through his, revealing pirates encircling her. A single tail swipe knocked three off their feet, and she snapped at the fourth, latching onto his arm and hauling him into the air. A woman shouted something, only to be swept aside by the dragon's large claw, talons tearing skin.

Cassian blinked, stunned. He was still in his small home. The table where Red and he had shared Seaman's Water was to his left, the bottle of liquor nearly empty. His head pounded, his left eye throbbed from where Red struck him, and his knee ached. Ironically, he wanted the arrogant pirate God back. Their encounter was preferable to the nightmare he had just awakened t o.

"Tell your dragon to stop or I'll make sure she loses a few more toes."

Cassian struggled, wanting to free himself, but his hands didn't obey. Skin strained against rope. Panic teased his emotions, taking hold of more and more of his reason until the flush sensation of terror engulfed him whole. This wasn't supposed to happen. He wasn't supposed to fall asleep, and based on the dusky dark hue of the sky, the night wasn't over quite yet, but dawn would come soon. By the sea, he shouldn't have ever agreed to talk and drink with Red. That was a horrible mistake. He and San'yila were supposed to be in the air, soaring over the sea, and with the Crown of Gods.

"I'm not really into this kind of foreplay," Cassian wheezed. "Just ask next time."

Ey'kon spit in his face. The warm liquid rolled down his cheek, leaving a slimy trail behind. It dripped off his face and sank into the fabric of his tunic. The Harvester tightened his grip. "Tell her to stop."

Cassian didn't want to call his bluff. The Harvester would do horrible things to her if he could—the twisted expression of brutal desire was the only proof Cassian needed. *Stop*, he begged. Her mind was shielded, covered in the blackened goo of wrath that choked out her other senses. It bled over onto his mind, making his hands tremble and his heart race. *Stop*. She didn't hear him.

San'yila! he screamed across their bond. The dragon stopped.

Her mind opened up, allowing for more manageable emotions. Sorrow and guilt came next. *I failed you. I should have warned you.*

The trembling in Cassian's hands lessened, but the fierce nature of her guilt made him feel like he was being crushed under cannonballs. Air was hard to come by. He choked. *You didn't. How could you see this coming?*

"Is she done?" Ey'kon asked.

Cassian tried to nod, but it was a poor attempt.

I should have noticed, San'yila whispered, regretful. Her words barely reached him. From her mind, he knew she was surrounded, but she didn't try to fight.

Cassian wanted to snap at her, to tell her she was being ridiculous and that he didn't have time to mop up her feelings. He couldn't bring himself to say what would be so easy to say to anyone else. She'd been on the beach, too far to notice anything. Instead, he wanted to run to her and lay his head against her warm snout and tell her that he never blamed her for this. That it would be okay.

Easy, he told her.

Ey'kon hauled him up by his shirt and shoved him into the other pirate. "Kinson is waiting for us."

At sea, the only laws that applied were those made by the most fearsome pirates. The Sea Laws were easy to follow for Cassian—keep his head up and don't step on the wrong toes, and he'd live another day. Everyone lived like that, so he was no different than other pirates in that regard. When a problem arose? Trade some Krye or fight it out and move on. Someone spreading false accusations? Enact one of the Sea Laws and kill the man in an equal duel. Seven laws that translated to not being a backstabbing asshole to the crew he worked for. Didn't work all the time, but most pirates had enough morals to respect them.

The Queens were different—savages, beasts, barbarians. The only laws they followed were the ones they made as they went along. The Sea Laws didn't apply to them. If a Queen had a problem, they could slit the throat of the other without declaring why or giving opportunity for a fair fight. They'd been raised to give respect only when it was earned. Hard work meant well-earned loyalty. The Queens' motto.

But as Cassian's knees landed in dirt and his cheek was slashed with the blade, he realized that this day would always have come, no matter how hard he worked or how well he took orders. They'd judged him the moment he'd been captured. He was an outsider—a risk, and a threat to the ancient practices that kept the Queens' culture alive. He'd been an ignorant fool to think he could talk his way out of this, or that he could earn some sort of trust to gain more information. They'd toyed with him, beaten him into the very submission he refused to bow to. And like a blind puppet, he flew off to *Red Pearl* with San'yila, salivating at the thought of releasing three moons of frustration, when he should have stayed and killed Kinson and Ey'kon and then taken the Crown before they had a chance to test its influence on the dragon.

Resentment and disappointment didn't even come close to how Cassian felt. The emotions were like open sores, oozing and inflamed. A dozen mistakes had led him to this moment; mistakes that he'd made in haste.

We'll be fine, he told San'yila. He didn't believe it, but it was all he could think of. As much as he hoped for the Gods' help, they hadn't stepped in in the past, and he didn't believe they would now.

The dragon wasn't convinced. *I could kill them all now.*

And risk me getting killed in the process or you getting hurt? Not a chance. Cassian strained against the rope binding his hands. Running now would do him no good.

Cassian didn't know whose home he was in. He'd anticipated being taken to Kinson's based on Ey'kon's threats, but this wasn't hers. Shelves stuffed full of vials and jars of different liquids and objects decorated the cramped galley, if one could still call it a galley. Specimens were suspended in the liquid, frozen and unrecognizable. To him, it looked more like a torture chamber. Chains sprouted from the walls, no doubt used to hold prisoners in place. A wood table that was covered in more grime and dried blood than an executioner's block sat to the right. Cassian's nose burned and his eyes watered from the pungent aroma of piss. Splatters of blood scattered the floor where the chairs should have been. A sickly sweet stench of vanilla wreaked havoc on his nose, a startling contrast to the horrific scene before him.

As he continued to scan the room, his eyes fell on the door across from him. Scratches cut through the weathered wood—fingernails. Dried red smears complemented the gouges. Cassian's stomach twisted. Prisoners who'd tried to run, to get out, only to fail and be dragged back to the table and chained to it. But next to the door, as stoic as the statues that guarded grand palaces, stood Kinson and Ey'kon, along with five other Red Queens who had their hands resting on the hilts of their swords. The crowd observing Cassian pressed tightly together, shoulders smashed into one another, so that they could all squeeze into the small room.

Cassian's heart dropped as his predicament became clear. Bound, unable to defend himself, and unwilling to drag San'yila into this mess, his life was as good as forfeit. She was bound to the Crown of Gods. If Kinson saw the dragon as any threat, the Red Queen ruler would exact terrible punishments upon San'yila, and Cassian could never live with himself if that came to pass. He saw the agony the dragon suffered earlier after their attack on the *Red Pearl*. He couldn't allow it again. Kinson stepped forward, folding her arms over her chest and observing him like a parent would before they scolded a child.

"I was hopin' to wait until the morning," she huffed, "but Ey'kon advised against it." The ruler was dressed in several leather pieces, which covered her breasts and groin area, and her hair was propped atop her head. Kinson looked like she had been waiting for this.

"Of course," Cassian remarked, dry. "He is such an honorable man."

Kinson didn't flinch at the comment. The woman who'd straddled his lap earlier was nowhere to be found. The woman who the world would come to fear if she got her way and pushed for territory expansion and more political control stood in her place. "I'd spare us the clever commentary," she warned. "A tired Red Queen be far less tolerable than a Tsu'ran." She jutted her chin at the Harvester. "Let's get this over with."

She stepped aside, and Ey'kon positioned himself in front of the others, dressed in a blue tunic that revealed the sun tattoo on his chest. He pulled his sleeve up, revealing a sheathed dagger in mahogany leather strapped to his forearm. The short blade had a curved gold handle, wrapped in the same color of leather for good grip. The metal was red with gold sigils carved down the spine of the weapon. The tip was fatally sharp. Cassian squirmed under the blade's hideous glare. Tendrils of darkness teased the edges of his mind. They moved with an intelligence and intention that made his skin crawl. It felt like someone else was in his head with him.

"Good luck, White Horn," Kinson stated before she motioned for the five Red Queen pirates to leave with her, leaving only Ey'kon and Cassian in the cramped room. The sound of the door shutting was final, cruel, and broke the last bit of confidence Cassian had for any of this to go his way.

Dread stormed his senses, turning his limbs frigid. Sweat sprouted along his brow as the tendrils strengthened their hold on his mind. San'yila's connection wavered. He grasped at her mind as tightly as he could. It was happening again. Once more, Ey'kon was severing Cassian's connection with the dragon, isolating him so that he was easier to work over.

Cassian shuddered, feeling his hold on San'yila slip away and the tendrils of energy squeeze every thread of thought. When he tried to find the bundle of burning light he'd seen in his last experience, the Harvester restricted him from moving, even within his own head. A prisoner, body and mind.

"There we are," Ey'kon hummed. He displayed the blade, letting the low lantern light reflect off the crimson metal. "The Krisár requires a powerful blade, one forged with energy, to be successful. I've held onto this one for a long time." He chuckled as if from an unheard joke. "Took it from the woman who trained me. She was a Sea Master—impressive, hm?"

Cassian didn't reply.

"I killed her and took this blade as my prize. She'd taken the blade from her trainer after she killed him, and the story goes on. It's cursed, some would say. Death's own weapon, forged by the blood of its owners. Have you seen it before?"

Again, Cassian didn't reply.

Ey'kon didn't care. The Harvester moved the lantern closer, setting it on the table to his left. "It has been around since before the age of the Rider Federation, when Dragon Riders reigned. My trainer believed it existed even before then, during the Vorelian Empire, but I have my doubts. Such relics are hard to come by, and they often don't look as loved as this one." He knelt before Cassian, meeting him at eye level.

Slowly, Ey'kon raised the short dagger and presented it to Cassian. Too close. The sharpened edge brushed his nose. "The Fangs had the relic for a long time. You know of them, don't you?" He smiled, eyes glittering with an incurable hunger. "The group that helped destroy the Rider Federation. Quite respectable people, really. How they came upon the blade is a mystery, although I dare say they might have had the help of a God to forge it." Ey'kon shrugged and studied the weapon as if seeing it for the first time. His callused fingers trailed over the spine, tracing the sigils. "They call it Peacemaker. Clever, hm?"

"No," Cassian replied. "It's a terrible name."

The tendrils tightened, and he wheezed, feeling all the air leave his body. Ey'kon didn't flinch. "I'd ask you if you could feel the energy emanating from this weapon, but you'd probably tell me *no* again, wouldn't you?"

A horrifying understanding settled into his bones. The corner of the Harvester's mouth twitched.

"You've never been properly trained. A shame, really. A Dragon Rider can almost always harvest energy. The bond you share with your dragon is beyond explanation. Even the most unlikeable, unskilled people can be given that opportunity. Dragons are bound to an energy no man or woman can touch—Chaos—and it gives people like you"—he poked Cassian hard in the chest—"capabilities that you didn't have before. Make sense?"

Cassian's head barely moved.

"You know so little, White Horn. It doesn't matter what they mark you with, you will always be a dirty-blooded scum pirate to me." Ey'kon eyed him like he was a barnacle on the side of a ship. "Chaos is ancient, the Mother of all energies, and the reason our world exists. That is a God's energy."

Too much information in such a short amount of time. Cassian wanted to ask more, wanted to figure out how any of that related to what he'd done, but didn't. Couldn't. His head swam violently, hardly within his own reach.

"I know you can harvest energy. You've made that clear with a few of your tricks." The last word came out with disdain. "Which means you can also feel energy. If you can harvest Light Energy, you have the ability to sense her sister, Dark Energy. You do know what that is?"

His dismissiveness made Cassian want to cut his tongue out, but he nodded.

"When you lied to me about feeling the Dark Energy, I knew we had a . . . *small* problem." Peacemaker hovered under his chin. The blade's coolness radiated onto his skin in waves, like a winter storm moving in on a desolate and quiet village. "Tonight, we'll take care of that. Wouldn't want you getting too ahead of yourself, would we?"

Ey'kon grabbed Cassian's bound hands. In one fluid motion, he dragged the Peacemaker across the palm. Skin sliced open, and Cassian jerked back. Agony flared. This pain was unlike anything he'd ever felt before. His hand went cold, and the sensation crawled up his arm like a thousand ice ants. Cassian shuddered, body reacting to the energy before he could even grasp what was happening.

San'yila roared, the sound ear-piercing. Ey'kon's smugness faltered. "Keep her under control," the Harvester warned. "I wouldn't want to chain a dragon. Stories say they never come back once you break their minds."

Please, he begged. San'yila's mind was a storm of untampered rage. *Don't.* He couldn't fathom anything happening to her. Not more than what they'd done. After all this, to come this far, only for her to act impulsively would crush him more than anything Ey'kon could ever do to him.

Let me, she insisted.

Cassian struggled to reply. The tendrils were creeping back up and around the sliver of thought he'd been granted. Her mind grew further from his reach. *No.*

"Well done," Ey'kon complimented. "You will make this very easy."

Ey'kon knew. The Harvester read Cassian's thoughts, knew his intentions. Anything he tried to do would be worthless. Ey'kon was one step ahead of him. This time, he wouldn't let him win. The Harvester had likely been dreaming of this moment for a long time.

Ey'kon reached down and dragged his fingers through the pooling blood. With meticulous care, he used the blood to trace patterns around Cassian. He continued to return to the blood, tracing over the same places until he was satisfied with the coloring and amount. Old Tongue sigils were placed inside the circle that now contained them both. Sigils he'd never seen before. Cassian tried to place any of them to help decipher the meaning of the ritual being performed, but he knew so little of the Old Tongue that it was useless. Lines intertwined with others, creating patterns of varying sizes. One design stood out, though—mockingly so. Two lines intertwined with a crescent moon. The same mark that Bauer had on his body. This was the language of the Gods.

Then he turned the blood on Cassian. "Don't move," he said. "Or you may damn us both."

Cassian obeyed. He hated the Harvester, but he didn't question the intensity of that command. Quietly, Ey'kon started to mumble phrases in the Old Tongue. The language was lost to most at sea, and the meaning was lost to Cassian. The Harvester cut the tunic down his chest and over his arms, peeling the fabric away from the inked skin without breaking his chant. Once the shredded tunic lay in a heap beside them, Ey'kon took more blood and started drawing the same sigils onto Cassian's skin. The blood was still warm, but it chilled with an otherworldly sensation as it settled into his skin.

An unseen wind caressed Cassian, charged with life and full of the putrid stench of death. The dead had arrived, the veil between their realm and the living was thin enough for them to be felt and heard, but not seen. Fingers poked him, hands dragged themselves over his arms and shoulders as shadows to Ey'kon's work, retracing what he'd drawn on Cassian's skin. Each curious prod was accompanied by the burning touch of ice. He shivered and flinched, only to be slapped by Ey'kon.

Low, haunting, and beautiful voices rose from the darkness. His mind went blank, succumbing to their calls. The chant grew louder. The room grew darker, the flame in the lantern flickered violently, but the Harvester never faltered. Cassian couldn't tell anymore who was talking—the dead or Ey'kon—but it all sounded so hauntingly beautiful that he didn't care. Cassian spasmed as a teeth-biting wind cut right through skin and wrapped claws around his heart and squeezed.

Peacemaker glinted under the low light. Ey'kon had drawn a sigil between his own eyes, which were now solid black. A few droplets of Cassian's blood rolled down the bridge of his nose. The Harvester grabbed Cassian's untouched hand and dug the blade in. The same frigid sensation seared his hand and pricked his arm. Too much was happening at once. His teeth chattered with the cold, but sweat poured out of him. The voices were promising things to him in words that he couldn't quite understand and didn't need to. He trusted them—yearned for them to come closer. Cassian's breaths grew wilder, more sporadic, and his fingers tingled. He looked at his bloody hands, only to see his veins blackened and *moving* under the skin like serpents.

Blood flowed and pooled into his cupped palms. Ey'kon raised Cassian's bound hands to his lips and tilted. Blood spilled into the Harvester's mouth and he gulped greedily. Cassian gaped, horrified and in awe, unable to stop any of it. When Ey'kon lowered Cassian's hands, his lips and teeth were tinged red.

Cassian opened his mouth, but nothing came out. Only a low-screech: unfamiliar, raw, and desperate. Ey'kon mumbled again, the chant gaining in speed and strength. The Harvester dragged Peacemaker over his own hand without ever flinching, slicing skin open before he set the blade down and pried Cassian's mouth open with an iron grip. Not that the brute needed to force it. His mind was no longer his own—he stumbled and struggled to form any coherent thought or to call upon his own limbs.

A sudden *thud* jarred Cassian's attention away from the haunting voices of the dead. *Thud. Thud.* His heart raced, frantic and quick, but he beamed, blissfully taken by the dead's embrace. The cold sensations morphed into an intoxicating warmth that swaddled him in comfort and safety.

Ey'kon's face twisted, satisfaction turning to horror. Blood leaked from the corner of his mouth, and the Harvester's skin dried and shriveled, sinking in on itself, even as his eyes appeared to bulge right out of his head. His grip on Cassian loosened before he slumped to the floor.

Damned and Dreadful

Red dropped to his knees and slapped Cassian's face to keep him awake, lifting his eyelids and twisting his neck like Cassian's body was made of clay. Red's lips moved frantically, but all Cassian could hear were the angry snarls and growls of the dead, their voices still fighting to get his attention and claim their prize. Cassian blinked, disoriented. Light returned, low and struggling. The countless vials and jars were swallowed by darkness as the faceless shadows passed over them, only to be spit out once more. They moved hungrily toward Cassian. He'd not seen these apparitions before Ey'kon was killed, only heard the voices and felt the claws of the dead sink further into his mind, fracturing his sense of reality.

"Can't you—" Cassian slurred, feeling cold and weak. "Hear them?"

Red squinted, looked around, and then he slammed his fist into the floor. He was furious. "Hear what?" he pressed, gripping Cassian's face with one meaty hand. "The dead? Are they talking to you?"

Cassian couldn't answer. The strength to speak left him. His eyelids fluttered closed, too heavy to keep open, but Red smacked him in the cheek.

"Don't listen to them, White Horn," the God warned. His voice, usually so bold and confident, wavered with uncertainty and dread.

Something was wrong. Horribly wrong. Cassian's eyes flicked to the looming shadows that were inching closer, hovering over Ey'kon's body. The voices of the dead were screeching in his mind, blocking everything out. He tried to reach for a single thread of thought, but the attempt was quickly snuffed out by the voices that only he could hear. The dead were calling to him, waiting. Along the walls, silhouettes reached for him, inviting him to take their hands. Cassian shrank from their reach. The dead wanted to devour him like prey.

In one swift motion, Red grabbed Peacemaker and dragged it across his own hand. More words spilled out that Cassian could not hear over the dead's cries. He eyed Red as holy blood welled up, aware but not understanding what was happening. Ey'kon was dead, so why was Red continuing the ritual? When had Red snuck into this cursed ritual space? Cassian tried to roll away and flee, but the strength to move didn't come when he summoned it. Red's face twitched, clearly uncomfortable, face paling, before he glanced over his shoulder toward the shadows that clung to the walls.

"Keep your eyes on me," Red said, his voice finally cutting through the phantasmal voices. "Not them."

Cassian blinked slowly. The motion didn't feel entirely like his own. His skin felt like it would split open, creating a chasm that would turn him inside out. The cold wind returned, sweeping across his bare skin like a kiss of frost. He shivered as he felt the slick fingers of the dead—not willing to let him go just yet—tease his arm. Cassian jerked, startled. The world felt like it was closing in around him.

Red raised his hand and let the blood drop into Cassian's open mouth, burning his tongue. He shuddered as his tongue moved with a will of its own, guiding the saliva and hot blood to the back of his throat and into the pit of his stomach.

The God's lips moved, his voice lost again, chanting unheard phrases over and over again in a desperate frenzy. The room shifted and light fought the darkness for dominion. Red quivered with power, and the flame danced with vibrance. He took hold of Cassian's hands and raised them to his own lips. Without hesitation, he drank the blood that still ran freely from Peacemaker's cuts.

The angry dead retracted their claws from Cassian's mind, and the shadows retreated, slipping between the boards in the wall and out into the night. The spectral voices ceased, and the room came into view, but only for a moment. Dead pirate bodies littered the floor in front of the closed door. A fiery eye watched from the single glass window. Cassian's entire body burned with pain.

"I'm sorry," Red whispered.

Cassian's muscles seized and he collapsed, head hitting the floor with a jarring thud. Drool foamed from his lips as he convulsed. Every fiber of his being was on fire, scorching him from the inside out. He coughed violently, tasting blood and rotten meat. Blackened mucus rose out of his gut and splattered onto the wood, coating his tongue with bile and gore, leaving him gasping for air. His bones creaked and protested, and he became acutely aware of the maddening agony across his wrist just as darkness engulfed him.

Cassian blinked. His limbs felt like he was shifting through mud. Muscles protested, pain hammered his skull, and his body shook like he had a fever. His wrist itched, and he scratched it. His fingers felt raised skin. Despite the aches, burning, nausea, and soreness, it was this small difference in his body that drew his attention. There was no scar on his body whose story he could not tell, save for this one. He sat up, which took almost all his energy. His head swam with a vengeance, threatening to spill the bile from his stomach aga in.

His wrist ached and he willed his eyes to focus as he stared at it. Along the base of his hand was a raised silver scar. He felt like he should recognize this one, too, and be able to tell its tale. Ey'kon hadn't cut him there. He fought the fog in his mind, searching for the memory.

Cassian shoved himself back, realizing his hands were no longer bound. The blood-drawn sigils still marked his arms, still partially wet in some places, smearing when he ran his hands over them. Scrawled across the floor were more of the same. To his right was Ey'kon, a bloody mess.

"You don't have much time," a voice whispered.

Cassian looked up at the table. Red stared out the window, arms crossed. San'yila's comforting presence embraced him like a long-lost friend. Her mind moved through his smoothly, pushing aside all the remaining tendrils of darkness that clung to the edges. He fought for a deep breath of air, feeling the muscles strain against his demands. Finally, they obeyed.

You're alive. San'yila was shaken up. Her voice trembled in a way that made Cassian flinch. Nobody had ever sounded so relieved to have him alive. And he didn't quite know how to deal with the relief that poured from him.

"I'm trying," Cassian mumbled. His life had been one disaster after the next. If he never saw a Red Queen for the rest of his life, he'd be all right with that.

No. That was a lie. Hate festered like an unpopped boil, tender to the touch and infected. He kicked Ey'kon's body as hard as he could. When that didn't satisfy, he did it again and again. He turned his rage to the shelves, smashing vials in front of him in one clean sweep. Glass shattered in a deafening chorus, but even that wasn't enough. Peacemaker lay on the sacrificial table, unblemished by the gruesome event this night had become. He grabbed the blade in a frenzy and stabbed the Harvester's body repeatedly. Blood only oozed now, with no heartbeat to make it flow, but his body was still warm. Muscles tore, blood coated Cassian's hand, and bone snapped underneath his fury.

When his rage was finally spent, he tossed the blade aside. It clattered, splattering crimson where it fell. He slumped back and sighed.

"Feel better?" Red asked.

Are you okay? San'yila pressed.

"Sure, I'm aces." The answer felt appropriate for both questions. "Just getting my legs underneath me." Cassian didn't move, though, glad to be down.

"Looks like it," Red remarked dryly. "Leave you out of my sight for a single breath, and you get yourself in the middle of a Krisár ritual." If Cassian wasn't covered in blood, he'd have laughed at the absurdity of it all.

His life was a disaster. A heist. That's all he'd been hired on for, and now here he was, barely alive and half bled out on a hidden island. Who knew what King Jair thought of his disappearance? Perhaps rumors had already circled in Greve's Point about a ship going down in the Grave. Maybe the king hadn't set a bounty on his head. Or maybe he had, believing Cassian had run off with the egg, which was almost the truth.

"Do you know what you've done?" Red's question came out in a deathly low whisper.

Cassian's mouth was dry. A drink was what he needed. And a shower and new clothes. His shirt lay destroyed, and he felt like a broken warrior stumbling through a battlefield. Skin was tender to the touch, the light from the lanterns was too bright, and he wanted only to sleep, but he couldn't. "No."

"A Dragon Rider bloodbound to a God. The Zyulë Bond wasn't made for such bindings. A Rider's lifeforce is complex in nature, married to the energies of the living realm and the dragon's. And now"—he stretched his arms wide—"you've given me no choice but to add a God's lifeforce to that. We are bound to Chaos already as it is, enslaved to serve Mother and destined to fulfill her needs for eternity, or until she says otherwise. How do you think this is supposed to work for us?"

Cassian threw his hands up. "How am I supposed to know?"

"A God's Bond!" Red yelled. Cassian flinched at the response. "We now have an equal bond made to serve both of us . . . all three of us. We are bound to protect each other. If you or San'yila are ever in a life-threatening situation, I will know. You will know if I am in danger. That scar along your wrist"—he raised his right hand—"I have the same."

Be patient, San'yila warned. Cassian could hardly hear her.

"You don't have to protect me," Cassian snapped. "Last I knew, you were gladly letting Kinson and Ey'kon have their way with me, and you didn't intervene once. So, why now? Why step in during this ritual and not when I was being mind-murdered and having the shit kicked out of me? Why not when they subjugated San'yila to the Crown?"

Red scoffed, cold. "If I hadn't intervened, you'd have been bound to Ey'kon to serve him in any way he deemed fit. A prisoner of the Red Queens. You'd never have a say in your own life again."

Resentment bubbled up. "Since when do you care?"

"Have you listened to anything I've said?" Red replied, ignoring the question. "Are you that dull?"

"You told me who you were, but I still don't know why you want to help now when you chose not to all the previous times I could have really used a hand," Cassian told him. "What is the point of being a God if you are only useful half the time?" Red didn't respond, his jaw muscle ticcing. Good. At least Cassian had finally gotten under his skin. That felt good. "I needed you far before Ey'kon dragged me here. I needed a bloody miracle on *Torment*, and again on the *Dread Deep*, and you stood by and didn't do a thing. Why?"

Red raised his chin. "Gods are bound to rules, just as mortals are." The answer came deliberately slowly. "I could spend a lifetime trying to explain our ways to you, and you still wouldn't understand. I have walked the realms for centuries, trying to figure it out myself, and I will go centuries more before I fully understand." Red swallowed, the sound audible between the stillness that stifled the air between them. "Do not dare stand before me and scrutinize my actions when I've saved your and San'yila's life."

Cassian's frustrations melted. He was in the wrong to challenge Red after what the God had just done. The silver scar that puckered the skin on his wrist was a commitment, a promise for protection and loyalty. They'd formed a complex brotherhood, if not yet a friendship. As much as Cassian wanted to argue and poke holes in Red's replies, he knew better. Red was telling the truth. Always had been, and now it was time Cassian accepted it.

A God stood before him. Another one. That couldn't be a coincidence. There was a reason for that, one Cassian knew.

San'yila's presence strengthened. *We will help change the world*, she said.

Everything Cassian thought he knew crumbled. He'd been so headstrong about proving his own worth that he'd forgotten that the rest of the world existed. Every decision he made would have consequences or benefits, or both. The Red Queens knew it, that's why they wanted to weaponize him and San'yila. In the wrong hands, a Dragon Rider could wreak havoc. The only people who seemed genuinely concerned about whether Cassian walked the *right* path or not were the Gods.

"Don't look so troubled," Red mused. "Didn't seem to bother you the first and second time I told you that."

"I'm sorry," he muttered, drained. "I guess now I actually believe you."

Red raised his hands and shrugged. "Still the same man you punched."

Cassian wanted to sink into the floor. If there were ever a time he wished he could pray away his mistakes, now was one of them. But if the Gods were really like Red, sailing the seas and intermingling with the everyday people, prayers meant nothing. The Gods didn't hear prayers. They didn't sit around, waiting for a whispered plea to reach their ears. They walked among the people, where they felt most comfortable, and helped when they could.

"You were stuck between realms," Red said. "Ey'kon's work was unfinished, but he was already too far into the ritual for me to pull you out without lifelong consequences, or death. Your lifeforce was compromised, vulnerable to the restless dead, and they were already having their way with you. Souls chained to the living are extremely dangerous, toxic to your mind and lifeforce. To counteract what was done, I had to draw on Chaos and perform a stronger ritual to protect your lifeforce from further being tampered with by the dead." Red scratched his face and added quietly, "What Ey'kon would have done to you would have been far worse. Your mind would have been nothing but a desolate field. Your thoughts would have been given to you by the Harvester, your actions would not be your own, and your soul would have been bound to the very dead you saw in this room."

Cassian swallowed down the bile and aged liquor that threatened to spill. Chaos. The Mother of all energies. The force Cassian knew so little about, but knew he must learn. He couldn't understand why he'd been so lucky. How a God had managed to find him at the right time and save his life. Without Red, Cassian would be a mindless weapon to the Red Queens, forced into servitude for however long they deemed fit.

"Why?" Cassian whispered. In that single word, he hoped to embody everything he felt. Words would do no justice to convey the gratitude and confusion he felt or how much his life had changed.

"You will need to move quickly. I have tampered with the surroundings as much as I can without causing any severe fluctuations in the energies. If too much Chaos is introduced, I risk creating an imbalance or causing a pattern of consequences which would be . . . unfortunate. Fish could turn up dead, sea beasts could come out from hiding after centuries—you get the idea." Red stepped forward. "Too much to tell you when we have such a short time." He gestured at Peacemaker. "Take her with you."

Cassian swallowed. "Her?"

Red looked baffled at the question. "A blade as old as Peacemaker is not just replaceable. You wouldn't replace a ship that carries you through the worst of storms, right?"

Cassian shook his head.

"Your blood was absorbed by her. You are her rightful owner now." He flicked his wrist at Cassian to pick up the blade. Slowly, he reached over and did so. It was still covered in blood. "Clean her up, and she will serve you well." Red raised his hand to halt the question rising in Cassian's throat. "Peacemaker didn't get her name by accident. She was never meant for the cruelty those like Ey'kon would inflict. She can sense the intentions of others. Place your hand on the hilt whenever you are in question, and she will guide you."

Cassian didn't know how that worked, but it was one more thing he'd have to learn. This was energy work beyond his slim understanding, and he knew they didn't have time to discuss Peacemaker in detail. Truthfully, he wanted to rid himself of Peacemaker, hand it back to the God who knew so much more about this world of strange relics and energy than he ever would. Possessing a blade like this was not Cassian's place. All he wanted to do was get off this island.

As if sensing Cassian's unease, Red said, "Certain weapons were never made for a God's use. In the wrong hands, a relic like this could destroy the lives of millions."

"But . . ." Cassian struggled to find the right response. He was a thief, one who bartered with royalty and stole jewels from whores when they weren't looking. How could anyone, let alone a God, trust him with such a valuable item? Cassian hardly trusted himself, afraid he might slip into old habits and find himself back at Greve's Point, selling Peacemaker off just for the thrill of the bartering. Too much, too fast. What he needed was a day of rest and to get all the answers he so desperately craved. But the passing moment would have to do. "What of the Crown? They did something to San'yila. Took her blood—"

"Let me worry about Rül'Cril," Red replied. The kindness in his eyes was gone, replaced with the heat of anger. "It cannot remain in the Queens' hands. They were never meant to involve themselves in these matters."

Cassian opened his mouth, puzzled.

Don't, San'yila urged. *In time, we will know the truth. But not tonight.* No room was left for argument. She trusted Red. The emotion bled across their bond with blinding ferocity. What followed startled him to his core.

Red promised her protection. Red's words raced across Cassian's mind, powerful, unrecognizable to the mischievous and snarky man he'd come to know. A God's vow.

We must go.

The urgency in her voice forced him to come to life. He looked like two-day-old shit—covered in his own blood and exhausted, but his wounds were healed. He hadn't realized that right away; he'd been too distracted to realize how well he felt physically. Healed, but still bearing the whipping scars that left their mark. He could feel the raised edges when he dragged his fingers over his shoulders.

Physically, he was fine. Emotionally, he held on by a thread, wanting to scream into a void.

"Here." Red tossed him a shirt that had been sitting on the counter in the galley. "I might've healed your wounds, but I wasn't going to bathe you. Let the sea take care of that when you've put some distance between the Queens and you."

Cassian stood, finding his belt on the table. "You healed me?" The answer was obvious, but he didn't know what else to say.

The God dipped his head in respect, an action Cassian never thought he'd see. "Tre'lang ungahr."

A Queen's farewell. "Tre'lang ungahr," he mumbled in return. In more traditional times, back when Red was still a mortal, the phrase was used for good luck rather than the finality it now usually denoted. Cassian knew he would see Red again—they were bound together now—but he hoped it wouldn't be too soon. He needed time to collect his thoughts and figure out his life—find the man he was and had lost along the way in all this madness.

Cassian donned the belt, checked the clasp, and tied the new shirt around a loop. No point in putting on a clean shirt until he washed off all the blood. San'yila was getting antsy. An image flashed across his mind from her—she still wore her saddle. He silently celebrated. The escape would go their way, after all.

Red stopped him before he made it to the door. Now, face to face with a man he knew to be a God, Cassian didn't know how to feel. A hundred questions rushed through his mind, but now was not the time. Half-finished strings of thought blew by before being sucked into the vortex of overwhelming panic and urgency. Nothing was worth discussing now. They were out of time. The Queens would stumble on this massacre any moment now.

"Do you want to know the truth?" The question was so random that Cassian froze, unsure. "I told you my story, but I never told you the truth."

San'yila nipped at Cassian's senses, feeding him with the desperate need to fly. He stared at the deity, reliving the stories he'd been told. All of it was true. A God had sailed the seas, and even after all this time, he still returned to this world of ships and endless water.

Red beamed, and for once, he looked ecstatic. "I came here for *you*."

The Forbidden Deal

Thirteen days later

Cassian slipped some Krye into the young boy's hands and quickly took the bundle of berries. The seller tried to say thanks, but Cassian turned and was gone, popping a berry into his mouth as he walked. He tugged at the hood of the cloak, making sure it was pulled as far as it could go over his head. The necklace was tucked under his shirt, the silver warm against his skin. Greve's Point was a hot spot for pirates, and one of the few places where no one asked questions. With his arms and face covered and gloves on, nobody could see the tattoos or the silver eyes.

Coming here was a rarity. Cassian only stopped in when he needed a few things that he couldn't procure any other way. Today, he'd replaced his gloves. Long days in the sun and reckless flights with San'yila caused him to tear the palm of his old gloves against a scale. A careless mistake, really. She'd been in a deep dive, and he'd let go of the horn in front of him. When she flared her wings, he'd nearly impaled himself, and his hand smacked against the dragon's shoulder, catching a scale and tearing instantly. Thankfully, he had the leather. If not, his hand would have been shredded.

You knew better, San'yila mused.

He scoffed quietly, weaving between two groups of people who laughed and shoved each other in hearty banter. *And you were trying to kill me.*

You're being a bit dramatic, the dragon remarked. With their connection, he could feel the wind brush over her. She flew far above, appearing more like a large bird than anything else. Nobody would ever think twice if they saw her silhouette from that high up. With the angle of the sun, she looked black, and no one would be able to accurately judge her proximity or size from the ground. At this distance, the strength of their bond wavered. The dragon's voice was quieter, her emotions less influential on him, and he was always eager to leave the small city of pirates to return to her. He couldn't imagine a life without San'yila's constant presence. In such a short time, she'd given him so much: affection, loyalty, companionship. Without her, he might as well rip a piece of his soul out and stomp all over it.

Learning to be a Dragon Rider wasn't easy. Cassian spent more time than he cared to admit scuffing his boot against sand, doubting everything he was. In the last thirteen days, he'd learned more about himself than he had known in his entire life. He was reckless, sure, but he was calculative about it. Risks didn't come without reward. Despite the many summers keeping his chin up and starting more fights than he could count, he never took action without some strategy. Life had been ruthless to him. Broken bones, scars, an armor of bravado and toughness, and he'd been molded into a man who'd cut the tongue out of any fool who disrespected him.

At night, when the hearts of lost queens and kings took to the sky—what many believed stars once were before grander ideas took hold—Cassian practiced his swordsmanship and survival skills on the small, desolate island he'd called home for the last thirteen days. There, far from the prying eyes of ships and Greve's Point, he'd swung his blade, parried with an unseen enemy, and pushed himself as hard as he could to learn the skills he'd need for this new life. When he was too tired for that, he sewed baskets for fishing with bark and leaves from the island, keeping an eye out for Captain Nibbs with a quiet wish to see the devious sea turtle again. He would place the wide basket in the shallow depths and sit back as the small fish wandered curiously too close. It took patience. One small movement and the fish would scramble. The first dozen times were a failure—accidentally twitching a finger, snatching the basket up too slowly, or a sneezing, and the fish would escape. By the fourteenth time, Cassian yanked the basket above water with two fish trapped and ready to eat.

Skin hardened, scars puckered, and the scruff along his jaw thick and unkempt, and he felt like a different person. Without a proper blade for shaving, he'd resorted to utilizing the beard as another trick to keeping his identity a secret. The scar along his chin wasn't visible anymore—a mark that so many knew him by. When life settled and he was far from here, he'd cut the beard. Until then, he would leverage the temporary look. Between the scruffy beard and the tattered attire, some might even believe he was living on the streets, begging for scraps of bread. The long days of flight with San'yila turned once-flawless fabric into torn and frayed pieces. He washed them in the shallow fresh water of the island, leaving them out to dry, but that didn't fix the tears.

The new gloves were stiff. He opened and closed a hand a few times to check the leather, the other hand still clutching the bundle of berries. The gloves would need some breaking in, but at least they weren't shredded. The sword was hidden under the cloak; he knew that the bold hilt design with the Krakí would gain the attention of a few buyers or curious thieves. Or worse . . . Red Queens. The less attention, the better. He never spent more than half a day when he needed to come here.

They'd found a small island a few leagues west of here. Trees bore fruit, roots were packed with nutrients, and the shallow waters off the coast made it optimal for fishing. San'yila had eaten fish and some small game she'd found, but it wasn't enough for the long term. The dragon grew fast. In just the thirteen days since they'd left the Queens, the leather straps of the saddle were already stretched close to their limit. He loosened them, but the saddle itself would need to be resized eventually as her shoulders widened to complement her growing bulk. He wasn't sure how big she would get, but if the stories were true, she'd be able to end wars with her presence alone.

A shoulder bumped into his with enough force to knock him off his feet and into the jewelry stand to his left, but he righted himself without ever turning his head. He mumbled his apologies and kept walking.

"Are you blind?" the man called. Cassian ignored him, his better sense now winning out over his temper.

Women called out to those who passed by, offering their bodies for a good time and an exchange of Krye. Breasts pushed out of their tightly-knotted corsets; hair coifed atop their heads with loose strands framing their faces. Their cheeks were rosy, they reeked of sickly-sweet perfumes, and they batted their eyelashes at the people who dared glance their way. Cassian would have paid good coin to spend the evening with one or maybe two of the ladies. The old him would have done it without thinking. The old him would have mauled the bastard who insulted him, too. But he was quickly learning that silence got him further than fury. The less he spoke, the more he heard. In these past few days, he'd also learned another valuable lesson: proper revenge against the Red Queens would take time.

Cassian didn't forgive the Queens for what they'd done to him and San'yila. He never would. They were greedy, too proud for their own good, and they believed they were entitled to every seafarer's fealty. Despite how starved he was to destroy them, he was stuck between running farther north or staying hidden. Cassian knew the Red Queens were searching for him, and he and San'yila would have to move on once the red-painted ships swarmed Greve's Point, which would be soon. Keeping San'yila hidden as she continued to grow at a substantial rate was becoming a real challenge. He couldn't just stick her behind a tree. She stuck out, crimson red against the green tropics.

Getting to Greve's Point involved fast and low flying. San'yila dropped him off on the other side of the island, where only the crabs and sea turtles were witness to their arrival. From there, he'd stroll into the small city, weaving his way to the market street. He kept his ears perked, always listening to the conversations of those around him, and he always kept an eye on the port.

Cassian spent days dreaming of what he would do to Kinson. At night, head propped up with his arms behind his head on the shore with San'yila next to him, he fantasized about the torturous acts he could do; anywhere from peeling her skin away to cutting her toes off and feeding them to her. He knew that he was in no position to return to Queens' Gate and bring them to their knees, to enact his revenge. He knew that would put San'yila at risk, and her safety was his number one priority.

Yet, he couldn't leave this part of the world. Not quite yet. He kept close to Greve's Point, watched the ships from afar, and missed the taste of the sea on his lips as he remembered tying a scum's knot or climbing to the crow's nest. No matter how hard he tried to justify these changes in his life and rationalize that he was better off now, he couldn't shake himself of the life he'd clung so hard to for so long. That had been his life, his identity—and now, he wasn't sure who he was or what he was supposed to do.

His hand slipped underneath his cloak to fiddle with the necklace. Glass would have known what to do. Without hesitation, too. His dead friend would have grabbed a bottle of Seaman's Water, laughed, and carried on without slowing. Instead, Cassian was walking the market street, inhaling the aroma of baked goods, fried fish, and the ever-present stench of rotten meat, the source of which no one ever seemed to be able to find.

Pirates were obnoxiously loud, a cacophony Cassian sometimes missed. They spat, tossed food, poured drinks in the middle of the street, and sang. They bought and sold without pre-set prices, bartering, trading good times and work. Little was hidden. Pirates spoke and bragged openly about their deals, jobs, and payouts. The news of the day typically featured White Horn movement, a pirate who killed another over a stolen rusted dagger, a heist gone wrong, and now—a Dragon Rider.

Cassian slowed, slipping between two rickety market stands so that he was out of the way of those who still walked.

"The Queens struck a deal with a king," a woman said through a giggle. "I hear the Red Queens will supply a Dragon Rider to the king, too. Rumor has it that the Queens want land."

"Seas forbid," another remarked hotly. "Queens wouldn't ever work for anyone."

"You're all out of your mind," a man added. "Anyone got Krye to trade for a game of knives?"

The woman snorted. "I heard some pirates spotted a dragon heading south, to Creitón."

Cassian strained, wanting to make sure he heard right.

"A black dragon. Can you believe it? You think that's the one?"

"I still think this is all just stories," a man commented, unimpressed. "Ain't been Dragon Riders for centuries, and now you're telling me one's flying around and nobody knows what it looks like or where it's from?"

Cassian pursed his lips, amused.

"I hear there's more than just one Dragon Rider. A black one was spotted north of here some time ago," the woman shot back. "Queens are going a bit nuts right now. Spoke to Delik this morning, and she said she's never seen them so frazzled. Delik was passing report to the Queens, you know. She's good friends with the crew on *Salvation*."

"What do you think of all that?" muttered a voice in Cassian's ear.

He jumped. To his right, Red stood there, rolling a coin across the backs of his knuckles like a juggler. He pocketed the coin and offered a wave as if catching up with an old friend. He was dressed in his trademark white tunic and red sash.

"Doing well?" Red asked.

"Better," Cassian whispered, swallowing the surge of memories with the dying taste of berries.

That dreadful night back on Queens' Gate, when he nearly lost his soul to Ey'kon, returned like a nasty sore that some pirates got on the bottom of their feet with old boots. Cassian sucked in air, suddenly feeling oppressed by the memories that swarmed his head. The silver scar on his wrist itched, a reminder that he was bound to the God before him.

San'yila nudged him from his spiraling thoughts, pouring affection into their bond. *The past will devour you whole if you allow it,* she advised gently.

Cassian nodded, despite her not being able to see him. She was right. He'd worked hard in the last thirteen days to regain some semblance of normalcy. Underneath that desire, he knew that what he used to think of as normal was impossible now, being a Dragon Rider, but letting go of who he once was wasn't an easy journey. Turning to Red, he asked, "Why are you here?"

The God motioned at the berries still in Cassian's hand. "Can I have some? Big fan."

Cassian eyed the bundle, hesitant. He'd wanted the berries when he bought them from the boy, but with Red's appearance, his appetite evaporated. He relented and handed the small bundle over, making a silent promise to himself that if his appetite returned, he'd get more.

Red took the berries like a starving boy, popping a few in his mouth instantly and chewing. "I came here for you," Red answered.

"Of course you did. You can track me now, too?"

Red shrugged. "Any God can track you or any other Vorelian, Cassian. I just have it a little easier with the Zyulë Bond." He raised his wrist to display the silver scar like he was proud of it. "A Dragon Rider's lifeforce is like a burning ball of light in the dark when you compare it to the rest of the world's energy. Hard one to miss when there are only a few of you. I made a guess that you might still be hanging around close to home."

Cassian tilted his head, intrigued. "There are more Dragon Riders? The stories are true?" Maybe what he'd just overheard had some truth. Perhaps a black dragon was heading south.

"Where's Peacemaker?" Red ignored the question.

"With San'yila," Cassian answered. He wanted to learn more about the Dragon Riders, but he knew better than to press. The God had proven he wasn't fond of being forced into any answer he wasn't ready to give. "I don't come here often. Only twice to replenish supplies since I found a little island a few leagues west of here."

Red shook his head, clearly disappointed. Cassian felt like he'd just let down an older brother. They'd had their differences and clashed, but he'd come to enjoy Red's company, even if he was no good at showing his appreciation.

"You need to keep her close," Red scolded, plopping another berry in his mouth. "What good is she if she can't be of use to you when you need her?"

Cassian crossed his arms and lowered his voice. "Why are you here?" In these past thirteen days, he'd been more at peace than ever before. It was the first time he and San'yila were able to truly enjoy each other's company and explore what it meant to be bonded. It was the first time they had felt *free*.

"Anyone here could be your enemy. A Queen or Nighthunter could be watching for you. Are you even looking around you, or are you blindly strolling?" Red asked.

Cassian chewed on his response, knowing he should have been paying more attention to his surroundings. San'yila hummed, amused at him being chastised. The God cared about their well-being, and Cassian should be grateful, especially after everything Red had done for them, but the only thing he wanted to do was tell Red to leave them alone. With the God's arrival, Cassian knew something would be needed of him. Nothing was ever free, not with pirates, royalty, divine beings, or even the dead.

"I'm here to make a deal with you," Red said so plainly that he might as well have been talking about supper.

The statement deepened Cassian's souring mood. "I'm not doing deals with you or anyone." He spoke too quickly, too frantically, like a bilge-sweating fool. After everything he and Red had been through, Cassian should have dropped to his knees and kissed the God's hand, but he wouldn't. The small peace he'd built in the past few days was being threatened.

Red raised his brow, as if he could read Cassian's mind. "You don't even know what I have to say. What if it's good?"

"Nothing you'll bring up is good," Cassian replied. "Are we done here?"

"No." Red pulled an item from a larger pouch on his belt, wrapped in purple cloth. He unveiled it, revealing the Crown. "I have this."

Panic electrified Cassian, and he covered the relic with his hands, quickly looking around to ensure nobody had seen. He pushed Red back so that they were removed from the path of the onlookers. "Have you lost your mind? Who would bring *that* to the marketplace?"

"Eazon," the God replied, bowing as though this were their first introduction. He smiled like he'd just told the best secret of his life. "Might as well give you the right name, yeah?"

The God of Luck. Cassian's jaw went slack. He wasn't sure what he was expecting—he knew a deity was before him, had saved his life, and was bound to him with the Zyulë Bond—but he'd not given much consideration to *who* that might be. The night Cassian fled the Queens, he'd also run from the memories and the questions.

Everything that happened, all the perfectly-timed interventions, or what Cassian had called luck . . . had it been Red's doing all along?

"I waited a few days before coming to find you," Eazon continued. "I figured you needed some decompressing after those three or four moons." The God displayed the Crown again. This time, Cassian got a full view of it and didn't try to cover it. They were deep enough in the alleyway that no one would see. It gleamed silver with red gems that decorated three points. Silver vines were expertly crafted to wrap around the band. The immense power that radiated from this relic was enough to make Cassian rub his face and shake his hands out. It made him uncomfortable.

"Dark Energy will do that, make you feel like you want to turn and run," Eazon mumbled. The hum from the energy grew loud in Cassian's ears, like a roaring maelstrom. "But there's far more involved than just that. Forged with the blood of a Cer'han, and treated with the metal scavenged from Volkeri Island, where the veil between realms is thinnest. What you feel is a call to the Soul Realm, where the dead call home."

After all this time, Cassian wanted nothing to do with it. He'd been so invested to find and sell this relic, but now, staring at it, he wanted to throw it into the sea and hope it sank to the bottom. "San'yila?"

The God nodded, understanding the meaning. "I stripped her blood from the relic," Eazon explained. He looked up, as if he could see San'yila himself. "I fulfilled my promise to her."

Cassian opened and closed his mouth, struggling to find words. He followed the God's gaze upward, willing San'yila to come closer. He couldn't wait until he could press his head against her snout. All this time, he'd carried the weight of worry, knowing she'd been bonded to that forsaken Crown. All this time, he dreamed of how he could right that mistake, or outrun it. Knowing the man across from him had risked so much to save him and San'yila from a cruel fate tugged at a piece in his heart that he'd thought was shriveled and dead. Kindness wasn't a gift Cassian knew how to accept.

In an instant, he no longer saw the world as he'd been taught to see it—merciless, each man for himself—but as it could be. Softer, filled with fleeting moments of compassion, and with genuine moments of beauty. He would spend the rest of his life indebted to the God.

"How?" he finally managed.

The usual cheer in Eazon's expression faltered, too quick for Cassian to be sure what he saw, but he sensed an underlying anguish. "Manipulating a relic like this takes a significant amount of sacrifice. I had help." The curve of his lips returned, but the playful nature of the act did not meet his eyes. "I had to make a promise. It has been done."

Every answer led to more questions. Maddening, but he was relieved to know San'yila's blood was cleansed from the Crown of Gods. For once, Cassian was all right with not having all the answers, so he changed the subject, afraid that if he prodded too much, the God would tell him it was a joke. He knew better, but the fear was still there. "Why are you showing me t his?"

Eazon wrapped it up. "I want you to take this to Morei Geral."

"Excuse me?"

"The Crown was always meant for him," Eazon told him without hesitation. "Certain matters require him to have it. Things that I cannot necessarily tell you without involving you in situations that would get you killed. In time, you will come to know more, but not now."

"I'm going to get killed anyway, aren't I?" Cassian laughed, strained. He was a rotten barnacle to think he could outrun his destiny.

"Not today. And not by running this errand." Eazon tilted his head and motioned to the small city. "What do you have left here, anyway? Why do you continue to return to a place you can't comfortably call home anymore?" He didn't wait for Cassian to answer. "You are terrified of what lies ahead. Change scares you. Rightfully so. Destiny was not kind to you this past season. I can understand wanting to hide from it and seek the peace that familiar routine brings. But it will only take you so far." Eazon licked his lips, flashing his eyes upward before he asked quietly, "Does San'yila deserve a life of hiding?"

Cassian closed his fist, tempted to smack the Crown from Eazon's hands and stomp on it. Damn it all. He knew what Eazon was doing—tempting him with purpose. It was all he wanted, all he'd ever wanted, and now, given the opportunity, he wanted to tuck his tail and run. Not because he was scared of losing his life, but because he worried about the dragon who'd given him a new chance at life.

"You are not my keeper. Nor San'yila's," Cassian whispered, but his voice shook with doubt. Gratitude didn't come easy for him. Deep down, he knew he owed the God everything for saving their lives, but he wanted more of an explanation. Morei was his chance at crushing the Queens once and for all, and he'd wanted to seek the mad king out, but not like this. He wanted to do it on his own terms and in his own time.

Sekar's words haunted him, taming his impulsiveness. *Revenge is beautiful, but only when it's done right.*

"The deal benefits you, Rider," Eazon replied softly. "Seek the King of Monsters out, and he will offer you sanctuary and purpose. You won't have to hide, San'yila will be accepted and revered, and you won't be enslaved to a cause you resent."

Cassian bit the tender flesh on the inside of his cheek, wrestling with warring emotions. On one hand, he was glad to see Red and know the God believed in him. On the other hand, he was upset that the man seemed so confident that he knew what Cassian wanted. "A cause? What am I, your puppet?"

The God didn't flinch. "Your deflections don't fool me, Cassian. I know you crave purpose. I can see it in your eyes. You are desperate to find something that you can commit yourself to. If you understood your own restlessness, you would've flown far from here the night you left the Queens. But you don't. Most of us go our whole lives trying to find a cause that we can stand behind—a reason to live." Eazon re-wrapped the Crown and extended it to Cassian. "But you have found yours."

Cassian stared at the bundle, still feeling the sensations wash over him and make his skin crawl. Eazon was right, and he knew it. The wall of defense that he'd carefully crafted shattered into a thousand pieces. Cassian didn't have a counterargument anymore. His usual temper dissipated into dust, leaving him exposed to the feelings he was a stranger to. In different circumstances, he would have brought Eazon into a brotherly hug, buy the man a drink, and have a good laugh about what they'd been through. But he didn't do that. Eazon was a divine being. A hug felt inappropriate, presumptuous. In fact, everything he'd said before this moment was wrong. He'd been an asshole. Cassian had been so busy trying to prove to himself and the God that he was in control of his own destiny that he'd forgotten just how much Eazon had risked for him and San'yila.

"Don't you want to see what this world could offer you?" Eazon asked. By the tone of his voice, he already knew he had Cassian's attention. "And if you find you are unsatisfied, then you'll be free to go. I cannot force you to stay anywhere. But I do advise that you think with your head, not your heart, when you meet Morei." A smile teased the God's lips. "He is a bit complicated, but I do think you two might see eye to eye on a few things."

San'yila? Cassian couldn't think of anything else but to go to her. She was so wise, far more than he, even at such a young age.

The dragon was silent for a moment before responding. *Eazon has not led us astray yet. I don't think we have any harm in seeking this king out to see what he can offer us.* She hesitated, then boldly declared, *We bow to no one. Ever.*

Slowly, Cassian reached out for the Crown, certain it might burn him if he touched it, even through his new gloves. Eazon didn't move or pull away. Cassian braced himself for an onslaught of sensations but stopped just before his hand touched the cloth. "Why?"

Eazon raised a brow.

"Why any of this? Why me?" Cassian clarified. The next question was lodged in his throat, and he fought to spit it out. Never in his life had he asked such a question, and he almost decided against it, but he needed to know. "Why do you care about *me?*"

In the heartbeats that passed, a season slipped by. Time slowed, the dragon's presence was warm against his mind, constant. The commotion in the street behind them went silent. Eazon settled the Crown into Cassian's hands. In a quiet voice, he said, "I've seen the world at its darkest point. In you, I see the chance for a new era. One that will bring everlasting peace."

Cassian smiled. He knew what he wanted.

Cassian and San'yila will return in book five of The Vorelian Saga,
The Ballad of Dragons

Vore Terminology

Ashýon (*Ash-ee-on*) – Outer region of the Soul Realm. It has become the home to the majority of the demons and is the most dangerous region of the realm. No Guardian will travel to this territory. Beyond demons, great beasts roam the area that are not seen anywhere else.

Assane *(Ah-sane)* – Northeastern city of Diyră. One of the only major cities to still allow for smaller territories to be ruled by tribes, the tribal territories make up the vast landscape of Assane. The primary income varies between tribes, but eccentric and unique gods are well known to come from this region.

Barnăl *(Bar-nahl)* – Eastern city of Creitón. A brutal past with strong armed forces. Historically remembered as the city that enslaved its princess. Supplies cities with ships, gathering supplies through a deal with the ancient Venkar City.

- Tyrik Village – Small and quaint, but best known as the village massacred during the White Horn pirate raid approximately 434 summers ago.

Binter – Often confused for Yavinks. Tiny creatures with translucent wings that live in the tropical forest of Creitón. They are attracted to humid climates, fruit, and wherever they can hide under leaves. They are known to be grumpy and prefer to be left alone.

Caster – Eastern city of Sorréle. Known for its high crime rates and violent culture, the city's economic income weighs heavily on the production of wines and trading. All goods, exported or imported, must pass through Caster's Port, giving the city a significant advantage over all others.

Cer'han (*Ser-hahn*)– A flying creature that comes from the Soul Realm. Many have referred to it as a 'demon dragon' because it embodies similar characteristics, such as wings, snout, powerful jaws, and talons. They live for decades and can be as small as a hand or as large as a home. Aggressive, territorial, and hard to kill.

Chaos – Often referred to as 'the mother of energy' or 'Mother.' Without Chaos, there would be no Vore World. Dark Energy and Light Energy are both sub-energies of Chaos. All things, including the realms, are linked to the mother of all energies.

Creitón (*Cre-ton*) – Nicknamed 'pirate country.' There is no clear record of whether Creitón or Eiyrăl came first, and the answers will vary by individual. This country is well-known for its ports, ships, and the cultural significance of the sea. It is true that most of the pirates Vorelians meet consider Creitón their home, but it is certainly a well-established country with strong values. Main cities: Barnăl, Saveen, and Delion. Lesser cities: Venkar City, Ruby Village, and Tyrik Village.

Crescent Blade – An honorable dagger forged out of gemstone, harvested from the depths of Crescent Lake. This blade isn't meant to be fought with but to store mass amounts of Light Energy. It is a ceremonial weapon presented to those identified as invaluable by the Yavinks. Very few are made. The hilt is narrow, made of dark leather and braided leaves, and the pommel is flat. There's no handguard. The blade is pink, translucent, and wavy.

Crystónity *(Cris-ton-ity)* – Branch of Drügalism. This monotheistic religion only celebrates Sekar and does not consider the other deities significant. Crystóns are secluded worldwide, but the City of Liral is the only location to practice openly. Also known as Dreamer's Faith.

Cu'cel *(Su-sel)* – Sinister illness responsible for the deaths in Geral. Old Tongue translates to 'evil' or 'ungodly.' Refer to Grënyl for a description.

Dark Energy – A more prominent form of energy, sometimes referred to as 'the sister of Chaos' or 'the dead's power.' This energy is raw, untampered, and pure, derived from the souls of the damned locked in the living realm and unable to pass into the Afterlife. Dark Energy is nearly impossible to master by an Energy Harvester, given the incredible power of the force. This power is often known to consume and kill the harvester and is considered a bad omen by most Vorelians. Dark Energy is embodied in the purest elements: water, wind, metal, and fire. Historically, only two have mastered the energy: Selena Delcate (wind) and Henry Junok (metal). Morei Geral (fire) is now the third Vorelian to master it.

Death's Sword – The blade of the Guardian. This weapon is forged using metal harvested from Volkeri Island. The creation requires Dark Energy and the blood of the selected Guardian, creating a customized weapon that will not break under high stress. It can withstand the strength of Chaos, as proven by Syra, and acts as a transportation tool for Guardians to form portals. This sword is highly prized in the living, with some extreme underground traders willing to kill to obtain the weapon. The actual process of how the blade is forged remains a secret, but it is akin to a God's sword, able to kill a Guardian, slay ancient beasts, and end souls.

Delion *(Dee-le-on)* – Northern city of Creitón. A quiet city that keeps to itself. It is commonly referred to as the heart of Creitón because of its central location, although the city remains compact and smaller in stature, unlike Saveen and Barnǎl. Do not be fooled by the city's quiet demeanor, as the toughest citizens live here, with many working the sea as their source of income.

Díanzon Prophecy *(Die-an-zon)* – As old as time itself. This prophecy focused on the rebalancing of the realms. It spoke of a man born with the power of a God, but with the violent tendencies of a monster—a delicate symbolic dance between the living and dead. Centuries of stories have been passed down, which have tampered with the literal meaning of some terms. The one who would act as the catalyst for this change is known as the King of Monsters, but due to time, has come to be known as the Demon King.

Die Cux'erial *(Dee Cuk-er-al)* – An ancient belief that a series of specific deaths would lead to a world-ending event (i.e., Diyrǎllian Massacre, the Great Fall, and the fall of the Vorelian Empire are a few). There is confidence that all lives are interconnected somehow, and that decisions lead to certain outcomes. This belief is often shared with Ghrynál, although they are not related. Hyle is a firm believer in this ideology.

Diemon *(Di-mon)* – Northwest city of Sorréle. The city of gems, or as some refer as 'the gem city.' Stationed up against the Releuthian Mountains, its primary income is from mining and jewelry.

Diyrǎ *(Di-rah)* – Founded over 1,500 summers ago and well-known for its gruesome history. At the height of the Lirallian Empire over four centuries ago, Henry Junok led a bloody domination that slaughtered millions, now known as the Diyrǎllian Massacre. Main cities: Assane, Raveer, and Junok. Lesser cities: Nighthunter Federation, Jasper Village, and Whale Village.

Diyrǎllian Massacre *(Di-ral-lian)* – The largest massacre in Vorelian history that occurred over four centuries ago. The Lirallian Empire carried it out under the guidance of Henry Junok. Millions of lives were lost across Diyrǎ, and the summer has become known as the 'Blood Summer.'

Don'sul *(Dawn-suul)* – A ritual that restricts Energy Harvesters from harvesting. This ritual is considered dark and is prohibited across all four countries. Most successful when performed on a child less than five, but it is still used on adults, although results vary.

- This was performed on Cyrus by Henry Junok.

Drügalism *(Druug-al-ism)* – The primary religion of Vorelians, embodying all five Gods: Helyna, Greve, Hyle, Eazon, and Sekar.

Duraloc *(Der-ah-lock)* – One of the original demons of the Soul Realm. This demon is bound to a Guardian of Death during the Commitment Ceremony, and what gives these warriors their features and enhanced abilities. The demon lives in cave systems and is a soul eater. Also used as part of the eternal punishment provided by Guardians.

Eazon *(E-zon)* – God of Luck. Ritual of Contact: a bundle of Krye placed on a cloth and surrounded by candles.

Edanzín Blade (*E-dan-sin*) – The blade used in the Commitment Ceremony of the Guardians. While the vast amount of information surrounding the process of the Commitment Ceremony remains a secret, this blade has been confirmed. The user of the blade is specially trained and must undergo a mental evaluation after each use to confirm that the power of the blade has not negatively impacted the person (in this case, Guardian). The master of this blade is called a Herän (*Her-ahn*).

- Only one Herän can exist at any point in time. The blade is bonded to the chosen individual until they relinquish that. In any case, relinquishment can be through death or by choice. In unique cases, by force.

Eei'on Rü *(Ee-I-on Ruh)* – 'Peace of the World.' This is the core value of the Rider Federation. It is referenced as 'the code of all codes' or simply the Code and represents the overall goal of the Rider Federation: achieving world peace by any means necessary. This philosophy was expected to be adhered to by every member during the federation's reign. Failure to abide results in punishments and formal hearings.

Egunsar *(E-goon-sar)* – Pesky and aggressive rodent-like creatures that have an appetite for eyeballs. They live in the Soul Realm and can attack in hordes.

Eiyrặl *(Eye-ral)* – An ancient country with conflicting settlement records, although many agree it was well over 2,000 summers, with some estimations as high as 3,000. With no clear indication, it is well-known as the Dragon Riders' home. The ancient country holds traditional Vorelian values that are entirely lost to many outsiders. More interestingly, Eiyrặl is withdrawn from many political movements and is independent of a lot of activity with other countries. Main cities: Kalic, East Razan, West Razan, and Rider Federation (destroyed in the Great Fall).

Ferguson – Northeast city of Sorréle, more commonly referred to as 'the silk family.' Ferguson's economic income is primarily from clothing, specializing in silks. An eccentric group of people that remain withdrawn.

Firóle *(Fur-ole)* – Giant serpents that once ruled the lands of Diyrặ and traveled openly. One of the ancient beasts. The Firóle were hunted for their scales and fangs during the height of the Dragon Riders, driving them to extinction. Very few remain and stay in hiding. They are ancient beasts and possess many characteristics like a dragon, such as telepathic communication and intelligence.

Fräurune (*Fraah-rune*) – Translates to 'Lady of the Dead.'

Geíon (*Ge-ee-on*) – A highly evolved and intelligent species of demon. They are violent, bloodthirsty, and constantly seek control. They are active users of Ön'grusah with theories stating they have evolved because of their use of this force. They loathe the Honuyál.

- Ka-Geíon (*Kah-Ge-ee-on*) – A higher and more powerful Geíon. Have the capability to conjure their own bodies, so they can look like anything. Many of these Ka-Geíons take the body of people because it allows them to walk among the living.

- Gor-Geíon (*Gore-Ge-ee-on*) – A lower and less powerful Geíon. They cannot conjure bodies like their brethren, so they possess the living. Any possession or soul bondage with a person is not permanent. This is because their own lifeforce slowly devours the lifeforce of their victim.

    ◦ Morei Geral, prophesized Demon King, is soul bonded to one.

Geral *(Geh-ral)* – Western city of Sorréle and nicknamed 'the blacksmith's city.' Geral's economic income weighs heavily on the trade of metals, including armor and weapons. A city that takes pride in its strength and independence.

Ghrynál *(Ghrin-all)* – A philosophical belief quite literally translating to *'the path forward.'* Everything has a cause and effect; every action dictates a different path. The mother of energy, Chaos, knows all paths forward. It was once revered in traditional Vorelian culture but has since become less known, specifically in Sorréle and many parts of Diyră. Guardians of Death adhere to this philosophical approach.

Gods' Realm – The original name for the living realm.

Gonsín (*Gone-seen*) – Translated from Old Tongue to 'leader.' A high form of respect when this term is used.

Gray Realm – The space between the living and Soul Realm. Often believed to be the realm closest to Chaos. Given its vast and uncontrollable environment, no one goes here, and it is acknowledged by Energy Harvesters or Vore scholars. Very few cultures address the Gray Realm. Sekar is believed to be the only God who freely travels to and from the Gray Realm, using its volatile and secretive nature to his advantage. With so little knowledge of this realm, no one truly understands what or if anything lives there.

Grënyl *(Greh-nal)* – Ailment associated with Sekar. Old literature discusses Grënyl to be the mark of the Dark Lord and how he identifies his next victims. Symptoms include black rotting pieces of flesh, fever, and mental deterioration. Sekar utilizes this tactic to weaken the life force and bring them to the Gray Realm, a space between the living and dead realms. Ancient texts theorized Grënyl only came to those with fractured loyalty to the Gods, such as Greve, Hyle, Eazon, and Helyna.

Greve *(Greeve)* – God of Strength. Ritual of Contact: wooden posts with letters nailed to them, followed by a hand gesture over the heart.

Guardian of Death – Warriors that belong to the Soul Realm. They are responsible for the guidance of souls from the living to the Afterlife. Guardians are also responsible for the protection of the Soul Realm against all forms of threats. They are mortal boys taken before ten after a tragedy and raised in the realm of the dead. Countless summers of training and mastery of their skills and emotions make them savage competition in a swordfight. Upon training completion, they undergo the Commitment Ceremony, which involves the bondage of a lesser demon to their soul. The ultimate test is surviving this ritual, and those who do are honorably gifted Death's Sword and become a Guardian of Death. Details of the Commitment Ceremony are not shared; Guardians do not speak highly of the seven-day ceremony and a few that have emphasized that it is un-bearable. The iconic characteristics—pale blue skin, red eyes, black hair, and Marking—all result from the ceremony. In cultures where they are less accepted and perceived as bad omens, they are called 'Death Seekers.'

- Shevana ceased all further training of Guardians, and the numbers are now the lowest they've ever been.

Gýshin *(Gee-shin)* – The purest form of the Old Tongue language. Spoken by the Yavinks. Translated to 'true tongue.'

Helyna *(Hel-e-na)* – Goddess of Love. Ritual of Contact: a glass of wine with use of the phrases 'Love is endless' and 'Helyna bless you.'

Honuyál *(Hon-u-al)* – A grotesque and ruthless species of beasts. They are power-hungry and feed off souls. They follow traditional values and place a high emphasis on female rulers. Noted traits include leathery skin, large and strong bodies, dagger-like teeth, slit noses, and tusks. They have amassed numbers in the Soul Realm.

Hyle *(Hile)* – God of Courage. Ritual of Contact: silver beads with a small wooden sun, widely named 'Hyle's Beads.'

Indül (*In-duul*) – A flower harvested on the outskirts of Venkar City. The flower produces a toxin that can be fatal in high doses. Ingestion of the toxin will create hallucinations and other symptoms. Only a master herbalist should work with a flower this dangerous.

Inere (*E-near*) – One of the ancient beasts of the Vore World. This giant beast is covered in shell-like armor. Large pincers, a dozen beady eyes, and ten legs. The Inere burrows underground and comes above ground only when threatened or curious. Can live up to 400 summers.

I'num (*E-num*) – The sigil of the Dragon Rider. Translates from the Old Tongue to 'loyalty,' and was used to symbolize the dedication Dragon Riders held for one another during the Rider Federation. Acts are made in the best interest of the Dragon Riders. Failure to uphold this was considered punishable. I'num is considered closely tied to Eei'on Rü.

Junok (*June-oke*) – Northwest city of Diyră. The largest territory of all Vore cities and best known for its gory history and rich Energy Harvesting bloodline. The Junok family is most notably known for Henry Junok, despite the family's expulsion of the prince and his title from the family lineage. Junok's Port is the major port of all trades for Diyră, making up a significant amount of city income.

Kalic (*Kal-ick*) – Eastern city of Eiyrăl. One of the smallest cities in the world. Well known as one of the only cities to enslave people still. Its brutal punishment system and predefined roles make the city ancient in its practices. Primary income is weapon and armor production.

Kan Sëri (*Kahn-Sar-e*) – Translates from Old Tongue to 'Master of the Sea' or 'Sea Master.'

Krakí (*Kra-kee*) – One of the ancient beasts of the Vore World. Eight tentacles, larger than any ship, and territorial. In some cultures, like Creitón, these beasts are revered. They live deep underwater and occasionally come up out of curiosity. Highly intelligent and hold grudges. Can live up to 1,000 summers.

Krisár *(Kris-har)* – One of the dark rituals of old Vorelian practices. Involves the consumption of the participant's blood and the recital of an ancient text spoken in Old Tongue. A blade of power must be used in the ritual for it to be successful. It is forbidden in most cities across the Vore World, given its highly dark association with the dead and curses. The ritual was outlawed after the fall of the Lirallian Empire and all books associated with Krisár and equally dangerous rituals were said to be burned.

Kultón *(Kuhl-tune)* – The most prestigious title a Guardian of Death can be given, similar to a commander in the living. Dryl held this title for many summers before it was stripped from him.

Ku'sar *(Kuh-sar)* – Old Tongue for 'Death Dancer.'

Leangé (*Lee-an-gee*) – One of the most important books of the Soul Realm. This book possesses all sorts of information regarding the history and creation of the Soul Realm, along with natural laws. This book is one of the few that was saved when Shevana, the current and longest standing ruler, set fire to all material in an attempt to withhold information and increase her political power.

Life Eater – A serpent-like creature that lives in the Vore waters. Often described as having blue or purple-colored scales, massive talons, and horns. Old stories of the sea speak of it as a water dragon. Extremely territorial, aggressive, and will stalk its prey up to a full moon before striking. Can live for centuries. Younglings are not considered adults until about 200 summers.

Lifeforce – More commonly known as soul. This is the energy that makes up every living thing or object. Depending on what region of the Vore World visited, one will hear either soul or lifeforce.

Light Energy – The weakest but most malleable form of energy, as it is impure and tampered with. All life is made of Light Energy. All Energy Harvesters lean heavily on this form, as its ease and stability make it reliable. Commoners often refer to this form as 'magic,' which indicates a lack of education in energy.

Lih'rel *(Lie-rehl)* – An ancient religion that worshipped the Vore beasts, including the dragon. Followers of this practice believed the Gods were not in control, only servants to the original masters of the realms.

Lunga *(Luun-gah)* – An ancient Vore beast that lives in the water. Known for its highly aggressive nature. Few have seen one and lived to speak about it. The creature will hunt a ship for countless leagues.

Ly'rün *(Lie-rune)* – A potent mixture of chemicals that combusts into a deadly fire when used. A fatal gas is released during this, which can spread for half a league in all directions. Anyone who inhales this will experience swelling of the lungs, hallucinations, and bloody tears. No records exist of any survivors.

Móermism *(More-mism)* – Spiritual religion. Followers place their value and respect in energies and are considered extremely spiritual, often praising Mother, or Chaos, as the ultimate deity. This old practice is seen rarely but is scattered throughout the world, and followers are known best as Móers.

Mo'lüre *(Mo-lah-ure)* – The commoners call it a unicorn. The creature is created with pure Dark Energy and has been nicknamed the 'Walker of Realms' because of its ability to dissipate and reappear wherever it wants. Nobody can touch the creature without permission. Doing so will cause the Mo'lüre to consume the lifeforce of the person. Ancient stories say that to see one is a good omen for this creature does not show itself to anyone without intention. There are only a handful of sightings throughout Vore history.

Nighthunter – The best assassin in the world. Trained for up to eight or more summers under the guidance of skilled assassins and must earn their sword in training. They hold tremendous value in the Old Laws and will hunt anyone.

  • Upon the formation of the Nighthunters, a deal was made with Junok. In return for land, the Nighthunters would never take a bid against the Junok family.

Nighthunter Federation – A southwest city located on the panhandle of Diyră. The city is well known for its zero-crime tolerance and is the only city in the world to offer asylum to all refugees. However, the Nighthunters are more than just soldiers, but the best assassins in the world. An underground market allows travelers from around the world to come and bid for a Nighthunter. The federation is a hotspot for illegal trade.

Old Laws – Old text written over 200 summers ago. These laws were the original promises of the Nighthunters and define the guild. To break one of the Old Laws is to break the oath of a Nighthunter.

Ön'grusah (*Ohn-gru-sah*) – Translated to 'evil energy.' This is a form of energy that has been abused, contorted, and twisted into an all-consuming force. While many of the Soul Realm believe the Ka-Geíon are responsible for this, it is still unconfirmed which species of demon is to blame. However, it has been confirmed that Ön'grusah is responsible for the current state of the Soul Realm.

- Studies on Ön'grusah are few. Those that have spent time researching this malicious power have theorized that it is alive and moves with the intelligence of Chaos. This could be the result of evolution—the force growing stronger and smarter when faced with any form of threat. Although one theory is that Ön'grusah was created with the use of a God's heart, which would explain the theory that there is a direct link to Chaos. There are no confirmed reports. To study Ön'grusah, one would have to venture deep into Ashýon, where it is believed the heart of this evil energy lies. This is extremely dangerous.

Oth'al (*Ahth-al*) – The book dedicated to the Guardians and their laws. All information regarding the Commitment Ceremony, their order, and training is covered in this book. As of current, the book is lost.

Peacemaker – a relic from the Vorelian Empire, forged with the aid of a God (deity unknown). This blade can sense the intentions of people, offering protection for the wielder. Blood creates a bond between the blade and wielder, only breakable in death. It was lost for centuries after the Fangs abused it during the reign of the Dragon Riders over 800 centuries ago.

Rauna (*Raw-na*) – In old stories, she is the ancient queen who fell in love with the God, Zyne. She was killed by her own citizens.

Raveer *(Rah-veer)* – Eastern city known for its brutality and ancient values in Diyră. The city has become revered for its armed forces; they are trained for twice the number of summers than the standard soldier observed in other Vorelian cities. The primary city income is metalwork.

Regule *(Reh-ghoul)* – A large, four-legged beast from the Beutóne Mountains. Incisors that extend past the jaw, and white fur speckled with orange stripes. Infamous for its iconic glacier-blue eyes with slit pupils. Prone to lashing out when it feels threatened. Can live up to 300 summers.

Renuri *(Ren-yuri)* – An expert in poisonous explosives. An outlawed practice by most cities, but that does not stop rulers from seeking out these experts.

Rider Federation – North city of Eiyrăl, or the remains. The city was destroyed over 800 summers ago during The Great Fall. The city's remnants offer sanctuary to strange beasts, volatile energy, and secrets. Often, citizens of Kalic and Razan come to offer gifts and say prayers.

- When it stood, the Rider Federation was glorious and home to some of the most influential people in the world. The federation kept peace among the cities worldwide and led massive explorations.

Rider's Sword – A prestigious and irreplaceable weapon custom-made for each Rider who passes the rigorous summers of training. Once inducted, Riders are gifted this as a symbol of their status. A Rider's Sword is forged with the blood of a dragon and meticulous ceremonial work. They can't break and they possess a lifeforce. Cyrus carries Darrin's, once a Master

Rider who soared the skies with Vikter and Hyle during the reign of the Rider Federation.

Rubal *(Ru-ball)* – A desert flower that, when crushed into a paste, can cause near-fatal reactions in the body. It is used in the underground market as a method to fake deaths. It is risky to use because, at times, too high a dose can be fatal.

Rül'Cril (*Rah-Cril*)– Translates to 'Crown of Gods.' This relic was one of the three forged by Henry Junok in his reign. It earned the name because it has the power to make any beast a mindless slave to the wielder. Sekar remains the only God with the knowledge on how it was forged. Henry Junok thankfully never got the chance to use it.

Rü'shane *(Ruh-shane)* – Translated from Old Tongue to 'God's Soul.' This is the proper term for a raven. Souls unwilling to pass into the Afterlife for one reason or the other. Once bound to the Soul Realm but managed to break free. These souls are forever bound to wander between the living and dead, too stubborn to pass.

Saveen *(Sa-veen)* – Western city of Creitón. Saveen drives global trades of jewels and unique goods. The city is known for its exquisite architecture and attitudes, but they are masters of the seas and should not be misunderstood.

- The prince of Saveen, Dameon, is the second Dragon Rider to soar the skies in over 800 summers.

Sea Master – An individual who is both an Energy Harvester and captain of a ship. Few Sea Masters have successfully lived long, due to the insatiable thirst for power and control that arises within them.

Sekar *(Seh-kar)* – In traditional culture, known as the Dream Walker or God of Dreams. More recently, heavily regarded as the Dark Lord, God of Darkness, and unacknowledged by some cultures altogether for the belief that such action brings bad luck.

- Ritual of contact as Dark Lord: blood sacrifice and recital of cursed text. Punishable by death if caught performing this ritual in most cities.

- Ritual of contact as Dream Walker: Prayer before bed. The method of contact is through dreams, so many would pray to Sekar for him to visit and guide them while they dream.

Sorréle *(Sor-rel)* – The youngest country of the Vore World, founded over eight centuries ago. The establishment of this country originates in a political dispute between families in Diyră. Main cities: Geral, Ferguson, Diemon, and Caster. Lesser cities: Gamer's Village.

Soul Realm – The realm of the dead. Commoners refer to this location as the 'underworld,' but this is inappropriate, as the Soul Realm lives parallel with the living—not above or below. Souls pass into the Soul Realm and exist until they are ready to be guided to the Afterlife. It is ruled by a select family who the Gods chose to uphold the responsibility of caring for the dead. The Soul Realm is critical to the living—it brings order and balance to the energy system. If the Soul Realm fails, the living will follow, and vice versa.

- The Soul Realm was once notably beautiful, with flowing rivers and vivid colors. It has since become the embodiment of ghastly and horrible imagery. The malevolent forces entered with permission under the guise of promised power and slowly devoured the land.

Soul Speaker – People who have a connection to the dead. They see, hear, and speak for the deceased. Some cultures regard Soul Speakers as bad omens, while others revere their gift.

Syckl Blade *(Sick-ill)* – One of few weapons that can kill a Guardian of Death. It is forged with the toxin of a Cer'han, and it is known for its yellowish-colored blade. This is the execution weapon used on punished Guardians, though that was a rare ceremony. The blade was held on for more hideous purposes.

Tre'lang ungahr *(Tray-lang uhn-gar)* – A Queen's farewell. It means Destiny herself loves the sea, and anyone who denies her what she wants has no right to call the sea their home.

The Great Fall – The fall of the Rider Federation. Upon the death of her Rider, Vikter, Aythen went mad with rage and destroyed the city. It is said only a handful escaped the carnage, but what happened to the survivors remains unknown.

- Prior to The Great Fall, two Dragon Riders fled in the middle of the night with their weapons and gear. What became of them remains undetermined—no further dragon sightings were reported, and no one by the iconic silver eyes was documented following the destructive events. Cyrus is believed to possess one of the Rider's Swords that was saved before The Great Fall.

Trembar *(Trem-bar)* – Originally from the Dark Forest. A four-legged creature with spiral-like horns that cover its jaw and head. It has tan fur, hooves, and four eyes. Will chew through anything except iron, and is known for its voracious appetite.

Tsu'Ran (*Su-ran*) – Shapeshifters of the sea. They live in hordes and call the Grave their home. They transform into anything their victim most desires. Souls are what they consume. Powerful creatures that in their natural form look closer to a small Krakí.

U'can *(You-can)* – A fierce and territorial mouse found in the Releuthian Mountains. Also the name of an obscure and small tribe of pirates.

Ve'hem *(Veh-hem)* – Old Tongue for 'the burdened one.'

Viv'an *(Vee-van)* – Old Tongue for 'daughter of the Red Goddess.'

Vor'gal *(Vore-gal)* – Old Tongue for 'the pit' or 'underworld.'

West and East Razan *(Rah-zan)* – Western city of Eiyrãl and second largest in the Vore World. Rich in ancient culture and values and is considered one of the oldest cities. One of the only cities in the world where people will walk without a weapon in the streets. Energy Harvesters are welcomed and highly regarded. The Razan family occasionally opens their gates and allows citizens to explore the vast palace. An extensive underground tunnel system accommodates the palace. Income varies, given the city's adaptability to economic changes.

- West Razan was once known as Suniyr (Sun-ear), a city of occult followers. Approximately 1,100 summers ago, Suniyr was dissolved by Razan after a political war. The Suniyr family was executed publicly.

Wurok *(War-ak)* – Massive and ghastly worm-like creatures that live in the Starved Sands. They sense through vibrations, noted by the ripples left in the sand when they move. Described as having hundreds of incisors and black. Extremely territorial and stalkers of their prey.

Wynzer *(Wine-zer)* – A creature created through mass experimentation and Dark Energy. Similar build to a dragon, small, and with an abnormally long tail. No scales, extremely intelligent, and observant. Only one exists, which resides in Caster, and is endearingly named Savage after he bit the head off a mouse.

Xaxer *(Zax-er)* – A bird-like creature that lives in the Soul Realm, once believed extinct. It has long, scaly legs and a disproportionately large body. Its dark, orb-like eyes and white beak starkly contrast with its black wings tipped in purple. Curious and passive.

Yalahnder *(Yah-lan-der)* – A violent beast with the bulk of a dragon but the body of an Onye. Bred for blood, thrives off destruction, and is infamous for the gouges left behind at the Soul Realm palace. Nearly driven to extinction but has since disappeared. The last known whereabouts remain unknown.

Zimbórism *(Zim-bor-ism)* – Branch of Drügalism. This religion identifies Greve as the primary God and is heavily recognized in Diyră, although there are a small number of Zimbór followers across the Vore World.

Zyne (*Zine*) – A Vore God who many believed was the moon in ancient Vore beliefs. He fell in love with a mortal, Rauna.

Zyulë Bond *(Zule)* – A type of energy bond that doesn't identify a master. The equal relationship that results is often referred to as a God's Bond. Both individuals must remain alive; the death of one will result in the partner's death. This peculiar characteristic makes it both dangerous and extremely useful. Both participants must adhere to the rules of Krisár. Individuals of Zyulë Bonds possess a silver raised scar on their wrist and are extremely valuable in some traditional cultures.

Acknowledgment

I'm quietly debating another hot cup of coffee, but I want to write this, and I don't want to lose my train of thought. I am in the final stages of prepping *The Dragon of Dread Deep* for the world. Kind of crazy to imagine, actually. I wrote this book in seven weeks at the beginning of 2025, consumed by a vision. And while the story came easy, the journey for it to reach you was not.

The editing journey was full of trials and errors. Mistakes were made, and I will spare you the details that, quite frankly, kept me up at all hours of the night a few times. Editing is an intimate partnership between the editor and author—something I could go on about for the next century. That bond was broken pretty early, and the story went on quite a journey following that. And no, this is not The Emperor of Editors, Dylan, that many readers are already familiar with (my goodness, he scares me, but I love him and can't wait to work with him again). *The Dragon of Dread Deep* went through a few hands, but it finally landed on Jennifer Bell's desk at Busy Quill Press. It was there that the story flourished.

I want to take a few sentences to acknowledge her undeniable passion for editing and this story. Jennifer gave *The Dragon of Dread Deep* exactly what it needed—a good beating and a pat on the back. Her attentiveness and enthusiasm gave me the boost of confidence I was quickly starting to lose as both a writer and in this story. Not because I didn't love Cassian and San'yila, but because the editing journey prior was anything but kind or fun. It was grueling, stressful, and full of gut-wrenching moments where I regretted certain decisions. Jennifer made me laugh, challenged the plot and characters when I knew work was still needed, and groomed the manuscript with a fine-tooth comb that would challenge the Editing Gods. So, thank you, Jennifer, for embracing this story, hearing my experience, and being a guiding light in what was quickly turning into a madhouse of doubts and festering anxiety. You breathed life back into the editing experience and reminded me why I love it so much—this is where the magic happens.

I also want to acknowledge Brian Lynch, Bryan Kamtsios, and Micah Campbell—all extraordinary storytellers. You lads make me laugh every day. Not sure how we ended up in the same circle, but I couldn't be more grateful for it.

Bryan—I am in awe of your kindness. The world needs more people like you. You continue to prove just how beautiful friendship can be. I will forever be indebted to you for teaching me a valuable lesson: Friendship never comes at a cost. It is a gift, and it should be cherished. The gifts you've provided to the Vore World continue to blow me away. Thank you for the chapter header and everything you've done!

A special shout-out to HD Bergen for encouraging me to do the impossible. It is safe to say my entire perspective on being an author has changed because of you and your insane time management. This will be the greatest year in my author career, and I owe that to you.

To every Vorelian who has joined this Empire—thank you. I often find myself sitting in my chair, thinking about every single one of you and the love you've given this world. This journey wouldn't be possible without you. You not only gave these characters a home, but you gave these stories a heart. And every laugh, tear, and reaction means more to me than any review ever will. Before *The Blood of the Lion*, not a single soul had read my work. I went years writing in private, nervous about sharing. But you all embraced this world and characters with enthusiasm and dedication, and for that, I can't thank you enough.

To Cherie—the saga, this world, is what it is because of your passion and creative eye. Every cover embodies so much more than a vision—it's a part of the story's soul. I am so unbelievably grateful to call you a friend. We have worked together since day one. This Empire would not be what it is without you.

And, finally, to my family. Thank you for letting me turn into a gremlin who listens to too much music and daydreams about grand worlds. Life can be wild and overbearing, but because of your unwavering support, I have been able to make my dreams come true.

Keep your swords sharp, Vorelians.

www.ingramcontent.com/pod-product-compliance
Lightning Source LLC
Chambersburg PA
CBHW061043310726
48969CB00004B/1066